A NEW BREED

"Nothing is normal about a Class Ten," Asplundh explained. "Lewis's tissue sample revealed nonstandard DNA fragments. He has amino acid analogues that mimic the building blocks of normal human DNA, but are subtly different. This isn't just human DNA that has been altered, it's DNA that's intrinsically different because it contains a component that's not human."

A vision of Lewis nearly overwhelmed me, but I desperately forced the memories away. "Well, if it's not human and it's not animal, what the hell is it?" I demanded.

Asplundh just spread her hands in a gesture of both helplessness and apology. "I don't know . . ."

Also by Karen Ripley
Published by Ballantine Books:

PRISONER OF DREAMS

THE TENTH CLASS

Karen Ripley

A Del Rey Book
BALLANTINE BOOKS • NEW YORK

A Del Rey Book
Published by Ballantine Books
Copyright © 1990 by Karen Ripley

Library of Congress Catalog Card Number: 90-93286

ISBN 0-345-37033-3

Manufactured in the United States of America

First Edition: January 1991

CHAPTER
ONE

I think that he was probably the one person in all the known systems I would have been happy to see right about then. And so when he spoke my name, as I turned to face him, there already was a huge and helpless grin pulling at my lips. Then he was hugging me hard and exuberantly, spinning me around so that my feet actually left the floor for a moment, and I felt a buoying rush of relief and pleasure in the simple security of his embrace.

"Jo!" he exclaimed enthusiastically, setting me back on my feet with his hands still gripping my forearms as he looked me up and down like a triumphant trader who had just made the deal of the millennium.

I was still so surprised, so genuinely pleased, that all I could do was parrot him, announcing his name with a breathless laugh. "Taylor!"

His big hands squeezed my forearms fondly, and he gave me a cheerful little shake. His sienna-colored eyes dancing, he said with a grin, "So, I hear you're looking for an advocate."

Recovering my breath, I retorted with equal humor, "You're not even a lawyer, much less an advocate."

"True," he conceded. His hands slipped down my arms to grasp me by the wrists. "But I bet I know the name of at least one good advocate in every inhabited system in this quadrant."

"Only because you've had need of their services at one time or another," I said. Then I had to break off and just study him for a moment. "Powers, you're looking good," I declared.

We were standing in a cluttered aisle in Buttley's, one of the more popular independent refitters on-planet; even as we had stood speaking, several flightsuited freightmen had already skirted around us, glancing at our obvious reunion with varying

1

degrees of amused tolerance. Then, as one of Buttley's harried clerks—a Class Four, I thought, with muscles like an ox—guided a hoversled laden with cartons up the narrow alleyway toward us, Taylor stepped back, drawing me with him, to lean against a towering stack of crates of food synthesizer substrate. Pressed against the smooth fabric of the front of his sleek gold and bottle-green flightsuit, I closed my eyes for a moment and just breathed in the faint, familiar essence of his unique scent. It had been over a decade since I had first met this man; any change in him had only been for the better.

Pulling back, I looked across into Taylor's eyes. He had maybe a half inch of height on me, no more. "I thought you were working for Longuard," I said, realizing that almost anything I said at that point would be something of a non sequitur. "What the hell are you doing on Porta Flora?"

His hands resting casually on my waist, Taylor flashed me a crooked grin. "I could ask you the same thing," he said, "only the news of your deeds has preceded you." His head gave a little shake, sending the layered locks of his blond-tipped chestnut hair bouncing. The golden-brown eyes were more serious then as his voice dropped slightly. "What you did at New Cuba and Heinlein hasn't exactly escaped public notice . . ." His hands tightened a bit on my waist. "But what happened to you—and what *almost* happened to you—is not exactly the kind of thing freightmen are going to ignore, either."

"Yeah?" I responded quietly. "Well, I was kind of counting on that. That's why I'm in Porta Flora."

For a moment Taylor just gazed at me, his usually open and ingenuous expression tempered somewhat by a look of thoughtful consideration. Then he released my waist, taking me by one hand. "Come on," he said. "You here by yourself?" As he gently tugged me, he glanced around the refitter's. "Let's have lunch—my treat."

Holding back, I shook my head. "I'm here with—"

"—Raydor," Taylor completed for me as the mentioned party stepped around a pile of crates and into the aisle where we were standing. Taylor dropped my hand and held his out to the towering man whose blue and silver flightsuit matched my own. "Hey, good to see you again," he said, greeting my second in command.

"It's a surprise to see you, Taylor," Raydor countered adroitly. Behind the concealment of the mandatory face wraps, Raydor's expression was unreadable; he shook Taylor's proffered hand firmly but without enthusiasm. Given the acuity of his hearing, I was certain the Tachs had heard everything that had been said between Taylor and me, no matter where in Buttley's he'd been at the time. But I also knew with the same certainty that Raydor would never offer an opinion, particularly in a social situation, unless I specifically asked him for it. And that was something I wasn't likely to do where Taylor was concerned.

If Taylor had interpreted Raydor's somewhat noncommittal greeting as an insult, he gave no sign of it. Rather, he took my hand again and flashed a winning smile. "Come on along," he said to the larger man. "We're going to have lunch."

"I can't," I reiterated, trying to cut through Taylor's enthusiasm, although I made no attempt to pull free from his hand. "I've got an appointment at two hundred hours." My voice dropped slightly, even though no one in the busy supplier's was paying any attention to us, as I added, "With the Ombudsman."

"Oh," Taylor said, his eyebrows arching slightly. Then his expression brightened again. "But it's not even one hundred hours yet; we've got plenty of time."

This time I did disengage my hand from the clasp of his warm fingers, gently but firmly. "I can't," I repeated. "I've got another meeting first . . . with Rhaine."

"Ohhhh." This time the word was drawn out in a manner that demonstrated Taylor's sudden comprehension. "Okay," he said evenly, "let me walk along with you then, anyway." He gave a little shrug, the corners of his mouth lifting crookedly. "We can grab something from one of the grill pits along the colonnade." He spared Raydor an obvious inquiring look. "That shouldn't screw up your plans, huh?"

I could read in my crewmate's huge dark eyes the hint of an expression that I suspected Taylor was blissfully oblivious to; it was not a reaction the chestnut-haired man was accustomed to provoking, and I doubted he could have recognized it in this, its most subtly manifested form. But Raydor just made a low grunting sound and said to me, "Go ahead; I can finish up here."

I gazed up into his deeply hooded eyes for a moment, knowing Raydor could read me as deftly as I could read him. "I'll see you later," I told him.

Outside Buttley's it was raining. It rained about eighty-five percent of the time on Porta Flora, and after being there for a day or so, no one hardly even gave it any notice. Nearly all the thoroughfares and walkways in the settlement were protected in some fashion, either covered with awnings or canopies or glassed in. The arrangement not only repelled the constant rain, it also held in the artificially generated cooling. The city was located near one of the planet's poles, but even there the average ambient temperature was close to 35°C.

Out on the throughway, Taylor once again reached for my hand. I gave it to him willingly. When I admitted it to myself, I was almost embarrassingly happy to see him again. It seemed like the first really good omen I'd received since we'd made planetfall. And there just was—and had always been— something infectiously cheerful about the man. Just being with him again made it not only possible but almost necessary to feel better.

The pedestrian walkway was fairly crowded at that hour, but Taylor strode along as though the additional companionship of hundreds of total strangers was more of an added bonus than an inconvenience. I hadn't been to Porta Flora in years; with its emphasis on service industries and relatively small retail and manufacturing base, it wasn't the sort of place out of which I usually worked. Therefore, we didn't encounter anyone I knew. And yet, in another way, all the people there were people I knew: jumpsuited Authority workers out on their lunch hour, shop workers and small merchants hustling between calls, personnel from the local medical complex, and the occasional odd freightman, several of whom were gawking like tourists at the elaborate network of awnings and rainshields. Even walking hand in hand, Taylor and I didn't attract any particular notice.

In its own unique way the settlement was strangely beautiful, and the mix of residents was agreeable. The planet had first been colonized by the Civilian Authority over a century earlier and originally had been used as a sort of botanical warehouse for hundreds of varieties of tropical and semitropical Old Earth plants. Ironically, despite its receptive climate, the only native "flora" on Porta Flora had been a few species of primitive sea plants. Freshwater oceans covered much of the planet's surface, but the colonists' specimens thrived in the peripolar regions. Over the years, as the surrounding systems had been explored and utilized, Porta Flora had lost its function as the quadrant's greenhouse, but the results of that early role were still evident everywhere in the current settlement. Although the city had become a relatively minor center of government, the service professions, and medical care, lush vegetation still flourished throughout the settlement, climbing the walls and columns of buildings, towering over the water conduits, and spilling from ornamental plots and plantings in a verdant flood of green.

Tugging me along after him, Taylor abruptly swerved out from the flow of foot traffic and stopped in front of a food booth located in a leafy alcove. Even though it was midday, the vendor was not especially busy, and when I glanced at her list of offerings and the prices attached to them, I understood why.

"What'll you have, Jo?" Taylor asked me as the mouthwatering smell of real meat wreathed around us in the humid air.

"Taylor," I protested, "this is—"

"My treat," he finished neatly, fishing a credit chit out of the breast pocket of his flightsuit. "One of those steak spears, please," he told the woman behind the counter. Then he cocked an expectant brow at me, an expression that brooked no further polite demur. "Well?"

My stomach had kindled hopefully; I could almost feel the inviting texture of the savory real meat between my teeth. "Uh, the same, I guess," I said.

"Two, please," Taylor told the vendor, passing her the chit. The woman, a middle-aged Normal with the kind of dewy skin whose youthful complexion was no doubt at least partially courtesy of Porta Flora's climate, flashed Taylor a smile that owed its radiance to more than just the size of the sale. Taylor had an effect on women—all women, it seemed. He was aware of it, but I don't think I'd ever seen him use it deliberately. He didn't have to. Taken separately, none of his physical attributes or facial features was particularly striking or memorable. But something in their composite total, something in Taylor's very demeanor, spoke unfailingly to other people, especially people of the opposite sex.

Within moments his joking comments had the vendor giggling like a young girl as she passed us the aromatic spears of juicy steak chunks. He complimented her on the color of her jumpsuit's cowl, and she nearly forgot to give him back his chit. Smiling, shaking my head, I followed him back into the tide of pedestrian traffic. I bit eagerly into the steaming real meat, relishing the luxury. Taylor attacked his own steak with gusto, weaving with ease among the other people on the walkway, teasing me about my obvious appetite. He flirted outrageously with me; before I had half finished the cubes of meat, he was regaling me with a loud and considerably embellished account of how ravishing I looked. I laughed so hard that I was in some danger of wetting my suit liner, and for a brief but happy time my meeting with Rhaine and with the Ombudsman—and the entire predicament that had brought me there—was gloriously forgotten. And as I watched him, glancing sideways at him as we walked along the gleaming, perpetually wet pavement, it was as though the intervening years of our separation had never happened. The Taylor I saw beside me then dovetailed so easily with the Taylor I had known before. Time and experience had changed me considerably, and probably not for the better; they seemed to have changed Taylor not at all.

Like me, Taylor was a Class Two, and like me, even though he had been exempt from a compulsory period of Service, he had opted to Volunteer, where we had met in Commercial Regulation. Although we had been nothing alike, we'd become fast friends. Taylor was good at making friends, but our relationship was still significant, because I was not. At the time I had thought it was a shame that someone with his natural gregariousness hadn't elected to go into government instead of wasting his gift in merchanting. But since then, having seen firsthand how easily and corrosively corruption could eat at those people in positions of power, I was glad that he hadn't.

Rhaine's office was in a building in a section of the settlement the locals called Little Venice. The reference was obvious: Porta Flora's natural abundance of precipitation had been channeled into a picturesque series of tree-lined canals and waterways, more ornamental than functional, although you could rent small watercraft for the scenic tour. And, ironically enough, even those man-made streams were covered with canopies to protect the passersby from the ubiquitous rain. Like most of Porta Flora's structures, the building was mostly underground, taking advantage of the natural cooling effects of the subterranean design. The upper portion was devoted to shops and small plant-festooned eateries, most with glassed-in roofs, across which the rain still poured in endless rivulets.

In the lobby, a cathedrallike expanse of glass and green, I turned to Taylor. "Thanks—thanks for everything," I said, feeling suddenly awkward.

"I'll go down with you," he said.

"Taylor, you don't have to—"

But he just interrupted me, taking my hand again as if strolling into the lift with me was the most natural and obvious thing to do. "Of course I don't have to," he agreed, making that a given. "But I want to."

I had never been much good at resisting his particularly sunny form of logic; it was no wonder he had been the first man with whom I'd ever joined.

The interior of the building's lower level, where we exited the lift, was so brightly lit and pleasantly decorated that it didn't give the appearance of a subterranean structure. Taylor followed me to a small central reception area that probably served the entire level. Behind the semicircular counter a stout man with closely cropped gray hair looked up from his Integrator access and raised one bushy eyebrow inquiringly at us.

"Captain Jo-lac, of *Raptor*," I told him, "to see Rhaine."

"Yes," he replied, as if it had been a question. He touched a button on his access, still glancing surreptitiously at Taylor and frowning slightly.

Almost immediately a door down one of the corridors slid open and a woman strode out. She was tall, nearly my height, and casually dressed in loose trousers and a brilliantly colored print overshirt. As she drew closer to us, I could see that the cut of her clothing skillfully minimized her almost skeletal thinness, although she certainly looked healthy enough and her ruddy complexion shone with vigor. She had her hand out as she approached me, and her voice was surprisingly resonant for someone so slender.

"Captain," she said, grasping my hand in a hearty clasp. "If you'll—" Her voice broke off, her eyes darting to my companion. "Taylor!" she exclaimed.

"Hi, Rhaine," Taylor responded with enthusiasm, taking a step forward and giving Rhaine a quick, friendly hug. Then he grinned, shaking her shoulders. "Powers, woman—don't you ever *eat*?"

It might have been an unexpected coincidence, but somehow I wasn't surprised. Taylor had worked for years in public relations for Longuard, one of the quadrant's largest shipping concerns. He must have known thousands of people; at times it seemed as though he might have known half the people in all the settled worlds. It could hardly come as a surprise, then, that he would know the more or less unofficial head of all the independent freightmen in the quadrant.

Rhaine looked from Taylor to me, then back again. She had sleek salt-and-pepper hair cut in short layers so that it framed her thin face like black and gray shingles. I guessed her to be barely middle-aged. She was normal, with cheekbones too sharply angular to be pretty, but the smile that Taylor had put on her face made her look almost winsome and certainly less intimidating.

"How long are you on-planet?" she asked Taylor bluntly, as if I had not even been there.

Taylor shrugged, a gesture both self-effacing and engaging. "A while," he said.

The woman studied him a moment longer. "Good to see you again," she said. Then she nodded to me, gesturing down the hall. "Captain?"

Because the position Rhaine held did not officially exist, the room to which she escorted me was not exactly her office, but the term would do for lack of anything more precise. Unlike the Teamsters, the independent freightmen did not have an organization or elected officials. But if we had, Rhaine would have been our head. When a label was necessary, she usually referred to herself as our "spokesman." Basically her function consisted of two things: mediating disputes between competing freightmen, whether between two independents or between independent and Teamster, and usually involving contracts, real or imagined; and protecting freightmen's interests in conflicts, official or not, with the Authorities.

The room we entered was ornamented almost to the point of clutter with an eclectic collection of bric-a-brac from half the settled planets in the quadrant. While the woman's lean face and steady brown eyes suggested a certain severity of style, I suspected the room reflected her true nature: an aspect of curiosity, an inveterate sense of acquisition, and more than a little nostalgia. She pointed me toward a low-slung upholstered couch and rapidly crossed the textured yellow carpet to her desk, where the same cheerful clutter held sway.

"Coffee?" she asked me, using her own huge mug to gesture toward a large urnlike pressure coffee maker. "It's the real stuff," she added by way of clarification, "not synthetic."

I shook my head, somewhat nonplussed. "No, thanks." My nerves were already strung tightly enough; I hardly needed caffeine.

"I drink too much of this stuff myself," Rhaine confided casually as the dark liquid jetted from the urn's stainless-steel nozzle, filling the air with a rich, heady aroma. "A vice," she continued, turning from the desk, "I've developed from decades of drinking every wretched coffee substitute known to man, on colonies from here to the New Beacons." She deftly spooned a small mountain of artificial sweetener crystals into the mug, concluding, "Being able to get the real stuff has really spoiled me."

I knew a little about Rhaine, but just the kinds of things every freightman knew. She had been born into a merchanter's line and had found that the work suited her. As her reference to the dregs of the systems' synthetic coffee indicated, she had traveled widely for most of her life. It puzzled me that she had ever agreed to take on this unofficial position as freightmen's advocate and had tied herself down to a colony world like Porta Flora, especially after having tasted the freedom of space for so long. But then, I also suspected that this was not a position you either "took" or not; it was a position that acquired you.

I guess maybe the obvious question showed on my face, because as she crossed the room again to perch on the padded arm of the couch where I was seated, Rhaine's calm brown eyes were regarding me with a certain bemused inquiry. "Not what you expected?" she asked, lifting her mug.

I appreciated her bluntness. "I was just wondering why you do it stay here, I mean," I said, gesturing vaguely around us, "and why you gave up freighting."

Taking a deep draught of her coffee, Rhaine glanced around the well-filled room, her lean face strangely impassive. For a moment the only sounds were the soft hum of the air-conditioning and the faint far-off drumming of water on metal. I thought perhaps I had asked a question to which she would not offer an answer. But then she shrugged lightly and said simply, "I guess I had too much stuff to have to keep hauling it all around."

For several moments longer she just studied me silently. Despite the tentativeness of her posture, perched on the couch arm, she seemed totally self-possessed and thoughtful. Finally she said, "I've reviewed the vidchip you sent me."

There were several reasons why I had chosen Porta Flora as the Authority center where I sought Intervention; Rhaine and her reputation had been one of them. When I had arrived on-planet, I had sent her a vidchip I'd prepared of the events that had necessitated my confrontation with the Authorities. Most of the chip was composed of the memory record of Handyman, *Raptor*'s shipboard Integrator. That part of the account was automatically legally admissible as fact, since an Integrator could not be made to prevaricate. The rest of it was my own testimony, augmenting and clarifying Handy's factual record and taking sole responsibility for *Raptor*'s actions over New Cuba and

Heinlein. That part, too, was the absolute truth—as far as it went. Along with the chip, I had sent a simple request for a chance to meet with Rhaine before I went before the Ombudsman. For although he would be the professional intercessor, the one who would represent me by formally bringing my grievance before the Authorities, I still found myself in need of another kind of counsel. Thus I found myself sitting in that comfortably cluttered office, watching that wiry woman's noncommittal face, waiting for her to go on.

Dropping her gaze, Rhaine took another long sip of coffee. As she lowered the mug from her lips, she said, "First of all, you can forget about the incident over New Cuba."

I must have actually jumped off the couch, for I suddenly was nearly face to face with Rhaine. "*Forget* about it—" Someone in New Cuba's Port had tried to *kill* me—had given my ship's Integrator defective coordinates for the pull, had tried to send us right into the path of a Military Authority cruiser—and I should "forget" it?

To my surprise, Rhaine's reaction to my outburst was more one of bemusement than of reproach. "I didn't mean 'forget it' like it didn't happen," she quickly explained. "I just meant it's already been taken care of." As I sank back onto the couch, embarrassed but mollified, she went on. "You had plenty of witnesses on that one, independents and Teamsters. Even if every Authority worker in Port had been conspiring against you, they couldn't've stood up to that kind of stink." She stared into her coffee mug, frowning slightly; then she took another long swallow. "You won't have any more problems with Port on New Cuba. Let's just say the people responsible for that incident won't be planning their next vacation for quite some time."

Detainment, I thought, with a stab of malicious satisfaction. Interference with the regulation of the pull was a capital offense; it wasn't a matter solved by paying off some fine. Of course, technically what I had done—switching to unauthorized pull coordinates, delaying against Port's command—was also a capital offense, but it didn't seem likely that I was going to face any repercussions from it, not even a written reprimand. Considering the circumstances, it would have been like getting cited for illegal pedestrian access because you'd had to jump into a vehicles-only area to avoid being hit by a ground car that was trying to run you over.

I shifted to settle back into a more civilized posture on the overstuffed couch as Rhaine drained the last of her coffee and cradled the big mug in her long, almost delicate hands. "The rest of it is more . . . complicated," she conceded.

" 'Complicated,' " I echoed with an ironic little grimace. "That's a tactful term for it." If only she had known the whole of it; and she'd *really* have "complicated."

"Of course," she continued, rolling the empty mug from side to side in her hands, "the fact that the person of highest authority on Heinlein also happens to be your maternal aunt has helped uncomplicate it a bit."

I flashed her a quick, appreciative grin, a grin that could only widen as Rhaine went on.

"Mahta was, shall we say, extremely displeased with the events surrounding your forced departure from the planet." Rhaine's eyes came up to meet mine, and there was a thinly veiled spark of amusement, perhaps even satisfaction, glinting in them. "I don't think I need to inform you that the Military Authority no longer enjoys stationing privileges on Heinlein. In fact, both the Military and the Civilian Authorities are currently codefendants in a rather large and complex class action suit being brought against them by the populace on Heinlein."

It didn't really surprise me, but I still almost had to laugh aloud at the consequences of incurring Mahta's wrath. The fact that she was defending her planet, not just her niece, did nothing to diminish my appreciation. "Am I likely to be brought up on charges?" I asked.

The mug was still then, the pale and sinewy fingers quiescent. The peppery-haired woman eyed me silently for a moment. Then her thin shoulders traced a slight shrugging motion. "It's possible," she told me matter-of-factly, "but if you want my gut feeling, no." She shifted a little on the couch's arm, leaning fractionally closer to me. "First of all, Mahta has put both of the A's in a pretty untenable position as far as anything connected with Heinlein is concerned—at least for the foreseeable future." Her dark brows came together in a quizzical little arch. "I'm sure this lawsuit wasn't instigated just for your benefit," she said in a tone that implied she wasn't sure of any such thing, "but it can't do anything but help your cause. And then there's the matter of this mess with the research complex."

I had to struggle to keep my expression neutral and not let Rhaine see just how much her blunt assessment had delighted me. Raydor and I had not even made port on Porta Flora before the newsvids were full of what the information services had quickly christened "the Camelot tragedy"—a misnomer if ever

I'd heard one. To my way of thinking, a rogue asteroid devastating a populated world was a tragedy; one of MA's biggest research complexes, on the remote wasteworld of Camelot, inexplicably imploding with a loss of the entire facility was more like a monumental screwup. Raydor's immediate evaluation of the news had agreed with my own: The use of the term, along with the way the whole story was being handled, was good news for us. Obviously some factions in MA were wildly scrambling for damage control, and there was some industrial-strength ass covering going on.

"Heads started rolling in MA with that little fiasco on Heinlein," Rhaine continued as if she had read my thoughts, "and most of them haven't stopped rolling yet. When that research complex went prime on them, I think their first priority became damage control; their public image is so shaky right now, it'd have to improve considerably just to make it up to piss-poor."

Again I had to grin at her frank evaluation. Like most Citizens, Rhaine seemed to have a reluctant acceptance of the role of the Civilian Authority and an openly jaundiced view of the Military Authority. "Meaning it's not going to look too good for them to go witch-hunting after one freightman captain right now?" I asked her.

"Meaning I don't think they can afford to have you bring up anything else that might make them look any worse right now," Rhaine said, "even if you did fry a couple of their picket ships over Heinlein."

I sobered as she reminded me that if I did face charges on that, I was looking at multiple capital offenses, not small-time stuff. I guess I must have been frowning, because suddenly Rhaine set aside the mug and laid one of her bony hands over my forearm where it rested across the back of the couch. The touch was unexpected, and her words were surprisingly gentle, coming from this relative stranger.

"You've sent the Ombudsman what you sent me?" she asked me. When I nodded, she continued. "Don't worry, it's convincing." She squeezed my arm, then released it and slid gracefully to her feet. "You're going there from here?"

I nodded again.

"Then I just have one piece of advice for you," she told me. With a slight motion of her sharp chin, she indicated the direction of the reception area beyond the hall, where I'd left Taylor waiting. "Take him with you."

I involuntarily glanced in the direction she'd gestured. "Taylor?" I asked, puzzled.

Rhaine nodded. "Don't take him into chambers—don't even introduce him," she continued evenly. "Just have him along, like he is here." Seeing the glimmer of comprehension forming in my eyes, she said, "If you need an ace in the hole, he's it. Even if the people over there don't know him, he's got PR written all over him."

As she saw me to the door, that shrewd and perceptive woman took one last long, appraising look at me, a look that suggested that she knew damn well that the account I'd given her was by no means the extent of my story. Then she added one final caution. "Just remember when you go in there: Having Taylor along is going to be like having a fusion grenade with the pin pulled. You don't want to go waving him around or making threats or this whole publicity thing could just as easily go off in your own face."

As I nodded, I was thinking, If only she knew the whole of it. Then she would have realized that I had felt like I'd been carrying a fusion grenade with the pin pulled for quite some time already, ever since I had met Charles Alan Lewis.

CHAPTER TWO

I had been well aware of my options when I'd made the choice to come to Porta Flora. If someone found herself in a position of major disagreement with either the Civilian or the Military Authority, there were two courses of action open to her: She could seek Intervention, or she could run. If she ran, she essentially exiled herself. Space, even within the known systems, was virtually limitless. People could effectively disappear in even the colonized worlds. But then they would lose the one thing worth having—Citizenship—and become nonpersons. Even if the Authorities never caught up with them, they would have no status, no credit, no legal ownership of property, and no protection under the law. Citizenship was integral to my way of life. That was one of the reasons I had never considered running after Camelot.

Seeking Intervention was neither an admission of guilt nor an accusation against the Authorities; it was merely the first step in a process of fact-finding that would hopefully resolve the dispute between a Citizen and the A's to the relative satisfaction of each party. Intervention was like a very narrowly focused investigation, initially involving only two people, the Citizen and an Ombudsman, who functioned as sort of an idealized advocate for both sides. The result of Intervention could be a negotiated settlement, a formal lawsuit on the part of the Citizen, and/or legal charges filed against the Citizen by the Authorities. Obviously, the first outcome was considered the ideal.

There were a lot of reasons I'd chosen to come to Porta Flora, and none of them had involved the weather. One reason had been Rhaine. Although she had no legal status and no authority to represent me in any way, she had done exactly what I had hoped she could: She had reviewed the details of my complaint and had advised me just what she thought the Authorities' response would be. And from a freightman's point of view she was an excellent barometer of public sentiment and the prevailing mood concerning what had happened—or, rather, what was *perceived* to have happened—at Camelot. She had told me what I had hoped to hear, and although I had not been completely frank with her, I had revealed as much of the truth as I had any intention of revealing to the Ombudsman.

And then there had been the matter of her parting advice; using Taylor's serendipitous presence to my possible advantage probably never would have occurred to me. I wasn't sure yet just how I felt about that. I was certain that Taylor had already intended to come along with me to the Ombudsman's, but I couldn't shake the nagging feeling that I was somehow using him, even if his presence was voluntary and quite innocent.

As I came back down the hallway to the central reception area, I found Taylor leaning across the semicircular counter in animated conversation with the gray-haired receptionist. In fact, it was the older man who glanced up as I approached, breaking off their exchange with a polite smile. I nodded to him as Taylor turned to me.

"Everything okay?" Taylor asked quietly, reaching for my arm.

His concern was genuine; I had seen enough of the manufactured variety to know the difference. "So far," I replied. "Come on, let's go."

As we started for the exit, Taylor turned back to the formerly dour-looking receptionist, whose expression was now quite pleasant. "Nice talking to you, Pointer," he called out to the man. "Thanks for the suggestions."

The gray-haired man actually gave us a little wave of farewell.

As we rode the lift back up to the ground level, I eyed Taylor with bemused skepticism. "Suggestions?" I repeated.

"Yeah," Taylor said. "The guy's lived here since the place was still part of the Botanical Reserve. He knows a lot of stuff about the old colony." A self-satisfied grin decorated Taylor's expressive mouth. "He gave me the names of a couple of really good places to eat—not the usual tourist traps, either, but places with *real* food."

I had to grin back at him. "You and the food," I teased him, feeling a small and probably transitory but very welcome surge of confidence.

Outside the building the rain had temporarily stopped, and

sunshine, hard and bright, was beating down on the dripping awnings and canopies and sparkling off the glassed-in roofs. Despite the best efforts of the coolant cyclers, the heat and humidity were considerable, and steam rose from the damp walkways in stifling waves. Innately seeming to understand my preoccupation, Taylor was silent as we walked along the throughway. He stayed nearly shoulder to shoulder with me—easily now, since most of the midday crowds were gone—but he didn't touch me.

The building where the Ombudsman had his office was only a short distance away, in the older section of the settlement. The structure looked like one of the original housing units for the botanical workers; it had been carved out of the dark native volcanic rock and featured a huge multistory domed atrium that had been well maintained and was still lush with a riot of exuberant plant growth. As we entered through the front lobby, the air became deliciously cool; as was usual on the colonized worlds, it seemed the original equipment was the only kind that still performed up to expectations.

Because the building, like many of the other older constructions, housed residences as well as offices, the entry security system was arranged a little differently. We stopped first in a small foyer equipped with nothing but a staggering array of plant life while I fed my ID into an Integrator access slot in the highly polished wall. Within a minute a dry voice announced, "Captain Jo-lac; enter, please." I pocketed my card as we stepped through into a more conventional-looking lobby.

The Ombudsman's position entitled him to Authority personnel, and so the woman who greeted us was a government worker, clad in CA's cream and navy jumpsuit. She was also, if I had my guess, an extensively Restructured Class Five. Differentiating such things had long ago become second nature to me, a sort of involuntary reflex whenever I met someone. She was slim and very pretty, with long blond hair and wide brown eyes. But her features were almost too perfect, and something about her face just didn't register as quite right to my automatic scanning. It was the symmetry, I think; government surgeons never seemed to have grasped the basic fact that normal people all have some degree, however subtle, of dissymmetry to the two halves of their faces. Most Normals were rigorously symmetrical; it was an unsettling effect, especially if it drew your eye, involuntarily and consistently, in every Restructured person you met.

The blond smiled sunnily at us. "The Ombudsman is ready to see you, Captain," she said to me, although her attention, however surreptitiously, was actually on Taylor at the moment.

I returned her pleasant smile and asked, "Is there somewhere convenient my friend could wait?"

"Of course," she responded just a fraction too promptly to maintain any credible illusion of disinterest on her part. She beamed at Taylor. "If you'd like to wait here," she told him, "I'll be right with you again." She made a small motion, probably an unconscious one, to smooth back the thick swag of her blond hair from her shoulder. "Perhaps you'd enjoy a tour of the atrium," she added.

"I'm sure he would," I said, shooting Taylor a knowing smirk. "He's very interested in the local culture, aren't you, Taylor?"

"It's surprising what you can learn," Taylor said, his malleable mouth grinning wryly.

The blond woman hastened to lead me off through one of the doorways. We traveled the length of a short, wide corridor, then she pressed the summons button on the last door and said into the speaker, "Sir? Captain Jo-lac."

The door cycled open, and I stepped through alone. I was in a small, square office, cozy yet almost Spartanly bare compared to Rhaine's. There was the usual Integrator access console/desk combination, a cluster of a few low upholstered chairs, and a liberal sprinkling of green plants. A man stood amid the greenery—which was, I could then see, grouped under a small skylight—watering can in hand. He turned toward me as the door closed behind me, and the corners of his mouth lifted ironically.

"We get nearly ten meters of rain a season here," the Ombudsman remarked, brandishing the can, "yet we still have to water our plants daily."

I just stared at him for a moment, honestly surprised by his appearance. Even clad in the traditional ankle-length, charcoal-gray-colored robe of his profession, he was not a physically impressive man. Actually, he was rather short and slightly built, and he was obviously moving past what could still accurately be called middle age.

"Won't you have a seat, please, Captain?" he inquired, gesturing toward the chairs. As he crossed to the console and set down the watering can, his expression was affable, with only the barest hint of amusement. "Can I offer you something to drink?"

"Just cold water, thank you," I said, dropping into the chair nearest the door and trying to study him without being too obvious about it. His skin was the dark, deep, rich color of burnished copper; he wore his long black hair, which was marked by two winglike gray streaks at the temples, plaited back into a single braid. He was used to the effect he caused; I could see that in his face as he bent to retrieve glasses from a compartment beneath the console. It was just that there was so little of the Old Blood left. The war had decimated his ancestors, and the Alterations had so drastically narrowed the gene pool that the necessity of interbreeding had pretty much eliminated what had been left of any kind of racial purity. His kind of coloration was uncommon, as were the distinctive set of his sharp cheekbones, the coarse texture of his black hair, and the hawkish jut of his nose. I let my scrutiny become more overt then, relaxing as I saw that he was not offended by it. If anything, I think he was proud of his uniqueness.

Pouring water from a tall metal pitcher, the Ombudsman glanced over at me again, his dark straight brows arching. "Ice?" he asked with a trace of the same ironic humor.

"Fine," I replied, quickly scanning the little room as he added cubes from a canister.

"So, Captain," he continued, lifting the two glasses, "now that you've been here a few days, how are you enjoying Porta Flora?"

Suspicious of all small talk just on general principle, I held my response until he had come across the room and handed me one of the glasses. "It's all right so far," I said as he slid gracefully onto the chair beside me, arranging the folds of his gray robe over his crossed legs.

"It's quite an interesting place," he went on, gently swirling the contents of his own glass, something vaguely milk-colored. His dark brows lifted again. "But then, I've thought that about every place I've served," he added with a self-deprecating smile. "There's a lot of history here, a lot of beauty. I hope you've had a chance to take in the old Botanical Reserve, the Cascades, Traders Row . . . Little Venice."

Taking a sip of the ice water, I eyed him over the rim of the glass. In essence the man was my advocate in this matter; it would have been a little disappointing to find out he had not taken care to inform himself fully. And my meeting with Rhaine had hardly been clandestine; I had made no effort to hide it.

And so my only response to his suggestion was a polite "Sounds like a lot to see."

"But well worth it," he assured me. He leaned back in his chair, and his expression remained benign but perceptive as he continued. "I appreciate the thoroughness of the record you've sent me, Captain. Your ship's Integrator is obviously very astute."

Thinking of how Handy would react to such an assessment, even one meant as a compliment, I replied neutrally, "It's part of his function to record everything that happens."

"And I've found that 'everything that happens' usually speaks for itself," the Ombudsman said, sipping from his glass. His heavily lidded dark eyes studied me in silence for a moment. "Are you aware that to this point the Authorities have not filed any legal charges against you?" he asked me.

I nodded, balancing the cold, wet glass between my hands and feeling its chill seep into my fingers. "Do you think they're going to?" I asked him.

He made a small movement with his chin, indicating his Integrator console. "Based on the account you've shown me, they have no real basis for any punitive action," he said. But his phrasing gave me the subtle message that he suspected I was withholding something from him. He spread the fingers of one hand, making an expansive gesture. "Quite apart from your own account, both the incident over New Cuba and the events on Heinlein are extensively corroborated by numerous witnesses. Your actions in both cases were justified self-defense; I can't conceive of any other verdict."

I could actually feel some of the tension run out of my body as he spoke, even though his tone remained level, almost bland, as he rendered his opinion. As I shifted slightly, taking another quick sip of water, he asked me matter-of-factly, "Do you intend to file a lawsuit against the Authorities in these matters?"

I swallowed too rapidly, almost choked, and then had to cough. "I don't know," I replied when I could speak. The smoldering rage that had burned in me when I had left Camelot had been diluted by distance and time—diminishing somewhat with every arrival and pullout we had made from a series of little backwater worlds as we had worked our way to Porta Flora—until finally I realized that my fury had gradually been replaced by a sort of dogged determination just to see the situation through and get it over with. I had become too concerned with avoiding being on the receiving end of legal action to really seriously consider offensive tactics. The random idea of inflicting slow death by dismemberment still entertained me, perhaps, but not the tedium of legal suits.

"It is one avenue open to you," the Ombudsman continued smoothly, resting his glass on one gray-robed knee. "However, I feel I must advise you that it has been my experience that if you are willing to waive your right to suit, the Authorities are more likely to relinquish their right to further legal charges as well."

I tilted my glass slightly, making the ice cubes clink together; my fingers had grown numb from the cold. "What you're telling me is that if I try to press this, the A's will probably just invent some charges—even if they don't have a case," I said carefully.

"In my opinion they don't have a case now," he said. "But if you did choose to bring suit, the case might face a considerable delay." There he paused, the corners of his mouth crimping faintly. "I suspect the Heinlein class action suit is going to tie up the Authorities' legal resources for a while. If your suit is delayed long enough . . ." He shrugged. "Other information could conceivably come to light—information which could unfavorably influence your cause."

It was not a threat; it was merely a dispassionate and probably accurate scenario for what was likely to happen if I did try to sue the A's. It was also another broad hint that the Ombudsman knew there was more to my story than what he was being told.

"In any case," he concluded, "if you are considering legal action, I would strongly advise you to seek separate counsel from a lawyer, preferably an advocate."

I was silent a moment, thinking. Then I asked, "If I waived my right to sue, the A's would waive their right to prosecute me?"

The Ombudsman gazed evenly at me—a warrior of the Old Blood then, this black-haired man, domesticated only by the charcoal-colored robe of his office. "That is what they have indicated to me, yes," he said.

But there was something else there, something in his demeanor that let me know that this was not quite the end of it. It wasn't to be that simple. I lifted my glass slowly and deliberately and drained the last of the ice water while the Ombudsman shifted his legs. After a few moments he spoke again, as I knew he would.

"The Authority liaison here would like to speak with you." He quickly held up one lean brown hand as if to forestall my inevitable and obvious response to that idea and continued smoothly. "You are, of course, under no obligation to talk with him about this or any other matter. And if you should decide not to speak with him, that refusal cannot be used against you in any possible future deliberations." He paused, his dark eyes narrowed to near slits beneath the craggy ridges of his brows. "But I would urge you to speak with him, Captain."

With precise deliberation, I set the empty water glass on the floor beside my chair; then I met his stolid gaze. "Why?" I asked.

The Ombudsman made a small, nonspecific gesture with one hand. "Because there is still too much you don't know," he replied simply.

I could have reminded him that there was still a hell of a lot the Authorities didn't know, either, and that I would just as soon keep it that way. But I didn't. Maybe partially because he had a point, partially because I was curious, and partially because he had been square with me; whatever the reason, I finally just nodded, giving him leave to go to his console and press the intercom button.

The Authority liaison had obviously been waiting, because it seemed to take him only about thirty seconds to come to the door of the Ombudsman's office. To my surprise, he was an older man, at least in his sixties, and not some green recruit. Places like Porta Flora were usually considered rungs one used on the way up the ladder; men his age were generally well into their careers and were posted on more prestigious worlds. I fought a momentary, almost reflexive aversion to the unbidden memory his maroon and navy jumpsuit stirred in me: the image of another liaison, Rollo, the little jerk who'd gotten me into all of this in the first place on New Cuba, a lifetime ago.

"John Leppers," he said, offering me his hand.

Again I felt surprise. The first name/surname combination was archaic, and few career Authority personnel still used it. With the elimination of traditional concepts of family and marriage, few people clung to the old system, especially those in government work. The fact that Leppers did told me something about him. I briefly shook his hand, quickly glancing him over. He was rather unremarkable looking, although he was normal: short graying hair, a blandly pleasant face, sandy brown eyes. Sometimes I thought that all of us had started to look too much alike—certainly the Normals and even some of the normals. It was as if the Alterations had forced us to eliminate most of what

was unexpected and diverse in human appearance. Especially
there, contrasted with the Ombudsman's almost heretical eth-
nicity, Leppers's physical conformity seemed especially pronounced.

The liaison dropped down into the chair beside me, where
the Ombudsman had been sitting only minutes earlier. To his
credit, he didn't make any pretense of small talk. Resting his
elbows on the chair arms, his forearms aligned perfectly parallel
to each other, he said without preamble, "We're having a problem, Captain, one that you can help us with."

I made a conscious effort not to look to the Ombudsman, who
stood a short distance from us, still at his console. I knew that
he had given a copy of the report I'd sent to him to the Authorities; that was part of the process of Intervention. I also knew
that Leppers's blunt statement had little to do with the carefully
edited series of events I had covered in that report. I made myself look instead at the liaison, my expression as noncommittal
as my voice as I responded. "What kind of problem?"

Unblinking, Leppers met my gaze evenly. "The incident at
Camelot," he told me.

I shrugged slightly, shaking my head as if I were mildly bewildered but still willing to be polite. "I've heard a little about
that," I said. "I really haven't had much time lately to keep up
on all the news."

Leppers shifted in his chair, leaning fractionally forward. Although I could not have described the exact difference, something in the expression on his totally ordinary face had changed,
and his voice contained an edge that had not been there before.
"Then that explains your choice of companions, I suppose," he
said, jerking his chin toward the doorway.

It took me a moment to realize that Leppers was referring to
Taylor and that his gesture had been in the direction of the outer
reception area where I'd left him. I let my brows rise in a cal-
culated arch. "Taylor?" I inquired owlishly. "He's just an old
friend."

The liaison grunted, his brow furrowing slightly. The sarcasm that crept into his tone added an odd rasp to his level voice.
"An old friend who just happens to work for MediaPlex."

No, he doesn't! The words that leapt into my brain were nearly
out of my mouth before I could catch myself, and I had to struggle to keep the surprise from showing on my face. Not only did
I have to suppress my surprise, I also had to instantly fabricate
an expression of puzzlement to successfully cover both my ig-

norance of this fact and my innocence of any reason why it should upset the liaison. Actually, I was stunned to learn that Taylor was working for MediaPlex—one of the largest multi-media information networks—and hadn't told me. No wonder Rhaine had thought the A's would find his presence intimidating. Good old Taylor, who probably was at that very moment down in the atrium, happily groping the Ombudsman's perfectly symmetrical little blond—damn him!

Luckily, I didn't need to come up with any witty response, because Leppers, still sternly frowning, continued. "We have reason to believe you were involved in what happened on Camelot, Captain."

"Reason to believe"—but no proof, or at least no proof that would hold up in a court of law. That was why we were sitting there in the Ombudsman's office trading insinuations instead of Leppers interviewing me through the bars of the visitors' area in some detention center. I let some of my newly burgeoning irritation leak through onto my expression, coloring my feigned confusion with some understandable annoyance. "And just what makes you think I had anything to do with that?" I demanded, allowing myself an exasperated glance toward the silent Ombudsman, who stood calmly with the backs of his thighs braced against his desk.

Leppers was poised so motionlessly in his chair, I almost felt like I should check him for breathing. His voice was flat, unemotional, nearly without inflection. "Because of Charles Alan Lewis," he said.

Time to check *myself* for breathing. Although it had not been entirely unexpected, hearing this relentless, colorless man speak Lewis's name made something inside me tighten painfully. Oh, no, you don't! I thought grimly. You're not using him as bait—not again! I now knew why the A's were interested in securing my cooperation, and I didn't want any part of it. I stared back at Leppers, my look almost offensive in its directness. "What about him?" I asked with elaborate nonchalance. "He was indentured to Heinlein, and I transported him there—as a run for MA, as a matter of fact."

Leppers exhaled softly, but neither his posture nor his tone changed. "But on Heinlein you bought his IS contract; then you released him from it."

I stared at him in blunt bafflement. "So?" I shook my head as if in puzzled irritation. "Is that against some law now?"

But Leppers was implacable, as stolid as a rock wall. "You took him to Camelot, didn't you?" he persisted.

I laughed, shortly and harshly. "Why the hell would I do *that*? Besides, the whole damned place blew up. If we'd been there, we'd both be dead!"

While his expression remained unchanged, Leppers abruptly altered his tack. "We have an offer to make you, Captain, an exchange of information: what you know for what we know."

"Not much of a deal for you, then," I retorted, "because I don't know shit!" I redirected my considerable ire, glaring at the Ombudsman and demanding, "*This* is what was so important that you insisted I listen to him?" Suddenly propelling myself up out of my chair, I encompassed both men with an irate glower and declared to the room in general, "I think I've given you both more than enough of my time. So long, gentlemen!"

I was quite genuinely willing and even eager to walk out, would have made it to the door in about three strides, in fact, had not the Ombudsman's unexpected intervention stopped me in my tracks.

"Tell her," he said softly to Leppers.

The liaison definitely had an expression now, although he was struggling manfully to suppress it; he was quite indignant and apparently more than a little shocked at the Ombudsman's audacity. "You're overstepping the bounds of your office, Hidalgo."

The Ombudsman did not move from his almost casual posture leaning against his desk, did not even raise his voice, and yet this black-braided man's tone contained a furious intensity that was like a hand reaching out and seizing the liaison. *"Tell her,"* he reiterated, "or I will."

Leppers looked from the Ombudsman to me and then back again. I hadn't been wrong in taking Leppers's measure; he was the product of his training and the years he had served. You didn't negotiate with terrorists; you didn't give something away unilaterally. He was almost physically unable to speak. "Only if she agrees to tell me what she knows," he finally insisted, his hands gripping the armrests of his chair.

The Ombudsman looked over to me, where I still stood with my hand hovering over the door release. "Captain?" he said.

But I shook my head. "No," I replied tautly. "Him first."

For the first time the Ombudsman moved, pushing himself off from the desk and standing erect. He addressed himself to the seething liaison. "Then tell her," he instructed calmly.

"But she has to—"

"She has to do *nothing*," the Ombudsman interrupted, his hawklike face fixing the hapless liaison with a piercing look. "She doesn't trust you—I doubt that I would either, given what's happened to her." He took a step closer to Leppers's chair, staring down at the gray-haired man, his voice so low, it was almost a coarse whisper. "If you want her help, you're going to have to *ask* for it, not try to bargain for it."

Duty and his decades of service warred on the liaison's face; the conflict he suffered was palpable. Under other circumstances I might even have felt sympathy for him, but not there, not then. The A's wanted my cooperation very badly, and I was determined to see just how badly. Leppers's capitulation, when it came, was both abrupt and harsh, his voice coming out like a hiss. "All right! All right, then!" He glared balefully from the Ombudsman to me; his fingers, clawlike, clutched the edges of the armrests until his knuckles were white. His eyes grew hard, almost defiant, as he began to speak.

"Anytime you have the kind of consolidation of power and wealth that the Authorities have assembled, you are going to have a socio-economic structure that will tempt a certain criminal element—call them 'renegades' if you wish." It was clear that Leppers, like everyone else in the Authorities, definitely preferred not to call them that; the term seemed to imply a certain maverick rebelliousness that vaguely suggested some justification or even secret admiration for their acts of subterfuge. "Over the years the Authorities have ruled, we have been continually weeding out these deviants." His tone almost seemed to dare me to dispute the A's righteousness. But much as Leppers might have been loath to admit to their existence, these renegades were one of our society's most poorly kept secrets. Despite that, any details on their identities or even their crimes were a lot harder to come by—I knew that for a fact, because during our meandering journey from Heinlein to Porta Flora, I had plumbed the depths of Handy's memory banks for anything even remotely related to that "criminal element," and had come up with little that I hadn't already discovered the hard way.

"For some time now," Leppers went on, "we've been aware of the signs of a particularly dangerous and subversive form of criminal activity. There have been certain . . . irregularities in some of the Authorities' operations." The fingers of one hand lifted slightly, tracing a brief, nonspecific gesture. "The diversion of funds from contingency accounts, atypical allotment of personnel, discrepancies in inspection reports—just little things, you understand, and scattered all over with no discernible pattern to them. But we never assume coincidence.''

He began to relax a little, falling into a sort of didactic mode that was probably closer to his usual method of operation than his attempt at brinksmanship had been. ''Eventually we discovered that the irregularities could all be traced to MA's Division of Research, but we still had nothing concrete. We were still casting about in the dark when Charles Alan Lewis came crashing back into the system.''

Leppers paused a moment, scrutinizing me quite frankly. I don't know what, if anything, he could read in my rigorously schooled expression, but whatever it was, he seemed satisfied. ''That was the first time we could connect what was happening with what was known about the Class Tens.'' Almost hesitantly, one of Leppers's hands stroked the smooth curve of the armrest; he glanced away from me and then, after a moment, back again. ''The information about the Class Tens is classified material; I don't have clearance for that level. Quite frankly, I wasn't even certain of their existence until this investigation involved me with them. So what I can tell you is only as much of the information as I have been given myself. After Lewis reentered the system as a Citizen, we knew Class Tens were being exploited in an unconscionable, criminal manner; after Camelot broke open, we found out what had been done to some of them. Unfortunately, most of our knowledge was after the fact, and the people involved are now dead. But we did have one informant we were able to apprehend from outside that group; he has been our primary source of what we've learned since the research complex was destroyed.''

I found that I had been holding my breath; I let it out then, slowly and deliberately, and eyed Leppers with a studied calmness. At some point during his narrative it had resumed raining; I could hear the faint drumming of water, like a muffled heartbeat, thudding on the office's skylight. ''I'm afraid I can't be of much help to you, then,'' I said levelly. ''It sounds like you already know everything that I do.''

''We think you can be of great help to us, Captain,'' Leppers said quietly, ''because you and the others who were with you were the only people who went inside that illicit facility and lived to tell about it.''

I felt my mouth pulling into a thin line; I met Leppers's gaze without flinching. "Assuming that I ever *was* even anywhere near Camelot," I reminded him acerbically. I shrugged and punched the door release. "Sorry I can't be of any help to you."

"Wait!"

Something in the tone of Leppers's voice made the single word more of a request than a command, and so I hesitated halfway through the open door and turned back to face him.

Leppers had gotten to his feet, but he seemed awkwardly poised there, as if even now that he was up, he had no intention of actually trying to detain me. "Perhaps you do know even less than I, Captain," he said intently, "but I can tell you this: There are still other Class Tens. We may not know their present location, but we know for a fact that they exist—and they are still in terrible danger from these renegades."

I considered that for a moment; then I took the half step back into the room that was necessary for the mechanism to allow the door to slide closed again. "What makes you think that?" I inquired, genuinely curious.

Leppers wet his lips; it was one of the few involuntary gestures that painfully controlled man had allowed himself thus far. If he'd had any intention of trying to withhold further information from me, the notion seemed forgotten then. I was finally to see how badly the A's wanted me.

"Immediately after the devastation on Camelot," he said softly, "substantial funds were withdrawn from certain 'liquid' accounts, accounts we hadn't even tagged as suspicious. We also believe that materials, equipment, and even some personnel have been abruptly removed from within the system, although we can't be one hundred percent certain yet; those things take a little longer to trace." He spread his hands, a gesture of acquiescence that was almost like an entreaty. "The rest of the Class Tens are still out there, Captain; the Authorities may not know exactly where, but we aren't the only ones looking for them. There is a renegade group within the system, still free to go after them again." His voice dropped even lower, and in that moment I had a sudden, surprising glimpse of the kind of passion that could be fired behind those bland and very ordinary features. "What has happened is intolerable to us—utterly intolerable. That it might happen again is beyond tolerance. That is why we're asking you to help us prevent that."

I met Leppers's eyes for several long moments, my own face kept tightly neutral. Then I reached out and hit the door release again.

"Captain!" the liaison called out.

From within the doorway I looked back at him. "You know," I said with perfect calm, "I delivered your IS to Heinlein, and I never even got the second half of my fee from MA."

Briefly stupefied, the older man just stared at me in complete surprise. "If I guarantee that you are reimbursed, then will—"

My eyes shifted to the Ombudsman's steely face. "Then I waive my right to suit," I told him, "if the Authorities waive their right to prosecution."

"We waive it!" Leppers nearly shouted, stepping forward even as I began to move into the corridor. "But Captain, will you help us?"

I didn't stop exactly, but I did slow my pace briefly as I tossed off over my shoulder, "I'll think about it."

CHAPTER
THREE

I covered the short corridor in a few long strides; the lobby area was deserted. I continued on through the connecting door to the outer foyer, where earlier I had presented my ID, and then out onto the throughway in front of the building. I neither slowed my pace nor looked backward as I swung into the relatively uncrowded pedestrian traffic beneath the curving canopy.

I was halfway to the next intersection before I heard the familiar voice calling my name. Lowering my head, I passed a group of puzzled strollers, who pulled back out of my way with as much alacrity as if I'd been carrying a drawn beam weapon.

"Jo!"

The voice was closer now, nearly right behind me. I cut to the left and out of the lane of pedestrian traffic, swerving abruptly across the center of the throughway. Out from under the protective canopy, I stepped into the thundering downpour of blood-warm rain, plowing through the ankle-deep tide that churned in the central gutter. Just as I reached the other side of the throughway, Taylor's fingers caught my shoulder, spinning me around to face him.

"Jo, for Powers' sake! Where the hell are you going?" His handsome, affable face was drawn with concern and confusion; his hand, grasping my upper arm, pulled me the rest of the way back under the protection of the walkway's overhead covering. He shook the water from his hair. "Why didn't you wait for me?" With his free hand he brushed at the darkened fabric of my flightsuit. "Stars, you're soaking wet! Haven't you ever heard of *crosswalks*?"

Perversely, the unguarded hurt and puzzlement in his eyes only served to goad my anger further. I rounded on him with a full load of indignation, twisting my shoulders to pull free of

29

his solicitous hold. "Why didn't you tell me you're working for MediaPlex?" I demanded.

Taylor pulled back from me, blinking; he was as totally startled as if I had just demanded, "Why didn't you tell me what you had for lunch two weeks ago?" Struggling to make some sense of my anger, he automatically reached out to touch my arm again, only to have me bat his hand away. "It never came up!" he blurted out, still baffled by my behavior. "Jo, I didn't know it mattered."

Aware that our altercation was beginning to attract some attention on the throughway, I shook back my dripping hair and began to walk again, moving with sharp, deliberate strides. But when Taylor matched my pace, I allowed him to stay at my side while I tried to rein in the reaction whose furious intensity was puzzling even to me.

"Jo, listen to me," Taylor said, his voice lowered but intent. He actually began to walk in front of me, backpedaling so that he could still face me, his brow creased with worry. "I left Longuard almost three years ago." He shrugged helplessly. "You didn't ask, and with everything you've had on your mind this afternoon, I just didn't think it seemed an appropriate time to bring it up."

I stopped abruptly, causing him to overshoot and forcing him to scurry forward to meet me again. I stared hard into his face, but all I could see in it was what had always been there: just Taylor, guileless and now filled with anxiety.

"I don't like him," Raydor had complained to me once, early on in my relationship with Taylor. "He's—*greasy*." And I had thought about it for a moment and then had just shrugged. "Yeah," I had agreed happily, "but it's a *sincere* sort of greasiness." That had never changed, and I was certain that Taylor was sincere now. Feeling somewhat foolish as my volatile anger evaporated, I reached up with a grudging frown and pushed back a wet lock of hair from his forehead.

Taylor took my hand and touched my fingertips to his lips, the corners of his mouth lifting in a tentative, hopeful smile. "Listen, if it'll make you feel any better," he told me, "next time I find you in a whole shitload of trouble with the A's, I'll just be totally insensitive and give you an endless, excruciatingly boring account of what *I've* been doing for the last few years first, okay?"

He made me grin; he always had been able to do that. Anger never stuck to him. He made me grin, and he wasn't pissed at me for acting like a jerk with him in public; how could I ever have doubted that he was my friend? I glanced around to see that the few passersby no longer seemed to have any interest in us once the shouting had stopped. I shrugged evocatively, letting him wrap my fingers in his. "Taylor, look—I'm sorry," I began.

But he stopped me, lifting my hand to his lips again, gently squeezing my fingers. "No," he said, telling me that apologies were not necessary. He searched my face for a moment, his eyes warm and concerned. "I've got some meetings this afternoon that I can't get out of," he said, "but I should be done by around eight hundred." His brows arched slightly. "Will you have dinner with me, Jo?" Reading the trace of hesitation off my face, he quickly continued. "There's that place that Rhaine's secretary told me about. It's down in the old central part of the settlement—not only real food but *live* music." He flashed his stellar smile. "C'mon, Jo . . ."

I pulled back a bit, slipping my hand from his. "I don't know if I'll be able to," I said.

"Okay," he said quickly, agreeably, "just think about it, huh? I'll come by later and see. What hangar bay are you in?"

I gave him the grid numbers, and he gave me a quick hug before we parted ways.

I was within walking distance of the port, but I was beginning to feel walked out. Since I was pretty well wetted down, the heat and humidity seemed especially oppressive to me, and the idea of shanking it even a half kilometer or so didn't exactly appeal to me anymore. I followed the covered walkway to the next intersection, where there was an entrance to the underground automated beltway, and rode the conveyerlike device to an intraport exit in our hangar. The beltways were always fairly crowded, even in midafternoon, especially near the port. It seemed that many of the freightmen, like most of the nonresidents of Porta Flora, had little tolerance for trekking around aboveground in the omnipresent rain and muggy heat.

I climbed a short ramp to the hangar level, feeling my entire suit liner sticking unpleasantly to my body. If anything, the heat and humidity were even worse in the hangars than they had been on the throughways. By the time I'd reached the section of the vast structure where my ship was berthed, I felt totally drained and vaguely depressed. Even the sight of *Raptor*, poised gracefully on the damp pavement of her designated bay, failed to give my spirits their customary lift.

As I palmed the hatch access on the sleek little freighter, I remembered the way I had turned on poor Taylor. When I thought about it, I understood where the unexpected blast of anger had come from, because I realized that I wasn't even really angry—I was afraid. And it didn't take a whole lot of brilliant personal insight to figure out just why I was frightened.

Forgoing the relief my cabin, a cold shower, and a change of clothing would have provided, I instead took the short passageway to Integration and palmed the hatch lock. As the hatch hissed softly open, the cool sweet air of Handyman's domain wafted out to greet me. Stepping through into the cheerily lit golden-colored room, I sank down gratefully into one of the padded chairs in front of his main access console. Immediately, the lights of his panel flickered to life.

"Hi, Handy," I said, resting my hand on the curve of his primary access.

"Hi, Jo," his deep voice rumbled. There was a beat, presumably devoted to his optic scan, before he went on. "Is it raining out?" he asked.

Wiseass! He always monitored the planetary weather, right down to the last drop of precipitation. "It's *always* raining on this place," I muttered, finger-combing back my damp and tangled hair. "Is Raydor back yet?"

"Back and gone again," Handy informed me. "They finished loading the stuff from Buttley's about an hour ago; then he went out. He said if you got back first to tell you that he'd be at the Port Authority office."

That didn't surprise me. At many ports the PA office functioned as sort of an informal gathering place for freightmen who were between runs. They hung around exchanging various rumors, gossip, and the occasional smattering of fact. Raydor wasn't especially interested in rumors or gossip, but he was a collector of fact, and you could learn a surprising amount by just listening around the Port Authority.

I tugged absently at the neckline of my suit liner where it clung to my sticky neck. "What about the Authority Integrator bank?" I asked. "Did you get into it?"

Handy made a grating noise, disconcertingly like a human's snort of contempt. The radical advances in Integration technology not only had compounded Biological Matrix Integrators' abilities, they also seemed to have exacerbated their emotional sensitivity. Integrators like Handy weren't machines, they were personalities—people, extraordinarily gifted people who, in his

case at least, were capable of maintaining an affectionate tolerance for my chronic if inadvertent underestimation of his skills.
"Of course I got into it," he responded. "Do you want me to
screen it for you now?"

The coolness of the room was beginning to cut into the le-
thargic despondency I had felt out on the throughway. "Just the
summary," I told him, knowing he had already prepared one.
"We'll save the details for later, if we need them."

I was slouched casually in my chair, studying the glowing
green lines of Handy's access screen, when the hatch softly
*whoosh*ed open behind me. There was only one other person
who could get into that room, and I didn't even need to turn to
greet Raydor, because he was already dropping into the other
chair beside me. He glanced at the material on the screen, and
I looked over at him.

Raydor's face wraps were unwound but still hanging in long
gray loops around his neck, as if he had discarded them in casual
haste somewhere during the trip from *Raptor*'s hatch to Integration. He was not perspiring—I didn't think Tachs sweated—but
the crepelike texture of his Altered face and neck were slightly
flushed with an unaccustomed pink color, and he had unfastened
the top portion of the seam of his flightsuit a few inches.

His eyes lifted from Handy's screen, and he studied my admittedly somewhat bedraggled appearance for a moment in
thoughtful silence. "How'd it go with Rhaine and the Ombudsman?" he asked quietly.

I leaned back in my chair, pulling up one knee and locking
both hands around it. Then I told him what had happened. With
Raydor, it was not necessary to embroider the account with a
lot of subjective response; he was skilled at reading nonverbal
nuance. To him, the facts were just the framework that he filled
in with the emotions he read so adeptly off me. The only thing
I left out was my little altercation with Taylor on the throughway,
even though it would have explained the soaking I'd taken. Raydor didn't particularly approve of Taylor; he grunted deprecatingly when I told him about the way Leppers had ambushed me
with the information about MediaPlex. Other than that, he made
no comments until I had finished my account.

"So," he said, "you trust him?"

I automatically assumed Raydor was referring to Leppers,
since trusting an Ombudsman—a professional sworn to an oath
of loyalty to Citizens that was more binding than any priest's
vow—was as much a given as taking your next breath. "To a

point," I replied, adding, "Not that it matters much if I trust him or not—with the renegades, he can't even trust his *own* security."

"But you're clear of charges," he reiterated, as if to assure himself.

"Yeah," I confirmed, dropping my raised knee back down again. I stared at Handy's screen. "But it looks like that's about all I'm clear of."

Silently, Raydor studied the data summary with me. From the information Handy had been able to pirate out of the Authorities' main Integration bank, it appeared Leppers had given me a pretty accurate and complete overview of what the A's knew, or at least what they were willing to commit to record. I had a feeling most of their data on both the renegades and the Class Tens was mnemonic and wouldn't be found in any bank. Even Handy had been unable to find specifics. As I read through the summary, I realized with some disappointment that I'd almost been hoping the liaison had lied to me, that he had exaggerated the extent of the A's problem in an effort to elicit my help. But if anything his brief revelations had understated what the A's, and the Class Tens, were still up against as long as those particular renegades remained uncaptured. If there was one thing that I had been made brutally certain of, it was this: These people, whoever they were, whatever their motive or method, would not back down—and they knew that I was their link to Lewis.

As the last lines of the summary scrolled off Handy's screen, Raydor's big dark eyes met mine. He didn't comment on what we'd just reviewed; he didn't need to. All he said, in that low and oddly soft voice, was, "We're all refitted; we could have everything set and calibrated in a few hours, and it'd take about ten minutes to square us with Port."

I gave him a small, ironic smile. "Be nice not to have to blast our way out of here, huh?" I remarked drolly. I turned back to the Integrator. "Handy, what's ship's status?"

"All systems optimal, pending calibration, Jo," came the prompt reply. "Want me to start the preflight rundown?" he added helpfully.

I had told Leppers I would think about helping the Authorities. Well, I had thought about it, and all I could think of was blood in the water: being used as the bait to draw the sharks.

"Yeah, start it," I told Handy.

* * *

Several hours later, our calibrations completed, Raydor and I were both in the corridor on our way to Control when the hatch buzzer sounded. I hit the intercom switch on the bulkhead.

"Jo?" came Taylor's voice. "Permission to come aboard?"

I punched the hatch release button, and a moment later the chestnut-haired man was bounding up the ramp. He glanced briefly at Raydor but reserved his exuberant greeting for me, rumpled flightsuit and all. "I'm glad I caught you," he said enthusiastically. "I know I'm a little early, but I was able to rearrange the rest of my schedule, and I thought maybe—"

"We're lifting," I told him flatly, hitting the hatch reseal.

Taylor's eyebrows lifted quizzically. "Now?" he said with surprise. "But what about dinner?"

The priorities evidenced in his response were so typically Taylor that I almost laughed aloud at him; instead, I just gave his shoulder an apologetic little squeeze and said, "I'm sorry; there just isn't time to explain—not now, anyway."

Taylor glanced again at Raydor, whose expression was about as self-satisfied as a Tachs would ever reveal, and then looked back helplessly to me. I honestly don't know if it was Taylor's forlorn disappointment or Raydor's almost smug satisfaction at it; maybe it was at least partially my own desire for some reliable, familiar comfort in the midst of the seemingly endless morass of trouble I had gotten myself into. Whatever it was, I found myself suddenly saying to Taylor, "Look, why don't you come along with us?"

"With you?" he echoed, his shoulders tracing a small shrug of confusion. "Jo, I don't even know where you're going!"

"Heinlein," I replied, turning and starting up the corridor again to Control. As I strode away, I added over my shoulder, "And we're leaving now."

"Wait!" Taylor called out, slipping past a visibly disapproving Raydor and hurrying after me. "What about my stuff? I have to go back to my lodgings and get—"

I halted outside the hatch to Control, letting Taylor catch me by the arm. "There's no time for that," I told him as I swung to face him. "Run up to Port and call the manager—you've got ten minutes."

For a few seconds, Taylor was speechless, and I briefly looked him up and down. "If you're coming . . ." I concluded.

The old grin was back then, feral and engaging. He gave an elaborate leer. "Oh, I'm coming," he suddenly announced, with a raffish wink, "on one condition."

"Oh, yeah?" I said. "And what's that?"

"On what's in it for me." His brows waggled suggestively. "You still got that great collection of golden oldies audio-chips?"

CHAPTER
FOUR

I had pulled out from planets thousands of times over the years, first as my mother's apprentice and then as *Raptor*'s captain. I never had exactly enjoyed it, but there were times when I genuinely appreciated the phenomenon that had given us the power of interstellar flight. Fortunately for all concerned, the actual physical phase of the magnetic acceleration pull was relatively short—or at least it seemed that way subjectively, in the pull's weirdly distorted time frame. You got used to the sensation from an intellectual standpoint, but your body never really became acclimated to it no matter how many times you pulled out.

I had made most of those thousands of pulls with just Raydor beside me in Control. The few passengers I had ferried had always proved to be more of a nuisance than a help. That's probably why with Taylor it seemed like such a pleasant change to be sharing Control with someone else who I knew would not only not get sick on me but could also actually be of some use. Immediately after Raydor and I had fastened our chair harnesses and he had taken one of the ancillary chairs behind us, Taylor leaned forward and reached for something on the panel alongside me. I glanced back to see that he had snagged the remote board for Internals. It took him only a brief perusal to familiarize himself with its format; then he was deftly running the pre-pull checklist.

I shot a look over at Raydor, but the Tachs was bent over his comm board, his big hairless head cocked into the pickup in his ear. I knew damn well he had noticed what Taylor was doing, but his stolid Altered face registered neither approval nor disapproval. I figured that sooner or later he and I were going to have a little talk about the wisdom of having brought Taylor along, but I knew it wouldn't be just then. Raydor was all busi-

ness when it came to the running of the ship, and right then the
upcoming pull had his complete attention.

Handy adroitly maneuvered us out of the bay, through the
maze of hangar alleyways that gleamed slickly with condensation, and onto the vacant launch apron we'd been assigned. Then
he lifted us, *Raptor* rising strongly but smoothly into Porta
Flora's night sky. I willed my body to go limp, letting the thrust
flatten me against my padded seat, only peripherally aware of
the constant stream of data that Handy bled across our access
screen while Raydor made occasional terse comments to Port.

That time of the evening was an off-peak period for pull traffic, so we were given almost immediate clearance. As Handy
fed the coordinates for our destination to Port, I was aware of
Taylor reading the screen over my shoulder.

"I thought we were going to Heinlein," came his puzzled
query from behind me.

"We are," I replied, leaning forward to punch the final clearance into Handy's access, "eventually. We're just going to take
the scenic route."

Taylor studied the screen further. "Locus IV?" he read, still
perplexed. "That's not even a real port; it's just a—"

"Don't worry," I interrupted to reassure him, "we won't be
there for long."

"Ready to start acceleration for the pull," Handy informed
us placidly, his screen blanking to its standby mode.

I leaned back more deeply in my chair. But before the familiar
torque could begin to take us, Raydor suddenly held up one
broad hand in an unmistakable gesture of interception. His crepey head was cocked sharply into his pickup; he was on the
verge of speaking when Handy abruptly interjected, "Incoming
message, Jo."

I felt a trickle of adrenaline—not a sudden flood in my veins
but more like a warning stab. "Port or the A's?" I snapped out
tightly.

"From CA," the Integrator promptly replied.

"We're still clear to pull out?"

"Right now," Handy replied, but our circumstances made
the purpose of his deliberate distinction perfectly clear.

I had perhaps seconds to make my choice, but I didn't need
time to think; I just reacted. I punched a switch on the console
before me. "Blank us out," I told Raydor. "Kill comm—let
them think we haven't received it. Then get us the hell out of
here!"

Behind me, Taylor stirred in the ancillary chair. "But Jo—don't you think you should—" he began, but the rest of his words were snatched from his mouth.

Raptor leapt, diving into her spiral. I braced the back of my skull against the padded headrest of my chair as the ship started into the huge, sweeping acceleration curve that would wrench us free of Porta Flora's gravity and ultimately send us racing toward the coordinates Handy had programmed. Speaking would have been impossible then. Taylor might have had some comment to make, either in query or in protest, but it was lost as *Raptor* surged into the pull. For then not only speech but orderly thought as well became something beyond the human capacity.

Once, out of frank curiosity, I had asked Handy just what he experienced when we went into the pull. "It's fun!" he had immediately enthused. Hardly the term I would have chosen for it, but when I had pressed him to elaborate, he had atypically been at something of a loss. "It's like . . ." he had begun, but then his deep bass voice had trailed off. Whatever frame of reference he had been about to use, he must have realized that it was something I could not possibly have shared as a common concept. Despite the popularly held perception that Integrators were essentially pure consciousness, without physical form, I knew that at least in Handy's case that was not strictly true. *Raptor*, the ship herself, was the physical extension of his being—his "body," if you will. But I was still unable to fathom what Handy, and the ship as his corporeal extension, felt as they were swept into that timeless maelstrom of supralight speed.

When the pull released us and both the thrust and the vague sense of vertigo that accompanied it faded, the first thing I heard was Taylor's voice, going on as if nothing had interrupted our exchange.

"At least see what that was all about?"

I postponed responding to Taylor for a moment, however, scanning Handy's reactivated screen as I asked him, "How're we doing?"

"All systems optimal, Jo," Handy promptly reported. "We're within audio range of the navigation beacon."

Surreptitiously, I glanced sideways at Raydor's board, where his blunt fingers spanned the buttons on the comm log station. Without even turning his head, Raydor gave me a minute nod, letting me know that he had captured the incoming message that our "malfunctioning" comm system had ostensibly missed. With a barely perceptible tilt of his thick wrist, he angled the small scan-slot of the log bank so that I could read the few truncated lines that glowed across his comm board:

CAPT. JO-LAC OF RAPTOR:
MALFUNCTION INCIDENT/SUBTERRANEAN BELTWAY—
LEPPERS, JOHN GIVENS/DECEASED—
CA REQUIRES YOUR IMMEDIATE AVAILABILITY FOR INQUIRY—
:PORT OF PORTA FLORA

I exchanged the briefest of looks with Raydor. Then, my expression studiously neutral, I returned my attention to Handy's navigation screen, where a glowing green stream of numbers was scrolling by. "How far out?" I asked him.

"Thirty-three minutes, ship's present speed," the bass voice announced.

Raydor looked across from his board. "The flyway grid is clear," he remarked evenly. "We should be able to get back into the pull without any delay."

"Good; just keep us blanked to any incoming on comm."

Behind me, a summarily ignored Taylor fidgeted almost audibly in his chair. "Jo," he reminded me plaintively, "are you going to explain this to me?"

Releasing the top few catches on my harness, I twisted around in my chair to face him. "And just what is it that you don't understand?" I asked him innocently, deftly mimicking both the phrasing and vocal pitch of a much-reviled instructor we'd both suffered under when we'd been in Volunteer training together.

Taylor grinned appreciatively at my effort. "Let's start with something simple," he said, "like why the hell we pulled out to this unmanned backwater station in the first place."

Taylor's unflattering assessment of Locus IV was pretty much on target. The station wasn't even located on the planet itself; it had been built on a long-dead but more geologically stable moon. It was basically nothing more than a navigational beacon ensconced on a rather unattractive chunk of rock. But Locus IV's scenic potential wasn't its primary appeal to me.

"What, you don't like my idea of a sight-seeing side trip?" I asked wryly. "This place has everything: It's convenient, no crowds, no admission charge, and it's got nice rocks."

On-screen, Handy was merrily rolling out telemetry data, but Taylor's eyes were not on the console. He watched my face for a moment, his scrutiny keen and acute. I could see the glimmer of comprehension as it kindled in his eyes.

"You're laying down a false trail," he said. "But why? If there weren't any charges filed against you, and your ship wasn't under any hold on Porta Flora . . ." His eyes narrowed. "Unless—"

I knew what he was thinking, and I moved as firmly as I could to deflect his speculation. "It's very important that we get to Heinlein," I interrupted him, all trace of humor suddenly gone from my voice. "And I don't want anyone knowing that's where we've gone."

From my right, Raydor announced, "We're within range to recalibrate, Jo."

"Lock us in, Handy," I instructed, straightening myself in my chair and facing forward again.

"Flyway grid's clear," Raydor said again. He cocked his head at me. "What coordinates?"

Refastening my harness snaps, I quickly scanned Handy's board. We had been lucky at Porta Flora. Whether or not CA realized we had received their last-minute message, we had gotten away clean for once, without any shots being fired. But Port knew where we had gone from there, and we could be followed to Locus IV. It seemed that once again we had become fugitives.

"Gunderson's System," I decided briskly. "The relay station off Gunderson's eighth planet."

Bewilderment plain in his voice, Taylor interjected, "Why aren't we just going to Heinlein now?" I almost had to smile at the confused tone of his question. While he was perplexed, there was no trace of exasperation in Taylor's voice. I don't think I could have been so equanimous in his place.

But I obstinately shook my head, watching as the pull schematics assembled themselves on Handy's screen. "No, I'm not taking any chances," I told Taylor grimly.

"We can go to the pull in nine minutes," Raydor said.

I glanced over at him, my face set. Malfunction incident, my ass! The big Tachs could deduce as easily as I had just what Leppers's untimely death signified: Terrifyingly enough, somehow the renegades were already on to us. The moment we had asked Port for clearance to lift, we had inadvertently betrayed him by revealing that I had no intention of conceding to the liaison's urgent request to cooperate with the A's in finding the Tens. Whether or not Leppers had realized it, it was appallingly clear to me that the renegades had infiltrated the system to the point where they were already one step ahead of him. And at the moment we had requested lift clearance, John Givens Leppers had become less than useful to the renegades, more of a threat to their secrecy than a tool, however unwitting that tool may have been. He was no longer worth anything to them alive, and his suspicions and what little he may have learned from me could have ultimately led him closer to them. And so his death was just one more blunt maneuver in an on-going process of covering the renegades' tracks. In a bizarre way, by leaving Porta Flora, I had sealed his fate.

"All systems optimal," Handy rumbled smoothly, cutting into my morbid thoughts.

Taylor sat back in his chair with a baffled sigh and dutifully tightened his harness again. It was obvious he could not understand my elaborate paranoia; I doubt that most Citizens would have. But then again, most Citizens had not had the edifying experience of having their own government—or renegades under the guise of their own government—try to blast them out of existence a few times. I knew my terse explanation had not answered many of Taylor's questions, and he certainly had the intelligence to figure out that the message I had refused to acknowledge, and presumably had not even seen, had something to do with our precipitate departure from Porta Flora. But I also knew that he would not press me further, at least not then. Out of the corner of my eye I saw him pick up the Internals remote board again and patiently start back through the prepull check sequence.

We weren't quite as lucky coming out of the pull to the Gunderson's System's relay station. Our coast time—that unpredictably variable distance from our destination when we came shooting out of the pull—was nearly seven hours. Only one thing kept me from chafing visibly at the delay: taking this second little added diversion had been my choice. At least I was certain no one could have tracked us from Locus IV.

As the postpull figures began streaming across Handy's screen, I freed the fastenings of my chair harness and bent forward over the console. Behind me, Taylor stood and replaced the remote board in its niche on the bulkhead panel. Then I heard his voice, nearly in my ear.

"Why don't you just take a break, Jo?" he said quietly. His hands landed softly on my shoulders, massaging them briefly. "I can help Raydor finish up here; you've got plenty of time to clean up and relax before we can pull out again."

"You suggesting I need a shower?" I demanded with feigned defensiveness, not turning from the console.

"Well, now that you mention it . . ."

I turned in the chair then and looked up into his smiling face. The thing was, he was absolutely right. I was suddenly aware of a monumental weariness, something that reached deeply into my bones, beyond mere physical stress. I was beginning to feel the accumulated weight of the tension of my last day on Porta Flora and, on top of that, the added uncertainty of CA's curt missive. I stood slowly but steadily and gestured inclusively at Handy's board. "You sure you remember how to do this?" I asked as Taylor slipped past me and dropped into my chair.

Glancing over at Raydor, who gave every appearance of being totally absorbed with the comm board, Taylor assured me, "I'm sure if I run into any problems, Raydor'll set me straight."

I let my hand rest lightly on the back of Taylor's neck, just beneath the soft fringe of his hair. His skin felt incredibly warm against my fingertips. "The spare cabin's stocked," I told him. "If you want to shower, there should be at least one spare suit liner in there that you can use until we can run your stuff through the laundry cycler."

Taylor didn't look up, but I could read the mock indignation in his voice. "Are you suggesting that *I* need a shower?" he asked.

Laughing, I gave his back a playful little slap. Our hasty departure from Porta Flora had barely given Taylor time to contact the manager of his lodgings; he hadn't been able to have any of his things sent over to Port before we'd pulled out.

Looking back over his shoulder, Taylor assured me, "Don't worry; whatever you've got'll be fine. Besides," he added, turning back to Handy's console with a wolfish grin, "I've always wanted to go to Heinlein in nothing but a suit liner."

As I left Control and started toward my cabin, I was reminded once again of two things I had neatly managed to ignore since I'd taken Taylor on board: One was that he was being his usual incredibly good sport about the whole business; the other was that I was very possibly placing him in some danger by having taken him. But those things, like so much that had happened that day, were things I couldn't afford to think about too much just yet.

In my cabin I stripped off my rumpled flightsuit and its sticky liner. I spent an inordinate amount of time in the shower, letting the needlelike jets of water buffet me. I didn't expect rejuvenation; I just wanted the pulsing spray to numb me. Only when I began to consider that I might be exceeding the temporary reserve capacity of the water recycler did I finally step out and under the drier. My hair, which had responded to Porta Flora's constant humidity by reorganizing itself into an intractable frenzy of frizzy little coils, had returned to its usual state of casual limpness. I combed it quickly, wrestling almost fiercely with it, and then dressed in a clean liner and flightsuit. As I transferred things from the pockets of my old suit to the fresh one, I tried determinedly to think of some way to distract myself for the next six-plus hours. I didn't think I could sleep, and I didn't know if I could concentrate well enough to tackle any ship's business. I felt restless and anxious, thoughts of the mess I'd left behind entangling with thoughts of the mess I had yet to face. Then I remembered Taylor's joking comment about coming along with us only because of my audiochip collection.

Seated on the edge of my bunk, I opened my chip case and began to sort out some of the golden oldies I knew Taylor had always been partial to. It was probably one of the more unusual conditions for passage on *Raptor* that I'd ever paid, I thought ironically, forming a small pile of the chips off to one side. If only he'd known what he was getting himself into.

He doesn't have to get involved in this, I told myself firmly. He's just going along as far as Heinlein—he won't be in any danger there. The thought had barely formed in my mind when another little internal voice, this one sharply sarcastic, reminded me, Yeah, just like Lewis was "safe" there. I tried to block off the new voice, but it went on insistently. You took Lewis off Heinlein once because you knew he *wouldn't* be safe there; now you've sent him back there with Alexandria and Redding—and he's *still* in danger.

Standing abruptly, I had to literally shake my head to silence my nagging conscience. All I needed was to bring Alexandria and Redding into the unproductive loop of thought as well. It was not the time to start rehashing the shadowy past of the enigmatic woman who had been my mother's best friend or the possibilities of what could yet develop with the laconic, gray-eyed freighter captain who might or might not be my father.

I was not even aware of having paced across the cabin, but I was standing right beside the hatch when my summons buzzer sounded. It startled me so much that I nearly dropped the little handful of audiochips that I was equally uncognizant of having carried from the bunk. "Come!" I barked, a bit too loudly.

The hatch *whoosh*ed open, and Taylor stepped in, eyeing my tense stance with mild curiosity. I nearly burst into laughter when I saw him; he was wearing nothing but a suit liner, and he was carrying one of the galley's insulated plastic trays in one hand. The liner was obviously one of Raydor's, because although liners were a unisex garment, they were hardly one-size-fits-all. That one hung on Taylor like a sack; he looked like nothing more than a little boy dressed up in his older brother's sleepers, an impression that was only enhanced by the tousled locks of his uncombed and hastily blow-dried hair.

"Well, I promised you dinner," he told me, presenting the covered tray with a flourish.

Grinning at him, I gestured toward the bunk. "I've reserved our usual table," I told him wryly.

When we both were seated on the bunk with the tray resting between us, Taylor hesitated dramatically with his hand hovering over the lid. "I know I promised you *real* food," he continued, "but your food synthesizer seemed to think I was joking." He raised the cover on the tray with another grand flourish, and a cloud of fragrant steam rose up from the food containers. "Tah-dah!" he announced; then he bent forward to peer with exaggerated intensity at the culinary offering, as if he'd never seen it before. "Hmmm," he murmured, cocking one brow. "Here you are—something greenish and something . . . brownish?" He shrugged innocently. "Well, whatever it is, Raydor assured me it was something you'd eat."

Laughing, I let the handful of audiochips tumble onto the bedcover and reached for one of the dishes.

Taylor rearranged the contents of the tray, setting out eating utensils and coffee mugs while making a few more disparaging remarks about the obvious decline of my dietary habits and the limitations of my food synthesizer. Then he folded up his long legs, sitting cross-legged on the bunk, and said, "And now that I've got you trapped here, I'm going to make good on my threat and bore you to death with absolutely everything I've been up to since I saw you last."

Taylor proceeded to explain and expand, often in great detail, exactly that. But he was quite wrong about one thing; he was never boring. Taylor didn't so much tell a story as he *performed* it, and I liked to think that he had realized just how preoccupied and stressed I was and that he had deliberately carried out his "threat" to distract me in the simplest and most direct way he knew. His history was simple: He had left Longuard three years earlier to join the ranks of MediaPlex for what he claimed was the basest of reasons—more money. But knowing Taylor, I thought the reason had less to do with money than it did with leeway. If there was one thing I had learned very early on with Taylor, it was that he was a man who needed a lot of leeway. Longuard was a relatively conservative employer, and their PR men had to be fairly circumspect. On the other hand, calling MediaPlex liberal was being tactful; it was downright anarchic at times, and I was sure Taylor fit right in with their philosophy. Taylor related those facts with considerable embellishment and frequent forays into his offbeat observations; several times he had me laughing so hard that I nearly choked on my brownish stuff.

Peering at me over the brim of his coffee mug, Taylor concluded, "So after I finished up that Rhinderpest thing, they thought I deserved a bit of a break—and I agreed." He lowered the mug and balanced it on one bent knee. "I was able to hitch a ride out on one of Carson's little yachts, so that's how I ended up on Porta Flora: precipitation capital of the known systems." He shrugged ingenuously. "I didn't know you'd be there; I hadn't even picked up on the freightmen's gossip until we'd made planetfall."

There was a pause, a moment of silence between us, while I spooned up the last of Raydor's idea of dessert—candied tubers—and Taylor calmly studied me. "So," he said, his voice deliberately casual, "was all the gossip right? Or are you going to tell me what really happened."

The last was not a question, and I took my time replacing the dish and spoon on the cluttered tray that sat between us. When I looked up at him again, I wished I had some well-rehearsed lie that would correspond nicely with all that Taylor had heard. But I don't think I would have lied to him then, even if a lie would have worked. He was my friend, and honesty had always been part of the history that bound us together. And so I did the next best thing: I told him the partial truth, the same edited version I had recorded so dutifully for Rhaine and the Ombudsman. Since I had settled, after a fashion, with the Authorities, the record I'd given the Ombudsman would become official and hence public. From there, it was only a matter of time before it became "news." At the very least, I figured I owed it to Taylor to give him first crack at it.

I began my story with my ill-fated meeting with Rollo, the A's liaison on New Cuba, my introduction to Lewis, and the fabricated run for MA to Heinlein, which had nearly ended before it began in disaster at the pull. Then I explained what had happened to us after we'd reached Heinlein. Detailing the renegades' attack on us in port gave me the opportunity to digress about the current situation with Heinlein's class action suit against the A's. By the time I'd finished with that, I figured I'd given Taylor enough original and intriguing information that he wouldn't notice if my story had had a rather hazy ending and that I hadn't referred at all to the mysterious message I had so arbitrarily scuttled as we'd pulled out from Porta Flora.

"Stars, Jo," Taylor said, shaking his head, "no wonder the A's were so eager to turn you loose. I think I'd've been tempted to sue their collective asses ten ways to infinity!"

I stretched out my legs and then pulled up my knees, bracing my elbows on them. "Well," I said, "there's always the class action suit. Nothing in my waiver on this Intervention prevents me from taking part in that."

Taylor gave a delighted hoot of laughter and set his mug down on the plastic tray. "I can see why you're in such a hurry to get back to Heinlein," he said.

We both grinned over that for a moment. Then Taylor casually picked up the littered tray full of empty dishes and set it on the bedside table. As he turned back to face me again, I could see that his expression had sobered. "Then there really are Class Tens," he said. "I had always thought they were just a figment of the A's imagination."

"The A's have no imagination," I responded dryly.

"So," he continued almost offhandedly, "what ever happened to Lewis?"

I hesitated a few seconds. Considering he'd soon find out for himself, there seemed no point in evasion. "He's on Heinlein," I replied, equally nonchalant.

Taylor nodded and gave me a knowing wink. "Another reason to hurry back," he teased me—fairly innocently, I was certain; he had no way of knowing how desperately right he was.

I thought then that Taylor might pursue the subject or backtrack to his questions about the puzzling paranoia that had led me to bounce us all over the quadrant, or at least that he might ask me why I'd ignored CA's last message to me. But he suddenly seemed strangely free of curiosity. As his gaze fell on the little scatter of audiochips beside me on the bunk, he asked hopefully, "Those my golden oldies?"

"Yeah," I said, and began scooping them up. "I think I still remember what you like."

"Jo," he responded playfully, cupping his hands around mine and claiming the chips, "you've *always* known what I like."

Suddenly, with a ferocity of feeling that caught me quite by surprise, I slipped my hands up and captured his wrists. His eyes met mine, his sun-colored brows quirking quizzically, his lips half-open in unspoken query. *What?* he must have been thinking, but I couldn't have given him a logical answer.

"Will you stay with me?" I asked, my voice softened to almost a whisper.

"Sure, okay." Taylor shrugged gently, scarcely moving my hands where they still gripped his wrists. "On one condition, though: that you get some sleep." Sensing imminent protest, he slipped one hand free and put his index finger to my lips. *"Sleep,"* he repeated emphatically. "You look like shit, Jo."

I dropped his other wrist. "Thanks!" I retorted, but Taylor only shrugged again, not in apology but in simple acknowledgment of the facts.

I flopped back onto the bunk and lay looking up at him with a sort of hazy expectancy. I couldn't help but remember the first time I'd ever lay down on a bed with him . . . or the last time. Somewhere in my memory, amazingly close to the surface, I still carried the very real physical sense of him: his hardness, his softness, the way his warm, golden body had fit into mine.

Taylor was still looking at me oddly, his brows tented in bemusement, and so I said, "Did you ever wish sometimes that we still . . . you know . . ."

Taylor's eyes softened; his lips curved in a smile, and his hand went gently to the side of my face. "Yeah, sometimes," he admitted. "But maybe it's better this way, Jo. The other—you never know if that will last. But this, the way we feel about each other now, well, that's something we can have between ourselves for the rest of our lives."

When I fell asleep, he was stretched out beside me on top of the bunk, his arm slung companionably over my side, one of my best golden oldies audiochips throbbing in his ear.

By the time we pulled out from the relay station at Gunderson's eighth planet, Taylor's clothes had been through the laundry cycler and he was again dressed in his usual gold and bottle-green. In a way it was a shame, I thought, since he really would have been a hit on Heinlein dressed in nothing but a suit liner.

But then again, Heinlein was the sort of place where Taylor wouldn't have had any trouble being a hit no matter what he was wearing.

The relay station was unmanned, and just like Locus IV, it was basically just a set of coordinates to which and from one could exit and enter the pull. I was sure we weren't the only ship that had used or would use the station for nothing more than that. In spite of CA's zealous regulation of the pull in any ports under their jurisdiction, most of the pulls made in the known systems were probably made outside of their control. Any ship with a functional Integrator and a set of coordinates could manage very nicely without any outside direction.

Pulling out three times within the same twenty-four-hour span was not exactly high on my list of sought-after experiences, but we got lucky with our coast time when we left Gunderson's; we exited the pull less than three hours out from Heinlein. This time I dismissed Taylor from Control and ran the postpull check with Raydor myself. But I was only partially motivated by a sense of hospitality for my last-minute guest; I needed to talk to Raydor, and I figured he had some things to say to me as well. This might be our last chance before Heinlein complicated things even further.

We worked in companionable silence for the first twenty minutes or so, exchanging only brief bits of information or readings off the board. Then, when most of the check had been completed and we each were just finishing up at our own stations at the console, the Tachs glanced sideways at me and, without missing a beat in the cadence of pushing buttons on comm, asked gruffly, "What're you going to do, Jo?"

Raydor and I had lived together on *Raptor* for so long and knew each other so well that we tended to communicate in a sort of verbal shorthand. I knew without having to think about it that what he meant was, what was I going to do when we got to Heinlein—what was my plan for dealing with the situation that first Leppers's unwelcome revelations and then his unwitting death had placed us in?

I didn't look over at Raydor; I just kept staring at my console, even though I had already blanked Handy's screen. "We're going to get Lewis and get out," I said finally.

Raydor's head turned again; this time he kept his gaze on me, and his big fingers rested motionlessly on the edge of the comm board. "Where?" he asked.

Again I knew what he meant. With that simple one-word

query he was asking me if I really thought that we could evade the remaining renegades within or outside the system, especially now that they obviously knew with whom they would find Lewis. "I don't know where yet," I replied, still staring down at the blank screen. "But then again, they won't know, either."

When Raydor failed to respond to that bit of bravado, I looked over to him, studying his dark, unnervingly wide eyes for a moment. "What?" I said. "You think I should have cooperated with Leppers? Joined up with the A's finest and gone out on their witch-hunt?" My eyes cut away, my voice dropping harshly. "No thanks; I've already had my fill of playing Junior Space Patrol. If I'd done that—if we'd stayed on Porta Flora—the renegades would have had both of us by now."

Raydor had undoubtedly considered that probability already; throwing it in his face only served to vent my own frustration and fear. His reply, when it came, was soft, almost contemplative. "Leppers said that the other Class Tens were still in danger," he reminded me.

I looked back again, glaring at his placid Altered face. "Yeah? Well, it looks like *he* was the one in danger, doesn't it? And besides, *one* Class Ten at a time is about all I can manage." I glanced down at my board, snapping one of the last active switches off with far more force than was necessary. "Leppers just wanted to use us as bait—to find the renegades and the rest of the Tens," I said. "Let CA ride to the rescue this time. I'm sick of getting shot at!"

Raydor just sat there quietly, his huge hands folded quiescently over the comm board. He knew why I was so angry, and he was smart enough to know that it had nothing to do with him. Still, I was a little surprised when he took the subject any further. After a few moments he commented, as if in summary, "You don't intend to get involved with trying to find the other Class Tens, then, or with helping the A's search for the renegades."

I stared sharply at him, considering possible levels of belligerence for my response. But it was just Raydor, and I knew he wasn't trying to provoke me. If anything, the worst that could be said about his questions was that he was playing the devil's advocate in the matter, a role into which my actions had often forced him in the past. And so I ended up just nodding affirmatively and grimly reiterating, "No way in hell!"

Raydor's reaction to that was a grunt, an all-purpose sound that seemed to encompass both understanding and agreement.

With a grace and smoothness incongruous in a man of his size, he slipped out of his chair and stood, but he didn't move immediately to step away from the console. Looking down at me, his scrutiny both candid and incisive, he asked, "How much does he know?"

The very slight lift of Raydor's broad chin toward the hatch was not necessary; I knew exactly to whom he was referring. I stretched my legs out in front of my chair, willing the tension out of them. "Just what everyone else in the quadrant probably knows by now," I replied with a little shrug. "Not about Leppers."

But Raydor still studied my face, and suddenly I saw again in that familiar look what had always been there for me: care, pure and simple. I knew he was well aware that Taylor had spent several hours of our last coast time in my cabin, and I had no trouble imagining what Raydor would have assumed we had been doing. But his disapproval of Taylor, even his disapproval of the presumed relationship between Taylor and me, did not translate into disapproval of me. Raydor was just doing what he had always tried to do: look out for me, cover my back, give me support.

"And I told him that Lewis is on Heinlein," I added after a moment.

Now it was the Tachs who shrugged, a gesture that seemed partially good-natured acceptance, partially mere acknowledgment of the inevitable. "He'd find that out in a few hours, anyway," he noted.

"Yeah," I agreed. But what I was thinking then was that it wasn't all that Taylor was about to find out.

We didn't make audio contact with Heinlein Port until we were well within their range. Even then, I let Handy and Raydor handle most of the necessary communication to get us clearance and grid coordinates for the landing. Taylor had joined us again in Control as we came down. He watched Handy's screen and then the viewer in relative silence, somehow sensitive to a mood in me that he could perceive, even if he didn't exactly understand it. His occasional comments were light and bantering and did not require any direct response.

I couldn't have explained my state of mind to Taylor anyway, because I didn't think I really understood my own feelings. If anything, this return to Heinlein was even more emotionally booby-trapped than the others in the past. I had always felt a deep ambivalence for the planet that might have been my home had fate kinked in a slightly different direction somewhere along the line. And then, beyond even that, I was profoundly puzzled that I did not feel more simple elation at the prospect of finally being reunited with Lewis. Even the fear that Leppers, by his disclosures and then by his death, had instilled in me did not seem to satisfactorily explain the sense of apprehension that colored my thoughts of seeing Lewis again. I had the vague and nagging impression that the reasons for my decidedly mixed emotions were there somewhere, just on the fringe of my awareness, like a formless shadow hanging on the periphery of the ship's sensors. But the more I tried to reach for them, the more elusive they became.

It was early evening, planet's time, and as we descended in a graceful arc over the stunningly precise geometry of Port, the field lay bathed in lemon-yellow light. Oblique rays of sunlight still glinted off the glass and steel of the nearby buildings, and both the city's numerous parks and the low surrounding hills gleamed an almost painfully intense shade of green. As we dropped lower, the vast shapes of the hangars resolved into distinct structures laid out in a network that had a functional beauty all its own.

Our landing clearance had been handled very routinely, and we had made no special requests for contact. Yet as Handy locked the landing gear stabilizers and began to shut down, I saw a familiar solitary figure approaching the ship across the smooth pavement of the massive docking bay. It was Mahta.

"Beginning standard docking shutdown," came Handy's casual rumble. But I was already out of my chair, moving past Taylor and out the hatchway from Control.

The landing ramp settled gently onto the tarmac, the surface of the pavement still checkered by huge alternating squares of shadow and the sunlight from the hangar skylights. I strode determinedly down the ramp's incline, my eyes on the slender figure in a taupe-colored tunic and pants whose booted heels tapped rapidly across the bay floor to greet me. Mahta's delicate and ageless face was alight with genuine pleasure as she lifted her arms; I stepped willingly into her embrace.

"Jo!" she exclaimed, pulling back then to look at me but not releasing my arms. "When we'd gotten the news about your Intervention, we knew you'd be coming back soon."

If she wanted news, she hadn't heard anything yet, I thought sardonically. But damned if I wasn't glad—truly glad—just to see her again. I slipped free of her hold at the same moment she released me. "Yeah," I said, "everything worked out pretty well there."

"Good!" she enthused, shaking back her long pale hair with a raffish and ready smile. "We could use some positive legal precedence. But you can tell me about that later."

She didn't need to remind me that much of my own success with the A's had probably stemmed from the legal fusillade she had leveled at them from Heinlein, and it wouldn't have been like her to bring that up. I didn't even need to make any comment on her remark, because by then Raydor and Taylor were coming down the ramp, and Mahta moved to greet them.

"Raydor," she said warmly, wrapping her slender arms around his huge torso and hugging him affectionately, "so nice to have you back again. Especially without someone shooting at you."

Raydor took her effusiveness with equanimity despite his usual disdain for public displays of tenderness. "Yeah, well, no shooting was the only condition under which I was willing to come back," he retorted.

Taylor had circumspectly kept himself in the background up to that point. Then Mahta turned toward him, her brown eyes gleaming, as I quickly said, "You remember Taylor, don't you? He was in the Volunteers with me."

Mahta spared me a sharp glance. "Jo, that was *years* ago," she reminded me with mock exasperation. Then she beamed at Taylor and announced, "Of course I remember Taylor." Apparently she remembered him in a good light as well, because she caught him up in one of her enthusiastic embraces, an expression of approval that Taylor thoroughly returned.

When Mahta stepped back, she surveyed all three of us with obvious satisfaction. "I'm so glad you're here," she said, only reiterating the self-evident. "Well, let's not stand here in this hangar all evening. You have other people here who are really going to be eager to see you again, Jo." And although she used the plural form of the word, I knew full well there was only one person to whom she was referring.

We started to walk across the bay floor toward the rampway, Mahta on one side of me and Taylor on the other, with Raydor bringing up the rear. "Yeah," I said casually, "is Redding still here?"

Mahta's eyes narrowed, her fine brows arching in her child-like face as she regarded me closely. "Redding?" she repeated as if I had just added something truly incongruous to the conversation.

"I didn't see any of the *Nimbus* shuttles in the outer bays when we taxied in," I continued matter-of-factly, "so I figured he might be gone." With a freighter of *Nimbus*'s class and capacity, time was too valuable to waste hanging in orbit; there was no way Redding could have afforded to leave her idle that long.

Frowning slightly, Mahta explained. "*Nimbus* pulled out again, but Redding stayed. He's in the country right now." She studied my face carefully, keeping pace as we reached the nearest hangar ramp and began to climb it to the overhead walkway.

"When's he going to be back?" I persisted, perplexing her even further. "I want to see him as soon as possible."

"Later tonight, I should think," she replied, still curious about my intense interest in *Nimbus*'s captain.

As we stepped out onto the glassed-in walkway that arced over the hangars, Port and the buildings of Immigration and Central Services glistened beneath us, their smooth surfaces aflame in the sinking sun. Mahta paused, enjoying Taylor's obvious appreciation of the sight. He scanned the view from the hangars to the skyline and beyond, to the horizon and the Koerber Range. Then he grinned happily at us. "Suns' Light, there isn't another place anywhere quite like *this*!" he enthused.

I couldn't have disagreed with that, even if for entirely different reasons. As we began walking again, heading toward the Central Services building, I glanced below us at the deserted courtyards and verges and throughways and remarked, "Where is everyone, anyway?"

Mahta laughed. "Jo, it's Sunday!" she reminded me.

I shrugged almost indifferently. Given the wide variance in planetary years, seasons, and days, few worlds still adhered to any semblance of the Old Earth week. Heinlein was one of maybe a handful of places that still observed the days of the week, including the quaint and archaic notion that Sunday was largely a day of recreation.

Mahta reached out and took my arm. "Come on," she said redirecting our path. As was usual with her, it was not exactly a request.

We bypassed the main Services entrance and continued on the upper walkway. "Where are we going?" I asked her, striding faster to keep up with the pace she set.

"Everyone's down by the pools this evening," she said guiding us toward a sensor-activated moving rampway that hummed into action at our footfalls and began to convey us down from the elevated walkway. She smiled back at Raydor and Taylor. "Have you eaten supper yet?" she asked them. "We had a buffet at the pool house, and I'm sure there's still plenty left."

I noticed Taylor's eyes light up at the mention of food, and for a moment the mundane familiarity of his enthusiastic reaction calmed the raging anxiety in my mind. But food was the farthest thing from my thoughts right then. Considering that I'd shot out of Porta Flora like someone was about to ignite a fire under my ass and had then proceeded to bounce us all around the quadrant, I was feeling less than relieved to finally be there on Heinlein. In fact, I was still experiencing a lot of confusion as to just exactly what it was that I was feeling.

The moving rampway deposited us at the ground-level entrance to the pool house. It was a massive building with a high vaulted roof and surfaces composed almost entirely of huge louvered panes of glass. Like a freestanding atrium or a giant greenhouse, it had been designed to take in the maximum amount of sunlight. Within its transparent walls, on a sublevel slightly below the ground-level entrance, were a series of elliptical-shaped pools of varying sizes, depths, and water temperatures, separated only by little decks with chairs and loungers. From our elevated perspective, the collection of pools looked almost like the curving petals of some exotic hothouse flower—smaller petals that were childrens' wading pools, their water blood-warm; intermediate-sized petals that were the main pools utilized for socializing; and the larger, elongated petals, which were filled with cooler water for the serious swimmers. Around the edges of the pool area, partially emptied buffet tables still attracted a straggle of diners, most in swimsuits or robes.

When I was a child visiting Heinlein, I used to love the pool house. I especially loved the story my aunt relished telling about how it had been built on the site of Heinlein's original MA complex, arguably one of the ugliest structures on the planet and one of the first to be torn down when Heinlein's Citizens had voted for deregulation. But by the time I was a teenager, I grew disinterested in going to the pool house; I had become gawky, shy, obsessed with other things. I couldn't remember the last time I'd been there.

Mahta steered us along the carpeted walkway that surrounded the entire pool complex. From its vantage point, we could survey all the pools. Most of them were asplash with activity:

Mothers with frolicking children, groups or couples cavorting or just lanquidly floating, and the occasional actual serious swimmer doing laps. The pools had always been a popular Sunday gathering place. But the crowds might just as well have been invisible; my eyes sought out only one person in that bright and watery amphitheater. And even though I had known, from the point when she had led us from the hangar, just exactly to whom Mahta was taking me, my heart still lurched in recognition when I actually saw him.

In one of the intermediate-sized pools near the periphery of the pool house, a small group of adults was engaged in a spirited game of water ball. They dived, leapt, and splashed, all to the accompaniment of squealing and laughter. I recognized Mimosa, the head of Port and Immigration and Mahta's protégé; Mahta's man, Jim; and several well-endowed young women who looked vaguely familiar and probably worked either in P & I or with the Mothers. Had any of those women been wearing swimsuits in the same distinctive colors as their usual jumpsuits, I think I would have been able to tell where I recognized them from. But that was a moot point, since the tiny scraps of cloth they wore were so small I could hardly tell what color the suits were. And in the midst of the fray, exuberantly bounding after the particular young woman who currently held the ball, was Lewis.

As I watched from the walkway, two of the other female players moved, one from either side, to intercept Lewis's pursuit of their teammate. Both of them tackled him, enthusiastically slinging their long bare arms around his neck and ducking him under the water. As he surfaced again, sputtering and laughing, the woman on his left tossed back the wet locks of her dark hair out of her eyes and bobbed forward, kissing him full on the mouth. Lewis twisted sideways, pulling free of her lips, only to have the lighter-haired woman on his right latch on to him with an equally emphatic kiss. I didn't know which of the Services those two specific women worked for, but apparently they weren't being paid well enough—not enough to be able to afford tops for their skimpy little swimsuits, anyway. Twisting again, Lewis managed to evade the second woman as well and, amid shouting and laughter, resumed his chase after the ball.

Mahta did not call out to them; I was certain of that when I thought about it later, even though it seemed like the logical conclusion at the time. Nevertheless, Lewis suddenly lurched to a halt in midpursuit, his dark head lifting, his lean body coming around in a tight curve in the water. He looked up, rapidly scanning the walkway, glancing at and passing over the other people on our level. Then he saw me, and for a few breathless seconds I felt literally frozen in the grasp of those vividly blue eyes.

Mahta waved at the group below us; the others in the pool, their game interrupted, had paused to discover the reason. I had not been aware of when he had moved, but suddenly Lewis was no longer with them. He reached the side of the pool and without hesitation was surging out over the edge like a seal, water sheeting off his slick body. He crossed the distance to the raised walkway in a few hasty bounds, drops of water still flying from his limbs and hair.

"Jo!" he cried out. And in that moment I felt my heart—which had, from the time I had first laid eyes on him, been banging wildly against my breastbone—abruptly squeeze down with crushing force as if some stifling hand had suddenly closed over it.

He stood directly below me, maybe two meters away, but the distance could just as well have been a quadrant or more. For I could only stare down at him, rendered speechless by a stupefying wave of fear and longing. Suns, he was beautiful, even more beautiful than I had remembered. Those few weeks of relative calm on Heinlein had filled out his body again, giving him an almost feline grace. He stood there on the pool's apron, poised so uncertainly, his upturned face filled with trust and joy and hope, all in equal measure. Water still dripped in shining rivulets from the gleaming blue-black mane of his hair, still ran down his hard shoulders and across his smooth torso, still winked in droplets that glistened like diamonds caught in the fine dark hair of his forearms and thighs . . .

My body stiffened as though I had taken a blow, and I could think of only one thing to do. I had to force the words from my mouth. "I'll talk to you later; right now I have to see Alexandria."

Then, with a wrenching effort of will, I pushed myself forward and began to move away from him, along the upper walkway.

CHAPTER FIVE

I didn't pause or look back as I began to stride rapidly along the pool house's elevated walkway, but I heard two voices call out after me; one was Lewis's, and I think the other was Taylor's. My legs felt strangely rubbery, and I had no clear idea just where the hell I was headed, but I picked up speed until I was walking so fast that I was nearly jogging. I just wanted to get out of there—away from him—as quickly as I could.

The blue light marking an exit ramp caught my eye, and I swerved abruptly toward it. Just as I reached the railing, I heard Lewis's voice right behind me.

"Jo, wait!"

I didn't know how he could have gotten up onto the walkway so quickly. I could have run then—not that I could have outrun him, not with my wobbly legs and thudding heart—but one thing made me swing around and face him instead. Anger, fierce and almost exhilarating, came rushing through my veins like a manic jolt of adrenaline.

Lewis had been reaching out to touch me, but as I turned on him, something in the furious look on my face stopped him. He stood there, wet and slightly goose-pimpled, his hand still poised uncertainly in the air between us. "Jo?" he entreated, those stunning cerulean eyes wide and bright.

Over Lewis's shoulder I could see Mahta, Taylor, and Raydor still standing where I had so precipitately left them, nearly half the length of the building away. Mahta was leaning over the walkway railing, speaking to Mimosa and the others in the pool below. Raydor held Taylor by one arm, evidently restraining the younger man from trying to follow me. Following my gaze, Lewis glanced in their direction as well. I don't know what he read into Taylor's obvious gesture of protectiveness toward me,

58

but something in those bottomless blue eyes flinched in un-guarded recognition.

I glared at Lewis. The swimsuit he wore wasn't even big enough to be called a brief. It looked like a codpiece with straps and fit the curves of his body like wet silk. The image of the topless players' easy familiarity with him suddenly strobed through my mind, and I felt my stomach cramp acidly. I stared pointedly at the carpeting beneath him. "You're dripping all over the floor," I said caustically.

Confused, Lewis glanced down at his feet. His shoulders hitched helplessly, his hand still held out to me. "Jo, it's a pool house—the floor is *supposed* to get wet," he said in bewilderment.

I think if he had stood up to me then, if he had fought back against my senseless and unfair attack, I might have been able to purge myself of the painful hostility I felt toward him at that moment. Stars, how he scared me! I had almost forgotten just how badly. But in some perverse way his passivity, his very willingness to be so reasonable, only served to inflame me further. And so I just dismissed him with a sharp but negligent wave of my hand, saying, "Go on—get back to your little game. I have to see Alexandria now; I'll talk to you later."

Above his thick, jet-colored eyebrows, Lewis's forehead furrowed in confusion. "But Alexandria isn't here," he explained helpfully. "She's with Redding—at Firerange."

I tossed my head rebelliously like a surly horse. "I'll *wait* for her, then," I retorted. "Go on—get back to your friends."

I knew that if I had stayed there a minute longer, Lewis would have overcome his reluctance to provoke me and would have reached out to touch me in spite of the overtly hostile way I'd been treating him. And I couldn't let that happen. So I swung around again and began to stride swiftly down the exit ramp, desperately hoping that he wouldn't try to follow me.

The ramp deposited me onto an open pedestrian walk outside the pool house. The evening air was warm and smelled faintly of cut grass. I hesitated, glancing around in the dimly ruddy light of the sunken sun, and tried to figure out just where the hell I was in relation to Port. Then, from out of the corner of my eye, I caught sight of a familiar figure coming out the exit behind me. I just stood, waiting with calm resignation, until the reassuring hand had landed on my shoulder.

"You okay?" Raydor asked softly.

I nodded, still keeping my face averted so that he wouldn't

be able to probe my expression for the explanation of my surprising little performance back in the pool house. As Raydor's hand slid from my shoulder, I saw Mahta and Taylor coming down the exit ramp after us. Perhaps a half dozen strides behind them, and moving up fast, came Mimosa, her long red pool robe flapping. She passed them before they reached the doorway and exploded into words before either of them could speak.

"Jo—how *could* you?" she demanded, nearly elbowing Raydor out of the way in order to stand face to face with me. In a tone I had not heard her use with me since we both were children, she continued reproachfully. "That poor man has done nothing but talk about you, think about you, *wait* for you since he's been here—and then you treat him like he—"

Mahta stopped her tirade before I could even try to, grasping Mimosa firmly by one robe-clad shoulder, but the instant the younger woman fell silent, I snapped back. "Yeah, I can see what a *hardship* it's been for him here!" With a tremendous effort of will, I reined in my almost pathological desire to continue to shout at her and went on instead in a tone of dry sarcasm. "With all the attention he's been getting around here, I'm surprised he's still got the strength to even remember my name!"

Ignoring Mahta's grip, Mimosa shot back, "This is the *first* time he would even come to the pools with us!" Mahta must have tightened her hold, because Mimosa actually had to take a step backward, but she continued determinedly, if in a somewhat more subdued manner. "As for the rest, well, *of course* they've all been trying to get to him—unsuccessfully, I might add." She was still glaring at me, royally infuriated. "He doesn't even have the faintest interest in anyone else; for some unfathomable reason, he's been waiting for *you*."

For a few moments the two of us just locked eyes, as much at an impasse as we had always been. While we had stood arguing, Taylor had edged around from the other side of Mahta to a position near my side; the literal significance of where he had placed himself did not escape my notice. Good old Taylor; he didn't know what the rules were or even what the hell the game was, but he was always in my corner. He and Mimosa knew each other only slightly; it had been dislike at first sight. You would have thought that the two of them would have had a lot in common and that, both being inveterate flirts, they would have become fast friends. But in spite of that—or maybe because of it—they had never seemed to have much use for each other.

It was Mahta's calm voice, quite typically, that broke the moment. "Mimosa, why don't you take Raydor and Taylor back to the buffet," she suggested with quiet authority. "I'm sure they'd like something to eat. Jo and I have some things to discuss."

Mimosa hesitated a moment; in the faint and dusky light, her wet, cinnamon-colored hair shone like flame. Then it was she and Taylor who exchanged stares, but he was the one who looked away first, his eyes moving back to me.

"Go ahead," I told him steadily. "I'm all right."

Raydor's brand of query was much more subtle; I doubt if anyone else there could have read the expression on his impassive face. "It's okay," I repeated, mostly for his benefit.

Mahta cocked an expectant brow at Mimosa. Mimosa shrugged slightly, pulling the red robe more tightly around her shoulders, and nodded curtly. "All right," she said stiffly.

When the three of them had disappeared back up the ramp to the pool house walkway, Mahta just looked at me for a few moments, her expression one of either amused irritation or irritated amusement. Whichever it was, I had seen that look on her face often enough during my long career of running at cross-purposes to her. She sighed delicately and gestured. "Shall we walk?" she said, a command, not an invitation.

In the near darkness I led the way along the paved and curving walk. I wasn't sure where the path led, but I doubted that it would matter very much, anyway. Mahta walked just behind me, slowly enough that I had to readjust my stride several times to keep from outdistancing her. The concept of strolling was alien to me, but Mahta seemed in no hurry. If she expected me to speak, she gave no indication of it. I knew that I would hear from her when she was good and ready.

After a time I grew accustomed to our leisurely pace. The walk merged with a wider concourse, leaving the pool house and cutting across a grassy verge to the broad throughway of the deserted Services district. Heinlein had no moons; when the sun set, the darkness rapidly became intense, but the night sky was awash with a cold glitter of stars. Even in the city, artificial lighting was held to a minimum and was directed for effect; on a clear night like that, you could see a spectacular star field from even the most populated areas. I slowed my pace even further, glancing back at Mahta. Then she touched my arm, indicating one of the spiral rampways that led to an open elevated walkway.

As we climbed, she said, "You can quarter in one of the guest apartments in Central Services again if that suits you." One finely drawn brow rose in an eloquent arch, and she added dryly,

"I assume you don't want to be in the same quarters with Lewis."

Same quarters? Right then I didn't even want to be in the same *solar system* with him! But I just nodded agreeably, refusing to feed Mahta's amusement with any more of a reaction to her comment. Besides, I found that I no longer felt the same blind anger toward Lewis that had sustained me such a short time ago. Worse yet, I was beginning to understand just what that anger had really been a facade for, and—my shouting match with Mimosa notwithstanding—I was discovering that it'd had considerably less to do with him frolicking with a bunch of bare-breasted women than I liked to consider.

Up on the walkway, Mahta paused, forcing me to retrace my last steps. She leaned casually against the rail, placidly scanning the star-strewn sky. Then she looked across levelly at me. "I can hardly wait to hear what all this is about," she informed me candidly. "You're even more wound up than the last time you were here—and look what happened then!"

I made a small, rueful snorting sound. It seemed incredible to me that the last time I'd been on Heinlein had been only a few short weeks earlier. In some ways it seemed like something that had happened to someone else or, if to me, something that had happened in another lifetime. If nothing else, Mahta would surely appreciate the irony of how similar my circumstances were once again. I rested my hip against the railing beside her and began to tell her the story of what had happened on Porta Flora.

Mahta listened with avid attention to my account of my unexpected reunion with Taylor and subsequent meetings with Rhaine and the Ombudsman. It all seemed like pretty dry stuff to me by then; I had already been through it a few times before and could recite it almost by rote. But when I got to the part where the Ombudsman had urged me to speak with the Authority liaison, I had to pause a moment, because the rest of the story was something I had discussed only with Raydor, and I found it necessary to organize my thoughts before I continued. Although nothing in her posture changed as she listened, I could see Mahta's focus narrow when she knew we were getting down to the heart of it.

I tried to summarize Leppers's revelations and his proposal to me as dispassionately as I could, but Mahta was astute enough to see through even my most detached delivery. About halfway through my terse explanation, one of her small slender hands reached out and found mine, squeezing it gently. To my horror, I found my voice begin to waver for a moment as my throat closed. Furiously, I pushed on, repeating Leppers's dire disclosures about the Authority renegades and the danger to the Class Tens in a steady stream of words. I had to stop and draw a deep breath before I could tell her the last of it: CA's communiqué on the verge of our pullout from Porta Flora. Her mouth tightened as I spoke, and I saw her compressed lips whiten, but she did not interrupt me to offer the obvious.

For a minute or two after I had finished speaking Mahta did not stir. She leaned against the railing, her eyes half-closed, the warm night breeze lifting the ends of her long pale hair. Even the touch of her slim hand over mine was quiescent, as if inside her head she was still replaying the last of what I had just said. When she did speak, her voice was a soft, husky whisper, and she did not say what I expected to hear. "No wonder you're so frightened, Jo; no wonder seeing Lewis again scares you so."

Various protestations—automatic denials of any fear or longing—tumbled through my mind, but none of them would come out past my lips. For it was true, the same truth I had tried to evade when I had left Lewis at Nethersedge: I loved him so much that my need for him terrified me. And to top it all off, we both were still in terrible danger. What was even worse, I was bringing that danger right to him, like a plague ship sailing into an unsuspecting port. But as always, I could see no alternative. And so I just leaned there against the walkway railing, helplessly silent, staring out with unseeing eyes over the quiet city.

After a time Mahta seemed to have organized her thoughts; her tone was more businesslike as, dropping her hand from mine, she went on. "If you have a system of government—any system—then you also have a system of corruption. There've always been criminals in our society. Of course, in the past *most* of them have made the mistake of trying to operate outside the system, and that makes them a lot easier to catch."

Understanding her point, I noted, "But these renegades have managed to get away with a hell of a lot by staying inside the system."

She nodded, her lips narrowing again. "Until now," she reminded me.

I shifted slightly, turning to face her. "Are you trying to tell me not to worry?" I asked. "That the A's will catch these renegades like they've always caught the rest, so Lewis and I aren't in any danger?"

But Mahta shook her head. "No," she said. "I can't tell you not to worry. You both are in a hell of a lot of danger."

Hardly cheered, I just nodded grimly. "That's why I've come to take him away from here," I told her. Although, to her credit, Mahta didn't interrupt me with any line of crap about Lewis being safer there on Heinlein, I still felt obligated to explain. "It won't take the A's long to figure out where I went when I left Porta Flora, and anything the A's know, the renegades seem to know about ten seconds later. Intervention or not, now that Leppers is dead, CA is going to have a Writ out for me. So as soon as I can talk to Redding and Alexandria, we're lifting."

Unlike Raydor, Mahta did not ask me where I was planning to take Lewis, but she did repeat one of the questions he'd asked me. "You're not going to try to help the A's trace the renegades, then?"

"And get stuck in the middle of a shoot-out?" I fired back at her. "The renegades are the A's problem."

"And the other Class Tens?" she persisted in that same calm tone.

"That's their problem, too," I said, shaking back my hair with an irritated toss of my head. Since when had I become the official intergalactic custodian of the entire Tenth Class? "Considering the A's track record, the Tens are probably better off if the A's never find them," I said. "Besides, we've already got enough trouble." Before Mahta could respond to that mercenary little bit of philosophy, I abruptly shifted topics on her. "If Redding comes back tonight, I want to talk to him. Can you post a message with Port for me?"

Allowing the sudden segue, Mahta just gazed at me for a few seconds, her dark eyes huge in the dim light. "Of course," she said simply. "He and Alexandria are at the resort at Firerange, though; I don't expect them back until late."

I looked back into her delicate almond-colored face; beneath those childlike features, the woman was pure steel. How much did she know, I wondered, about Redding and me, Lewis and me, about everything? She revealed only what she chose to, and even that in her own good time. As we stood there, she arched one eyebrow slightly and almost ironically at me and said with maddening practicality, "Let's see you to quarters now." She made a small, economical gesture. "You need to eat and get some rest; you'll have a hard run ahead of you."

We began to walk again along the open and deserted walkway. She kept abreast of me, but she still set the pace. After we had gone a few minutes in silence, she looked over to me, her expression calmly thoughtful. There was something unsettlingly familiar about that considering look, and like a reflex I felt an involuntary spasm of apprehension twinge in me.

"Before you lift," Mahta said, "there's someone you and Lewis should speak to."

I resisted the urge to stop moving; glancing sideways at her as we walked, I responded casually. "Oh, yeah? And who's that?"

"Asplundh," she replied, adding, "She's one of our researchers at the center."

Still eyeing her, I pointed out, "We're not going to have much time. Can't this wait?"

Typically, Mahta took the circuitous route to her reply. "When Lewis and the others returned here and we learned what all had happened on Camelot, I insisted that they be examined by one of the Health Center's physicians. You know that we've always required a physical examination for all Volunteers and immigrants." Mahta gave a small, wry smile. "Lewis, Redding, and Alexandria weren't exactly immigrating." She shrugged, concluding with droll understatement, "But then again, we so seldom have visitors who have been touch-healed."

The walkway curved, crossing the throughway that ran below it. At the T intersection on the other side Mahta wordlessly indicated the direction we should take. I turned obediently but persisted. "I don't understand what you're getting at. Is Lewis sick or injured somehow from what happened on Camelot?"

Mahta quickly shook her head. "Oh, no, not at all. But the physician who initially examined them consulted with one of our people in Genetics." She continued evenly. "Asplundh was extremely eager to have the chance to study the cause and effect of Lewis's touch-healing. Lewis, Redding, and Alexandria all agreed to have her take tissue samples to further her research. Did you know," she suddenly interjected, "that tissue that's been touch-healed is virtually indistinguishable from other tissue, except for the absence of the usual wear and tear and cellular damage that's typical of what we consider normal?"

Fascinating stuff, but hardly so crucial that I could not leave Heinlein without knowing more about it. The tense anticipation in me tightened another notch, and it was all I could do to keep from stopping short and confronting Mahta about just getting to the point of all this.

She walked beside me for a few moments without speaking

while a small group of pedestrians passed by on the dimly lit throughway below us. Then she said, "Asplundh is a particle geneticist; her specialty is the study of submolecular—"

I finally halted, swinging to face her. "I *know* what a particle geneticist is!" I snapped. "What the hell does this have to do with me and Lewis getting out of here?"

Placidly winding her way around me, Mahta continued to walk, forcing me to either follow her or be left standing there alone like an idiot. As I caught up to her, she went on as if I had not caused any disruption in her explanation. "Because she'd never had the opportunity to work with touch-healing or a Class Ten, Asplundh ran a series of DNA indexes on all three tissue samples, including a Riekert's Chromosomal Index. Something unusual showed up on Lewis's sample." Stopping then, too, Mahta faced me squarely and said matter-of-factly, "I think both of you should speak to her about this before you leave planet, Jo."

Confusion and irritation sharpened my voice. "Look, I'm sorry if taking Lewis out of here is going to screw up her research, but—"

"This is important, Jo," Mahta said, interrupting me, her tone calm but imperative.

"Then what the hell *is* it?" I exploded. "Why can't Lewis just tell me about it later?"

Her voice was level but intense. "Because he doesn't know about it yet." Holding up one pale, slim hand to forestall my predictable protest, Mahta quickly went on. "This was a voluntary research study, not treatment, so the ethics of medical confidentiality don't exactly apply here," she told me quietly. "Still, Asplundh never would have told me this without Lewis's permission if it hadn't been that she knew how much he matters to you." As she stood facing me, her long hair nearly colorless in the starlight, that self-possessed expression suddenly became transparent enough to reveal the very tender woman beneath it. "And she knows how much you matter to me," she concluded softly.

Dread, like a rush of cold water, sluiced into my veins. Things were bad enough already. Why did Mahta have to make them any worse? I could only stare at her, mutely pleading for her to finish.

"Asplundh did submolecular electrophorectosis on a strand of Lewis's DNA." She reached up and touched my forearm, the gesture almost one of compassion. "The analysis revealed non-standard DNA, Jo."

I gaped at her for a few seconds more, puzzled; then I burst out with unfettered irritation. "Of *course* he's got abnormal DNA—he's a damned *Class Ten*! What the hell did she expect, a normal genotype?"

But Mahta was just calmly shaking her head, gently tugging on my arm as if in a bid for my attention. "I didn't say abnormal, Jo; I said nonstandard," she reminded me quietly.

Baffled but still irate, I shook my head. "What the hell do you mean by 'nonstandard' then? If it's not abnormal, why isn't it standard?"

Mahta's voice was so low, only her proximity to me on the empty walkway made it audible. "Jo, Asplundh says it's not human."

Confusion had temporarily blunted my sense of fear; I scrutinized Mahta's upturned face as if seeking direction there. "What else is there?" I asked, honestly perplexed. Then a sharp shaft of comprehension pierced the armor of my puzzlement. "Are you telling me he's got *animal* DNA?"

For some reason the only image that came to mind in that moment was the infamous spectacle of the "gorilloids," the nearly classic example of a genetically engineered fiasco. In the chaos following the Old War, a group of desperate research geneticists had sought to create an immediate improvement in the nearly-depleted normal human gene pool by producing a hybrid creature using artificially cloned gorilla genes. Of course, instead of the physically superior, intelligent humanoids they had hoped for, all they had succeeded in creating were some spectacularly hairy and singularly stupid hunchbacks who were more interested in swinging from girders than in designing spacecraft. The horror that image evoked must have shown in my expression, for Mahta quickly moved to reassure me.

"No—no, that's not what I'm saying, Jo. Please, you'll have to speak to Asplundh; she still hasn't finished her analysis."

"I want to talk to her tonight," I insisted. "Does she think this DNA is synthetic, then, or what? And what—"

Mahta's fingers closed over my forearm, which she had to squeeze with some pressure to interrupt me. "You won't be able to speak with her until tomorrow, anyway, Jo; she's in the country for the weekend. She wouldn't be back tonight unless it's very late."

What the hell was this—the whole damned planet closed down

for the weekend? I shook off her hold, sidestepping a few paces down the walkway. "I don't care how late it is," I said vehemently, "I want to talk to her the minute she gets back!"

Her voice firm but reasoning, Mahta gazed at me calmly across the small space I had created to separate us and assured me, "This variance isn't the result of any tissue damage, Jo. Asplundh is certain of that, so it isn't from anything that MA may have done to him. It's something intrinsic, something that's always been there. It isn't going to harm him now."

But as she watched her words of reassurance having something of the opposite effect on me, Mahta's look narrowed, suddenly becoming intensely scrutinizing. "But that isn't what you were worried about, is it?" she said softly, almost to herself. Her direct gaze brooked no evasion. "Just why is this so upsetting to you, Jo?"

I met her gaze, keeping my expression almost aggressively set. "Because if I'm going to risk my life with him again, I want to know just what the hell I'm dealing with," I said brusquely.

That was logical enough; with anyone else but Mahta, it might have worked. But this tough little woman just studied me shrewdly and then shook her pale mane of hair, unconvinced. "No," she told me, "that's not it." She reached out to me again, deftly grasping my forearm; this time I did not try to pull free. She looked up steadily into my fiercely guarded face and asked implacably, "Why are you so agitated about the status of Lewis's DNA?"

The few moments of dry silence with which I tried to deflect her question seemed to burn inside me like a large gulp of something drunk too hot, swallowed too rapidly, so that I was forced to let the words spill helplessly from my mouth. "Because I have an embryo that was fertilized by him," I blurted out. Then, ever the child of my excellent grounding in the sciences, I automatically corrected myself. "Well, it was the ovum he fertilized, but what I have now is an embryo—second degree," I added compulsively and uselessly.

Mahta gripped me with both hands then, on her upturned face an incongruous mixture of didactic reproach and maternal delight. "Jo!" she exclaimed. "Why weren't you using—"

I managed to silence her with a simple hard stare of patent disbelief; she must have known that I was one of the least likely people in the quadrant to have needed the antiovulants—before Lewis, at least. "I'd kind of gotten out of practice," I remarked dryly, pulling back to free myself of her hold.

There was no mistaking the look in her eyes. In spite of the unfortunate circumstances surrounding the conception, Mahta was happily astonished. "Then you didn't discard it?" she asked me with cautious hope.

My stare must have revealed my incredulity. "Discard it?" I echoed. "No, of course not; why would I do that?" The thought quite simply would never have occurred to me. I had been taught from birth to revere the potential of human life; we Heinleiners regarded our embryos with all the fervor of zealots protecting their religious idols. "It's back on Porta Flora, at the medical complex."

Mahta popped forward on her toes and gave me a quick, spontaneous hug, which I was too surprised to evade. "Oh, Jo," she said, "this is wonderful!"

I was tempted to remind her that while that had never been the term I would have used to describe the fact, it had been a whole lot closer to "wonderful" before her latest revelation. My ambivalence about what I had let happen between Lewis and me had only deepened. But I saw no advantage, no purpose, in deflating Mahta's joy.

Stepping back to look into my face again, she asked me quietly, "Are you going to tell him?"

"I don't know," I admitted candidly. "I guess it depends on what I decide to do." And just how bad things get, I added morosely to myself.

Mahta smiled softly at me, the wisdom of generations of my ancestors shining in her eyes. In the thin silver starlight she looked like a child, innocent, with her simple clothing and long straight hair. But she had a woman's determination on her face as she admonished me, "Come on, let's get you to quarters now."

As she began to usher me along the elevated walkway, I resisted, reminding her, "I want to see this Asplundh as soon as she gets back; I don't care how late it is."

"I promise," she said. "I'll see she speaks to you the moment she gets back. But for now I want you to get something to eat and then get some rest."

I glanced back at her as, with remarkable efficiency, she hustled me along. "Where is Lewis quartered?" I asked her. I was feeling increasingly uncomfortable with the way I had treated him; the look of hurt and confusion on his trusting face haunted me. "I think I should—"

"You should eat and get some sleep," Mahta corrected me

briskly, barely pausing in her stride to adroitly palm the access key to one of the Central Services building's lower entrance doors. "Lewis is with Raydor and the others now; there'll be time to talk to him later." She looked sideways at me as we waited for a lift, her mouth quirking wryly. "And don't worry, Jo; in spite of your little performance back there at the pool house, I can guarantee you he realizes how you really feel about him." As we stepped through the doors into the lift, she added, "Mimosa was telling you the truth, you know; despite the heroic efforts of some of Heinlein's finest, he's been untouched. He really was waiting for only you."

Abashed, I remained silent as we rode the lift to the upper residential levels of the massive, elliptical-shaped structure. When we exited on the floor Mahta had chosen, she assured me, "And I'll see that Raydor and Taylor know where you're quartered."

I didn't bother to explain to her that Raydor would probably spend at least part of the night at the hangar, dutifully making sure that *Raptor* would be prepared for tomorrow's lift. And it was probably obvious to Mahta that on Heinlein there wasn't much likelihood of Taylor needing to seek me out to find a place to spend the night.

Although I felt strangely exhausted, sleep eluded me. Even a good meal, a warm shower, and the comfort of clean sleepers in a luxurious bed were not enough to automatically push me over the edge. The spacious apartment was even stocked with an excellent selection of audiochips, including a couple of Autasia chips I hadn't heard in years. When I finally succumbed, my sleep was fitful and filled with disturbing dreams.

I didn't know what time it was when I was shaken awake, but it seemed to me as though my head—which still felt enormous and unwieldy from emotional tension and physical fatigue—had just hit the pillow. Groaning in protest, I rolled partially away across the bed, trying to evade the insistent disruption.

"Jo? Come on, Jo, wake up."

Only when my stuporous mind made the necessary connections and recognized Mahta's voice did I begin to yield reluctantly to her demand. Struggling to open my recalcitrant, sleep-weighted lids, I blinked up sluggishly into the glare of the bedside light. Mahta was seated on the edge of the bed, gently shaking my shoulder.

"What is it?" I croaked up at her. "Is she back yet?"

But Mahta's head, a blurry silhouette above me, shook negatively. In her diaphanous ivory-colored robe, she looked like a diminutive angel bending over me. "No, it's not Asplundh, Jo, it's Redding."

I tried to lift my head. "He's here?"

Seeing my lack of comprehension, Mahta helped me pull my wobbly body up into a sitting position before she corrected me. "No, he's gone."

Rubbing at my gritty eyes, I stared torpidly at her. "What do you mean, gone?" I echoed stupidly.

"He's pulled out, Jo—and Raydor and Lewis have gone with him."

CHAPTER SIX

I doubt that contacting a live electrical conduit could have brought me awake more completely or more quickly. I stiffened and jerked up so abruptly on the bed that I nearly knocked heads with Mahta. I glared incredulously at her. "How could you let them pull out without telling me?" I demanded, furious.

Her wide brown eyes flashed with indignation. "First of all," she informed me archly, "this is a free port, and all three of them are Citizens—and grown men, I might add. They hardly need my permission, or anyone else's, to pull out from Heinlein." Her voice dropped slightly both in volume and in vehemence as she continued. "And secondly, no one knew they were going to pull out."

I started to kick free of the bedcovers, still staring at her in disbelief. "What do you mean, no one knew?" I repeated angrily, ducking past her to scramble to my feet. "They'd've had to have had clearance. What the hell was going on at Port? Everyone take the joining weekend off?"

Mahta stood, keeping clear of me as I swung clumsily around, searching the vicinity for my clothing. Although she was still dressed in sleepers and a robe, she managed to convey an air of calm dignity that I sorely lacked. "They didn't pull out from Port," she explained levelly, bending smoothly to pick up one of my deckboots, which in my haste I had just kicked under the edge of the bed frame. As I snatched up the boot, she said, "They lifted from out at Firerange."

Pausing with my flightsuit and liner both wadded up into a ragged ball in my hands, I looked sharply at her. "Where did they get the ship?" I asked.

Calmly and deftly, Mahta reached out to catch one boot as it began to slip from my grasp. "Redding and Alexandria have spent the last few days out at the resort," she reminded me, her voice amazingly even considering the ferocity of my reaction. "They had *Kestrel*, one of the Services' yachts. Redding lifted from Firerange and went directly to the pull by nonregulated access."

Just as I had, twice already, on the way to Heinlein.

"Great!" I said, nearly ripping the seams on my sleepers in my haste to free myself from the garment. "Then no one knows where the hell they've gone!"

"What makes you think no one knows where they went?"

At that familiar gravelly voice, my head jerked up. In the bedroom's doorway, her frenzied mop of grizzled gray hair and her broad shoulders backlit by the outer chamber's lights, stood the one woman from whom nothing should have come as a surprise to me: Alexandria Moore. In her dun-colored, cross-belted tunic and baggy trousers, that boldly craggy face set in sardonic query, she looked more like a demented pirate than an eminent scientist. I had known her to be each, both at the same time. And although we had reached the point in our somewhat turbulent relationship where nothing about this truly unique woman should have dumbfounded me, for a moment I found myself just staring stupidly at her as if I'd never seen her before.

"Hello, Jo," she greeted me, moving into the room. "I'm glad to see you're still in one piece."

Half-naked, the top of my sleepers drooping down around my waist, I confronted her with newly invigorated wrath. "What are *you* doing here?" I demanded. "I thought you were with Redding!"

Before Alexandria could reply to that accusation, another familiar form appeared in the bedroom doorway. Taylor, his sun-streaked hair rudely tousled and his flightsuit slightly misfastened as if donned in great haste, burst into the room. "Jo, are you okay?" He ignored Alexandria and strode right past her to my side. "I heard all the shouting," he explained, his hands going automatically to my bare arms. He glanced at me up and down, his boyish face creased with concern. "Are you all right?" he repeated.

With some surprise, I realized Taylor must have been right in the adjoining bedroom. I was also quite aware that Alexandria was missing nothing, from Taylor's state of mild disarray to the casual way he overlooked my own partial nudity. Refusing to acknowledge the knowing smirk that pulled at her mouth, I accorded Taylor a moment's reassurance. "I'm all right," I told him. "I'm sorry I woke you."

Giving me a few seconds' more scrutiny, he then glanced first to Mahta and then back over his shoulder at Alexandria, throwing her a scalding look. "Who the hell is this?" he insisted, not mollified.

Although I kept my voice deliberately neutral, I knew my lips must have curled slightly. "Alexandria Moore," I told him.

I watched that engaging but slightly befuddled face as Taylor ran a quick memory check on the name. Then his eyes widened, and he threw Alexandria another quick look as he said in utter perplexity, "Alexandria Moore, the Integration expert? I thought she was dead!"

"She was," I assured him cryptically, "but she got over it." Before he could pursue that further, I quickly went on. "Redding pulled out," I explained grimly. "And Raydor and Lewis went with him."

Still baffled, Taylor searched my face as if something there would clarify that string of seeming contradictions. "But I thought Lewis was going with you," he said. "And Raydor—"

Our lopsided exchange was interrupted by a loud, insistent buzzing sound from the outer room. Mahta, who had wisely chosen to stay on the sidelines, started toward the doorway. "It's the summons mode on the Integrator access console," she offered over her shoulder as she passed us.

As she disappeared through the bedroom door, I gently twisted free of Taylor's hold and, stepping past him, confronted Alexandria again. "And where the hell were you?" I repeated testily.

"At Port," she explained simply, reaching out to nonchalantly tug my suit liner free from my hand. "As soon as we got word that you were back, Redding and I came in from Firerange." She held up the liner by its neck like a mother dressing her child. Absently, I thrust my bare arms into it, but I kept my eyes on her mildly amused face. "When we got in to Port," she continued, helping to arrange the undergarment, "Raydor and Lewis met us at the hangar."

A brief look passed between us; it was the merest of glances, but it was an exchange of utter understanding. She did not have to tell me more than that; I knew what Raydor would have told Lewis after I had left them at the pool house, and I knew that the two of them then would have told Alexandria and Redding everything. What had happened not only had ceased to be an outrageous surprise, it was fast becoming an inevitable consequence of everything that had gone before.

With an obvious and cynical look in Taylor's direction, Alexandria casually pulled the bottom of my sleepers the rest of the way down. Automatically, I helped her by kicking free of them and bent over to step into the legs of my suit liner even as she concluded. "I was up in the commissary at Port when they lifted to go back out to Firerange." She shrugged with total aplomb, eyeing my liner-clad body with the indifferent scrutiny of a ship's mechanic checking out a newly fitted thermal coupling. "They had pulled out from there before I could even get off the ground again at Port."

Helplessly aware of the futility of my rage, I nevertheless glowered balefully at her calm, leathery face. "And so you just let them go?" I asked caustically.

Her shaggy brows lifted slightly, but the heavily lined face remained infuriatingly placid as she took hold of my crumpled flightsuit. "Jo, I wasn't exactly in a position to stop them," she reminded my dryly.

I jerked the suit away from her and began to pull it on. I would have said more—probably much to my regret—had not Mahta reentered the room at that point.

"That was Mimosa," she reported tersely from just inside the doorway. "Port has an unidentified vessel approaching—within sensor range but still out beyond audio." Her youthful face was composed, nearly expressionless, but there was a certain tautness to her voice. "Scans make it for an Authority cruiser."

Blood in the water . . . I thought with curious dispassion. It was possible the A's had just decided to cover all bases in their search for me, but that didn't seem really likely. Whether the ship was legitimate or renegade-controlled, they had come to Heinlein with good reason. I didn't believe in luck.

"I'm going up to Port," Mahta concluded. "I'll keep you informed, Jo."

Taylor watched the slim form cross the commons area and disappear beyond the outer door. Then his eyes swung back to me. "I thought Raydor was supposed to look out for you!" he exclaimed indignantly, interposing himself between me and Alexandria, his hands reaching automatically to help pull up the back of my flightsuit over my shoulders and straighten its seam. "Why the hell would he run off like this? Why would any of them run off now, without you?"

The uncharacteristic anger was directed at what Taylor presumed to be Raydor's poor judgment in the matter. Acutely aware of Alexandria's keenly assessing look, I sealed the front of my suit with one firm, determined sweep of my hand. Then I touched Taylor's upper arm in an almost placating gesture and quietly said, "That's exactly why Raydor's doing this—to try to protect me."

It was almost stunningly clear to me then; not only had I made Raydor's leaving a possibility, I had made it a near certainty. When we had spoken during the coast to Heinlein, he had scrupulously made sure that I had no intention of looking for the other Class Tens or of helping to hunt for the renegades. But he hadn't been trying to talk me into it, I realized belatedly, he had just been determining that I intended to try to stay out of danger. Damn him and his Tachs honor—I had practically given him my blessing to go!

"What do you mean, 'protect' you?" Taylor insisted. "He's going to protect you by deserting you?"

I just squeezed his arm and said, "I don't have time to explain it all right now, Taylor; I've got to get the hell out of here."

I could see I wasn't helping matters much; Taylor's brows seemed to be developing a permanent arch. "You're leaving?" he asked in surprise. "But we just got here!"

"Yeah, well, it seems it's been long enough," I replied, starting toward the door.

"Wait," he protested, grabbing hold of my arm and digging in his heels. "I'm going with you. Just let me get a message off to Porta Flora; if I don't tell my boss I'm extending my leave, I'm going to lose my job."

I didn't need to consider his offer. "Okay," I agreed, swinging around so that I was then pushing him toward the door instead, "run up to the Port Authority. You can send him a message from Mimosa's office." I shook free of his hold, giving him a firm shove in the right direction. "Just hurry; we're lifting immediately."

Taylor made it as far as a few strides into the outer room; then he suddenly halted, pivoting around to face me again. "Wait. Where are we going?" he queried plaintively.

I swung to meet Alexandria's stolid face. It was somewhat disheartening to find that when it came to her involvement in the matter, I felt more a sense of resignation than one of actual anger anymore. "You said you knew where they were going?" I asked wearily.

But she shook her grizzled head, her mass of frizzy hair bouncing. "That's not exactly what I said, Jo," she said. Before I could interrupt her in sheer exasperation, she continued. "But I do know where they *should* be going: Earthheart."

For once my own expression probably appeared more baffled than Taylor's. He hesitated only a moment, long enough for the name to register, and then he remarked somewhat ingenuously, "Oh, the place with the animals." Then he resumed his course across the commons and out the door.

I had been ready to take off at his heels until Alexandria's words put a temporary halt to that. "Earthheart? Are you sure?" I asked. It was Raydor's homeworld, but it still seemed an unlikely destination for the three of them. The planet was under Interdiction; Citizens required special clearance even to land there.

But Alexandria seemed to pay no attention to my skepticism. "Aren't you forgetting something?" she said, staring pointedly at my feet.

I spun around and came back into the room, scrabbling for my boots. As I hopped clumsily on first one foot and then the other, too stubborn to take the time to just sit down in front of her to pull them on, Alexandria gently shook her head. I threw her a baleful glare, but she seemed unaffected by my irritated haste.

"Where'd you pick up Slick?" she asked, jerking her thumb in the direction Taylor had gone.

I headed out the bedroom door, not bothering to look back to see if she was following; I knew that she would. "He's a friend," I said over my shoulder, hitting the release on the outer door. "An old friend," I added. "A *good* friend."

In my annoyed rush I nearly ran headlong into Mahta's Jim, who was approaching down the outer corridor. He had to reach out and grasp my shoulders to keep both of us from being knocked sideways on impact. "Jo!" he exclaimed, setting me back straight on my feet. His bearded, usually genial face was drawn and sober as he quickly explained. "Mahta sent me to tell you: They have audio contact with that Authority vessel; it's the light cruiser *Sumatra*, out of Porta Flora." As he spoke, he urged me along the corridor toward the lift. Deftly punching buttons, he continued. "They're demanding permission to land, but Mahta has been refusing them clearance. She's not in a very good mood," he offered in his typically understated manner.

Giving Alexandria a rueful glance, I said, "Neither am I, Jim—not lately."

We exited the lift on the level of the covered walkway to Port. The predawn sky was murky, the color of muddy water, and streaked with feathery bands of cirrus clouds. In spite of the early hour, the walkway and the throughway below it were dotted with a surprising number of people: Services workers, shop employees, personnel from Port. Monday morning on Heinlein, and the city was getting back to work. Alexandria and I followed Jim silently; he didn't even turn back to look in our direction until we reached the down ramp at the hangar. Then he paused, politely and automatically, to let us precede him down the incline.

In the airy cavern of the huge hangar, *Raptor* looked strangely normal, sitting solidly on the smooth pavement of the docking bay. In a world full of unexpected rebukes, my ship suddenly seemed like a very welcome oasis of reliability in the midst of chaos.

As I started across the floor of the massive structure, I heard Jim's voice call from behind me. "There they are now, Jo," he said. I turned to see him pointing down the long, broad aisle between the other docked vessels to where Mahta and a woman I did not recognize were rapidly approaching our berth. As Mahta drew nearer, I could see that her face was still traced with unaccustomed lines of stress and her lips were compressed into a firm line. As soon as she was close enough, she began to speak without preamble and without introducing her companion.

"*Sumatra* is demanding clearance, Jo." The earth-colored eyes were resolute, their gaze steady on my face. "They say they have a Writ of Inquiry issued in your name in the matter of the death of John Givens Leppers."

Behind me Alexandria made a rough, grunting sound; its tone suggested exactly what she thought the A's could do with their Writ of Inquiry. The other woman with Mahta just looked rather confused—an epidemic problem around there. Ignoring them both, I asked Mahta tersely, "How long can you put them off?"

Mahta's expression was determined but calm, her brows canting slightly. "Long enough, I think," she said. "The Writ gives them the legal right to land, even in a deregulated port—even with the restraining order imposed by our class action suit." Her brows climbed fractionally. "But it is a Monday morning, and we're a very busy port. It might take some time to accommodate their request."

Fighting back the urge to grin at her audacity, I asked her, "Have you seen Taylor?"

"He was just coming up to Mimosa's office when we left," she said. "We only spoke briefly, but he should be down directly."

The petite woman at her side shifted restively, glancing from me to Alexandria with a puzzled frown on her face. But I still ignored her, instead addressing Mahta's remark. "Good," I said, turning toward the ship. "I can get her prepped and be ready to lift in—"

"Jo, wait," Mahta interrupted. She gestured to the impatient woman beside her. "This is Asplundh. I want you to speak with her before you leave."

I briefly surveyed the geneticist. She was dressed in a leisure jumpsuit, not her medical colors, and looked as though Mahta had intercepted her just as she'd come in on an early-morning shuttle from the country. She was much younger than I had expected, perhaps even a few years younger than I, with the kind of hard, trim figure that suggested she did more than just lie around on a chaise during her weekends off. Her short smoky-brown hair was a mass of ringlets, and her tawny eyes were widely set in a neatly oval-shaped face. In short, she was the kind of Normal who shot to hell my pet theory that we all were becoming too depressingly homogeneous in appearance. But I just shook my head at her. "There's no time to talk now," I said shortly, turning again. "It'll have to wait—we're lifting."

Asplundh was apparently unaccustomed to such a summary dismissal. She snagged the sleeve of my flightsuit as I turned and effectively halted me. "Captain, this is important," she insisted.

"So is getting the hell off this planet before they have to let *Sumatra* in," I snapped, pulling my arm free.

Visibly exasperated by my brusque treatment, the geneticist turned back to Mahta. "Just what is this all about, anyway?" she asked. Her eyes shot to Alexandria, and she displayed an air of expectation born of some familiarity. "Alexandria, are you leaving, too?"

"Looks like," Alexandria replied.

I had resumed striding toward *Raptor* when, behind me, I heard Asplundh suddenly demand of Mahta, "Is this about Lewis? You said he'd left. Is he in some kind of danger?"

Something in Asplundh's tone made me pause and turn back. I had to stare at her for a few seconds to satisfy myself that she had not been one of the two bare-breasted women who had been cavorting in the water with Lewis the previous night. My eyes narrowed. "What if he is?" I asked, daring her to explain why she should be so concerned.

Asplundh used my hesitation to stalk up to me again, eyes flashing. "He's a very special person, Captain," she said stiffly. "Whether or not you're willing to take the time to talk to me about him, I still happen to care about his welfare."

"Then why don't you come along with us?" Alexandria suggested.

I turned farther, glaring at the big frizzy-haired woman. "This isn't a—" I began.

But Alexandria just plowed on through my objection like a heavy-duty crawler flattening some insignificant bit of debris on a landing field. "She's smart, tough, and she's got medical training," she said, "and we could use the help."

"We don't need any more help," I insisted. "We've got Taylor."

Alexandria just gave a short, coarse laugh. "Taylor's not help—he's entertainment," she said deprecatingly. "What do you say, Asplundh?"

Furious at the way Alexandria had overrun my objections and usurped my prerogative, I turned on the curly-haired geneticist. But the woman stood up to my irate glower, meeting my eyes with a stubborn stare of her own. "If Lewis is in any danger, I'd like to help in any way I can," she said quietly.

She was loyal, I had to give her that. She didn't even ask where the hell we were going, and even Taylor had questioned that. Never mind that the possible source of that loyalty caused a sudden sharp pain, like the sting of an unexpected slap, to reverberate through me. It was beginning to appear that she had more than just a dispassionate professional interest in Lewis. But Alexandria, for whatever her reasons, wanted Asplundh along, and I was rudely forced to face the fact that I would not be able to get very far on Earthheart without the help of the big, brash former liaison to the Tachs. So I bit down on my anger and my misgivings and just shot Alexandria one final baleful look. "All right, then, have it your way," I told her. "But we're lifting *now*."

"Fine," Alexandria responded with equanimity. "Here comes Slick, too."

I glanced back across the huge hangar. Taylor was striding rapidly up the broad aisle, following the course Mahta and Asplundh had just taken. By the time he reached us, he was nearly jogging. From the way his eyes skimmed over Asplundh, I assumed Mahta had introduced them up at the PA office; his gaze came to rest on me. "Are we ready to lift, Jo?" he asked with obvious concern.

"I'm ready," I assured him, adding dryly, "Let's see if we can get out of here before Alexandria decides we need any more crew."

"Jim and I are going back to Mimosa's office," Mahta said, before Taylor had time to puzzle over my caustic comment. "I don't know how long I can stall *Sumatra*, Jo, or how you're going to get around them once you're up there, but—"

This time I cut her off, probably astonishing her—and certainly surprising myself—by darting forward to embrace the slender little woman, still clad in her bedrobe, in a quick, fierce hug. Jerking back before she had a chance to respond, I told her, "Just hold them off as long as you can; we'll think of something." Then I turned and headed off toward *Raptor*'s belly.

As I palmed the ramp key access, Taylor and the others caught up to me. Waiting as the ship's boarding ramp curled down from her sleek underside, Taylor asked me quietly, "Does that Authority cruiser up there have anything to do with that message they were trying to send when we pulled out from Porta Flora?"

As the ramp's padded feet landed on the tarmac with a soft thump and I stepped past him to bound up the incline, I heard Taylor answer himself with a certain glum resignation. "Or we can talk about that later." But I noted he was the first one behind me when I rushed up the corridor to Control.

I slid through the hatchway before it had entirely opened and threw myself down into my chair in front of the operations board. Palming Handy's access, I asked without preamble, "Ship's status, Handy?"

"All systems optimal, Jo," came the prompt response in that deep bass voice. Raydor had not neglected his duties the previous night. The rest of Handy's commentary came rumbling out before I could interrupt him. "I've been monitoring communications from Port and *Sumatra*, and I've set up the prepull check; I can implement it as soon as you give me input. Hello, Alexandria."

"Hi, Handy," Alexandria replied heartily, brushing past Taylor to drop her bulky form into Raydor's chair at comm.

I glanced back to see that Taylor had taken the ancillary chair right behind her; I knew he would have taken Raydor's board had not Alexandria beaten him to it. Asplundh dropped into the second ancillary chair, right behind me. I reached across my board and punched the necessary button; instantaneously, the blur of prepull figures began pulsing across Handy's screen.

I looked across at Alexandria, who was scanning the comm panel with almost casual ease. No matter what I might have thought of her manners, I was willing to admit that I was lucky to have her filling Raydor's seat. Aggravating as she could be, the woman had probably been designing Integrator-accessed comm boards like that one since before I was born. Her blunt and callused fingers found their way to the right positions on the board without her even needing to glance down. Instead, her eyes were on Handy's screen and the stream of data that flowed across it.

"Handy, have we got launch clearance?" I queried, beginning to reach automatically for the straps of my chair harness.

"We have clearance, and we're ready to taxi," the Integrator responded.

"Then get us out," I told him. Behind me, I was aware of Taylor and Asplundh fastening their own harnesses. Alexandria had clipped the pickup over her ear and sat back with her frizzy head cocked, her expression impassive as she listened. *Raptor*'s engines came up, the deck plates shivering delicately beneath our feet. Handy pivoted us around in the docking bay, the ship's nose dipping slightly; he adeptly began maneuvering us out into the aisle and toward the hangar doors.

"Get me Port," I instructed Alexandria. As she punched audio, I leaned forward in my harness across the small space between my chair and the board and waited for Mahta's voice to come over the speaker.

"Jo, we've had to reroute some incoming traffic, but we've got you clear for immediate lift."

"What about *Sumatra*?" I asked her.

"They're getting a bit . . . testy," Mahta responded with a true Heinleiner's flair for understatement. "It's going to be difficult to hold them off much longer."

"Just a few more minutes," I said grimly.

Outside the massive hangar, sunlight streaked the field in low, oblique shafts, burning away the tattered remnants of a light morning fog. The ship accelerated slightly across the tarmac, sending the mist scattering, as Handy swung us to pick up the taxi lane. I bent over his access, punching in coordinates with methodical expertise.

"Ready to lift, Jo," Handy informed me.

"Jo," Taylor said from over my right shoulder, his voice level but taut, "you don't really think you can outrun that cruiser, do you?"

"No, but we won't have to," I replied. I turned to Alexandria again. "Call Port," I told her. "Tell Mahta to stand by to give *Sumatra* clearance to come in."

Her big square teeth bared in an appreciative grin of comprehension, Alexandria deftly punched out my request to Port.

I could hear Asplundh shifting in the chair behind me. "I don't know why the Authorities are after you," she said in a puzzled tone, "but if you let that cruiser come down now, we'll never be allowed to lift."

"Stand by to lift, Handy," I said. I shot another look to Alexandria on comm. "Tell Mahta, *now*."

Still grinning, Alexandria punched it through. Smoothly, scarcely glancing down at the board, she keyed the ship-to-Port feed through her pickup and began monitoring *Sumatra*'s communications. "This is really going to piss them off, you know," she commented, "once they figure out what you're doing."

"Let them be pissed," I said, my fingers curling lightly over Handy's ENABLE switch.

"What exactly *are* we doing?" Asplundh asked from behind us.

Ignoring the geneticist's perplexed question, Alexandria continued blandly. "Even light cruisers've got high-beams. They get pissed enough, they just might get a little trigger-happy—Heinlein or not."

Let them try it! I wanted to respond, but I reined in my roiling sense of frustration and instead just replied tightly, "I don't intend to present them with much of a target."

"What is—" Taylor started from behind us, but at that moment Alexandria interrupted him by abruptly lifting one big hand in a gesture of constraint.

"Okay, they're coming down," she announced, her grizzled head cocked into the pickup.

"Let me know when they hit the atmosphere," I told her, pressing my finger lightly against the enable. "Ready, Handy?"

"Jo," the Integrator grumbled, sounding mildly put out, "*I'm* always ready."

By that time Taylor had figured out for himself what I intended to do. His voice was even, almost with a touch of curiosity, as he asked me, "How long before a cruiser with that mass can accelerate to lift again?"

"If we let them get low enough, they won't be able to," I explained, scanning Handy's screen.

"You mean they'll have to land before they can lift again," he said.

"Of course, if we let them get that low before we lift," Alexandria reminded us helpfully, "we're going to make a pretty good target down here."

"Not necessarily," I remarked.

Asplundh had listened to our exchange with growing impatience; she had kept silent as long as she was able. "An Authority vessel would never fire on a civilian ship in this port," she insisted indignantly. "No matter why they're after you!"

Alexandria and I just threw the geneticist nearly identical glances of patent disbelief. But, of course, Asplundh would have had no way of understanding the depths of our bald skepticism concerning Authority ships. She might have known about Camelot, but she probably thought the Authorities had things under control; she didn't know what had happened to Leppers, and she didn't realize that *Sumatra* was probably manned by renegades. And so I slightly softened my reproach at her naiveté. "Maybe normally they wouldn't, but this isn't a very normal situation."

Before Asplundh could respond to that, Alexandria cut in. "Ten seconds to atmosphere," she told me.

I counted off the time in my head; even had I misjudged, Handy would have corrected me. I must have done pretty well, though, because I hit the enable without any feedback from him. Almost instantaneously, I felt the smooth surge of acceleration, and my body was forced back into my padded chair as *Raptor* began to lift from the field.

From beside me, Alexandria relayed the information from monitoring *Sumatra*'s comm. "They've picked us up on ground scan," she reported. Even though she was flattened back against her chair's headrest, her craggy face wore an irrepressibly self-satisfied expression. "They're hailing us, demanding that we return to Port." Her head turned fractionally toward me, her lips parting just enough to show those formidable square teeth. "How shall I respond?" she asked.

"No response," I said, my eyes snapping back to Handy's screen.

Alexandria listened in silence for a few moments. "Yeah," she drawled then, "I'd say they were starting to get a bit pissed."

"Jo, maybe you should—" Taylor said a bit anxiously.

"Uh oh," Alexandria interrupted, holding up her hand again. "*Now* they're pissed!"

"They're dropping their high-beams, Jo," Handy translated matter-of-factly for me.

My hand darted out, punching a button on the navigation panel. "Lateral thrust, Handy," I said. *"Now!"*

Artificial gravity generators, even on ships of *Raptor*'s size, were remarkably efficient, but some maneuvers defied the efforts of even the best AG systems. Pulling out was an example of one such maneuver that immediately came to mind; lateral thrust was another. At my command, Handy slewed us sideways in an almost instantaneous ninety-degree deviation; *Raptor* shot away nearly horizontally from Port's airspace and away from *Sumatra*'s high-beam cannon. Unfortunately, in the seemingly endless seconds until the gravity compensators could catch up, all four of us were crushed back into our chairs with breathless force. Whether or not the cruiser would have actually fired upon us became a moot question as we quickly accelerated beyond the range of their weapons. I intended to continue to do everything I could to keep it moot.

"Handy," I grunted as soon as I was able, "how long before we can go to pull?"

"Three-point-seven-six minutes, once we resume vertical thrust," he said brightly. I was teetering on the edge of adrenaline breakdown, and he was probably having the time of his life!

"Resume it, then," I directed, hitting another button.

Beside me, I saw Alexandria pull her burly torso forward over her board, bracing herself for the sudden resumption of lift acceleration. I don't know what kind of communications were coming in from *Sumatra*, but I could well guess; Alexandria's leathery face was split by a crooked grin of satisfaction, and she gave a derisive little snort at something that was coming in over her pickup. She glanced over at me. "They're still going down— not very graciously, I might add."

But I couldn't spare much time to join in her somewhat skewed sense of triumph. As the gravity stabilized again and I was able to lean forward, I hung over Handy's panel. "I'm going to give you some pull coordinates," I told him, my fingers flying over the board. "I want you to feed them to Port—but uncoded and over the standard channel."

From behind me Asplundh said in surprise, "Why are you letting them know where we're going? I thought you were trying—"

But Taylor cut her off, interjecting with a tone of almost amused admiration, "Those aren't the coordinates for Earthheart." He was catching on fast; he hadn't even had to glance down at the navigation screen to come to that conclusion. But as he continued, his voice held more of a note of concern. "I hate to be the one to point this out, Jo, but there's a very good reason why what you're going to do is illegal. What if we're not clean when we go into the pull?"

"Mahta knows where we're really goi ̣g," I reminded him. I was trusting her to warn us if she couldn't guarantee us a clean spiral for the pull.

As the figures pulsed over the screen in a glowing green line, Alexandria said from comm, "These guys are out to set a new record for turnaround; they're coming back up!"

"How long, Handy?" I asked shortly, my arms braced against his panel.

"Point-eight-five minutes," he reported. The figures on the screen were scuttled, replaced by the schematic for the spiral for the pull. "Preparing for standard trajectory into the spiral."

"Wait a minute," Alexandria cut in, a frown replacing the glib smirk on that craggy face. "I'm getting something from Port—" She broke off, snapping the switch on the speaker. Then Mimosa's familiar voice filled the compartment.

"I repeat: *Raptor*, this is Heinlein Port. Your coordinates for pull have been received." Beneath the cultured calm I could detect the significance of the tight control in that even tone. "To expedite current incoming Port traffic, we request you delay your entry into the spiral and hold at the following coordinates."

Even Asplundh did not need a translation this time: Mimosa was warning us that there was an incoming vessel in a position to interfere with our entry to the pull for Earthheart. She was also telling us, by the coordinates she had sent for our supposed holding pattern, to just where she was hastily diverting the intervening ship.

"Shit!" Alexandria muttered, listening intently to her pickup. "*Sumatra*'s initiating lateral thrust."

Adrenaline began sending its familiar flood of ice through my veins; even as its tingle reached my fingertips, I hit Handy's access. "How long, Handy?" I snapped.

"Any time, Jo," the Integrator responded. "We're at optimal altitude for entry into the spiral."

If that was the case, then the altitude was the only optimal thing we had going for us right then. "Jo," Taylor said cautiously, reasoningly, leaning forward in his harness to touch the tips of his fingers to my shoulder, "why don't we just pull out to somewhere else—lose them and then make the pull to Earthheart from there?"

What he suggested made sense, and it wasn't like I hadn't already played plenty of interstellar hopscotch on our way to Heinlein for exactly the same purpose. But not now. I just couldn't take the chance that we'd be stuck crawling along with some three- or four-day coast time at some backwater world—not with the lives of three very important men in danger.

"Handy," I said quickly, "how much of a deviation can you make in the spiral and still get us into the pull for Earthheart?"

"Jo!"

"Captain!"

The two protesting voices rose simultaneously from the ancillary seats. Alexandria didn't say anything, but her head swung about abruptly, the riotous mass of her unfettered hair bouncing manically, her sharp stare speaking quite eloquently for her.

Plunging onward, I hastily continued. "Can we dodge this incoming ship and still make the pull?"

Handy's deep voice was mild, typically unperturbed. "That would be a violation of Port regulations, Jo."

There had once been a time when I probably would have exploded angrily at that automatic observation, but I had learned to view it for what it was: merely programming. I had also learned that the fact of Handy reminding me of the illegality of an act was not tantamount to his refusing to perform that act. So I just repeated with quiet urgency, "Can we?"

There was the briefest of pauses while he deliberated, a minute lapse in the Integrator's response as his hypertrophied neurons surged into action, calculating the complex equations with stunning speed. Seconds later he responded, "We could do it, Jo."

"Jo, this is crazy!" Taylor exclaimed from behind me.

I couldn't argue with that, so I just replied, "Yeah, I guess you're right," at the same time I was palming Handy's access and instructing him. "Let's go, then."

"Entering the spiral for the pull," Handy said.

"This is *not* a good idea," Alexandria remarked, stoically bracing herself against the comm board.

Her words were the last thing I heard before we dropped into the spiral and the lunging distortion of the pull flung us beyond any hope of taking back my decision.

CHAPTER
SEVEN

My recent shipboard experiences had not made me any more fond of the pull than I'd ever been. But if nothing else, I'd figured that my frequent exposure to the phenomenon on the way from Porta Flora should have at least served to slightly inure me to the worst of its physical effects. No such luck. Ordinary pulling out was bad enough; whatever it was that Handy'd had to do to divert our spiral around that incoming ship seemed to have added an element of major turbulence to the maneuver. I had never before been aware of any specific sensation of direction or acceleration during the pull, but that time it felt as if whatever might otherwise have been normal velocity was dramatically altered. *Raptor* lurched and shook wildly, as if the ship were hitting the edge of an atmospheric field without the benefit of stabilizers. I was dimly aware of a few small objects—things that had always been secure during pullout—flying crazily about the compartment. My head, pressed back painfully into my chair's padded headrest, felt enormous and dangerously fragile. The typical sense of vague nausea that always attended the pull for even the most seasoned of freightmen had burgeoned frighteningly then; I was sure if I'd had the misfortune of having eaten anything that morning, my breakfast would have already been decorating the inside of Control. But worst of all, the normal and forgiving sense of timelessness that should have accompanied the pull was somehow skewed, making me excruciatingly aware of everything I was experiencing. Just when I thought that I might very well vomit, after all—as an expression of opinion, at least, even if the act would have been lacking in substance— the terrifying grip of the pull released us, and *Raptor* went into coast.

As I hastily struggled to straighten myself in my chair, my

senses were assailed by the unpleasant constraints of real time. "Handy—" I started, then had to pause, nearly gagging at the sour smell that seemed to fill the small compartment in a suffocating wave. I also was suddenly aware of a raucous, unrelenting noise: the panicky whooping of Internals' malfunction alarm. The pulsing sound drilled through my aching head like shots from a hot-riveting gun.

"It's okay, Jo," the Integrator immediately assured me, his deep voice maddeningly calm above the din. "There's no major damage."

No major damage? We must have blown out every cross-stem on the ship! The ship's schematics flashing on his screen, from Internals to Navigation, were lit up like a pyrotechnics display, strobing with color-keyed malfunctions codes. I just shook my bloated head incredulously and demanded, "I thought you said we could do this!"

"We did do it," he replied with infuriating equanimity. There was a brief pause; if Handy had still been a human being, he would have been shrugging. "I didn't say we could do it without sustaining any damage," he said.

"Terrific!" I snarled, lashing out clumsily to hammer at Internals' main switch. The abrupt movement made my vision swim woozily. "Cut the joining alarm, will you?"

In the sudden relative silence I heard Alexandria beside me, grunting as she struggled with the catches on her chair harness even as she pulled herself forward over her board. She shot me a baleful glare; I noted with a vengeful twist of satisfaction that even her usually implacable face looked a little nauseated. "Bloody Stars!" she cursed, catching sight of the damage display on Handy's screen. "What did we do, burn out every damned system on the ship?" She glowered at me. "I *told* you it was a bad idea."

"Yeah?" I retorted, my eyes stubbornly glued to the Internals board. "It *worked*, didn't it?"

"Okay, so it was a bad idea that worked," Alexandria shot back. She twisted awkwardly around in her chair to check on the occupants of the ancillary chairs. Gingerly, I followed suit, uncomfortably aware of the somewhat uneven reestablishment of ship's gravity.

Taylor looked shaken but essentially none the worse for wear. Asplundh had been spectacularly and miserably sick to her stomach; whatever she'd had for breakfast on her way back to the city earlier had done nothing for either the decor or the atmosphere in the small compartment.

"You all right?" Alexandria asked her solicitously, but the geneticist could only slump in her harness, her face a pale oval framed by brown curls.

"Get her out of here," I ordered the compartment in general. The odor of vomit was goading my own unsettled stomach, and whatever sense of sympathy I might have felt for my hapless fellow traveler was being overridden by my annoyance and a nagging feeling of urgency.

I saw Alexandria and Taylor exchange looks; they had barely met, but already they seemed to have established a protocol of locking horns over everything. I expected and hoped that it would be Alexandria who would tend to Asplundh, since she at least knew the woman. But it was Taylor who moved, carefully unfastening the catches on his harness as he quietly said, "I'll take care of her."

As I turned back to Handy's strobing screen, Alexandria quipped with some of her usual asperity, "I'll flip you for the vacu-mop."

I threw her a sour glance, saying, "It was your idea to bring her along—you clean up after her." But the caustic comment was made more as a matter of habit than as an expression of true anger, and Alexandria probably knew it. It was difficult to maintain any real anger at the big woman; she was one of the few things we had going for us right then. Of course, I wasn't about to acknowledge that dependence on her any more than I was about to clean up after Asplundh.

Momentarily ignoring the graphic damage report on the screen, I leaned over Handy's console again and asked, "How far out?"

"Twelve-point-six-three hours, Jo," he replied immediately, adding casually, "Actually, we sort of overshot the planet, so we'll be coming in from the other side."

Overshot? Beside me, Alexandria's head jerked up. I had never heard of overshooting a planet; we had probably broken some kind of record. We were also probably lucky to be alive.

I fumbled to release my own chair harness, instructing Handy, "Categorize all these malfunctions for me, then prioritize the most critical for repair."

"Where do you want me to start, Jo?" Alexandria asked nonchalantly.

I stood, determinedly fighting the shakiness in my legs, and reached for Internals' remote board. "I want you to start with the vacu-mop," I replied bluntly. "Then you can do the postpull check for me to log in when I get back."

"The check shouldn't take too long," she responded, glancing at the screen, "with half of your functions blitzed out." She eyed me mildly. "Where are you going?"

"Down into the maintenance well," I answered, holding up the remote board. "We won't be able to maneuver, much less land, with some of these burnouts."

From the look on her weathered face as well as from past experience, I half expected some kind of disagreement from Alexandria. Thus I was somewhat surprised when her expression instead slowly softened into an ironic grin and she just shook her grizzled head. "Powers, Jo—sometimes I just don't know about you," she said. The look in her eyes was almost fond. "You've got three men who love you, all trying to protect you, and you still can't seem to keep the hell out of trouble!"

At first I didn't make the connection. I just made the automatic assumption that she was counting Taylor as the third man until I realized that she really didn't know or like him well enough to give him that kind of credit. Then I felt the fuzzy sting of adrenaline numb my limbs, and I just stood there, the remote board gripped in my nerveless hands, staring at her with a suddenly evolving sense of comprehension. She didn't mean Taylor; she was referring to Redding. Then I knew what she had just so casually confirmed for me: The maverick freightman was indeed my father.

"You *knew*!" I said, my hoarse whisper not so much an accusation as a furious exclamation of anger. "You *knew*, and you never *told* me!"

Her mouth quirked wryly, but there was surprising gentleness in her hooded eyes as she replied. "Tell *you*? Hell, I never even told *him*!"

Momentarily taken aback, I could only stare mutely at her as, with a candid shrug, she went on. "Jo, I promised your mother I'd never tell either of you."

My confusion was only compounded. "Then—then he doesn't—?"

"Oh, he knows now," Alexandria explained matter-of-factly. "He had the tests on Heinlein. That's why I figured it's okay to tell you now, too," she added, shrugging again. "I don't think she'd care anymore now that you two've found each other on your own, anyway."

I had thought that I'd already experienced the greatest impact of whatever shock that knowledge could impart in that tense, perilous, and almost surrealistic moment in the research complex on Camelot when Redding had first told me that he thought he might be my father. In the intervening weeks, in spite of all the other concerns that had filled my mind and my time, I don't think the possibility he'd raised had ever really been far from my conscious awareness. I had considered both sides of the potential outcome—that Redding was mistaken or that he was indeed my father—in endless detail. But in that moment I found, much to my dismay, that the truth still had the power to surprise me, even if the information was delivered in such a calm and dispassionate manner by a woman as terminally blunt as Alexandria Moore.

"So you see," Alexandria remarked into my continued gaping silence, "he left Heinlein without you for the same reason Lewis and Raydor did: They all just wanted to protect you."

Oddly, the first question that occurred to me then had nothing to do with our present situation or even with the three men's timely defection from Heinlein. "Why didn't she ever tell me?" I asked Alexandria, my voice so low, it was nearly a whisper.

The big woman shifted slightly in her chair, the swivel mechanism squeaking sharply in protest. "I'm not sure," she admitted. "Maybe because she thought if you knew, you'd want to know why she didn't stay with him—or give him a chance to stay with her."

The question, automatic and helpless, was out of my mouth before I realized that I probably already knew the answer to it. "Why didn't she?"

Those wide, dark eyes, fathomless beneath the formidable ridge of her weathered brow, just regarded me in silence for a moment. "Because she was afraid," she said quietly. She didn't need to add what her look had already told me: *And you know of what.*

Yes, I knew of what, all right. I had become intimately acquainted with the same fears. My mother had been afraid of the inexplicable strength of what she had been capable of feeling for him, of what it might have made her willing to do, of what he might have been willing to do in return. She had been afraid of losing herself—as if love could become an abyss, an emotional black hole that would pull more and more of herself into it, until finally there was no way to go back, no hope of returning to what she had been. She had been afraid of what I was afraid of: the irrational, inexorable power of love.

Something in the expression on my face made Alexandria glance down for a moment. She made a small, negligible gesture, spreading her broad, callused hands over her knees to smooth the rumpled fabric of her trouser legs. When she looked up again at me, her lip curled in gentle amusement. "I hear you really gave Lewis the stiff-arm last night at the pools," she said.

Startled from my morose musings, I stared at her in surprise. "He told you that?" I blurted out.

She shook her head. "No, of course not. The man's got it so bad for you, you probably could've whacked off his balls with a dull blade and he wouldn't've even said 'ouch.'" She leaned back again in her chair. "I heard it in the commissary. You know how Port workers like to gossip."

Port workers weren't the only ones, I decided acerbically.

Alexandria was eyeing me candidly, her leathery face curiously open. When she spoke, her gruff voice held an unexpected tone of compassion. "I told you to be careful with him, Jo," she reminded my softly.

"Yeah," I shot back, "but you told me that too late."

I don't know what further comments Alexandria might have offered if I had given her the chance, just as I didn't know what further painful things I might have revealed. I didn't want to find out. Clutching the remote board to my chest like a shield, I turned and strode out of Control and into the corridor.

Unfortunately, the term "maintenance well" was aptly descriptive. Except for the fact that the passageway extended horizontally, not vertically, down the long axis of the ship, *Raptor*'s service access was a claustrophobically cramped tunnel, tightly packed with the cross-stems of nearly every function core affecting ship's systems. The cross-stems were basically like fuses; overload a circuit and the cross-stem blew rather than destroy the core. Armed with the remote board from Internals and a small portable Integrator relay, I had spent scarcely twenty minutes in the well before my back and shoulders were aching and my head was formulating the beginnings of a stupefying headache. For perhaps the tenth time in as many minutes I wondered how the hell Raydor managed to scramble around in there without killing himself or going nuts. Perspiration was trickling irritatingly through my hair, and my suit liner was already sticking doggedly at my neck and belly as I tried to balance the remote board in such a position that I could see its indicators and still speak into Handy's relay at the same time.

"Well, I already tried that," I reported impatiently to him, "and I still get a dead circuit. So what else—"

I broke off with a little yelp of surprise as someone goosed me in the rear. As I jerked around, nearly braining myself on the cross-stem I had pulled out, I knocked the remote board over, but I didn't really mind, because the cheerful grin on Taylor's face was well worth any temporary inconvenience his impetuous form of greeting might have caused.

"Figured you could use some company," he said affably as he crouched in the low tunnel behind me.

"What I could use is some *help*!" I retorted, thrusting the board at him.

"That, too," he agreed, pulling himself in closer behind me. He looked considerably more comfortable than he had when we'd come out of that pull. His skin and tousled hair smelled faintly of soap. I was entirely happy to see him. "What cross-stem are we retooling?" he asked.

I began to explain what I had been doing or, rather, what I had been trying to do. He took the remote board and edged ahead of me in the well, quickly punching in codes as I again tackled the stubborn circuit. Despite the fact that his choice of career probably allowed him little opportunity to make use of what he had learned, Taylor had received an excellent grounding in the basics of ship's mechanics. He had a good grasp of Integrated circuitry and was undoubtedly far more adept than I was at making those kinds of repairs. To his credit, as we slowly and painstakingly progressed along the length of the cramped tubular space, repairing the damage our unorthodox departure from Heinlein had wreaked upon the ship's delicate nervous system, he never once reminded me of that fact. He also never mentioned the obvious: that my furious haste could have torn the ship apart.

For a long period of time we worked in comparative silence, communicating only in the short phrases and strings of coded data necessary to our work. It was only once we had finally gotten the last circuit on Handy's "most critical" malfunctions list operational again that I even glanced at my chronometer and saw that Taylor and I had been at it for almost three hours. I knew that I couldn't have gotten that far alone in even twice the time.

Seeing that I had paused with the relay resting canted against my thigh as I reclined sprawled on my side on the floor of the well, Taylor lifted his brows inquiringly. "That can't be it already," he remarked wryly. "Not after *that* pullout!"

I flashed him a self-deprecating but appreciative grin. "No," I admitted, "but that's the worst of it. The rest can wait for now."

"Are you sure?" Taylor asked, feigning disappointment. From a kneeling position he sat back, stretching out his long legs parallel to mine. I noticed that the legs and sleeves of his gold and bottle-green flightsuit were smudged with traces of maintenance well "dirt," a distinctive blend of component lube and the inevitable dust and particulate matter carried in by any human intrusion. His teeth shone in a teasing grin. "And here I was just starting to have fun."

"Great," I shot back promptly. "Then you won't mind finishing up the rest of this later on."

With an amused snort, Taylor gave my arm a little poke with the edge of the remote board. "Fine," he said, "that'll give you the time to take a badly needed shower!"

He was only joking, but unfortunately, he was right on the mark; everything that had happened since Mahta had gently shaken me awake in my bed on Heinlein seemed to have conspired to make me dirty, sweaty, and tired. Then Taylor's expression softly sobered, and he fixed me with a look of patent concern. "You really do need a break, Jo," he said quietly, reaching out to touch my shoulder briefly.

I made an exaggerated sniffing sound. "Yeah? Well, I really do need a shower, too," I conceded. I switched off the power on the portable relay. "That reminds me," I said. "How was our eminent geneticist doing when you left her?"

"Asplundh?" Taylor made a small but hardly indifferent shrugging movement. "Just a slight case of 'situational emesis'—which almost struck me, too, by the way. I put her in that little cabin off Control. She was all right once we got some reasonable gravity back again." His gaze was direct and typically level. "Don't be too hard on her, Jo," he said. "She's a good person; she only wants to help."

I merely looked critically at him for a moment, analyzing possible motives for his quiet defense of the woman. In the end, the most likely reason turned out to also be the simplest one: He was just being Taylor. "Well, she hasn't been much help yet," I remarked. I studied him for a few seconds longer before adding with a fond and mollifying smile, "Unlike you, of course."

He shrugged again. In our positions, sprawled out side by side and head to toe on the well's grated floor, the brief motion caused his upper body to bump lightly against my one raised knee. "Yeah?" he said with a crooked grin. "Well, unlike me, some people expect to know what the hell they're getting themselves into before they tend to get very cooperative."

Guiltily, I quickly glanced away. It was simply not a part of Taylor's nature to complain, but I had also taken shameful advantage of his friendship in the few days since we'd been reunited on Porta Flora. There was no longer any way I could avoid telling him the truth.

"You know what I told you about what happened to Raydor and Lewis and me?" I began slowly. "The stuff with MA—why I needed Intervention?"

His sun-colored brows lifted slightly. "Yeah," he replied, more curious than suspicious.

"Well, I didn't tell Rhaine or the Ombudsman everything. I didn't tell you everything, Taylor," I confessed.

His shaggy head canted closer, his expression still open and interested. "That message before we pulled out?" he said.

But I cut him off, reaching out to touch his casually bent leg. "That's part of it," I explained, "but it goes back farther than that—to what happened weeks ago." Then, as quickly yet as thoroughly as I could, I began to tell him everything. I took him from what he already knew about what had happened on New Cuba and Heinlein to our urgent passage to Camelot, our joining forces with Redding and Alexandria's pirates at Nethersedge, and that nightmarish descent into the research complex's manmade hell. Throughout my clipped and quiet narration Taylor did not interrupt me; he scarcely even moved. But a changing progression of expressions flitted across his familiar face as I related my story: surprise, incredulity, outrage. But above all, and always, concern.

As I filled him in on the rest of what had happened in the Ombudsman's office—Leppers's revelations and the A's bid for my help—Taylor's hand slipped down to where mine still rested on his thigh; he grasped my fingers, squeezing gently. "So they were trying to stop you already, even back on Porta Flora," he said. "That message—"

I was mildly surprised to find that my muscles were unpleasantly tensed. "That was a Writ of Inquiry," I told her. I paused, then said, "Right before we lifted from Porta Flora, Leppers was killed. An accident, they said, but you can bet it was about as much of an accident as the things that've been happening to me."

Taylor's fingers tightened on mine so abruptly and near painfully that I involuntarily jerked back. He stared at me in open-mouthed shock. "Leppers is *dead*?" he repeated incredulously.

I wasn't sure which discovery was more distressing to him: that an innocent man—an Authority liaison but a man just doing his job and innocent nonetheless—had been murdered by the renegades or that twice already I had blatantly evaded a Writ involving a death—a capital offense. Either way, Taylor had the right to be upset with me since my continued deceit had involved him so deeply and unwittingly in this morass.

Carefully twisting our entwined fingers, I encouraged him to ease his biting grip. "I'm sorry, Taylor," I told him sincerely, feeling my cheeks flush slightly with shame. "I know I should have told you everything that had happened before I let you leave Porta Flora with us." I had to lower my gaze then, because the look in his eyes was still too disturbingly shocked. "Suns, Taylor, I hated misleading you like that! But I kept thinking that if you didn't know about it," I offered lamely, "I could somehow still keep you out of it."

For once, in all the time I had known him, the expression on his usually unshuttered face was something I could not clearly interpret. He blinked, looking down for a moment at our joined hands as if at least temporarily he could not fathom what their juncture signified. Then, slowly, with an almost tangible focusing of concentration, his expression became more normal again. And as he lay there beside me, our bodies stretched out only inches apart in the cramped service tunnel, I was aware of the irony of our juxtapositioning. We were so close that the movement of his shallow breathing caused his body to bump gently against mine, so close that even the smallest of things, like the tiny gold hairs on the back of his big hands and the way his eyes darkened as his pupils dilated, seemed incredibly immediate to me. Suddenly then, I saw Taylor for exactly what he was: an ex-lover who still loved me.

"It's okay, Jo," he said quietly, giving my fingers a little squeeze. "If you've got trouble, I *want* to be here. And as for not telling me all this sooner . . ." He gave a slight shrug, a gesture so characteristic that I nearly smiled despite the gravity of the moment. His eyes caught mine, holding them without a trace of reproach. "You only did what I would have done. We both want to protect our friends."

When I got back up to Control, the compartment was empty. I expected Alexandria was making use of Raydor's cabin to clean up and get some rest. Powers knew when the woman had last had any sleep, and her long-range chances still looked pretty iffy. I checked ship's status and position with Handy, then logged in Alexandria's postpull check and went back to my cabin.

Taylor had had the right idea; even a quick shower and a change of clothing made me feel remarkably better. Good enough, in fact, to face the next duty I had to perform. As I punched the hatch buzzer outside Asplundh's cabin, I wondered absently whether the little compartment was well stocked enough for her to have been able to adequately clean the vomit off her jumpsuit. My mind made an instantaneous segue to the last passenger on my ship to have had that particular problem, and, caught completely unaware by the intensity of my emotional reaction, I was stunned by how painful the sense of fear and loss evoked by even those most mundane memories of Lewis could be.

As the hatch shushed open, it took me an obvious moment to jerk myself back into the present. Asplundh stood right inside the hatchway, her tawny-colored brows raised quizzically at my undoubtedly ambiguous expression. Before she could speak, however, I managed to blurt out some appropriate words.

"I thought I'd better check and see if you were doing okay," I said.

She looked slightly abashed and nodded ruefully. "I am now," she said, stepping back and gesturing for me to enter the cabin. "Your friend Taylor was very helpful."

As I stepped through the hatchway, I quickly looked her over. As far as I could tell, her jumpsuit looked immaculate again; either she or Taylor knew some pretty good tricks. "Yeah," I remarked, "he tends to be."

She ran a quick hand through her hair, adding with a self-effacing smile, "I'm sorry for the mess I made, Captain; I haven't puked my guts out quite so gloriously since the *last* time I pulled out."

The hatch hissed shut behind me. I just made an abbreviated dismissive gesture with one hand and said, "I came close to that myself; it wasn't exactly your standard pullout."

But Asplundh's self-deprecating smile only widened. "I wouldn't know. They *all* feel like that to me."

"In that case," I responded, "I hope you don't have to do much interstellar travel in your line of work."

She raised her right hand, palm out, as if mimicking the taking of an oath. "None—not since I came to Heinlein," she averred.

I was a bit surprised. "You're an immigrant?" I asked, frankly curious.

The geneticist took the couple of steps to the little cabin's bunk, inviting me to sit with a quick wave of her hand even as she sank down on the edge of the bed. She made a wry face. "It's the Restructuring," she said ingenuously, without a trace of self-consciousness, even as I found myself automatically re-examining her features. "It's good enough to be Heinlein's, I know. But I'm from DoubleNew York. I've been on Heinlein for almost eight years, though," she added helpfully, as if that fact could somehow account for my having made the apparently common error about her origins.

I lowered myself onto the edge of the bunk and sat facing her, preparing myself for what I had come to discuss, when she spoke again. "I want to apologize for the way I've acted, Captain" she said quietly, "both at Port and here on your ship." She spread her hands. "I'd been looking forward to meeting you. I'm sorry we got off on the wrong foot."

I was about to interrupt, to offer my own apology, which was one of the reasons I'd come there, but she was doing such a great job for both of us that I hated to interfere. Besides, she seemed quite comfortable with making apologies, and she sure was a hell of a lot better at it than I was.

"I was just worried about Lewis," she continued. "I really do want to help him, and I hope that we can be friends."

I just nodded sagely, offering magnanimously, "We hardly met under the best of circumstances." I tactfully refrained from adding that I really didn't see the situation improving any in the near future.

Asplundh pulled up one leg, locking her hands around her raised knee. "Alexandria just explained to me why we had to leave Heinlein so quickly—what happened to you on Porta Flora and why Lewis left." Her expression narrowed, her brow furrowing with genuine distress. "He's an exceptional person, Captain," she told me with heartfelt conviction. Then, catching herself, she quickly noted, "Well, I guess I don't have to tell you that. But I understand why this is so important to you."

I wasn't about to debate that assertion with her. Besides, I had begun to feel mildly uncomfortable with the turn the conversation was taking. Swiftly, I moved to divert it toward the other reason I had come to the cabin. "You know that Mahta told me about Lewis?" I asked. "About what you had discussed with her?"

Asplundh nodded, her smoky-brown curls bobbing. "She had someone meet my shuttle at Port. She told me it was imperative that I talk with you before you left Heinlein." She flashed a quick grin. "Well, that's not exactly the way it turned out, but as long as I'm here . . ."

Despite my initial misgivings and Alexandria's aggravating peremptory attitude concerning Asplundh, I found myself beginning to honestly like the geneticist. With her disarming ironic sense of humor and her down-to-earth candor, she would have been a difficult person not to like. Still, there would be nothing easy about what I still had to ask her.

"Mahta told me that you had discovered something—" I almost said "abnormal"; I was fumbling noticeably for another, less damning term when Asplundh rescued me.

With a little hitch of her shoulders, she made a curious but evocative gesture with the thumbs of her laced hands. "There's nothing 'ordinary' about any aspect of a Class Ten," she stated simply. "It's been an incredible opportunity for someone in my field, Captain; I'm just so grateful that Lewis gave me the chance to study his genetic material." Something in my expression must have made her pause, and when she began again, she redirected her response back to my truncated question.

"Theoretically, we've known the molecular basis for touch-healing for ages," she explained. "What's remained open to doubt is that touch-healers actually even existed. Individuals with that Talent are able to rearrange cellular matter at the sub-molecular level, to affect the chemical bonds between—" She broke off, realizing she was losing me. Abandoning the scientific approach, she shifted tack. "It's a lot like biofeedback, really; you train the mind to recognize changes that can then be consciously effected in the body. In fact, you might call touch-healing biofeedback carried to its logical extreme."

"Yeah, except for one thing," I reminded her. "Anyone can learn biofeedback."

But Asplundh held firm to her comparison. "Yes, but in theory anyone could touch-heal, too—if they had the neural conditioning to be able to focus their awareness that way. A Talent just has that kind of neural conditioning built in.'' Shrugging again, she quickly continued with her explanation. ''Anyway, what I was doing with my research was comparing the touch-healed tissue to the 'normal' tissue from Alexandria and Captain Redding. That led me to do the submolecular electrophoreutosis on samples from all three of them.'' She paused, visibly selecting her terms. ''Lewis's sample revealed nonstandard DNA fragments. He has amino-acid analogues that mimic the building blocks of normal human DNA and obviously perform the same functions but are subtly different.''

I rested one hand flat on the surface of the bunk beside me, propping myself with deliberate casualness on that outstretched arm. ''So,'' I prompted her with a cool and totally feigned calm, ''is that the reason for his Talent?''

Asplundh eyed me silently for a moment; it was unlikely that my display of detachment had fooled her. ''I suspect that it is,'' she replied simply.

My heart felt like an overwound spring coiled like some great serpent in my chest. Everything in that Spartan little cabin suddenly appeared both amazingly discrete and painfully familiar, and the plain, purely physical memory of Lewis—his eyes, his voice, the touch of his skin—moved in to nearly overwhelm me. But I desperately forced the memories away, concentrating instead on Asplundh's pale oval face. ''You know what he went through on Camelot, how he had been fused with Lillard?'' I asked.

She nodded. ''Yes,'' she said softly, ''he told me.''

''And you don't think that had anything to do with this nonstandard DNA?''

The geneticist shook her head almost reluctantly. ''No, I'm sure it didn't. This isn't just human DNA that's been somehow altered; it's DNA that's intrinsically different because it contains a component that's not human.''

I stared sharply at her, momentarily forgetting both my aching memories and my thudding fear as I echoed the query I had made earlier to Mahta. ''Well, if it's not human and it's not animal, then what the hell *is* it?'' I demanded. ''Synthetic?''

But Asplundh just spread her hands, a gesture of both helplessness and apology. ''I don't know,'' she admitted. ''That's what I was hoping to find out. Synthetic genetic material has never been successfully integrated into the human DNA structure—not before this, at least.''

I stood abruptly, taking one sweeping stride away from the bunk, and then swung to face Asplundh again. I had only two questions left. ''Does Lewis know about this?'' I asked her.

The geneticist's hands were still now, draped quiescently over her drawn-up knee. ''He knows that I found something interesting, something unusual,'' she replied. ''I didn't feel that I should tell him more until I could be more specific.''

The dread coiled behind my breastbone shifted, taut and waiting. It had taken a lot of shapes in the past few weeks, but it had never been far from me. I looked down steadily into that openly compassionate face. ''This nonhuman component,'' I put to her, ''can it be genetically transmitted? Is it a heritable trait?''

Perhaps she didn't realize the reason for my particular interest; perhaps she lacked Mahta's uncanny sense of intuition where I was concerned; perhaps she saw nothing unusual about the question. Perhaps.

Asplundh was silent for a moment. ''I'd have to speculate,'' she replied softly, ''but I'd say yes.'' She shrugged helplessly. ''Or where else would Lewis have gotten it?''

''Yeah,'' I echoed numbly, turning toward the hatchway. ''Where else?''

I didn't see anything of Alexandria again until we were nearly within audio range of Earthheart. Taylor and I were in Control, where I was logging the last of the systems repairs into Handy's access. Not only had Taylor finished up the rest of the less critical cross-stem work, he had also rechecked and filed a maintenance supply list on everything he and I had done together earlier. I'd found him waiting for me in Control when I'd come in, relatively fresh from several hours of sleep.

I had just instructed Handy to call up the meager specs we had on Earthheart when Alexandria leaned in through the hatchway and asked gruffly, ''How far out are we yet?''

I glanced over my shoulder at the big woman; she certainly didn't look like she'd gotten any rest. The bags under her eyes looked like week-old bruises, and the weathered skin on her face and neck resembled the creased fabric of a cheap flightsuit that had been slept in—repeatedly. ''Not far,'' I replied. ''We're almost to audio range now.''

"Good," she replied. "Don't hail. What kind of thermal gear have you got?"

Momentarily stymied by the apparent non sequitur, I hesitated briefly before responding to the first, most intelligible part of her comments. "What do you mean, don't hail?" I asked, swiveling around in my chair. "We're going to be approaching Port in—"

"Port on Earthheart isn't run by the Tachs," Alexandria interrupted, her bulky form filling the open hatchway. "It's an Authority facility; they're the only ones who can fly in and out of here." Her big square teeth showed in a quick grin. "No Citizens allowed, remember?"

"Then how the hell are we going to land?" I asked. "I thought you still had some influence here." Suns! If I had brought that aggravating woman along for nothing—

Alexandria's grin just widened wolfishly. "If I do, it sure as hell wouldn't be with the A's!" she retorted. "Just keep on course and don't hail. I'll give you new coordinates in a minute."

"What does she mean thermal gear?" Taylor asked. But she had pulled back from the hatch and was gone, leaving his question hanging uneasily in the air.

"Shit," I muttered, turning back to Handy's screen. I hastily scanned the glowing green lines of data. "Is this all you've got?" I demanded irritably of him.

"It's considerably more than the Authority's main Integrator banks have," Handy replied placidly. Obviously, Raydor had added his own contribution to the nearly skeletal information on the Tachs homeworld that was available in the official data banks. But I had never before had either the interest or the need to learn much about Earthheart, and it was a little late to be taking a crash course. Beside me at comm, Taylor stirred in his chair, drawing my attention back to him.

He glanced back over his shoulder toward the hatch again, then looked to my face. "If Citizens aren't allowed on Earthheart and we can't land at Port, what are we doing here?" he asked.

Good question! I thought glumly, but for his benefit I just shrugged and said, "Alexandria served here for years as the A's liaison; she must know a lot of Tachs. If Port is controlled by the A's, we sure as hell wouldn't be safe coming in there, so it makes sense to land somewhere else." Like another quadrant, I added silently.

There was another observation that I didn't voice to Taylor. It was obvious to me that it wasn't just a coincidence that the A's, legitimate or renegade, had found me on Heinlein. If they had been smart enough to figure out that I'd head for my home-world for help, there seemed to be every probability they'd be smart enough to be looking for us on Raydor's homeworld as well. Coming here at all was looking more and more like a bad idea; maybe, if we were lucky, it'd turn out to be another bad idea that worked.

"Why would we need thermal gear?" Taylor persisted with a puzzled frown.

"I don't know," I admitted. "Here," I added to forestall any further questions to which I had no answers, "take a look at this stuff for me, especially the geographic surveys." I hit the transfer button, unloading Handy's Earthheart data onto the smaller screen set into the comm board. "See if you can find us a reasonably settled-looking place to set down."

"Belay that," came Alexandria's predictably dissenting voice from the hatchway. She strode into Control, her very posture that of a woman used to assuming authority automatically. Hell, it was like a reflex with her, something done without conscious decision, like holding your breath underwater. She threw me a quick, tolerant glance. "I told you I'd give you the coordinates," she said.

"Fine, I'm waiting with bated breath!" I responded, but I suspected the snap of sarcasm went right over her head.

Alexandria leaned over me, rapidly punching in a series of numbers on the navigation panel's board. Pulling back again, she nodded to me. "Okay, log it in," she said.

"Not until you tell me where the hell it is we're going," I insisted.

Alexandria's bushy brows quirked in mild exasperation. "Dayne's Prairie," she replied, enunciating each syllable with exaggerated diction. "Now, would you log it in before we get close enough to Port for those cod-swabbing A's to pick us up on their security scans?"

It hadn't been much of an answer, but I couldn't argue with her logic. I hit Handy's access but also instructed him, "Reference Dayne's Prairie, Handy."

While part of his massive neural circuitry logged in Alexandria's coordinates and instantaneously altered the ship's course to accommodate them, another small part of his faculties promptly met my request. His screen scrambled, then reassembled, bearing only a half dozen words: "Dayne's Prairie—Northwest Octant—data incomplete."

"We're only about ten minutes from reentry," Alexandria said as I stared morosely at the screen.

"Nine-point-seven-nine minutes," Handy interjected.

"Better get Asplundh up here," the burly woman went on, throwing Taylor a pointed look.

Taylor didn't even bother to glance over to me in an effort to either protest or question Alexandria's rude treatment of him; among other things, the man knew when it was worth making a fuss about something and when it was simpler just to cut your losses and acquiesce. Unfortunately, where Alexandria Moore was concerned, one tended to find oneself doing less and less of the former and more and more of the latter, anyway. Standing, he wordlessly skirted around Alexandria's bulky form and disappeared through the hatchway.

As Alexandria casually slipped into his chair at comm, I briefly debated the merits of reproaching her for her attitude toward Taylor, but I discarded the idea not as unwarranted but as ill timed. Instead I studied her for a moment and then commented succinctly, "I understand why we're avoiding Port, but it would be very helpful to have some idea just what in the hell kind of place you're taking us into."

She looked over at me, her expression a familiar one of wry amusement. "The A's Commerce Commission keeps this planet under a pretty tight surveillance net; they have to, or the place'd be overrun by free marketeers. The Prairie's a relatively safe place to come in. It's remote, but they've got a small field, and the location'll be convenient."

"What do you mean, remote?" I was certain that I liked this idea less and less all the time.

But I was denied even the admittedly slight possibility of an answer from her by Taylor's reappearance at the hatchway. Asplundh followed him in, nodding to me in greeting, and the two of them took the ancillary chairs again. Then Handy's deep voice cut in, distracting me even further from what Alexandria had said.

"Four minutes to atmospheric contact, Jo," he noted. "Do you want a landing schematic?"

"Sure, why not?" I responded fatalistically, automatically beginning to reach for the catches on my chair harness. Conditioned behavior took over then as I bent over the panel, my fingers making all the familiar movements over the board. At least temporarily, things like unanswered questions, irritation, and doubts were shoved aside, and only one thing mattered: the business of running my ship.

Unfortunately, Taylor didn't have quite the same duties to distract him as we began to come in. Leaning forward in his harness, he was studying the landing schematic on Handy's screen by peering over my shoulder. "Jo, what's wrong with your image?" he asked. "It's all blitzed out."

I took a moment to glance at the screen; within the usual gridwork of the fixed topographical lines, the expected boundaries of the planet's surface were obscured by a swirling electronic chaos. "Handy, can you clarify that?" I asked him, most of my attention still on Internals' board as we started to hit Earthheart's atmosphere.

Luckily, Handy's attention was divisible to an almost infinite degree, and while he was devoting the needed concentration to bringing *Raptor* down, he also promptly informed me, "That *is* clarified, Jo."

Alexandria had the pickup on her ear, apparently on the alert for any stray out-of-Port transmissions that might indicate the presence of any scout ships or remotes in our vicinity. Sparing her a glance, I asked Handy, "Are you still optimal on that circuit?"

The ship shuddered slightly as atmospheric friction began to drag at her skin; I felt my body start to sink leadenly into my chair while our AG's compensatory ability lagged.

"Two minutes to setdown," Handy interjected smoothly, then replied, "It's optimal, Jo."

From behind me, Taylor noted ruefully, "Yeah, that was *one* circuit we didn't burn out."

Internals' board pulsed with figures; Navigation was awash with a nearly incomprehensible flow of data. As the landing retros cut in with a low growl and our gravity briefly flip-flopped once again, I instructed Handy, "Give me viewer, then."

The turbulent incoherence of the landing schematic evaporated. When the image reappeared on the screen, there was only one perceptible change: the fixed landmarks of the grid lines were now gone. Across the glowing surface of the viewer, an impenetrable storm of particles whirled like a maelstrom of white static.

"By the Light—what *is* that?" Taylor asked from behind me.

"Sixty seconds, Jo," Handy said calmly.

But his was an equanimity I failed to share. As our gravity's rebound finally gave me the freedom to move again, I swung in my chair, confronting Alexandria's weathered and implacable face as she bent over comm. ''What the hell is going on here?'' I demanded angrily above the rising hiss of the retros.

But much as I should have expected, the big woman just showed me a flash of teeth and responded, ''Local weather.''

She was pushing me too far, and suddenly something in me rebelled. Maybe it was being reminded of the extent of our helplessness there—how completely I had placed my ship and my friends in Alexandria's hands, how totally dependent on her knowledge and judgment we were. Maybe it was just the accumulated weight of a lot of smaller things. Whatever it was, I felt the anger wash through me like a surge of adrenaline, filling me with the kind of fury that only that sense of frustrating impotence could raise in me. I reached across the small space separating us, seizing her beefy forearm in a tight grip; her solid flesh was corded like a metal cable beneath my fingers. ''What the Void are you getting us into here?'' I said, my voice a tense growl. ''What kind of place is this Dayne's Prairie, and why the joinin' Suns are we landing here?''

Whether or not Alexandria would have replied to my questions became of secondary importance to me then as my tirade lurched on, my fingers tightening on her arm. ''Even coming to this planet doesn't make any sense! The renegades and the A's are both going to be expecting us to come here because it's Raydor's homeworld. What makes you think he'd be stupid enough to come here even if Lewis and Redding needed help?'' I jerked viciously at her arm; considering the difference in our masses and strength, the attack was more psychologically satisfying than physically effective. I was nearly shouting as I concluded, ''All we're going to find here is more of those ball-less renegades—and they sure as hell aren't going to settle for serving me with any damned Writ of Inquiry, either!''

Throughout my verbal barrage Alexandria's calm expression had remained pretty much unchanged, even when I had tried to shake her. Sitting there then, breathing heavily from my useless effort, I realized that the retros were silent: We had just set down. My fingers were still dug tightly into the coarse fabric of Alexandria's tunic; I stared into those fathomless black eyes as she exhaled a patient sigh.

''If Lewis and the others aren't here yet, they will be soon, Jo,'' she said quietly, making no move to free her arm.

Behind me, I was subtly aware of Taylor and Asplundh's postures of tense anticipation. Before me on the board, Handy's viewer still swirled with the whirling storm of white. And within me, a cool and deadly calm core of dread had replaced the volatile heat of my previous angry outburst. Slowly, deliberately, finger by finger, I released my grip on Alexandria's arm. "Why?" I asked her tautly, straightening my body with elaborate dignity. "What makes you so damned sure they have to come here?"

The formidable gaze that met mine was unblinking, but the tone of her deep voice was almost gentle as Alexandria replied, "Because this is where the rest of the Class Tens are, Jo."

CHAPTER EIGHT

There were other worlds in the known systems besides Earthheart from which Citizens were prohibited. On some planets, such as Camelot, the ban was for security reasons; on others, there were severely hazardous natural conditions. Planets that housed detention sites were off limits for the obvious reason. But Earthheart was unique in that it was probably the only settled world whose colonizing residents actively supported their planet's Interdicted status. Stripped of their own Citizenship generations before—banished to that then-barren world for their dogged refusal to conform to the Authorities' Genetics and Reproduction Code, the Tachs had parlayed their exile into a story of tenacious success. They not only had not broken under their ostracism, they had had the temerity to prosper. It was not difficult to understand why those people still vigorously rejected the very rights of Citizenship that had once been so vindictively denied them.

"The place with the animals." That was the characterization by which Taylor had recognized Earthheart. The planet was a major source of the known systems' real food, things that had actually been grown as opposed to formed from Powers knew what. And they were undoubtedly nearly the sole source of such luxuries as real meat, real wool, and real leather. The Tachs were an agrarian sect, the last of the galaxy's farmers. Over a span of generations they had transformed a harsh and marginally habitable planet into a thriving agricultural colony. But their world was still Interdicted, and so the average Citizen knew very little about Earthheart or her people.

Politically and economically, Earthheart was a cautiously tended resource for the A's. From the beginning of the Tachs' exile, CA had put its Commerce Commission in charge of the planet's trade. But as with any commodity in high demand, there had always been a thriving black market operating out of Earthheart, zealously pursued by pirates and profiteers of all allegiances. In many if not most cases, the Tachs were said to support the black marketeers; they paid considerably more than the punitive prices set by the "Ceecee" bureaucracy. And I suspected that it also appealed to the Tachs' ingrained sense of stubborn independence to deal with anyone who allowed them to circumvent the stifling surveillance net the A's maintained on-planet.

Most of what I knew about Earthheart, I knew from knowing Raydor; even then, it still wasn't nearly enough. Until he'd accepted Alexandria's training, he'd lived as a farmer, and until he'd accepted the sterilization and hypothalamic alteration required of his Class, he'd lived as a non-Citizen. Whether there was pain in remembering or pain in forgetting, I was never certain. But for whatever reason, Raydor never spoke of his life before he'd left Earthheart. Now, as so often in the past hours of this harrowing journey, I fervently wished I had the big Tachs back where he belonged, sitting beside me in Control.

It didn't even occur to me to question Alexandria's quiet assertion about Earthheart and the Class Tens; why else would she have brought us there? But even before I could have opened my mouth had I been so inclined, she stated brusquely, "I don't have time to explain right now, Jo." She was rapidly unfastening her chair harness even as she spoke. "We've got to get some gear together and get out of here—fast, before any Ceecee scouts pick up on this ship."

"Wait a minute," Taylor protested from behind us. "I thought we landed here so the A's *couldn't* find us."

Propelling herself to her feet, Alexandria looked down at him from the advantage of her superior height. "We did, and they haven't—yet—but sooner or later they will. Come on, Slick," she went on, yanking on the sleeve of his gold and green flightsuit, not giving him the chance to respond even as he fumbled with the catches on his harness. "You can help me in supply."

"Wait a minute!" Taylor repeated, literally grabbing the back of his chair to keep the larger woman from pulling him to his feet. "What do you mean, supply? Just where are we going?"

Some small reflexive part of me rebelled even as the words came so automatically to my lips, but I found myself briefly turning from Handy's console and saying, "Taylor? Just do it— go with her, huh?"

He hesitated a moment longer, his face filled with concern, more for me than for the situation in general, I realized with a guilty stab of remorse.

"It's okay," I assured him as I gestured at the board. "I'm just going to shut her down."

"No," Alexandria interrupted, "don't shut her down." Flashing Taylor a feral grin, she actually did lift him to his feet; then, as she propelled him helplessly toward the hatchway, she threw back at me, "We'll be right back."

I exchanged a look of baffled resignation with Asplundh; the geneticist had only begun to free herself from her chair harness and now seemed uncertain if she should continue. I turned back to Handy and asked him wearily, "Ship's status?"

"All systems optimal, Jo," came the cheerful response. Apparently Alexandria's idea of a landing had been a hell of lot less traumatic than my idea of a pullout.

I glanced down at the viewer again, where the whirling chaos on the screen seemed to have assumed some random order. "What the hell is this shit, Handy?" I asked not sure that I really wanted to know.

"It's crystallized water vapor, Jo," the Integrator informed me.

"Snow," Asplundh translated from behind me, her voice touched with amusement. "It looks like we've landed in the middle of a blizzard."

"Terrific," I muttered, hitting the switch to kill the viewer. "It just gets better and better." At least that solved the mystery of why Alexandria had been looking for thermal gear. Unfortunately, she wasn't going to find much aboard *Raptor*.

"Would you like the planetary specs on the ambient topography and conditions, Jo?" Handy asked.

About that time I had a specific location in mind where I would have liked Handy to have stowed the specs on the ambient ambience, but I managed to temporarily throttle my irritation and doubts and just told him, "Screen them, please." With Asplundh reading over my shoulder, I began to run through the data Handy was churning out. In the next few minutes, studying the fragmentary information he had on file and the analysis of his sensor scan, I learned that we had set down on a tiny landing field about eighty meters from a cluster of low, blocky structures, surrounded by a vast, unbroken expanse of rolling prairie grassland—in the middle of a blizzard. Unsurprisingly, none of this impressed me as being particularly encouraging, not even the thought that the site would probably appear equally unlikely and inhospitable to any patrolling Ceecee officers.

There was a brief commotion in the corridor outside Control, then I heard Alexandria's inimitable voice growling, "*Set* it down—don't just *drop* it! We've got little enough to work with here as it is." Moments later her head poked through the hatchway.

Before she could launch any further orders, I gestured to the specs, still frozen on Handy's screen, and said glumly, "Let me guess. No hangars, right?"

"Right," she confirmed. "You're going to have to send her back up."

Taylor's head appeared beside Alexandria's, framed by the opposite side of the hatchway. "The ship?" he asked, glancing warily from Alexandria to me. His voice had taken on an edge of doubt. "You're going to send the ship back up?"

For perhaps the first time since we'd left Heinlein, I thought Asplundh was beginning to grasp the gravity and complexity of our situation. "But if you do that, won't we be stuck down here?" she noted almost plaintively.

No more enthused than either Taylor or the geneticist, I struggled to hold on to my shell of cool rationality. "We don't have much choice," I explained to them. "There's no place to get her under cover here. And sitting out on this pitiful excuse for a field, she'd be like a beacon for the scanners on any Ceecee remotes or ships in the area. Besides," I added, "we won't exactly be stranded. With one of Handy's remote relays, I can keep in touch with him from down here."

"Better get the orders logged in," Alexandria said. "Even with this storm, you can bet the A's have still got plenty of standard surveillance out scanning for unauthorized vessels. We've got to get clear before they stumble onto us."

Taylor's expressive face could not conceal his continuing desire to protest, but I effectively cut off his only recourse by swinging my chair back to Handy's board. Alexandria was right; even if the renegades hadn't tracked us there yet, normal Authority security procedures for Interdicted worlds would have gotten us apprehended and detained. Without the protection of some kind of cover, *Raptor* would be a liability to us, and she would be useless on the field. Palming Handy's access, I ordered him quietly, "Security Prime, Handy; independent mode."

"You've got it, Jo," he replied immediately. "Standard trajectory and holding pattern?"

I hesitated a moment, thinking furiously. Integrated control on ships was designed to have preprogramming capacity—"automatic pilot," if you will. But there were certain mandated, built-in limitations, a restraining system intended to keep an Integrator from literally taking over a ship under autoprogrammed situations. When *Raptor* had been converted from a private-use passenger vessel to a short-haul freighter, several "modifications" had been made. One such modification was the totally illegal high-intensity beam-weapon system she carried in addition to the standard nonmilitary beam cannon. Another illicit change was that the Integration restraint circuit had been bridged. Handy essentially had total discretion and free rein in any situation requiring his independent judgment regarding the welfare of the ship and her crew. As recently as several weeks earlier on Camelot, he had proved to me just how judiciously he was capable of wielding that power.

Sitting there, my hand resting on the curved access, I was acutely aware of the presence of the other three people there with me in the compartment. It went against all my instincts to separate myself from my ship like that, but I was prepared to do what was necessary to protect her—and us. I gently fingered the smooth surface of his access and said quietly, "Keep her clear, Handy. Just do what you need to do."

"Suns, would you hurry up?" Alexandria complained from the hatchway.

I reached across Handy's board and slid the small, palm-sized relay from its bracket on the side of the console. Slipping the slim rectangle into the breast pocket of my suit, I got to my feet.

In the corridor outside Control, Alexandria had assembled most of the expedition gear I had on board. It didn't look like very much, especially when pitted against the kind of climatic conditions Handy had shown us existed outside. We had only two thermal suits, mine and Raydor's; three power lanterns; an emergency pack; and a trio of beam pistols that probably hadn't even been fired in years.

"Asplundh and I will take the thermal suits," Alexandria said, thrusting mine at the geneticist and appropriating Raydor's for herself. "I'm the only one who'll fit in this one," she pointed out, beginning to toss other garments at Taylor and me, "and you two are tall enough that you'll be able to pile on extra layers."

As Taylor and I struggled to hastily don pairs of Raydor's oversized suit liners over our flightsuits, he voiced the question

I had been reluctant to ask. "Why do we need all this insulation?" he asked Alexandria, his tone mildly irate. "There're buildings here. Haven't these people ever heard of *heat*?"

"You'll see," Alexandria said, dismissing him brusquely and flinging one of Raydor's old flightsuits at him. "Here, put this one on over everything else." Her lip curled deprecatingly. "And don't worry—fashion won't count here, Slick."

The woman was starting to make even the congenitally affable Taylor bristle; I quickly tried to deflect some of Alexandria's needling attention from him. "Better check the charges in those pistols," I suggested, also tugging one of Raydor's capacious suits over my other layers of clothing. "They don't see much use." At least when you're not around, I nearly added.

"Already did," Alexandria replied, gathering up the weapons and the lanterns. She glanced at Asplundh, who looked only moderately frumpy in my too-large thermal suit. "All set?" she asked.

The curly-haired woman nodded, her hands thrust deeply into the front pockets of the suit. "There're extra gloves," she offered, holding them out to me with an almost apologetic expression on her face.

"Thanks," I said, slipping into them. Then I bent to retrieve the emergency pack.

"I can carry that," Asplundh said quickly, holding out her gloved hands.

Alexandria was already heading down the corridor toward the boarding hatch. Absently and without pausing, she dug into the pockets of Raydor's thermal suit and flipped the second set of insulated gloves in Taylor's direction. She was waiting impatiently when the rest of us caught up to her at the end of the passageway. As I palmed the ramp release, she instructed us tersely, "Be sure to stay close out there."

The reason for her warning became immediately and dramatically obvious. As *Raptor*'s hatch dilated and the ramp peeled down from beneath the ship's belly, we were treated to our first taste of the "ambient climatic conditions:" A fierce gust of icy wind pelted us with a fusillade of stinging snow. But Alexandria charged ahead into the whirling wall of white, nearly disappearing right before my eyes as I rushed down the ramp after her. Visibility was about a meter at best, and that was presuming you could keep your eyes open. I lowered my head, squinting into the pelting gale, and just had to trust that Taylor and Asplundh were following.

On the schematic on Handy's screen, the distance from the ship to the row of buildings at the edge of the field had looked insignificant. In practice, the eighty meters felt more like eighty kilometers. It wasn't a matter of the planet's higher gravity. The effects of the slight variance from Earth standard were so subtle that you hardly felt them; you only saw them over the generations. It was the force of the storm itself. Even with the wind at our backs, I found myself staggering awkwardly through knee-deep drifts, buffeted by the constant blinding whirl of driven pellets. The extra layers of clothing protected me from the worst of the cold, but the thin rain hood I had pulled out from the collar of Raydor's suit to cover my head was barely adequate, and my cheeks burned from the frigid and abrasive blasts.

Although I still couldn't see a thing ahead of me except for the occasional blurry outline of Alexandria's bulky body, I knew when we had nearly reached the buildings. A deep rumble reverberated across the snowy field, superseding even the howl of the storm, and I swore I could feel the frozen ground tremble beneath my feet. *Raptor* was lifting.

Unexpectedly, a sudden and overwhelming wave of desolation washed through me, and I momentarily paused, turning back, even though I couldn't see anything. My boots snagged in the deep snow, and the brutal wind slewed me sideways so that I nearly fell. It took every bit of concentration I possessed to keep myself erect—and to hold back the biting push of tears that suddenly swelled behind my lids. Then I felt Taylor's arm slip around my waist, and his face was pressed close to mine. His brows and the whipping strands of his hair that had escaped from beneath his hood were frosted with white.

"You okay?" he asked, shouting over the combined roar of the ship's engines and the fierce wind.

"Yeah," I lied, shouting back. But I seized his gloved hand with mine and kept his arm around me as we plowed along to catch up with Alexandria.

I didn't actually see Alexandria or Asplundh again until we reached the nearest building, although we all had probably never been more than a few meters apart. Ironically, it occurred to me only once we were actually standing in front of one of the low structure's wide, steel-sheathed doors to wonder how the hell we were going to get inside.

"How are we going to open it?" Asplundh asked, almost as if she had read my thought. Frosted with snow, the smaller woman looked rather waiflike in the cumbersome folds of my thermal suit. But I was strangely gratified to see that she had included me in her inquiry.

Nonplussed, Alexandria held up one of the power lanterns and briefly bent to inspect the door's lock mechanism. Then she shrugged. "Universal lockpick," she decided bluntly, digging into one of her thermal suit's pockets and producing one of the beam pistols. Stepping back, she leveled the weapon at the lock and casually fired. Sparks flared, and snow hissed against the hot metal. Then she stepped forward again, planting the full force of one booted foot against the base of the door. With a sharp shriek, like metal shearing, the heavy door swung inward.

Alexandria made a sweeping gesture. "Welcome to the Dayne's Prairie station," she announced mockingly.

As we stumbled inside, Alexandria passed out the other two power lanterns. Taylor struggled briefly with the heavy door to reseal it against the force of the storm; it protested, but when he threw his shoulder against it, the latch held. The building was not heated, but just being out of the wind and snow was an instant improvement.

Asplundh and I both held our lanterns aloft, sweeping them in long, divergent arcs through the interior of the darkened structure. We stood in a huge, nearly empty single-story room whose ceiling appeared to be the bare beams of the roof trusses. The only windows were small squares of opaqued glass set high up under the eaves at regular intervals. The walls and floor were unpainted poured-rock, and the lighting fixtures hung in unadorned rods from the overhead beams. The cool, dry air had a faint but peculiar scent to it that I recognized but could not immediately identify.

"What about the lights?" Taylor inquired, glancing around for some kind of switch. In the harsh illumination of the lanterns his breath rose toward the crude ceiling in ghostly puffs.

"This time of the season, the power's been shut down," Alexandria responded. Aiming her lantern, she began striding off toward a narrow doorway along the wall to our left. "We'll just have to restart it," she called over her shoulder as she pushed through the swinging door and disappeared into the formless darkness of whatever lay beyond.

For a few seconds we all just stood there silently like three children left waiting while the adults had left the room. Then Asplundh started to sweep the beam of her lantern along the far wall, exploring. The floor there seemed to have a recessed section, as if there was some kind of track or gutter running along the wall. She lifted her lantern higher, shining it along the ceiling struts, where a series of symmetrical metal loops connected by a network of smooth rails was now clearly visible.

Glancing around us, Taylor shook a melting gobbet of slush from his hair and inquired in genuine bafflement, "Why would anyone want to live where it *snows*?"

Shrugging sympathetically, I looked over to where Asplundh had wandered and was occupied curiously inspecting some feature of the building's floor. In the oversized thermal suit, against the blank backdrop of the nearly featureless wall, she looked even more like an abandoned child. I was just about to move to join her, to offer my lantern's beam to add to hers, when suddenly the vast low room was flooded with light. Alexandria had restarted the power.

In the revealing brilliance from the lighting rods, I could then see features of the room that had previously escaped my notice. The recess in the floor was indeed a gutter of some kind, and the rails and loops on the overhead beams appeared to be some type of conveyer system. At either end of the room, aligned with the track, were wide, steel-faced swinging doors. And built into the back wall was a recessed housing containing what looked like a long coil of water hose with a pressure nozzle.

Slowly rotating, Taylor's eyes swept the room. "What *is* this place?" he asked.

"I think it's an abattoir," Asplundh replied, studying the gleaming rails directly over her head.

"A what?" Taylor said.

"A slaughterhouse," came Alexandria's gruff voice from right behind us.

Startled in spite of himself, Taylor turned around, staring at the big woman. "Slaughterhouse?" he repeated. "I thought these people were vegetarians."

Alexandria had stowed her lantern again, but she carried another and unfamiliar implement in one gloved hand. She used it to gesture at the far side of the room, where the heavy hose lay draped over its carrier like the thick loops of a black snake. "They are," she responded, flashing that sardonic grin, "but the rest of the galaxy isn't." As Taylor's eyes followed the movement of her arm, then skittered quickly over the overhead track and the stark floor cut with its narrow gutter, Alexandria gave one short burst of her braying laughter. "I'll wager you fancy a bit of real meat now and then yourself, Slick," she noted with dry amusement. Her gesture broadened to include the vicinity in general. "What the hell did you think they raised up here on these high plains—carrots?"

"The Tachs raise most of the systems' cattle," Asplundh said, coming back across the room to rejoin us. "They have several strains they've developed themselves. Ruminants are about the only species that can utilize the tough forage up here on these dry, elevated prairies."

At my look of frank surprise and Alexandria's typical expression of bemused cynicism, the geneticist suddenly paused in her dissertation and hastily explained, "Most of the research tissue I get from animal sources comes from Earthhcart, so I know a little about how the planet's agrisystem works."

Still blatantly enjoying Taylor's obvious uneasiness with our surroundings, Alexandria took up Asplundh's explanation. "The Tachs only run cattle up here in the temperate months. The harvest is over before winter sets in; then they shut this place down again until next year. The nearest permanent settlement is a couple of hundred kilometers south of here, a farm commune called Springcamp."

Taylor was still warily eyeing the crude reminders of the room's function. His very expression suggested that he suspected he would regret his question, but he couldn't seem to keep himself from asking it. "Why would they build this kind of facility way out here? Why not slaughter the cattle at the settlement?"

Alexandria gave a deprecating grunt, a sound that eloquently conveyed the opinion that among his other demonstrable deficiencies, Taylor obviously didn't know much about farming. "Because it's easier to haul meat than it is to haul cattle," she said. Then she surprised me with another laugh, this one seemingly not directed at Taylor for once. "Besides," she added, "a lot of that meat gets 'lost' between here and Springcamp."

I hated to break up the lecture on animal husbandry, but we hadn't come that far just to bootleg real meat. "Is this Springcamp where the Class Tens are?" I asked Alexandria.

"No," she responded, "but it's a start."

I stared at her with unconcealed irritation. "Then why the hell did we land here?"

Alexandria just gestured again with the implement in her hand, and I finally recognized it as some kind of electronic wrench. "Because it's the middle of nowhere," she offered simply, "it's one of the last places on the planet the A's or the renegades would expect anyone to land."

"Unless they've ever shipped with you," I heard Taylor mutter under his breath. He waved one hand at the cold and empty room, saying more loudly, "And how do you plan on getting out of here through that blizzard—take the next cow out? Or are we going to wait for spring?"

As usual, any resistance only seemed to serve to deepen Alexandria's amused resolve in a situation. "If that's your preference, Slick," she said with another flash of teeth. "Personally, I'd prefer something a little quicker."

Without looking back to see if any of us were following her, she abruptly started off across the room, back toward the narrow doorway through which she'd just come. That door led to a short corridor with a few other doors spaced along its length. She strode straight down it to the end, however, where she exited through a wider doorway and into another vast room.

The sights and scents of this chamber were something I could easily recognize: It was a ground-car bay. It might have been a little smaller and more orderly than most such structures I was used to, but at least the form and function of the room were things I was familiar and comfortable with. A row of about a dozen single-passenger ground cars stretched along a series of recharger stanchions set into the poured-rock floor. Beyond them, parked in orderly ranks, were a variety of larger ground vehicles. There were no air or hover cars, but there was no shortage of ground craft.

"We aren't going out of here on those, are we?" Asplundh asked from behind me as she pointed to the sleek but relatively unprotected-looking ground cars and smaller carts.

"No, you wouldn't get ten meters in this storm on one of those," Alexandria replied. "They just use those for working the cattle." Slipping between the first row of craft, she gestured to a vehicle parked beyond them. "We're going to take that."

Taylor just gaped, staring from Alexandria to the conveyance she had indicated. *"That?"* he echoed in disbelief. "Stars, it looks big enough to be a troop carrier!"

But Asplundh had calmly followed Alexandria forward and was studying the huge, boxy vehicle with some interest. It was a Division-A ground truck with an articulated frame that formed a hinged point between the aft part of its cab and the capacious cargo bed. The cab was perched over the first of the truck's two pair of cleated treads, nearly shoulder-height above the ground and accessible only by a drop-down metal-runged ladder. The massive slat-sided transport box, supported by the second and larger pair of treads, was roughly the size and dimensions of a small building. "That's a cattle carrier, isn't it?" she asked curiously.

Nodding, Alexandria pointed again with her wrench. "It's the only thing here that can definitely get us across the kind of terrain and conditions we'll have to cover. All we've got to do is get the fuel packs charged up."

I eyed the monstrous truck skeptically. It must have had fuel packs the size of sofas. It was ugly and ungainly, and the cab—which had the unnerving appearance of the tiny head on some giant, bloated insect—would probably barely seat the four of us in comfort. But I couldn't argue with Alexandria's logic and so, ever mindful of our vulnerable position there, I quickly asked, "How long is that going to take?"

With a mocking grin, Alexandria said, "About two hours from whenever we get started." She waved peremptorily at Taylor. "Come on, Slick. You look like you'd be pretty good at shinnying under a truck."

"I'll help," Asplundh responded immediately.

But Alexandria put off her proposal. "I've got another job for you and Jo," she told the geneticist. "Every instrument and gauge on the console is going to need resetting."

I looked with resignation from the cattle truck to Alexandria's implacable face. Somehow, waiting for spring was starting to sound more and more like a viable idea to me.

If there was one thing in the universe that had remained unchanged, unmitigated by even the Alterations, that one thing was Murphy's law. The only surprising thing was that it had taken us only about a half hour of cold, cramped, uncomfortable work under and around the big ground truck to discover that no amount of charging was going to make the vehicle's fuel packs usable. The Tachs, apparently as a routine part of their shutdown and storage procedure, had removed the engine's enablers. The fuel packs would accept a charge, but they couldn't hold it, and the energy couldn't be transferred from the disabled pack to the power train. Taylor lay sprawled in a supine position on the cold, poured-rock floor beneath the carrier's engine compartment. When he had restarted the cyclers on the charger for the third time in ten minutes, only to watch the charge bleed right off the gauges again, even Alexandria had to concede that her plan wouldn't work.

The grizzled-haired woman had been leaning against the vehicle's frame, bent over with her head and shoulders down inside the opened engine compartment. She pulled back abruptly, heaving herself erect, and took a frustrated whack with the flat of her hand against the side of the truck. She swore vehemently, a phrase in some non-Standard language that I didn't need to understand to appreciate in context. Then she aimed a none-too-gentle nudge with the toe of her boot against Taylor's protruding legs. "Come on, you may as well get out of there," she snapped at him. "This isn't going to work."

Taylor inched backward until he could scramble out from under the engine compartment. As he got to his feet, he glared at her. "I told you that ten minutes ago!" he retorted, brushing furiously at the dirt on the back of the legs of his bulky flightsuit. "No enablers, no power!"

"What if we could find the enablers?" I said quickly, throwing Taylor a calming look. I couldn't blame him for his anger; she had it coming. But this was not the time for him to finally lose his patience with Alexandria. There was too much at stake.

Both he and Alexandria were shaking their heads, but it was Taylor who answered me. "No, that wouldn't help," he explained grimly. "Even if we could find where they stored them, it would take forever to reintegrate them into the packs, and we'd have to recalibrate them before we could begin charging again." He threw Alexandria a baleful look. "And besides, I doubt if they left the kind of equipment we'd need for doing all that out here in wonderful Cow City."

I recognized the gleam in Alexandria's dark eyes, and even someone unfamiliar with the big woman's temperament could hardly have missed the overt hostility in the tense stance of her burly body. Just as I was about to step forward and physically interpose myself between her and Taylor, Asplundh spoke up from the truck's cab, where she and I had been working.

"What about the other craft?" she asked, leaning out the open window. As we all turned toward her, she gestured vaguely around the bay. "Do you think the Tachs removed the enablers from all of these vehicles—even the smaller ones?"

There was a taut moment of silence. Then, in a measured tone, Alexandria responded, "I don't know; probably not."

"Well, then," the geneticist went on, glancing from one to the other of our faces, "what if we could find enough fuel packs that still had enablers?" She shrugged ingenuously. "If we could charge up and remove those packs, is there any way we could rig them all to power this truck?"

Almost unwillingly, Taylor and Alexandria exchanged a brief look. Then he turned the genuine charm of one of his dazzling smiles on Asplundh. "I don't know," he admitted, "but it sure as hell is worth a try."

But it was Alexandria's approval, though lacking the stellar charisma of Taylor's high-beam smile, that actually brought the hint of a blush to Asplundh's pale cheeks. "That's a very good idea," Alexandria declared. "Come on, let's see how many of these crates still have enablers."

The methodical frugality of the Tachs herdsmen was almost our undoing. The only vehicles they hadn't bothered to remove the enablers from were the dozen or so little ground carts.

"Will these be enough?" Asplundh asked, looking with unconcealed doubt from the row of small, single-passenger carts to the mammoth carrier.

"One way to find out, I guess," Taylor said gamely. Without further preamble, he cracked the case on the nearest recharger stanchion and began to pull out the power conduits.

Charging the carts' diminutive fuel packs would not take much time, but hooking each pack to its stanchion was a tedious pain in the ass, especially in those circumstances. It was bitterly cold in the unheated bay, and connecting the conduits' leads wasn't the kind of work you could do with gloves on. Without any protection, our bare fingers quickly became numb, and we had to pause frequently to rewarm them. Asplundh had never done that kind of work before, so she wasn't able to hook up a pack by herself. But she determinedly worked alongside me, and the two of us together accomplished the job much faster than I could have done it alone. By the time we'd started on our second cart, we had begun to get a system down.

"Joinin' cold!" I complained as the slender, threaded end of one of the conduit leads slipped for the third time from my fumbling grasp.

Her expression sympathetic, Asplundh glanced briefly around us at the brightly lit but brutally cold bay. "I guess they never saw much reason to heat this place, since they never worked out here in this kind of weather," she observed.

"I wouldn't work *anywhere* in this kind of weather," I groused, tucking my bare hands under my armpits.

The geneticist gave me a small smile of commiseration. "I've seen worse," she said. "There are climate zones on DoubleNew York where no one lives, even during the temperate months."

I gave a soft, cynical grunt. "That must be why you emigrated."

She seemed to have taken my remark fairly seriously, although I had intended it as mere sarcasm. "No," she replied as slowly, almost absently, her fingers separated and realigned the remaining conduit leads. "There just wasn't much opportunity there for someone like me—a Class Four, I mean."

So I took her response seriously as well, deliberately studying that attractively Restructured face as I observed, "But you were degreed and in a medical field. You mean to tell me you were denied advancement on your homeworld because of your Class?"

She suddenly seemed studiously absorbed in the intricate patterns on the lead's terminal. Skirting my question, Asplundh said, "Have you ever noticed how many Fours and Fives there are in the medical fields?" Her slim shoulders hitched slightly. "It's almost as if we're the ones who have the most to gain from expanding as far as possible the frontiers of what we know . . ." Her voice trailed off, and for a few moments I just watched the wispy tendrils of her frozen breath as it spiraled up toward the bay's stark ceiling. Then, abruptly, in what seemed to me at first to be a non sequitur, she looked directly at me again and asked, "Did Lewis ever touch-heal you?"

I thought for a few seconds, then nodded. "Yeah, but it was just for some little marks—nothing like Alexandria."

Automatically, we both glanced down the row of parked ground carts to where the broad, frizzy-haired woman was bent industriously over the engine case of one of the little vehicles. The deep hum of the rechargers we had already activated was loud enough that I was sure she couldn't hear us.

"In the preliminary work I've been able to do so far on Heinlein," the geneticist continued, "I've barely had the chance to scratch the surface of the entire electrobiochemical process of touch-healing. I still have more questions than answers." She toyed with one of the dangling leads as she went on. "For example, what if a touch-healer could consciously modify the effect of the process? I know that Lewis somehow focuses the ability through his hands, but is it possible to focus it from anywhere else?" As she warmed to her subject, Asplundh's voice and expression became increasingly animated. "If he can rearrange cellular matter from damaged back to undamaged, could he somehow learn to rearrange it from Altered to normal? Think what it would mean, Jo, if there actually was a way to repair, at the submolecular level, the genetic damage the Alterations have caused."

I was thinking about it, and it scared the shit out of me. If a man could do that, he would be worth anything—literally anything: worth taking any risk, breaking any rule, taking any life . . .

Asplundh paused, suddenly seeming a little abashed by her enthusiastic stream of words. "I'm sorry," she said with a soft, self-mocking laugh. "We scientists tend to get carried away with the self-importance of our own work."

But I just shook my head. "No, I've done a lot of wondering about Lewis's Talent myself—although," I added ruefully, "not with quite the same kind of authority you have."

We each shifted slightly, stretching our cold-cramped muscles. I found myself feeling a growing sense of camaraderie with the curly-haired geneticist, and not just because we shared a common element of risk in our venture. I simply liked her.

Asplundh bent to gather the rest of the conduit leads again, assuming that the conversation was over. But as I flexed my fingers and took up the next lead, I glanced over at her serious face and asked, "Do you think it's possible for a touch-healer to reverse the process?"

Asplundh's brows tented, and she frowned in puzzlement. "How do you mean?"

I hesitated, uncertain then whether I wanted to reveal to her what I had witnessed in the research complex on Camelot. In some way I almost felt that I might be violating Lewis's privacy, but Asplundh's perplexed look forced me to go on. "Instead of rearranging damaged tissue on someone else's body and making it normal again," I explained reluctantly, "what if they could take damaged tissue from their own body and—" I fumbled for a word. "—transfer it somehow to someone else's?"

The geneticist's frown only deepened. She studied my face as if trying to read there just what had prompted that unexpected question. "Do you mean using the Talent like a—a weapon?"

"More like in self-defense," I quickly corrected. Then I just stood there, becoming increasingly uncomfortable as those acute gold-colored eyes steadily took my measure. After a few moments of awkward silence I suddenly shrugged and deliberately redevoted my attention to the conduit lead in my hand. "I was just wondering if you thought it was possible, that's all," I concluded, feigning nonchalance. But I knew Asplundh was not fooled.

I was almost relieved when Alexandria's grating voice boomed from right behind us. "Come on, you two—let's get at it! We've still got six more fuel packs to charge."

Hooking up the ground carts' fuel packs to their stanchions and charging them proved to be the simplest part of our job; finding a feasible way to house and connect all the smaller packs and their enablers within the carrier's engine compartment was another matter entirely. Asplundh and I were forced to leave the main part of that task to Taylor and Alexandria. Working space under and inside the engine compartment was limited, and the two of them had a lot more experience with that kind of work. Unfortunately, the two of them did not also have what could by any stretch of the imagination be called a good working relationship, and neither the working conditions nor the amount of time we'd already spent in the frigid bay did anything to improve it.

"God's tit!" I heard Alexandria snarl from where she hung over the side of the carrier's engine compartment as, halfway into the increasingly cramped space, she struggled furiously with some recalcitrant piece of cobbled-together circuitry. Her head jerked back, and she glared down through the tangle of improvised fuel pack linkups to where Taylor's blue- and silver-suited body was flattened supine on the floor beneath the engine compartment. "I said on *alternating* posts, you Classless idiot—not odd-sided ones! Or didn't they teach you any power-train mechanics in that cod-swabbing charm school you went to?"

From where I sat in the truck's cab, I could not make out exactly what Taylor's response was, but I didn't need to understand his precise words to appreciate their mood. It was a tone of voice I didn't think I'd ever heard my even-tempered friend use. I began to scramble out of the carrier even before Alexandria could reply.

"What the hell do you mean?" she shouted at him in return, even as Taylor began to clamber out from beneath the engine compartment. "In case you haven't noticed, we're not finished here yet, Slick! So you just get your sorry ass back—"

Alexandria was forced to break off as Taylor lunged to his feet right in front of her, his face just inches from hers. He confronted her with a look of such volatile fury that for one breathless moment I actually thought he was going to take a swing at the bigger woman. I also thought, quite peripherally, that she would have soundly deserved it, although she probably would have swung back at him and done far more damage than he could have.

For a few tense moments the two of them stood frozen there, the mutual antagonism between them palpable in the icy air. I was afraid to move, to step forward and try to mediate the situation, as if any motion on my part might trigger some real violence from either one of them. Then slowly, by sheer effort of will, the heated flush of passion on Taylor's livid face began to subside. Stiffly and with elaborate contempt, he bent to retrieve his gloves from where they had tumbled to the floor at his feet. His spine rigid, he turned and wordlessly stalked away from the truck.

From the corner of my eye I saw Asplundh slip from the cab. Her pale face was tense and anxious, and she threw me a quick, inquiring glance. I followed her eyes to Taylor's departing back and gave her a minute nod. Silently, she started after him.

The instant the two of them had both disappeared out the bay's door, I rounded on Alexandria and made no attempt to check my anger. "He should have decked you!" I snarled. "Where the hell do you get off treating him like that? You've been riding him ever since we left Heinlein!"

Alexandria's face was like a great leathery mask, her dark eyes hard and brittlely set. "You said you brought him along to help," she reminded me tersely. "There's a lot of work to be done here and not very much time. We've got both the A's and the renegades to stay clear of." Her upper lip lifted slightly, revealing just the hard edge of those big even teeth. "This is serious business, Jo. I don't have time to appreciate him for his more . . . charming qualities. He helps, or I've got no use for him."

I found that my body was actually rigid with tension, poised so tautly that my muscles ached as I confronted Alexandria with no less a show of antagonism than Taylor had displayed. I made a conscious effort to ease off and deliberately let out my pent breath in a long, smooth sigh. "In case it's escaped your notice, he *has* been helping," I pointed out as calmly as I could. "He's done everything you've asked him to, the best that he could." I could not resist adding, "He's not one of your hired lackeys, and he's put up with more shit from you than I would have thought humanly possible."

The tightness in her broad shoulders eased perceptibly; the old amusement was returning to those imperturbable eyes. "And he's going to have to put up with some more until we get this crate moving.''

I just shook my head in frustration and irritation. ''You know, he'd do anything you asked to help if you'd just treat him with a little respect.''

One of Alexandria's bushy gray brows climbed sharply; she cocked her head and looked at me with keen suspicion. ''Are you and him—'' she asked bluntly, casually making a timelessly graphic hand signal.

So *that* was it, or part of it, at least. She was as bad as Raydor! I knew I could have put her mind at ease by simply telling her the truth—that Taylor and I loved each other but were not lovers. And yet, just as with Raydor, something in that same implicit disapproval of hers made me obstinately refuse to give her that satisfaction. ''That's none of your damned business,'' I replied. ''He's here because I asked him to come and he wanted to help me. So just do everyone a favor and stop riding him so hard.'' I paused a moment, lowering my voice to a more moderate tone. ''He's doing everything he can, and I'm damned glad to have his help.''

Alexandria studied me silently for a few moments. As always, her scrutiny gave me the vaguely unsettling feeling that she was considering me in the light of some information of which I was still woefully ignorant. Then the deep lines on her weathered face eased slightly, and she shook her head. ''You know we can't count on any outside help here, Jo. The A's are worse than useless to us. They'd just lead those renegades right to the Tens.'' She paused thoughtfully. ''He has no idea how important this all is,'' she said quietly, ''or just what we're up against. You never should have brought him along.''

I could have used the same argument against her and brought up Asplundh's equally inappropriate presence but for some reason the fight seemed to have gone out of me then. Maybe it was because I *did* realize how important it was and just what we *were* up against. Maybe it was because I had fought alongside that infuriatingly stubborn woman before, and for essentially the same cause. My mind suddenly flashed back to one fleeting but indelible image from my remarkable experience in Camelot's research complex: Alexandria as a young woman, laughing in the arms of Lillard, the Class Ten she had loved. I knew what drove her, even as I knew she could not expect Taylor to be driven with the same ferocity. Only I had the equal capacity to be impelled by that same passion.

"Yeah," I replied softly, meeting her fierce gaze unblinkingly, "you're right; I never should have brought him along." Her eyes widened slightly in mild surprise at my admission even as I went on. "It's not fair to him. You and me, we really don't have much choice, do we? But them—" I jerked my chin toward the bay door, where Taylor and Asplundh had disappeared. "—we've dragged them in over their heads." I spread my gloved hands, a gesture of both acquiescence and conciliation. "Let's just not make it any worse than it has to be."

Alexandria grunted, a deep, deprecating sound. But her gravelly voice was surprisingly even as she inquired wryly, "You think you can get him back in here?"

"Yeah," I replied. "You think you can manage to *keep* him in here?"

Taylor was already on his way back to the bay when I met him in the corridor, just outside the door. I didn't even have to say anything to him; he just shook his shaggy head at me in rueful resignation and flashed me a quick glimmer of that stellar smile. If anything, I think he was a bit chagrined that he had allowed himself to lose his temper, not because Alexandria hadn't deserved his anger but because having expressed it had somehow only demonstrated her ability to further control him. From the doorway, Asplundh merely shrugged at my inquiring expression and said nothing in explanation.

Within a half hour the huge carrier's engine rumbled to life. The mechanics of ground vehicles was hardly my specialty, but with Alexandria beside me in the cab, I began to pick up a hasty education as together we ran through a check of the instrumentation while Taylor finished putting the modified engine compartment back together again.

Leaning over our shoulders in the cab, Asplundh asked the obvious question. "Are we going to have enough power to drive this thing?"

Alexandria deftly punched a button on the monitoring section of the truck's console; she frowned slightly, but I wasn't sure if the expression was prompted by what she saw on the gauge or by the geneticist's query. "I don't know," she replied, hitting the button again. She glanced back at Asplundh. "You got everything loaded?"

"Everything?" I echoed. All we had were the bare essentials we had carried off of *Raptor*.

Outside the cab, Taylor snapped down the engine compartment hatches and stood back, looking up to us with his brows arched quizzically. Through the windshield, Alexandria gave him a thumbs-up gesture, and he started toward the bay's wide outer doors. He gave the control panel a brief perusal, then hit the appropriate switch. As the heavy doors began to grate slowly open and the icy wind sprayed snow in across the bay floor, Alexandria engaged the carrier's drive. With a reverberant shudder, the massive vehicle pulled out of its stall and started crawling toward the doorway.

Taylor had run back to shut down the power and manually close the broad doors. Alexandria didn't exactly come to a complete halt for him, but she did slow down sufficiently for him to hop nimbly up onto the running board of the truck's cab as he caught up with us. He scrambled inside, his clothing and bare head liberally dusted with snow. But he gave an exuberant little whoop and slapped me triumphantly on the shoulder as the truck, its engine growling steadily, plunged forward into the featureless white expanse of the blizzard-torn prairie.

"We did it!" he grinned, tossing back his wet hair like a high-spirited colt.

"So far," Alexandria grunted noncommittally, methodically scanning the gauges and indicators on the console. Without even looking up at him, she continued. "Ever handle an industrial-weight ground carrier, Slick?"

To my surprise, Taylor just shrugged. "Division C and D stuff; nothing quite like this."

Alexandria turned then, briefly but long enough to give Taylor a measuring look. "Get down here on these pressure and hydraulics monitors, then; I'll teach you what you need to know."

From practically the moment we'd cleared the bay doors, the squat buildings of the Dayne's Prairie station had disappeared, swallowed by the whirling wall of white snow. Visually, every direction—including up and down—had become identical. The carrier had navigational equipment, but to me it looked hopelessly primitive compared with the Integrated systems I was used to. The crude schematic of the horizon looked like a child's drawing. While Taylor monitored the engine's status, Alexandria set our course and maneuvered the huge vehicle. I had no idea how deep the snow was on the level; it could have come up nearly to the cab's windows for all I could tell. But the carrier's massive cleated treads bit in, propelling us steadily and relatively smoothly through the trackless storm.

Besides its mobility, the cattle carrier had several other advantages over the station buildings. For one thing, its cab was heated; by the time we'd gone a couple kilometers, the temperature inside the small cubicle had become quite comfortable. It smelled faintly of cattle, but I'd smelled worse things, and at least we were warm. The truck also had scanning equipment; it wasn't very sophisticated or powerful, but we weren't as totally blind as we had been sitting in the bay. And even though I still didn't have any really solid idea just why the hell we were going to Springcamp, at least we were on the move again, going *somewhere*.

Asplundh and I sat together on the padded bench behind the drivers' seats. "Well, it looks like we've got enough power," the geneticist said.

"So far," Alexandria just repeated dryly, her grizzled head bent over her section of the console. "This is still about a two- or three-hour trip overland—maybe more in this crate."

But Asplundh and I exchanged a look of guarded optimism behind her broad back.

I had resigned myself to the likelihood of a fairly long ride, and I doubted the scenery would become engrossing. The warmth of the cab, combined with the carrier's steady, slightly rolling motion, inspired drowsiness in me. Maybe the stupefyingly boring view had something to do with it as well. All that kept me awake was a dull cramping in the pit of my belly. Just as it occurred to me that the sensation was probably just hunger, a hollow, strangely muffled beeping sound filled the cab.

It took me a moment to figure out what the noise was and what it signified. As both Taylor and Alexandria glanced back at me and Asplundh watched in puzzled concern, I fumbled down through the many layers of half-opened suits and liners to extract the slender rectangle of Handy's remote relay from my breast pocket. Tilting it in the cab's dim light, I pushed the receiver and squinted at the tiny screen.

I don't know what my face revealed, but it was obvious that my expression must have changed as I strained to read the brief coded message that raced across the surface of the little device, for I could see that change reflected in Asplundh's expression. Her eyes widened, and her brows drew up in query and concern. "Jo, what is it?" she asked, her voice automatically hushed.

"Jo?" Taylor echoed, glancing back at me again.

"There's an air car pacing us," I replied, not looking up from the relay in my hand, "heading eight-point-eight-five and holding." I paused, lifting my eyes, only to meet Asplundh's alarmed face. "Someone is following us."

CHAPTER NINE

One of the funny things about the human body, even transmuted as it had been over the centuries, was that it could adapt to almost any kind of stimulation, even the hard push of adrenaline. The sensation that cascaded through my veins, numbing my limbs and making my heart surge furiously, had become amazingly familiar to me. And although it still fulfilled its physiological function, the phenomenon no longer had the power to startle me. If adrenaline had been an addictive drug, then I guess you would have had to say that I had become habituated to it.

Alexandria's voice was the first to cut into the little bubble of silence that my words had created in the truck's cab. "Give me that heading again," she instructed tersely.

Looking down at the relay, I had to hit its replay function to be able to recite the numbers for her. She bent over the console, manipulating the scanner.

"Maybe it's Tachs," Asplundh suggested in a hopeful voice.

"I don't get anything here," Alexandria said. "Very few Tachs own aircraft; besides, Tachs would never be out here in this sector during this season, especially in this kind of weather."

Of course, I thought glumly. Tachs had more sense than we did.

"The A's, then?" Taylor asked from his seat beside Alexandria. "A Ceecee patrol?"

But the big woman still expressed her doubt. "Maybe, but not likely. The A's do their surface patrols in picket ships, not air cars. And the only thing the Ceecees would have out here this time of the year would be remotes. Even if a remote had picked up on something suspicious, they wouldn't use an air car to follow up on it—not out in this storm."

132

"They also wouldn't be just pacing us," I reminded her grimly. If it had been the A's, they would have just apprehended us.

"Can you confirm their distance and heading?" Alexandria asked me, gesturing at the truck's scanner. "I don't get anything here, but then, Handy's equipment's got a hell of a lot more range and sophistication than this crate's."

As I began punching a brief series of numbers into the relay's miniature transmitter, Asplundh interjected in a puzzled voice, "I thought you sent the ship up out of their range."

"She did," Alexandria replied for me, indicating the relay with a wave of her hand, "but the range of *Raptor*'s scanners is a lot farther than the instrumentation on any picket ship. Handy can still keep an eye out for them without being close enough for them to detect the ship. As long as he keeps his transmissions short and scrambles the signal, they won't be able to trace it."

"Definitely pacing us," I announced. "They must have picked us up as soon as we left the station." I studied the relay's screen. "They're hanging along back there, just beyond the range of this carrier's scanner."

Alexandria locked eyes with me. "Shit," she said.

Shifting uncomfortably on the bench beside me, Asplundh asked anxiously, "Where did they come from? Why didn't your ship detect them sooner?"

"I don't know," I admitted. "But this snow makes it pretty hard to get a fix on something as small as an air car, at least from as far out as *Raptor* is. Maybe Handy didn't detect them until they were close enough to us to start pacing us."

"Could it be something else? Black marketeers?" Taylor asked, his voice calm as he looked over his shoulder from his monitors. "You're sure it's the renegades?"

"Who else would be pacing us in an air car?" Alexandria growled, bending over the console and roughly punching one of the scanner's locate buttons. Her voice rose with untempered frustration. "Who else could've followed us from the station? Who the hell else'd want to let us lead them right where we're going?"

There was a moment of taut silence; then Asplundh asked in bewilderment, "But how would the renegades even know we were at the station in the first place?"

Alexandria slowly twisted in her chair to stare at the geneticist. "Good question," she said. She glanced from Asplundh, to me, to Taylor. "How would they know, unless they've been following us all along, ever since we came in?"

Something in her question prickled at a half-formed thought that had been nagging at me ever since I'd left Porta Flora. I didn't believe in coincidences or in bad luck. The Authorities had been on to me right along, and so, by extension, had the renegades. "You sure the A's at Port didn't detect us when we came in?" I demanded of Alexandria.

But she shook her head. "I had a good ear on them: nothing but dead air."

I looked down at the little rectangle of the relay in my hand, thinking rapidly. "Then the A's probably still don't know we're on-planet," I said.

"Probably not," she agreed. "If Handy got the ship back up without being detected, I'm sure he hasn't had much trouble staying clear of their routine surveillance."

Ironically, it occurred to me then that we almost would have been better off if it *had* been the A's who had found us. They might have been pissed off because of the way we had torn out of Porta Flora, evading the Writ of Inquiry, but it hardly would have been a killing offense. At least the legitimate A's never would have tried to fry us the way the renegades in control of *Sumatra* had at Heinlein, the way the renegades following us in that air car might once we had unwittingly given them what they wanted.

"What do we do now?" Asplundh inquired, confusion and some honest fear etched onto her pale face.

"Well, I can tell you one thing we're *not* going to do," Alexandria replied brusquely, swinging back to the console to take up the carrier's controls again. "We're *not* going to just lead those ball-less bastards right to the Tens!" Even as she spoke, she jerked on the directional levers; on the truck's navigational grid, the stylized representation of the horizon began to shift abruptly.

"Wait a minute," Taylor protested, scrambling to adjust his monitors. "What are you doing?"

Alexandria replied without even looking up. "Just making a little course change."

"Yeah? Well, I wouldn't take too much of a scenic diversion," he reminded her dryly, his eyes on the gauges. "We don't even know if this bucket's got enough charge to get us to where we were headed in the first place, never mind the side trips."

Ignoring him, Alexandria just threw back to me, "They still pacing us?"

I punched the repeat-request sequence on Handy's relay; almost instantaneously he responded with a coded reply of the air car's coordinates. "Still pacing," I informed Alexandria.

"Good," she grunted. "Let's lead them a little farther afield, then."

Taylor did not reiterate his previous warning or even glance up; he just devoted himself to his monitors. But Asplundh didn't have any such duty to distract her, and her relentlessly logical mind had already progressed to the next obvious question. "Even if we do succeed in diverting them away from where we were going," she pointed out, "won't they just keep following us?" She made an economical but evocative gesture that encompassed the whole of the massive truck with all its built-in limitations. "We certainly can't outrun an air car in this; we can't even outlast them."

I just aimed my gaze at Alexandria's broad back; if the burly woman had something specific in mind, I was eager to hear it as well.

"We don't need to outrun or outlast them to get rid of them," Alexandria replied cryptically.

I glanced down, studying Handy's relay. "They're still pacing us; interval steady." The air car was following so closely that if we couldn't detect them with the truck's equipment, the range of our carrier's scanner must have been minimal. Then again, I realized morosely, all it had probably ever been needed for was to keep the truck from colliding with stray cattle.

Asplundh seemed to have assumed Taylor's mantle as chief questioner of the wisdom of Alexandria's ideas. "What do you mean, get rid of them?" the geneticist persisted, leaning slightly forward on the bench, as if proximity to the big woman might somehow compel Alexandria to answer more expansively. "You mean disable their car somehow?"

Alexandria just gave a little grunt. "Something like that," she said.

The geneticist's eyes were still wide with doubt, her tone openly skeptical. "They could have beam cannon on that air car; this vehicle isn't even armed."

Alexandria glanced sideways at the navigation display, but she did not spare Asplundh a direct look. "*We're* armed," she said.

Even Taylor's head lifted at that assertion; he turned from his gauges long enough to trade a look of patent incredulity with both Asplundh and me. "We've only got three beam pistols," he pointed out to Alexandria. "Just what were you planning on doing—flinging cow shit at them?"

But Alexandria's expression remained implacable. "If we have to, but I don't think it'll quite come to that."

In her bid for an alternate course of action, Asplundh turned her attention to me. "Couldn't you just call down the ship?" she asked me, a quick nod indicating the relay in my hands.

But I had to shake my head. "Not now—not for this. When we really need her to get out of here, I want her up there where I know she's clear of the A's. Besides," I continued with considerably more confidence than I actually felt, "if it is the renegades following us, they aren't going to start taking potshots at us; they *want* us to keep going."

Nodding in agreement, Alexandria flashed me an oblique look. "Still steady?" she inquired.

I consulted the relay. "Yeah, they're holding right off our tail."

Alexandria made a small sound, either of acknowledgment or satisfaction, or both. She directed her next query at Taylor. "You any good with a pistol, Slick?"

I thought I had begun to fathom just what Alexandria was up to, and I wasn't especially happy with her plan. But Taylor's expression was still innocently puzzled as he replied, "Adequate, I guess; I'm a fair shot." His brows rose, indicating with a little tilt of his head the general direction of the renegades' air car. "Not good enough to hit an air car at that altitude, though; especially from this distance."

"Don't worry about the distance," she told him matter-of-factly. "You'll be a lot closer than this. As for the altitude . . ." She shrugged, seemingly unconcerned. "Maybe we can give you a little help with that, too." Without turning or looking up or addressing Taylor's puzzlement any further, she said, "Jo, if you look in the equipment locker under that bench you're parked on, there should be a paint marker gun."

Asplundh and I got to our feet, and I lifted the bench's hinged seat. "A what?" I repeated, rummaging through a jumbled cache of unfamiliar implements.

"A marker gun," Alexandria repeated patiently. "It fires paint cartridges to mark cattle; it looks like a—"

Like a grenade launcher: I jerked the heavy gun with its long, wide-bore barrel out of the locker. "Yeah, I've got it," I interrupted her, holding the device aloft.

"Good," she responded blandly, her big hands steady on the

console's controls. "Now pop the power packs out of two of those beam pistols, and—"

Asplundh was already scrambling to follow Alexandria's instructions, but even before the beam pistols' cylindrical-shaped power packs could be freed from their housings in the weapons, I had mentally completed the picture. "And load them into the barrel of the marker gun," I finished for Alexandria.

"Just load one of them," the grizzled-haired woman corrected. "You try to launch two power packs from that thing at the same time, all you'll do is blow both of them up in the damned barrel."

Shaking my head, I took the pack from one of the pistols from Asplundh and fed it into the paint gun, remarking wryly, "Why do I get the feeling you've done this before?" The principle was self-evident; fired with sufficient velocity from the barrel of the marking device, the power packs would explode on contact, much like small impact grenades.

"There, that should help you out with the altitude problem, Slick," Alexandria went on. "As for the distance . . ." As she made some further adjustment to the truck's power regulator, the ungainly vehicle began to slow perceptibly.

"Wait a minute," I protested, still wielding the loaded marker gun. "Why does Taylor—"

"It's okay, Jo," Taylor interrupted. He turned from the monitoring panel, getting to his feet and reaching out to take the gun from me. "I think I know what she's got in mind."

I was certain that I knew what Alexandria had in mind. That was why I still resisted, holding the makeshift weapon clear of Taylor's reach.

"What are you going to do?" Asplundh asked Alexandria anxiously.

"She's going to drop him off the truck," I replied—drop him off into the storm to lie in wait for the pursuing air car, armed with nothing more than some stupid, half-assed cow gun. And despite her antipathy for him, I was damned if I was going to let her make him assume that kind of risk. I shook my head, insisting obstinately, "There's no reason for Taylor to go; I'll do it."

"No," Alexandria and Taylor both said simultaneously, rendering me momentarily speechless. It was the first time I had heard the two of them agree on anything concerning our whole ill-conceived mission.

"I need you here on that relay," Alexandria continued firmly.

"Besides, you're the only other one here who can manage these monitors."

"Besides, you're a lousy shot," Taylor added, leaning forward so that his hand closed around the barrel of the marker gun. His upper lip lifted, forming a crooked grin. "It's okay, Jo," he repeated, his voice pitched more softly. His grin widened, and he pointed out, "I may as well volunteer. If I didn't, she'd probably just pitch me out of here on my ass, anyway."

As I swiftly studied his raffish face, two things were immediately obvious to me: Much as his tone was bantering, Taylor honestly believed Alexandria was capable of throwing him out if necessary, and as much as it stymied me, he was genuinely willing to go. But before I could question his judgment or his decision further, he tugged the paint gun free from my grip and reached for the extra power pack. Then, winking broadly at me, he bent to engage me in a quick but energetic hug. "Wish me luck," he advised me, swinging toward the cab's door.

Alexandria had slowed the big carrier even further, but we still were moving at a steady clip. "They're only a couple of kilometers behind us," she told Taylor briskly, barely glancing up from the console, "so you aren't going to have much time to wait." She shot him a brief, sidelong look to where he hung against the cab's door frame, his rangy body poised almost indolently against the backdrop of the fierce storm that still raged beyond the protection of the truck. "Once you get out there, drop down and stay low; get on your belly and brace your elbows. That thing isn't balanced for a projectile with the density of those power packs, so it's going to fire short." Her square white teeth showed in a mirthless smirk. "And it throws one hell of a kickback."

I was watching Taylor as Alexandria spoke; he had slung the marker gun across his chest by the device's shoulder strap, and his expression was a bemused mixture of admiration and irritation. It was obvious that Alexandria had had some practical experience with the guerrilla tactics she was schooling him in; her casual confidence seemed to impress him. "You aren't going to be able to see much out there," she continued, "but you should be able to hear them once they get close enough, and you might be able to get a fix on their running lights. Let them pass over you; aim for the fuel cells on their belly. Even a tangential hit from one of those power packs will start a chain reaction that'll blow the engine apart."

Nodding, Taylor pulled on his gloves. He cracked the latch

and popped the door partway open; a gust of frigid air, replete with glittering flakes of snow, swirled through the narrow aperture and into the cab. Balanced in the door frame, he shot his burly antagonist a brilliant smile. "Aren't you going to wish me luck?" he asked her wolfishly.

But Alexandria's gaze had already returned to her controls. "Luck's got nothing to do with it, Slick," she tossed back evenly. "Remember, you've only got two shots—just don't miss."

I was sure I actually heard a hoot of laughter from Taylor as he agilely hopped out the door and almost instantaneously disappeared in the whirling maelstrom of the blizzard.

"Get up here on these monitors," Alexandria instructed me immediately, reaching out almost casually with one powerful arm to reseal the door. "They still pacing us?"

Sliding into Taylor's seat, I fumbled to prop Handy's relay on the console before me. I hit the repeat. "Yeah," I said after a moment. She might have grunted something in reply, but I was too preoccupied with my new duties to be sure. My focus had narrowed to the unfamiliar array of gauges and indicators in front of me, and although I could not have technically defined most of them, an almost instinctive grasp of their functions came over me, allowing me to quickly take over their monitoring. I was only vaguely aware of Asplundh's presence; she sat behind us on the bench seat, the third beam pistol still gripped, forgotten, in her hands.

Alexandria had been watching the carrier's odometer even as she kept the vehicle moving on course and at a steady speed. After a short interval she threw me another inquiring look.

I consulted the relay again, but for the first time the coordinates did not correlate. My initial reaction was one of mere confusion. I punched the recall function. Then adrenaline took over, sending the icy intimacy of its liquid panic sluicing through my veins. "What the—" I hit the replay once more, so hard that I nearly dropped it from my nerveless fingers.

"What is it?" came Asplundh's alarmed voice from behind us.

My gaze shot over to Alexandria's stoic face. "This can't be right," I protested even as I knew it was. "According to these coordinates, they've stopped pacing us." I swallowed, surprised to find that my throat was so dry and tense that even that simple action made it ache rawly. "They've dropped back. They're following Taylor!"

"Following him?" Asplundh echoed in confusion. "How can they be following him? He's not *going* anywhere!"

But the hulking woman beside me understood what was happening perhaps even before I did. Muttering some arcane curse, Alexandria jerked on her controls. The big truck swung sharply and began to turn, its nose bobbing as the cleated treads spun, throwing up a heavy spume of glistening snow that rattled like gravel across the blank windshield. The engine whined in protest as she hyped the power, but the lumbering vehicle came around and lurched forward again, its speed increasing in response as we began to retrace our tracks.

"What is it?" Asplundh demanded then, her fear overriding her habitual courtesy. She still held the pistol in one hand but had to use the other to hang on to the back of the bench to brace herself in the swaying truck.

"The air car has stopped following us," I explained tersely and distractedly, still consulting Handy's relay. "When we dropped Taylor off, they suddenly slowed up." I punched the repeat, then looked quickly to Alexandria's grim and weathered face. "They're coming up right behind him."

"But how could they know he was there?" Asplundh insisted, her voice rising sharply. "They couldn't detect something as small as one person on the ground—from that distance, in a blizzard—could they?"

"No, they couldn't," Alexandria agreed evenly, never looking up, "but they did." She checked the odometer again. "We should be almost—" She broke off, then resumed vehemently. "Why the hell hasn't he fired?"

I stared at the numbers on the relay's tiny screen. "Because they're still behind him," I told her tautly. "They've stopped moving." My monitors forgotten, I merely braced myself, clutching Handy's relay as the carrier's protesting engine whined an octave higher. Burning out the circuits seemed an inconsequential result at the moment; all I could think of was getting back to Taylor.

I had become so concerned with our progress back to the point where we had dropped Taylor off that I hadn't tried to keep consulting Handy's figures. The air car had come to a halt less than half a kilometer behind Taylor. Suddenly, as we approached from the opposite side, coordinates began to stream across the relay's little screen. The air car was on the move again. It was only then that I understood what had actually happened: the renegades hadn't slowed down to follow *him*; they had thought they were still following *us.* Only when we had abruptly reappeared on their scan, coming from the wrong direction, had they realized we had split up.

"They're moving again," I told Alexandria, quickly rechecking the coordinates. "They're almost on top of him."

"Good," she responded with a grim enthusiasm, bent over the truck's controls like the madwoman I had always suspected she was. "Let's hope Slick is a better than 'adequate' shot."

As desperately as I tried to peer through the whirling curtain of snow that beat against the truck's windshield, I could not see the oncoming air car's running lights. Inside the cab, I was effectively distanced from the sights and sounds of whatever was taking place out there in that storm. And so the explosion, when it came, was almost something that I could feel more than something I could see or hear. There was the faint physical sensation of concussion; then, for a moment, there was nothing.

"Sun's Light!" Alexandria breathed from beside me. She let up on the carrier's power, and for a few seconds the massive vehicle shuddered hesitantly, propelled forward only by its own momentum. Then she hit both the power and the steering again, and the truck began to slew sideways violently.

"What the hell are you—" I started. Bent over in my seat, I grappled with Handy's relay while trying to remain upright in the canting vehicle. But then I no longer needed Handy's figures to locate the air car, and there was no real need to finish my question. As I straightened up, I just had time to brace my arms and legs while I gaped helplessly at the scene framed by the truck's windshield.

Light from the disabled air car strobed through the flying wall of snow, dancing like a manic lightning storm. The burning fuselage set the swirling particles afire with a demonic wash of red and gold as the crippled craft sliced inexorably down toward us. Refracted glow filled the carrier's cab, painting Alexandria's craggy profile a garish hue as she clung tenaciously to her controls, trying desperately to get us out of the incoming vessel's line of descent. Looks like Taylor did it, I thought with a weird sense of detachment and no small satisfaction. Then a harsh, rising roar filled my ears, and the gaudy light's brilliance became unbearable.

The truck's cab tilted wildly, and I felt my head impact with some solid object. Somewhere above me I heard the windshield explode in a shower of glass. Frigid air and the cold, wet slap of snow hit my face. Then I felt nothing.

CHAPTER
TEN

Swimming up from unconsciousness was an arduous, uneven process. Although I felt no specific point of pain, my entire body was submerged in a wave of overwhelming malaise. I tried to halt the unpleasant course of my return to awareness by keeping my eyes tightly closed. I just let my other senses float and tried to interpret what they could tell me.

Other than a massive unwillingness to move, I didn't feel like I'd sustained any permanent damage. I was reclining at a slight angle on something firm, and my mouth felt smoky and dry. There was a peculiar scent in my nostrils—wet, like the snow, but musky, too—and the throaty howl of wind echoing in my ears. Then I felt the surface beneath my head and shoulders yield and shift slightly.

"Taylor?" I croaked, whether audibly or not I wasn't sure.

"Don't worry; he's all right," a voice above me assured me.

Reluctantly, I cranked open my unwieldy lids and blinked furiously. I way lying, partially propped, inside some kind of compartment; it took a tremendous leap of deduction for me to realize that it was still the cab of the cattle carrier, turned on its side and somewhat battered in. The surface beneath me was littered with snow, shards of glass, and various unidentifiable implements from the truck's equipment locker. The shaggy form that cradled the upper part of my body was so unfamiliar to me that for several seconds I had difficulty even registering it as human, but the face that was deeply framed by the woolly hood was completely familiar, right down to the crooked mouth, faint scar, and gunmetal-gray eyes.

"Redding," I rasped, trying to push myself up.

Dressed in the bulky sheepskin greatcoat of a Tachs herdsman, *Nimbus*'s captain steadied me by my upper arms. "Just take it easy,'' he said, helping me into a sitting position. "You've had a pretty good crack on the head, but Lewis touched you. He said you'd be all right in a minute or two." His lip curled slightly. "Or at least as rational as you've ever been," he added sagaciously.

"Lewis?" I glanced anxiously around me, a maneuver that caused my vision to swim alarmingly. "He's here? Where is he?"

"Hey, don't worry—he's okay," Redding reassured me, supporting me with one arm around my shoulders. "He's taking care of the others."

"Taylor?" I repeated, my voice gaining a little timbre.

"You mean the guy with that poor man's grenade launcher?" Redding asked wryly. Then he hastened to assure me, "He's fine; a little cold, maybe, but he wasn't hurt. But Asplundh got sliced up pretty badly by all this flying glass." He eased his hold on me even as I struggled to sit up straighter. "Lewis had to do some of that hocus-pocus on her and Alexandria."

Temporarily mollified at least on that score, my mind made the next logical connection. Looking into those canny slate-colored eyes, I asked hoarsely, "How did you find us?"

His mouth quirked again. "Wasn't too hard," he replied. "There aren't too many cattle trucks firing missiles at air cars out here, at least not this time of the year." Enjoying the growing frown of irritation on my face, Redding gave a little snort of laughter and offered with continued amusement, "The slaughterhouse at Dayne's—you guys tripped an alarm when you drove out of there in this ground carrier."

I couldn't help myself; despite my annoyance, I had to shake my head and smile ruefully. "Alexandria," I said by way of explanation. "Some queen of the pirates!"

I started to gather my legs beneath me, glancing around for something in the skewed cab that still remained in a usable position to help me pull myself to my feet. Smoothly and automatically, Redding rose, drawing me with him as he stood on the littered and slightly tilted panel. "We must've come in right after you," he continued. "We set down at Bluestem station— another one of those delightful cow camps. Only we had one of the Services' excursion air cars on board *Kestrel*, so we didn't have to steal a cattle truck. We'd just reached Springcamp when the alarm signal came in. The Tachs knew it couldn't be profiteers—not in this weather. All they knew was it was some kind of trouble." He shrugged as if the conclusion they'd drawn had been self-evident. "Who the hell else could it have been?"he finished simply.

Despite the less than fortuitous situation in which we found ourselves and despite the stormy uncertainty of our past history together, I suddenly felt a tremendous surge of warmth and gratitude toward this laconic, infuriating man. Looking into those calm gray eyes, I recalled my surprising conversation with Alexandria on our way from Heinlein. And for the first time I was able to view Redding not just in terms of everything that had already happened but with some expectation of what still could be. Just when I was about to act on that unfamiliar emotion and let myself say or do something completely sloppy and sentimental, I abruptly remembered the circumstances that had catapulted me out of bed back on Heinlein and had started me on this ill-advised trip. Pulling away from his hold, my spine reflexively stiffening, I glared at Redding and demanded, "Why the hell did you leave Heinlein without me?"

"Because I asked him to, Jo."

Those quiet words, spoken from right behind me and cutting clearly through the noise of the storm, caused me to wheel about so rapidly that I nearly fell. Lewis stood framed in the now-vertical rectangular gap from the decimated windshield, his woolly hood pulled back, a sprinkling of bright, pristine snowflakes glittering like crystals in the black tangle of his hair. As he stepped forward from outside, he had to angle his shoulders to slip the bulk of his sheepskin coat through the narrow opening. His lips were slightly parted, as if he was about to speak again, but I never gave him the chance. With a soundless sob, I launched myself into his arms.

There are some things that never need to be relearned because they are things that are never forgotten. In Lewis's hungry embrace I felt the substance of my life being given back to me. Beneath the thick, shaggy coat, his body was hard, lean, totally familiar. The contact made every nerve in my body rally enthusiastically, as if every synapse had been bathed in light. It was, I realized then, and with no small sense of wonderment, not a matter of want or even of need. It was simply a matter of *being*. Lewis was a thing that had become a part of me. I had tried once to deny that part, and then, failing that, I had tried to walk away from it. But the part was still there; it only waited for that reconnection.

Relief, exhilaration, desire—all those feelings and more flushed through me as I clung to him in the toppled cab of that battered truck. But I could not seem to pull back even long enough to kiss him; all I wanted to do was hold him to me, cementing the inexplicable bond that had existed between us from the first moment I had let down my defenses to him. I didn't even cry. I knew that Lewis understood what I felt; he understood it because he shared it. There did not seem to be any need for tears. His arms encircled me with a fervor that was both possessive and totally giving. And after a time I realized he was whispering something to me, his face buried in the disheveled locks of my wet hair.

"I was so afraid they'd try to hurt you, Jo—that's all. I was just so afraid . . ."

Redding's voice cut in then, typically insistent but strangely gentle. "Come on, we've got to get out of here. Can you walk?"

Pulling back from Lewis's embrace, still gripping the thick wool of his greatcoat, I found it took me a moment to register what Redding had asked. "Of course I can walk," I protested indignantly; right then, I felt like I could have *flown*. Then I took a step sideways and proved it by slipping on the broken glass beneath my feet, nearly pitching headfirst into Redding.

"You've had a concussion, Jo," Lewis remonstrated, helping steady me by wrapping one arm around my waist. "Believe me, I *felt* it!" Those brilliant blue eyes sparkled as he added, "We'd better give you a hand; you've had enough crash landings for one day."

I started forward again, almost bumping into Redding. And as I looked up into those gunmetal eyes, I saw the elusive shadow of the unwieldy emotions to which I had nearly confessed. I reached out quickly and deliberately to take hold of his arm as well.

Outside the cab, when the full brunt of the blizzard hit us again, I was grateful for the support of both men. I looked around, squinting against the driving snow, trying to orient myself in the featureless white landscape. Visibility was almost zero, but it wasn't due solely to the storm; night was falling on the prairie. In that growing gloom I heard what remained of the renegades' air car before I could actually see it; the sluicing sheets of icy particles *siss*ed loudly as they hit the hot metal of its burnt-out fuselage. I faced into the wind, straining to see where the wreck of the vehicle lay.

"They clipped the top of your truck when they hit," Redding said loudly, nearly in my ear. With a firm grip on my arm, he helped Lewis keep me moving in that impenetrable murk.

"Did any of them—?"

But Lewis cut me off, shaking his bare and snow-plastered head. "Incinerated, Jo; they never had a chance."

Good! I wanted to think, craving some feeling of satisfaction, some sense of triumph. But something in Lewis's touch had purged that feeling of vengeance from me, at least for then.

A half dozen meters before us in the swirling snow, I saw the flickering pulse of the Services' air car's running lights. A lone figure plowed toward us, his shaggy coat painted by the strobing lights, his broad shoulders bent into the storm. Lewis and Redding both released their hold on me as I lurched forward, falling into Raydor's arms.

Tachs didn't show much emotion and Raydor had always been particularly stoic even for one of his kind. I liked to think that I was able to see through his taciturn facade and that I could recognize even in his stony reserve that flux of feelings common to all humankind. But right then, as he enveloped me in his massive arms, I think even a total stranger could have read that big, habitually reserved man. He nearly lifted me off my feet; I hugged him tightly.

"I could have used you coming out of Heinlein," I said breathlessly into the wet wool of his coat.

As he gently set me back, I could see the exaggerated creases in the crepey skin of his Altered face. Those dark and depthless eyes regarded me solemnly from beneath the rimed fringe of his sheepskin hood. "Ship safe?" he asked with a grunt.

"For now," I assured him, then added with a rueful smile, "But wait until you see the cross-stems!"

With those words, something clicked in my memory. Suddenly I spun around, frantically patting the pockets of my oversized flightsuit. "Wait!" I exclaimed. "We have to go back to—"

His upper lip lifting lazily, Redding cut me off by reaching into the flap pocket of his greatcoat and holding something out to me. "Looking for this?" he asked. In his hand he held the slim rectangle of Handy's relay.

Too relieved to object to his teasing, I just snatched the relay from him and stowed it in the breast pocket of my suit. "You still had it gripped in your hand when we found you," Redding explained.

"Hey," Raydor suddenly complained, glancing me up and down as we all started toward the air car, "isn't that one of my suits?"

"Yeah," I said grinning up at him, "and it looks a hell of a lot better on you!"

If I needed any assurance that she was fine, the moment we reached the air car, Alexandria's jarringly familiar abrasive voice bellowed out at us from the open hatch. "Come on, get a move on! This isn't any cod-swabbing sight-seeing excursion. We've got to get the hell out of here before the friends of the deceased show up to view the remains."

Throwing Lewis a look of long-suffering commiseration, I murmured, "Well, I can see Alexandria is all right," as he and Raydor boosted me ahead of them into the car's rear passenger compartment.

Alexandria, looking slightly rumpled but none the worse for wear, sat in the front in the copilot's position. On one of the passenger seats Taylor sat with Asplundh, his arm slung supportively over her shoulders. Her thermal suit—*my* thermal suit, I realized belatedly and with some regret—was stained with blood, but she appeared uninjured, if still slightly shaken. Taylor himself looked surprisingly normal, except for the wet disarray of his chestnut hair and the sodden appearance of his clothing.

Not for the first time since my reunion with Lewis, I felt the weird juxtapositioning of what had been with what yet would be. As I slid onto the seat across from him, bracketed by Raydor's and Lewis's bodies, I locked eyes with Taylor, and what passed between us in those mere seconds filled me with both joy and sadness. Then Taylor winked broadly at me, a gesture so typically irrepressible that suddenly I was incapable of sorrow and felt nothing but pride and affection for him.

"You okay?" Taylor asked me.

"Yeah," I responded, thinking, Thanks in no small part to you, and knowing I did not need to say it. I glanced from him to Asplundh and then back again. "How about you two?"

"A little cold," Taylor admitted, then he grinned. "But no worse than it was in that ground-car bay!"

Shifting slightly against Taylor's side, Asplundh traded a quick look with Lewis before replying. "I know I've been badgering everyone about touch-healing," she said ruefully, "but I didn't expect to test my theories by becoming part of my own research."

Redding had climbed into the pilot's seat and sealed the doors. I could hear the hovers revving as he quickly ran through his instrumentation check. Warm air blasted from the heat vents along the vehicle's inner walls, melting the last of the snow from my flightsuit. Comfortably sandwiched between Lewis and Raydor, I glanced from the cockpit to the passenger compartment.

"I take it you've met everyone here?" I asked Taylor.

Taylor's boyish face wore an expression of self-effacing candor. "Uh, yeah; you might say that," he replied.

The air car was lifting, rising obliquely but steadily into the dark, turbulent air. Without turning his attention from the controls, Redding elaborated. "Your cowboy here nearly blasted us out of the air with that damned paint gun of his!"

"What?" I exclaimed, but the sudden image that came to mind was so incongruous that I couldn't keep from grinning.

"How should I have known who they were?" Taylor responded with an air of elaborately feigned defensiveness.

"Good thing you're not a crack shot, Slick," Alexandria said acerbically from beside Redding.

"No, good thing I only had one power pack left," Taylor corrected her.

"Well, you sure took your sweet time firing the first one," Alexandria said.

For a few moments Taylor said nothing; then, when he did reply, his tone had suddenly sobered. "Just what the hell was going on out there?" he posed. "Why did they stop following the truck?"

"You tell me," she shot back at him.

I straightened uneasily on the seat. I was not about to let their useless bickering spoil my fragile haven of hope and relief; food was the first diversion that came to mind. "I don't suppose you brought anything to eat?" I asked loudly.

"No," Lewis admitted. His arm was still around my waist, and he gave me a gentle squeeze. "We left Springcamp in kind of a hurry."

"There's a couple of thermal jugs of hot tea under the seat," Redding said without turning from his controls. "And we salvaged your emergency pack. What've you got in there?"

Raydor and I traded a quick look; I made a face. "Concentrates," I replied. But I knew that under the circumstances even the most prosaic of formedfood would have served as a feast; it was just that whoever had said "Nothing lasts forever" had obviously never tasted concentrates.

Within ten minutes I was sagging against Lewis's shoulder. Redding had cut the interior lights when we reached cruising altitude. Warm, temporarily sated on hot tea and concentrates, and lulled by the steady throb of the air car's engine, I had become helplessly drowsy. Lewis had unfastened the front of his woolen greatcoat; discarding my gloves, I slipped one arm in past the still slightly damp fleece and clung to the nubby fabric covering his firm side. From the front seats I could hear Redding and Alexandria conversing in low, terse voices, but somehow it seemed very distant and very unimportant to me. Across from us, Taylor and Asplundh slumped propped together, apparently asleep.

"You warm enough?" Raydor's soft, gruff voice came from beside me. But I knew his question was only the superficial part of what he was really asking me.

Turning my face against Lewis's chest, I mumbled groggily, "You know, you were absent without my leave . . . I'm going to have to start docking your pay."

Raydor just made a deprecating grunting sound but I felt his big leg bump gently against my knees, and I knew we were square again.

Touching Lewis, inhaling his scent, synchronizing my breathing to his, I promptly fell asleep.

Our arrival at Springcamp and disembarkation from the air car assumed the muzzy proportions of a dream. Later, I realized that I must have been awake at least part of the time, because I knew I walked more or less under my own power from the landing field, through the cold, crisp darkness of the Earthheart night, to some kind of warm and dimly lit building. But I had no real time frame or sense of continuity about any of it. The air-car trip shouldn't have taken more than an hour. I don't think the landing itself wakened me, but I vaguely remembered the deep murmur of unfamiliar voices, and someone, probably Raydor, had lifted me out of the vehicle. Stubbornly stumbling along at Lewis's side, I'd had a fleeting impression of the scent of smoke and wet earth and a brief glimpse of the night sky, incredibly clear and glittering with stars. Then we were indoors, where it was nearly as dark but warm, and I'd mumbled some automatic and halfhearted protest as layers of clothing were stripped from my somnolent body. That was the last thing I remembered before I fell soundly asleep again.

Awakening the second time, I had a better idea of the reason. But I was perfectly content to just lie still for a few minutes longer, silently assessing my surroundings. I was in a bed with Lewis, and we both were still clad in our suit liners, although my body was molded so closely to his, it was as though the thin garments didn't even exist. The heat of his skin was pleasant and reassuring. The bedding had a strange, faintly musky scent, but it was clean and comfortable. I was exceedingly reluctant to move.

Slowly lifting my head, I squinted in the near darkness. The only light came from one subdued illuminator on a far wall, but I was able to make out the relative dimensions of a large, low-ceilinged room. The room was filled with beds just like the one I found myself in, and several of the others appeared occupied. It took a bit more study as my eyes gradually adjusted to the gloom to recognize that the other sleepers were the rest of our group. I even recognized Raydor's soft glottal snore.

Gently, I pulled back from Lewis's embrace and slipped out from beneath the bedcovers. The floor beneath the soles of my suit liner was smooth and cool. Glancing around, I found the faint outline of the doorway and started carefully toward it. The first few beds I passed were empty. As I padded past the occupied ones, I could just barely make out the blanket-shrouded forms: the big mound of Raydor's bulk, Taylor's lanky frame, and Asplundh's small, curled figure. The last bed by the doorway was crowded with two bodies wrapped together in some indistinguishable tangle amid the covers. Grappling clumsily with the door latch, I could not keep myself from staring in frank surprise at the sleeping couple. When I pushed the door open, a slant of slightly brighter light fell across the bed, and one of the figures stirred. I hesitated in the doorway; just as I began to look away, Redding's eyes flipped open.

The outer room was apparently some kind of small commons area; it was plainly furnished with a couple of tables and a scattering of hard chairs. It surprised me to see that the tables and chairs, as well as all the flooring, appeared to be made of real wood. The walls were studded with pegs, most of them supporting objects I couldn't identify, although I did recognize the sheepskin greatcoats and several small food-related utensils. A narrow door opening off the rear of the room led to the facilities I required. The fixtures there were simple but clean; I'd had occasion in my travels to use far worse.

When I came back out of hygiene, I was startled to find the commons room occupied. Redding, clad as I was in only his suit liner, was rummaging casually through the contents of one of the cabinets that lined part of one wall. Without turning from his perusal of the shelves, he asked me quietly, "You hungry?"

Surprised, I had to consider the question for a few seconds. "Real food?" I asked hopefully.

The room was dimly lit, but my eyes had adapted to the point where I could see him fairly clearly as he turned to me, a couple of covered containers in his hands. His upper lip lifted slightly. "This is Earthheart, remember?" he said. He held out the containers. "It's *all* real food." He nodded toward one of the wooden tables, concluding, "Let's see what we've got."

He seemed so utterly unconcerned about lounging around in only his liner that I found myself feeling strangely comfortable in his presence. I pulled up one of the hard chairs. As I sat, I glanced around the little room and asked, "What is this place?"

Popping lids off the food containers, Redding let his glance briefly follow mine. "Herdsmen's barracks," he replied. Studying the contents of the containers, he added with a mild but unapologetic shrug, "These people don't get many visitors, and we asked for a place where we all could quarter together." He shoved a container across the table to me, continuing nonchalantly. "Here, what does this look like to you?"

Staring down into the plastic tub, I felt the faint heat of a blush begin to creep up from the collar of my liner. It looked to me like some kind of cracker, but what I said, without looking up, was, "In there—I, uh, I'm sorry if I woke you up."

I knew he had paused to gaze at me; there was no point in trying to avoid those steady gray eyes. Even in the dimness I could see the comprehension come to him. Before he could comment, I hastily went on. "I'm sorry; I just didn't realize that you and Alexandria—"

His soft snort of laughter interrupted me; he leaned back in his chair, his expression openly amused. "Alexandria and I aren't—and we weren't," he informed me. "We were just sharing contact." I could feel my flush deepen even as Redding dipped into one of the containers, popping something that looked like some kind of dried fruit into his mouth. Chewing diligently, he added, "Alexandria's more than any mere mortal man could handle!" His brows rose slightly as he reached for another morsel. "Although I'm flattered you'd think she'd have me," he concluded with a wolfish leer.

Still embarrassed by my presumption, for a few moments I devoted myself solely to the consumption of several whole-grain crackers. They were chewy but delicious. When I looked up again, I saw that Redding was watching me with an expression that I could not quite define, except that I was certain it was not mocking. "I'm worried about her," I told him. "She's pushing herself right to the limit with this." Surprisingly, I found that my concern for the congenitally overbearing woman was quite genuine.

But Redding seemed to take my opinion with confident calm. "Alexandria's tough," he said, chewing another lump of fruit. He pushed the container across to me and helped himself to a few crackers in the process. "And she knows what she's doing." He paused, then added, "I've known her for a long time; since before you were—"

Since before you were born, my mind automatically finished for him. I sat there, a dry chunk of cracker in my mouth and apparently a good bit of my heart on my face. From the way Redding studied my expression, I knew that he had discovered there just what I knew.

His gray eyes softened, warm as ashes, and I suddenly felt very vulnerable and totally exposed in their gaze. "She told you, didn't she" he said softly.

It was not a question, but I silently nodded anyway.

Glancing away, his eyes moved to some undefined part of the dusky room. He blinked several times. When he went on, his voice was so low that it was almost a whisper. "All those years, and she never told me." His long fingers toyed absently with a fragment of cracker. "I always thought she must have known, but she never told me."

It was a little omission on Alexandria's part with which I had already dealt, however ineffectually, and yet I found then that I had nothing I could say to Redding to comfort him.

And so I merely hesitated, awkwardly swallowing the wad of thick cracker while he studied the food containers with a certain blank intensity and composed himself. His hands fell quiescent, the crumbled cracker clenched in his fingers, his eyes still without focus. When he spoke again, his voice was low but surprisingly level.

"That was a crazy time then—for her, for me, for all of us." He deliberately reined in his gaze, forcing his eyes to return to my face. "I'd just gotten a job offer from Teitelbaum's; it would have given me a shot at a captaincy. And she was trying to help Alexandria, and starting to get so mixed up in—"

Redding broke off, dusting the bits of cracker crumbs from his long, sinewy fingers. A touch of the old familiar irony kindled in his eyes and pulled at the quirky curve of his mouth as he went on. "She encouraged me to take Teitelbaum's offer."

His shoulder hitched in a small shrug. "I just didn't realize it was her way of telling me good-bye."

I'm sure there was more he could have told me, but he had already revealed more than I ever would have expected from him. And there was a lot I could have told him as well. I could have told him that he had never been a random factor in my conception, that she had chosen him deliberately. But then, I think he already knew that. And I could have told him the one thing that only I was able to say: that I was convinced, finally and utterly, that she had chosen well: But when I did speak, I only asked him, "Where do we go from here?"

I realized that there were several ways that question could be interpreted, and I was relieved that Redding chose to take me literally. His eyes flicked up again, and he quickly popped what appeared to be some kind of nut into his mouth. Chewing, he replied, "Coldwell, to start with. There's a supply caravan leaving here in the morning, and they're willing to take us along."

I picked up a bit of dried fruit but did not lift it to my lips. "How far away is that?" I asked, quickly adding, "And what do you mean, 'to start with'?"

Redding shifted slightly in his chair; the wooden joints creaked softly beneath his lanky frame. His long legs were stretched out beneath the table, so close to me that if I'd moved my knee a few inches, I could have nudged him. He dug into the nut container again, casually spilling half a handful into the side of his mouth. "About four hundred kilometers due south," he answered. "It's a bigger settlement in a more temperate zone." He made a vague gesture with one hand. "More tillage, some craft industry—leatherwork, woolens, that kind of thing."

Eyeing him, the piece of dried fruit still suspended in my hand, I prompted, "Is that where the Class Tens are?"

Swallowing what he'd been chewing, Redding just shook his head. "They were," he said before I could question him further. "Apparently they moved from there when the news came out about what happened at Camelot."

He seemed so utterly calm about the fact that for a few moments I could only stare at him, mildly confounded by his seeming lack of any sense of urgency about a quest that had already taken us halfway across the quadrant and seen us nearly killed. Finally I had to ask, "Well, do you know where they would have gone, then?"

Licking his fingers, Redding just shook his head again. "No," he offered, "but someone at Coldwell probably does. There are people there who have been helping the Tens since Alexandria brought them here. If we make contact with those people, they can lead us to the Tens." He paused, popping more nuts into his mouth. "Assuming, of course, we don't bring the renegades along with us."

I gently squeezed the bit of dried fruit between my fingertips. "What do you think happened out there?" I asked him quietly, indicating the prairie with a vague little tip of my head. "Why did that air car drop back?"

Redding just shrugged, a gesture I had learned did not necessarily mean indifference on his part. "Thermal scanner, maybe," he suggested.

"Not exactly standard equipment on an air car," I reminded him.

"No? Don't forget who we're dealing with," he said. Then he indicated the piece of fruit I still held in my hand. "I'd chow down if I were you," he advised. "Breakfasts on this planet are a pretty dreary affair."

I tossed the fruit into my mouth and began to chew vigorously. "How dreary can real food be?" I muttered.

But Redding just grinned at me. "Well, I can tell you one thing: it won't be bacon and eggs. No coffee, either—Tachs don't drink it." He scooped up another handful of nuts, concluding, "Lots of whole-grain breads and legumes; this time of the year, maybe some potatoes."

Actually, that all sounded pretty good to me. I was mortally weary of formedfood, and shipping with Raydor had given me a taste for the Tachs' penchant for complex carbohydrates. But what I said as I calmly surveyed Redding's bland expression was, "You've been here before, haven't you?"

"Yeah," he responded immediately, crunching on the nuts. "Now and then, over the years. Used to run quite a bit of freight out of here at one time."

I straightened in my chair, regarding the lanky brown-haired man with renewed interest. "Freight?" I echoed, my brows rising. "*You* were a black marketeer?"

That mobile upper lip curled, showing just the sharp white edge of his teeth. "Independent contractor," he corrected, then he gave a brief, indifferent shrug. "It's good business for the Tachs; I paid them three times what those vipers from the Commerce Commission would allow them."

Technically he was a criminal, but ethically he was right. The A's brutal regulation of all trade on Interdicted worlds, especially Earthheart, with its wealth of real food and other natural products, was a direct invitation to piracy. If not for profiteers like Redding, the Tachs might never have made it economically, particularly in the crucial early years of settlement. I think the only thing that really bothered me about his disclosure was Redding's seemingly limitless capacity to come up with revelations that could surprise me.

I stifled a yawn. Suddenly the coming dawn was entirely too near, and the thought of being able even to just snuggle up with Lewis again presented a beguiling alternative.

Redding seemed to have read the thought right off my sleepy face. "Go on, hit the sack while you still can," he advised me. "Tomorrow we go native." As I got to my feet again and turned to start back toward the communal sleeping quarters, he said after me, "I hope you look good in leather!"

The next time it was Lewis who woke me—quite intentionally, I hoped. Moving against me, his sinewy limbs stretching, he gently brought me to consciousness. In the dim light, I looked across the pillow into those incredible blue eyes, his face only inches from mine.

Wordlessly, one of his slender hands slid up into that small, warm space between our bodies, and he caressed the long, curved plane of my side. Then, lids dropping, his head bent forward, his mouth reaching to meet mine.

The creaking of the room's wooden door was as abrupt and startling as a blast of beam fire, and it separated us just as efficiently. Our heads jerked apart so suddenly that I nearly fractured my nose on Lewis's chin. Glancing quickly around the semidarkened room, I realized the rest of the beds were already empty. That discovery would have been a pleasant surprise had not Asplundh been just coming in through the doorway.

The geneticist was dressed in a tunic and trousers, an unfamiliar combination of bulky woolens and suede leather that gave her the appearance of an underfed child clothed in some adult Tachs's castoffs. She entered the room cautiously, stopping when she saw we both were awake. "I'm sorry," she said, "but everyone else is already eating." Her mouth crimped in a little grimace. "And Alexandria was threatening to come in here and wake you two herself, so I . . ." She trailed off with an apologetic shrug, seeing that further explanation was probably unnecessary.

Lewis smiled affably at her. ''Tell Alexandria we'll be right out,'' he told her.

As Asplundh slipped back out of the room, I darted my head forward again, fervently capturing Lewis's mouth. As I reluctantly pulled back again, he caught one of my hands and quickly led it down the front of his suit liner. His cerulean eyes were bright, his cheeks slightly flushed, as he pressed my eager fingers against the insistent bulge that curved beneath the thin fabric. I felt an electric jolt of excitement go through me. ''There better be more where that came from,'' I teased.

Lewis redressed in the simple woolen shirt and leather pants he had worn the night before. I pulled on the clothing that had been laid out for me: a heavy woven tunic and suede trousers that were very similar to what Asplundh had been wearing. We both wore soft-soled leather boots that laced up the front. They were farmer's clothes, tough and practical, and although up close none of us would have been mistaken for Tachs, from a distance we now blended in. The last thing I did before we left the room was transfer the contents of my flightsuit's pockets to the belt pouch of my tunic.

Out in the commons area two of the wooden tables had been shoved together to accommodate our group's meal. Only Asplundh and Alexandria were still seated, however. And Redding had been right about the food; everything on the heavily laden tables was vegetable in origin. Taylor was standing stiffly near the front door. He greeted us with an amiable smile, but I could tell that he and Alexandria had already been locking horns over something. Redding, standing at a point midway between the two of them, seemed in my absence to have been forced into the role of a mediator. Looking up from her plate, Asplundh threw Lewis and me a quick, surreptitious look of wary resignation. He and I had barely sat down when the argument resumed in full force.

''Just because we haven't detected them again doesn't mean they aren't still following us,'' Alexandria said, waving her spoon for emphasis.

''But we've still got contact with Handy,'' Taylor responded, his voice level but dogged. ''If they were still on our trail, don't you think he'd pick up on it?''

I hated to be the one to correct him, especially in front of Alexandria, but I figured Taylor would take less offense if the challenge came from me, so I quickly pointed out, ''Only if they came close enough to reveal an obvious pattern.'' I took a hurried bite out of the thick slab of bread I'd snagged off one of the plates. "With all the Commerce Commission surveillance on this planet, there's a hell of a lot of routine air traffic even in these remote areas. Handy can't call us on every bit of vehicular movement he scans, even if it is near us."

"And you can bet those renegades aren't going to make the same mistake twice," Redding drawled, seemingly relieved to step down as referee. "Now that they've discovered we have a way of detecting them if they tail us too close, they're going to drop back."

"But they can't drop back too far," Taylor insisted. His hands were curled around a big earthenware mug, but I hadn't seen him drink out of it. His prosaic outfit of homespun and leather seemed curiously at odds with the stubborn edge in his voice. "No matter how they're tailing us, they'd lose us."

"I still think we should split up," Alexandria announced, dropping her spoon to the table with a clatter.

"No." The dissenting word came from both Redding and me at the same time, but I decided to let him be the one to tackle her proposal.

"It wouldn't help," Redding told her calmly. His hands spread evocatively. "And it's too risky."

"Risky or not, it just might be our only chance to trip up these bastards," she maintained.

I thought I knew what she had in mind. When you were being hunted, sometimes the only thing you could do was try to turn the tables and start hunting the hunters. If some of us split off or stayed back, we might have a chance of detecting whoever would follow the first group. But I also realized that Redding was right; we were hardly in a position to try to outgun an opponent with the kind of resources those renegades had demonstrated they had.

"We can't afford to underestimate these people," Redding said, as if he had read my mind. "They could just as easily follow two groups as one, and with good equipment and a little luck, they could still keep on evading our detection." He looked meaningfully from Taylor to Alexandria. "We stick together," he concluded.

Popping a sizable chunk of some kind of cream-colored vegetable matter into her mouth, Alexandria chewed with determination and then proclaimed obstinately, "I don't like it."

But Redding just grinned, the faint scar on his face crinkling.

"I don't like it, either, Alexandria," he said, "but it's what we've got."

While the others outfitted themselves in woolen greatcoats and gloves and Redding slipped out to confer with the Tachs, Lewis and I finished wolfing down a hasty breakfast. The warm haven of our bed was fast becoming only a memory. And although I was hungry and the food was welcomely real and actually quite tasty, the mealtime topic of conversation had taken its toll, and I found myself just methodically stuffing myself with little regard for what I was eating. Alexandria had been right, too, I was forced to concede. And all the unanswered questions and continuing threats still hung like a cloud in my mind.

The renegades might have figured out we would come to Earthheart for assistance, but that still didn't explain how the hell they had picked up on us so easily once we'd made planetfall. They hadn't counted on Handy's surveillance, so they'd made a mistake when they'd tailed us so closely from the station at Dayne's Prairie. But as Redding had also pointed out, those people hadn't gotten where they were by being stupid or by failing to learn from their mistakes. And Redding's assessment of their abilities had brought up another thought, one I was reluctant to consider. If the renegades had figured out how we had detected them out on the plains, then they would know enough to be looking for our ship. It was unlikely they would have to worry about spreading themselves too thin; they had the kind of resources we couldn't hope to match. As I saw it, sitting there glumly chewing on a chunk of fruitbread, about the only advantages we had over them were that we had at least a general idea of where to seek the Class Tens and that the renegades were probably even more eager than we were to continue to avoid the legitimate Authorities on-planet. Somehow, it didn't seem to add up to much of an edge.

When we had finished eating, Lewis and I joined the others outside the herdsmen's barracks. I was pleasantly surprised to find that the climate at Springcamp was a considerable improvement over the prairie station's. The morning was brisk and bright. The air was cold, but it was sunny, and there was only a sprinkling of snow dusting the short tufts of grass that dotted the flat yard. The little settlement stood on a gently rolling plain barren of trees or any other landmarks. There were some large cultivated areas that must have been planted with crops in season. The barracks was one of about forty or fifty low, stoutly built buildings that I could see from where we stood. Some of the others looked like storehouses or barns, but most of them appeared to be residences. The structures weren't arranged linearly but were scattered in random clusters; the roads or throughways just wound casually around to accommodate all of them. A sense of anarchy against the grid concept of building placement; it shouldn't have surprised me at all, coming from the Tachs, who had waged the galaxy's longest-running and most successful rebellion against conformity.

Other than the men by the trucks, the settlement seemed strangely deserted. Alexandria and Asplundh stood together near one of the adjacent buildings, deep in conversation. Taylor stood apart from them, seemingly preoccupied with some obscure detail of Tachs architecture. On the roadway in front of the barracks, a string of eight heavyweight carriers—quite similar to the cattle carrier we had managed to destroy out on the prairie— were parked head to tail. Raydor and Redding stood beside the lead truck, talking to a small group of Tachs. On Authority-regulated worlds you never saw Tachs Altereds without the face wraps; the coverings were mandated by the A's to conceal their so-called deformities. And yet the sight of so many unwrapped Tachs faces was not what gave me pause; it took me a few moments to realize that what seemed to be out of place about the scene was that several of the men were not Altereds.

I guess I had always known that not all the Tachs were Class Fours or less or, rather, what would have been classified as Fours or less had the Tachs chosen to leave their homeworld and take up the burden of Citizenship that would have allowed the system to be applied to them. But I had never seen an unAltered Tachs, and I had to make a real effort not to stare at them. Most of the Altered Tachs resembled Raydor, with his crepelike hairless skin, rudimentary nose, and dark, prominent eyes. The physical differences, particularly the pronounced facial changes, were to me so much a part of what came to mind when I thought of a Tachs that it took a deliberate act of will to see the obvious resemblance in those normal faces. And they were indeed normal, not Normal. The Tachs as a sect did not believe in cosmetic Restructuring any more than they believed in Classification or hypothalamic alteration. Besides, even had I not known that fact, the faces of those Tachs were far too imperfect, too delightfully unique, too filled with individual detail to be anything but normal.

Raydor was continuing to confer with the men, but Redding had moved off, strolling casually alongside the line of carriers.

Just as I was debating joining him, Raydor turned and gestured to me. Giving Lewis a small shrug, I left him and walked over to where they stood by the lead truck. A quick glance showed me that Redding was still wandering among the vehicles, appraising them with the almost studied indifference of a potential buyer.

Raydor did not reach out to touch me in any way, but as I came up beside him, I stood close enough to his familiar bulk to make our relationship clear to those men and he made no move to dispel the impression of fraternal solidarity that I'd created. "These are the men who'll be taking us to Coldwell," he told me. Then he introduced me to all of them. I would have had to confess that most of their names didn't really register with me; most Tachs names tended to sound like machinery parts, anyway, and I doubted if I could have put names to half their faces even five minutes later. But there werc two men, normals, who obviously were brothers, and I made a special effort to remember the names Raydor attached to those broad, strongly hewn faces. The eldest, Harley, was the man in charge of the supply caravan. His younger brother, Traeger, was unusually tall even for a Tachs and had surprisingly reddish-colored hair. Then again, to me, any hair on a Tachs seemed surprising.

Harley reached out one huge gloved hand to me; it easily engulfed mine. He had Tachs eyes, wide and dark, with very little white showing, and long brown hair that fell to his shoulders in loose ringlets. Beneath his woolly coat, his chest looked as broad as the barracks door. As he pumped my arm, he said heartily, "So, you're the one who wants to see the chicks."

"Chicks?" I repeated blankly. The word seemed vaguely familiar, but for a few moments I had trouble placing it in context and glanced over to Raydor for help.

"Yeah," Raydor prompted me, gesturing back to where Lewis still stood where I had left him, outside the herdsmen's barracks. "I explained to Harley how you and Lewis would really like a chance to ride in the back of the incubator truck with the chicks."

If it hadn't been that Raydor's stolid face was totally deadpan, I think I would have begun to blush as comprehension suddenly came to me. "Oh, right—the chicks," I quickly agreed. I gave Harley my most winning look. "Lewis and I haven't had a chance to see any chicks yet since we've gotten here," I told him with complete sincerity.

Beside Harley, Traeger was giving me a disarmingly perceptive look; he appeared to be about as close to grinning as a Tachs ever got. And Harley prefaced his response with a snort of patent skepticism. "Just don't spook the chicks," he said gruffly.

The supply caravan would be driving to Coldwell nearly empty, Raydor explained. Basically it was a run to pick up materials there that were needed in Springcamp. At this time of the year very little was produced at the smaller settlement for trade with the larger community to the south. We would be carrying some root crops, miscellaneous items made by the local craftsmen, and, in a specially heated vehicle at the end of the convoy, a shipment of newly hatched chickens. Apparently there was a fairly large hatchery in Springcamp, and the shipments were a regular cargo. The human cargo would be an unusual shipment, but there was plenty of room for us, and it seemed like the safest, least conspicuous way for us to travel to Coldwell.

By the time we were ready to roll, I was no longer paying attention to which vehicles Raydor and the others got into. The incubator truck was parked at the end of the line, and Lewis followed me to it with a perplexed look on his face. Harley himself accompanied us, unlocking the rear door of the carrier with a flourish. As Lewis boosted me up the steep step, the big Tachs straightforwardly reminded me and my puzzled companion, "Don't rile up those chickens, now."

Once we were inside, Lewis's expression quickly turned from confusion to delight. "Look, baby chickens!" he enthused, his face boyishly alight as he spun around in the truck's wide central aisle. On three sides of us the cargo area was stacked from floor to ceiling with individually lit and heated trays of golden, fluffy, incredibly animated chicks. It was undoubtedly the greatest number of animals I had ever seen together in one place. It would have been hard not to share Lewis's sense of exuberant wonder, but sometimes there were things even more precious than live animals.

"Yeah, cute," I murmured, reaching up to sling my arms around his shoulders. I buried my face in the soft, sweet-smelling skin of his neck. "We'll look at them later."

As he suddenly became fully aware of just what we'd been handed—by Raydor, Harley, and whatever gods you chose to believe in—Lewis's mood quickly adapted to mine. "Yeah," he echoed compliantly, his mouth brushing across my cheek to my ear, "later."

Eagerly embracing him, I laughed softly. "Do you think we should at least wait until we get under way?"

"No," Lewis replied, "we've waited long enough."

Our sheepskin coats spread on the aisle of the cargo hold made a surprisingly luxurious bed. And although we started out slowly, still fully clothed and just kissing, none of those conditions lasted for long. There was an urgency beating in me, but it was not quite the same urgency I had felt those first times with him. Then, I had been so frightened of what I had felt for him that I had been unwilling to admit it in any other way but that wordless and physically graphic act of joining with him. Maybe I was still afraid, but I was willing to accept that fear as part of the price of loving him. I still wanted him just as badly, but for a different reason. After what had happened between us with Lillard on Camelot, when his mind had briefly become a part of mine, I was sure of Lewis. And after what I had felt when I had first seen him again out on that storm-swept prairie, I finally was sure of myself.

Naked, skin against skin, he could not hold himself back. An unwilling moan escaped him as he slid fiercely over me. His body felt hot, slippery, like wet silk over steel. He tried to make it last both for my sake and for his own, but his urgency was too great. He held himself back as long as he could, even though I knew I was goading him mercilessly, shamelessly. But the strength of his desire and the intensity of his passion were part of what made him so desperately attractive to me, and when he finally did let himself go, his selfless zeal was complete and unstinting. His last thrusts were helplessly furious, almost uncontrolled; my name came from his lips in a long, pleading moan. At the final moment he was nearly motionless, buried deeply, clinging tightly to me. And that time, for all the intensity of emotion I felt, I didn't cry; I had no reason to weep.

We clung together, breathing raggedly, our bodies slick with perspiration in the hot, bright little space. I was amused to notice we had collected a faint dusting of chick fluff, sticking to our bare limbs like fuzzy down. Lewis tried to stay in me as long as he could, but everything has its limits, and post coital adhesion had never seemed to be high on nature's list of priorities. He had to content himself with holding me closely, one hand gently caressing my face and hair while our thundering pulses gradually returned to normal. At first I tried to resist the overwhelming stupor that came with the warmth of the compartment and the utter relaxation and comfort of my postorgasmic state. I even tried to distract myself by concentrating on the odd little things like the creeping liquid trickle across the

inner surface of my thigh and the way his body hair lightly
scratched me as our breathing bumped our bodies together. But
it was no use; against my will, I dozed off.

I had no idea how long I slept or if Lewis even slept at all. I
awoke to the touch of his slender hands on my breasts; smiling
happily at me, he began to use his mouth. The second time was
even better than the first: slow, smooth, and sweet. We found a
mutual rhythm that made each sensation a distinct step, building
in a series of teasing stops and surging starts toward a stunning
release. We wanted to begin a third time—Powers knew, our
spirits were willing—but his body proved, at least temporarily,
to be refractory. And so we lay on our sides, facing each other,
lightly touching at chest, belly, and thighs, content to wait. Our
faces were only inches apart, his dilated blue eyes intently
searching mine.

"I wonder how far out of Coldwell we still are," I mused
lazily, my hand slipping around his waist. The floor of the vehicle vibrated slightly beneath us; I had no concept of how long
the caravan had been under way. When Lewis's only response
was to plant a trailing kiss along the angle of my jaw, I added
judiciously, "I just hope Redding had the foresight to separate
Taylor and Alexandria for this trip."

Graciously acquiescing to my obvious penchant for conversation, Lewis brushed back a damp tendril of my hair from my
brow and offered, "She doesn't seem to have a very good opinion of your friend."

The tactful understatement in his observation caused me to
be blunter than the situation warranted. "Yeah? Well, she thinks
I've been joining with him," I responded without thinking.

But Lewis seemed completely unruffled by my insensitive
remark. He was touching my brows, delicately tracing their curve
with his fingertips, as if there were something innately fascinating about their very conformation. His own body—firm, naked,
still flushed—was so beautiful that I was still amazed that he
would offer it to me. And when he replied to my crude statement, his own jet-colored brows were lifted quizzically. "She's
usually more perceptive than that," he said, as if Alexandria's
oversight and not her accusation were what really concerned
him.

I looked directly into those incredible eyes. "Then you didn't
think—" I began.

"Jo, he's your friend," Lewis said simply, his forefinger following the curve of my lip, effectively silencing me. "I'm very

grateful to him for all the help he's given you. And yes, I know he loves you. So do Raydor and Alexandria and Redding.''

Relieved, I nipped playfully at his fingertip. "Raydor, yes," I admitted. "Alexandria, I'd be less sure of, and Redding—" I broke off, suddenly studying that familiar face with a new intensity. "You know about me and Redding, don't you?" I put it to him quietly.

On one of the many trays above us a brief altercation broke out, and cheeping chicks loudly squabbled in a miniature flurry of down. As the fuss died down again, Lewis cupped my chin in his hand. "He told me on Heinlein, when he knew for sure," he said slowly, "but I think I knew before that." There was an oddly intense but introspective look on his face. "On Camelot, when I touch-healed him . . ." He paused, as if he were uncertain how to explain something that obviously defied rational explanation. "I *felt* something about him, Jo," he finished softly, "something that made me know he was connected to you."

Random bits of my conversation with Asplundh in the groundcar bay came back to me then, unwillingly and with the indiscriminate force of a scattered blast of beam fire. *Think what it would mean, Jo . . .* Just what was Lewis capable of? The possibilities both excited and terrified me. I reached up and lightly clasped his wrist on the hand that framed my chin. "Lewis," I said hesitantly, "on Camelot, in the research complex, when you—when that guard wounded you and you—"

Grimacing, Lewis tensed in my arms. "That was awful!" he stated emphatically.

"But you said you hadn't known you could do that," I persisted, still holding his wrist. I regretted the painful memories I had just forced him to relive, but I was unable to back off then. "If you didn't know you could do that, do you think there might be other things—other kinds of physical reorganization—that you could do by touch-healing?"

The look on that unshuttered face was a mixture of mild puzzlement and anxious unease. His body stirred slightly, abruptly exposing more of my damp skin to the air. Suddenly I wanted to take back the words I had just spoken—cancel the question, just rewind the last part of that conversation and entirely shift topics—but there was no way to unsay what had already been said. Shit! What was it about that sweet and trusting torpor of afterglow, that gentle hiatus after joining when two people should just shut up and enjoy it, that instead seemed to drive them to all sorts of impulsive and tactless confessions?

Lewis's fingers curled, slipping down to twine with mine. He squeezed my hand urgently. "Jo, there's something that I have to tell you."

No, not now! I wanted to tell him, No matter what it is, any time but now! But I felt as helplessly driven as he was. "Listen, there's something I need to talk with you about, too," I whispered.

But he got ahead of me, hastily beginning, "On Camelot, when you fed that chip of my memories into Lillard, I regained more than just what had been recorded, I regained all of the past that I'd lost." A little shudder ran through him, and his fingers tightened again on mine. "There are things that I remember now, things about myself that you should know, and I—"

"No!" I interrupted him more vehemently than I had intended.

Taken aback by my protest, for a moment Lewis just gazed at me in mild surprise. Then, before either one of us could speak again, there was a loud thumping sound on the rear door of the incubator truck, and a familiar voice called out my name. Ironically, rather than reaching for our clothing or any kind of covering, the first reaction both Lewis and I had was to pull ourselves up and reach for the interior release for the door.

Cool air streamed in over our naked bodies, but Raydor's bulk filled most of the doorway, blocking it. The carrier was still moving slowly as he swung up onto the rear step of the vehicle. With him there was no need for any false modesty or sense of embarrassment about the circumstances in which he'd found us, but by the same token, there was also no need for him to be apologetic about having interrupted us. Although his broad, Altered face might have appeared expressionless to others, I could read the subtle urgency etched in his creased brow and the tension sparking in those huge dark eyes.

"You got Handy's relay?" he said tersely.

Nodding, I dropped back onto my knees on the sheepskin coats and searched for my tunic amid the jumbled pile of our discarded clothing.

"What is it?" I heard Lewis ask him quietly, but Raydor did not reply.

Groping in my belt pouch, I tugged out the little device. My eyes lifted to Raydor's where he loomed above us in the opened doorway.

"Can you raise him?" he asked me.

I glanced over at Lewis for a second, then back up to Raydor's face. "On the emergency frequency," I said, starting to feel the first tiny prickles of adrenaline nibbling through my veins. "But I don't want to risk—"

"Try it," Raydor interrupted me, his deep voice dead level.

I punched the code into the relay as I knelt there staring at the tiny display screen. My skin quivered with gooseflesh, and my nipples ached, but it was not just from the cool air.

"We received a distress signal from *Kestrel*," Raydor continued grimly. "Then nothing."

Nothing. Repunching the code, I stared at the blank screen on the small rectangle in my hand.

Raptor, too, was gone.

CHAPTER
ELEVEN

I was not sure exactly when I had started thinking of Handy and *Raptor* as one and the same, but it had been for so long that to me the ship almost seemed to possess a plural pronoun: they, not she. The freighter and the Integrator were so much a part of each other that I could not imagine either one existing independently of the other. Handy's directive was both to protect *Raptor* and to protect us at all times. When I had put him on independent mode back at Dayne's Prairie, I had essentially forced him into a situation where he might have to choose between us and the ship. If the ship was in immediate peril and we were not, then it was his duty to save *Raptor*, even if that meant pulling out from Earthheart. Whatever had happened up there, I was certain he had done only that with which I had always charged him: whatever he had to do.

"It doesn't necessarily mean anything has happened to the ship," I said with a calmness that had more basis in instinct than in fact. "We can't even be sure that he's pulled out; all we know is that he's had to move her out of the range of this relay."

We had all assembled in the cargo hold of one of the larger ground trucks, an area only partially filled with crates of craft items. The caravan was still in motion, but two of the Tachs had joined us, Traeger and an Altered, a silently watchful man who I was surprised to find that I remembered was named Cam.

Lewis and I had dressed in such haste that my unfamiliar Tachs clothing was still dusted with bits of chick down. I shifted my weight on the crate where I was seated and caught Raydor's eye. Then, elaborating for everyone's benefit, I said, "If there'd been any damage to the ship, I would have gotten a distress signal from him."

"If you would have heard it," Alexandria remarked.

I threw her a sharp look, but it was Redding who noted evenly, "She'd've heard it. Hell, you just heard for yourself how loud those damned things are when *Kestrel*'s went off." To me he said, "What's the range on that thing?"

I used the relay's own circuit to calculate it and showed him the figure on the screen. He gave a low whistle. "Pretty far out," he noted.

"He'd pull out if he had to," I maintained levelly, "but even if he did, he'd come right back in." I didn't bother to point out that *Kestrel* hadn't had the option of escape. The Services' yacht had been fitted with the standard remote control; she could be sent back out into orbit and retrieved again, but she could not have evaded a pursuer independently. The aborted distress signal meant one of two things: Either she had been seized by the A's or she'd been destroyed by the renegades.

Taylor and Asplundh were sharing a seat on one of the larger crates. The geneticist looked tense and anxious, both quite understandable reactions given the situation. But Taylor had a more thoughtful look on his face, as if he were considering some abstract problem of theoretical physics.

"How far are we from Coldwell?" I asked of no one in particular.

"About ten kilometers yet," Traeger promptly replied.

"Well, we're going to have to go on like we planned, ship or no ship," Alexandria said. "There's nothing we can do for *Raptor*, and there sure as shit isn't anything more we can do about *Kestrel*."

Touchingly put, but so true, I thought morosely. And I had been the one who had said I wanted to keep my ship out of danger. To my chagrin, I realized that I had been counting on her to keep *us* out of danger as well.

"Maybe there is," Taylor remarked quietly into the brief pause in the discussion.

For a moment no one spoke. Alexandria was the first one to recognize that his comment had been made in reference—and direct contradiction—to her last statement. "What do you mean, 'maybe there is'?" she demanded.

Taylor gave a little shrug, spreading his hands. "There must be some kind of a transmitting station in this area, right?" he said, not just to her but to the group in general. "There's communication between these settlements, so they must have the equipment and the parts. What if we could find the components we needed to boost your relay so that we could reach Handy again, even if he's way the hell out, coming in on coast?''

The idea made sense; it even held some promise. I could see that Alexandria was as annoyed as hell. I looked to where Traeger and Cam stood by the cargo hold's door. "Is there a transmitting station anywhere near Coldwell?" I asked them hopefully.

''There's a signal booster station near the egg farm,'' Traeger said, ''where we deliver the chicks.'' His broad face creased with a frown. ''It's just a local facility, though; I don't know if they'd have much of anything you could use.''

I exchanged a quick look with Raydor. He was beyond a doubt the closest thing to a communications expert we had, and I had seen him work miracles with far fewer resources. His big shoulders hitched slightly. ''It's worth a try,'' he said simply.

Stepping to the front of the hold, Traeger popped the release on the hatch to the driver's compartment and held a quick conference with the Tachs who was operating the truck. Pulling back into the hold, he announced, ''We'd better hurry, then; the incubator truck is just about ready to turn off for the egg farm.''

Traeger's use of the inclusive pronoun ''we'' had not escaped my notice. And as I passed Handy's relay to Raydor, Taylor hopped down off his perch on the craft's crate and said, ''I'll go, too.''

As could have been predicted, Alexandria's response to that offer was immediate and deprecating. ''You're not here to play with the little chickies, Slick,'' she told him. ''You'd better stick with us.''

To my surprise, and probably to Taylor's as well, it was Raydor who came to his defense. ''He knows more about transmitters and multiple-core circuits than any of the rest of you,'' he said evenly but pointedly. ''He'll be of a lot more use to me than to you, Alexandria.''

Traeger just looked from Raydor to Alexandria with barely concealed impatience; Cam was already opening the rear door. ''Whoever's coming, we'd better get going,'' he said. ''That incubator truck isn't going to wait.''

As Taylor moved past me, he quickly bent and planted a light kiss on my forehead. ''Wish me luck!'' He grinned, then he followed the other three men through the opened door, dropped off the end of the truck, and was gone.

''Luck!'' Alexandria snarled in frustration, as if Taylor had uttered an obscenity in parting.

But Redding, turning from relatching the rear door, just flashed her one of his all-purpose wolfish smirks. "Hell, Alexandria, we're stuck down here now without a support ship. Call it what you want, but I figure we can use all the help we can get."

Cargo carriers weren't exactly designed for sight-seeing, and riding in the back, we had missed most of the passing scenery. The convoy of vehicles slowed its pace and made several turns before finally grinding to a halt. My first impression of the settlement as we climbed out from the truck's rear cargo hold made me think that Coldwell was a misnomer. Dayne's Prairie had been arctic; Springcamp had been cold; by comparison, Coldwell's climate was downright balmy. The air temperature was pleasant, and the surrounding land was lush with green.

The line of carriers was parked on a broad lot or courtyard that served an entire square of sprawling one-story buildings. We obviously were well within the settlement, because the area was surrounded by rows and blocks of similar buildings. Never before had I been in a community where all the structures were built so low to the ground. If not for the addition of their rather steeply pitched roofs, the whole community's buildings would have looked unfinished, as if construction were still under way.

Alexandria noted my bemusement and gave me a cryptic snort. But before I could ask any questions, Asplundh tugged at my sleeve and said, "Look, no formblock or composite." She pointed to one of the nearest structures and continued, "It's all rock, or native brick, or real wood."

While Alexandria and Redding strode off along the line of trucks, apparently to confer with the Tachs drivers, Lewis slowly turned in place, scanning Coldwell's architecture. "I wonder why they've built everything so low," he mused, scuffing the uneven paving of the courtyard with the toe of his leather boot.

"They probably have a lot of tornadoes," I said, facetiously, realizing even as I said it that it was quite possibly the truth.

From the angle of the sun, I guessed it was just past midday. The air was warm enough that I was seriously looking forward to getting out of my heavy woolen and leather clothing and into something more seasonable. I scanned across the wide expanse of buildings, throughways, and small courtyards to the land beyond the settlement. We were surrounded by vast, gently rolling hills checkered with neat patches of gold and brown and green, crisscrossed by dark lines of what I could only assume were trees. Set into the hills, I could with further study just barely make out the blocky shapes of other structures, probably agricultural in purpose.

When I glanced over at Asplundh again, I saw that the geneticist was gazing around us with an almost reverential look on her pale oval face. "Isn't it beautiful?" she said happily.

Giving her the benefit of the doubt, I presumed she meant the whole settlement, not just the adjacent buildings. Briefly surveying the distant panorama again, I nodded in agreement and replied, "Yeah, it's nice." I tactfully refrained from mentioning that it would have been a hell of a lot nicer if we hadn't happened to be Citizens on an Interdicted world or if we weren't being pursued by renegades and hadn't lost contact with our ship. I gave her the moment. Something—or someone—would take it away from her soon enough.

Perhaps that someone would even be Alexandria or Redding. I saw they both were beckoning to us then from the head of the caravan. As we reached them, Alexandria said, "There's someone here who can help us if Harley can contact them. For now, though, we'd better get inside." She began walking, and we automatically fell into step. "There only are a few Authority personnel stationed in Coldwell, but one would be all it'd take if they spotted us here."

"Authority personnel?" Asplundh echoed, puzzled. "But I thought Earthheart was unregulated."

"It is," Alexandria responded, pausing to push open the heavy real-wood door on one of the squat buildings that lined the square. "Officially," she added as she ducked through the doorway.

The building we entered appeared to be some kind of eatery or common house. Actually, what it most resembled was what they used to call a tavern back when ethanol was used for effect. A long serving counter stretched along one entire wall, with plenty of tables and chairs scattered throughout the rest of the wide, low-ceilinged room. All the furnishings were made of real wood, and many of them were quite ornate. Once again I was surprised to find that a good number of the Tachs patrons, perhaps even the majority of them, were normals.

"The A's personnel here are Commerce Commission workers," Redding went on quietly as we stood together in a small cluster near the establishment's door. "The Tachs would never betray us, but those Ceecee workers aren't so stupid that they'd fail to notice we're off-worlders if they ran into us on the throughway.'' He gestured casually to one of the empty wooden tables. ''That's why we're better off waiting in here,'' he concluded, dropping down into a chair.

Sitting across the table from him, with Lewis seated beside me, I glanced surreptitiously around the big room. Most of its occupants were eating or at least drinking something from thick earthenware mugs. With their tanned and stolid normal faces and the roughweave farmers' garb they wore, they almost looked like a scene out of some ancient vid of Old Earth's American West: townfolk gathering at the local saloon. All that was missing was a smoky card game or a glitzy piano player . . . or a grim sheriff and the obligatory shoot-out, I thought morbidly.

''Who are we waiting for?'' I felt compelled to ask, even though direct questions had never gotten me too far before where Alexandria was concerned.

But it was Redding who replied. ''A local woman,'' he said. ''She lives near where we want to go, so we can follow her out there.''

For the first time I noticed that all the Tachs in the large room were men. It was only then that I realized I had never even seen a Tachs woman.

Asplundh was still gazing around the establishment with open appreciation. ''It's amazing, isn't it?'' she remarked, running her hand over the polished surface of the table. ''All this wood and ceramics and leather!''

I knew that Lewis shared to at least some degree her enthusiasm for natural things, but he seemed to be making a deliberate effort to contain his interest. He sat beside me, with Asplundh on his left, and confined his study of the room to brief glances. I didn't really understand the reason for his subdued manner, but the emotional state that I could once again read so freely from him didn't seem to be one of agitation or fear.

The heavy wooden door opened and closed a few times; men came in or went out. I hadn't seen Redding or Alexandria make any kind of signal, but presently an aging Tachs normal, who although unAltered was nevertheless almost completely bald, brought us a tray of the earthenware mugs. No payment was requested; in fact, no one in the place seemed to be paying for food or drink. I assumed the format was similar to Heinlein's numerous buffets and picnics, where food and beverages were provided gratis for those who worked in the community. I lifted one of the heavy mugs to my lips; the contents tasted like spiced cider, and it was delicious.

Lewis seemed so withdrawn that I didn't try to converse with him. I was content just to have him that near to me, his knee touching mine beneath the table, our hands just inches apart. And no one else seemed inclined to talk. It was surprisingly quiet in the whole room, considering it was half-filled with men eating and drinking. I occupied myself by covertly studying the Tachs, listening to the clink of their ceramic and metal dishes and the occasional murmur of conversation. I had been on their planet for a day already, and in that time I had traversed hundreds of kilometers of it, yet I still could not even begin to imagine what their lives were really like. What did those burly and taciturn men talk about over their cider and vegetable stew? Pirates and profiteers, anarchy and rebellion? Or last year's calf crop and the price of potatoes?

When the unusual silence at our table was beginning to get on my nerves and I was almost tempted to say something to provoke Alexandria just to shake her out of the silent funk she seemed to have fallen into, the common house door swung open again and a powerfully built Altered woman strode through. Her unswerving gaze moved immediately to where we sat, and she approached our table.

It didn't surprise me that Redding knew her, considering what he'd told me at Springcamp. But the first person to greet the big woman was Alexandria. She got abruptly to her feet and, leaning forward, seized both of the woman's muscular forearms with her beefy hands. "Brill!" she said, the intensity of her greeting giving the name a fervent emphasis.

Tachs seldom smiled, but the expression on that broad and crepelike face was a reasonable approximation of the Tachs equivalent. Brill grasped Alexandria's elbows with her own hamlike hands and gave her an enthusiastic shake. Then, spying Redding over Alexandria's shoulder, she gave a sharp bark of laughter. "Redding, you rascal!" she greeted him fondly. "I didn't think I'd ever see you again in this lifetime."

"Well, you almost didn't," Alexandria said, pulling back, but I could see that with the robust Tachs woman her brusqueness was all pretense.

Brill glanced quickly over the rest of us, but I had the distinct feeling those intense dark eyes missed few details. Her seamed and crepey face was similar to those of the other Altereds I had seen, but she had a few coarse dark hairs marking her eyebrows, and a wispy scattering of graying hair peeked out from beneath the turbanlike woven hat she wore. "Come on, then," she said, her manner as brisk as Alexandria's. "The day's on the down-side now, and I've still got work to do before dark." She gestured impatiently when Asplundh and Lewis and I did not all immediately jump to our feet. "Come on," she repeated, "my span is waiting."

If I'd been more familiar with the subtle differences in Tachs clothing styles, I might have recognized Brill's occupation from the type of trousers and overtunic she wore. As it was, I didn't make the connection until we had all stepped back out into the courtyard outside the common house and I caught sight of the half dozen shaggy creatures huddled nervously together on the crudely paved lot. They stood well over a meter high at the shoulders, with cloven hooves and long, coarse coats that hung nearly to their knees in ropy, tangled strands. I had never seen one except in educational vids, but there was only one thing they could possibly be: sheep.

Brill gave a sharp whistle, and suddenly a low shape was rocketing out from behind the tightly packed formation of sheep. If I hadn't been certain that it was a living thing and not some kind of missle, I would have jumped back out of the way, because the swift projectile aimed itself directly for us. Then, as abruptly as it had approached, the creature dropped into a crouch at Brill's feet. Tongue lolling, cinnamon-colored eyes slitted, it looked up at the big Tachs woman with keen attentiveness.

"It's a *dog*!" Asplundh exclaimed in delight.

My vid-assisted recognition of the animal was even sketchier than my recognition of the sheep, since dogs had come very close to extinction in most of the known systems. Earthheart might have been one of only two or three worlds where they even existed at all anymore. And I'm not sure even my Old Earth ancestors would have recognized the creature that was crouched before us as canine. It had a wolflike, bullet-shaped head with wide-set slanted eyes. The ears were small and tipped forward, and the tail was long and slightly flattened. The dog was covered with short, thick fur, a dun color that was brindled with darker stripes, and when it stood, I could see that its powerful shoulders were slightly taller than its haunches, so that it looked like it was going uphill. If anything, the Old Earth animal it most resembled was a hyena. But there was no doubt about the dog's function or its ability. Brill made a slight, almost imperceptible hand signal, and the dog was away again, a blur of action around the packed group of sheep. Within seconds it had all six of the woolly creatures moving again in a steady formation across the courtyard.

It took us only about ten minutes of brisk walking to clear the edge of the settlement. Once we left behind the confines of the winding throughways, I thought the sheep—which seemed by turns both placidly tractable and then obstinately skittish—would all scatter in the open fields along the roadway. But I had not reckoned with the skill of Brill's herd dog. Alternately intimidating, then cajoling, then subtly nudging the little span along, the damned dog did everything but stand up on its rear legs and whistle to keep the sheep just where it wanted them.

Both Asplundh and Lewis seemed to be totally absorbed watching with admiring fascination as the dog worked the big sheep, but I was more interested in the human interplay. Brill and Alexandria walked along together, matching their formidable strides and conversing in short, animated bursts. Redding walked slightly to one side of the pair, but they seemed to be including him in their conversation, because I heard him add an occasional comment. The three of us hung farther back and, at first anyway, were silent.

Although the sun's rays had grown weaker and more oblique, the day was still mild, and my heavy clothing became increasingly inappropriate the farther we walked. I wasn't exactly looking forward to a long hike, but I didn't see any sign of dwellings nearby. Here and there in the distance I could make out the blocky shapes of crawlers and other machinery with implements, growling along the far rows of crops. The land immediately outside the settlement was divided into cultivated plots of various sizes, ranging from about a quarter kilometer square to probably several square kilometers. Laid out in intersecting lines between many of the fields were rows of tall, slender trees, apparently planted as windbreaks. I didn't recognize the trees or any of the crops growing between them, but Asplundh did, and after a bit she began to offer a commentary on the fields as we passed them. She told us the windbreaks were made up of so-called junk trees, varieties like willow and European poplar that were unsuited for commercial use but grew rapidly and were resistant to temperature extremes and drought. I was surprised by the antiquity of some of the crops: things like cotton and flax and hemp that were probably literally no longer grown anywhere else in the galaxy but on that planet. By the time we'd been walking for a half hour, I had picked up a halfway decent working knowledge of Tachs agriculture from the curly-haired geneticist.

Lewis seemed much more at ease than he had been back in Coldwell. Besides watching the herd dog's maneuverings, he followed Asplundh's botanical explanations with avid interest, and he took in the sweeping vista of the surrounding hills with a look of genuine pleasure on his expressive face. We walked close together but had not been touching. Around the time the cultivated land began to give way to hay fields and pasture, he surprised me by reaching out and almost shyly taking my hand. When I glanced over at him, he gave me a small but significant smile, a smile that I felt all the way to the soles of my feet.

I still don't know if I would have called it "beautiful"; I was not a child of the land. I didn't think I'd ever spent more than two consecutive weeks of my adult life in any one place, and no planet ever pleased my senses the way the mesmerizing vastness of space could. But by the time we left the paved roadway behind and started up the gentle swell of a grassy hill, following a dirt track that looked like little more than a cow path, I was willing to concede that Earthheart had its merits. Once I had followed Lewis's lead and had unfastened the front of my heavy tunic to allow the breeze to reach my suit liner, the long walk had become a pleasant experience.

"Look!" Asplundh suddenly exclaimed, pointing to the swell of the next hill. "On that crest—cattle!"

Like most connoisseurs of real meat, I liked to think I had at least a passing idea of what cattle looked like, but the creatures Asplundh was pointing to forced me to rethink that notion. Then again, I guess they looked as much like cattle as that brindled hyena looked like a dog. There were about twenty of the beasts visible from where we walked, although they were scattered far enough apart to suggest that there probably were a lot more of them just over the rise of the hill, still out of our line of sight. Head on, they resembled ground carriers on legs. All of them were the identical color, with deep fawn backs and creamy pale undersides. And while there was nothing nearby that I could use for scale, their shoulders looked to be about the height of the top of my head.

"I didn't know cows were that big," I admitted, staring at them so intently that I almost tripped over a clod in the path.

"They're LaGrange," Asplundh explained enthusiastically. "It's one of the breeds the Tachs developed especially for Earthheart."

I had to concede that they certainly looked like they could have plowed their way through just about anything, including the blizzard we'd been confronted with out on the high plains. A brief and unbidden image of the abattoir came to mind, with its steel hooks and guttered floor. Like most connoisseurs of real meat, I also preferred not to dissect its origins too thoroughly. I stared down at the ground, where I finally noticed that the "clods" I'd been stumbling over were actually large dried flops of cow manure. I gave one a healthy kick and watched it fly apart.

"How come you know so much about this stuff?" I asked Asplundh curiously.

But she just gave a small, self-effacing shrug. "A lot of my lab materials come from here," she reiterated. "It's one of the systems' few suppliers of real tissue. And I've studied a lot of the earlier genetics work that was done here, right after the first settlement period, when they had to modify their existing animal stock to fit this climate and topography."

I gave her a quizzical look. "I didn't realize the Tachs were so big on genetics."

Again she gave a slight, almost dismissive shrug, her smoky-colored ringlets of hair bouncing. "Just because they reject the Genetics and Reproduction Code and Classification doesn't mean they don't believe in genetic modification as the basis of improvement for a species. They've done some really incredible things in a very short period of time by using sophisticated methods like gene splicing and cloning."

Again I was surprised. "They have the facilities for that kind of technology here, on this—"

Asplundh smiled wryly. "On this backwater, hick planet?" she finished for me. Then she nodded, gesturing toward the huge cattle, several of which had lifted their massive, blunt heads at our approach. "As a matter of fact, much of the groundwork in particle genetics was done here on Earthheart. The research that led to Riekert's Index was done here during the Tachs' development of their own strains of poultry."

The moment the words were out of her mouth, the geneticist fell suddenly silent. I met her anxious glance with a sharp look. Riekert's Chromosomal Index: the test that had led her to her disturbing discovery about Lewis's DNA. The three of us still had that unfinished bit of business between us. But when I looked sideways at Lewis, he seemed not to have reacted to the reference or to have noticed anything strange in the sudden pause in our conversation. He was studying the LaGrange, his expression one of simple fascination.

As we approached the area where most of the cattle were grazing, they slowly and casually moved away from us. Neither the dog and sheep nor the sight of a half dozen people on foot seemed to alarm them, but once they had satisfied their mild curiosity, they obviously preferred to keep their distance. We did pass near enough to several of them for me to determine that their size was not an illusion; they stood a good two meters at the shoulders and must have weighed close to fifteen hundred kilograms.

Once we had crested the long hill, several buildings were visible in the low trough of land between us and the next gradual rise. Most of them looked like some kind of livestock or equipment sheds, but at least one of the structures appeared to be a dwelling. There were clumps of a type of large tree with long, sweeping branches planted around the buildings; I recognized them then as willows. More sheep were penned in an enclosure off one of the sheds, and the closely shorn yard was alive with a bizarre assortment of brilliantly colored fowl. The chicks with which we'd shared our ride to Coldwell were far too ordinary to have ever been the antecedents of those birds. None of them looked even remotely familiar to my untrained eyes; in fact, no two of them even looked remotely alike. They had every conceivable length, texture, and hue of plumage, neck, tail, and comb. All they seemed to share in common was an industrious interest in whatever could be scratched or gleaned from the yard's short grass and earth.

Lewis and Asplundh were both delighted by the display of birds. "Look at their feathers," he said excitedly, squeezing my fingers. "They're almost iridescent!"

I had been watching Redding, Alexandria, and Brill; the three of them had slowed slightly, so that we were beginning to catch up to them as we came down the slope. Before I could reply to Lewis's remark about the birds, there was a flurry of activity from just inside the doorway of one of the larger sheds. Then animals began bursting out of the building, rocketing around in circles, yipping and barking. It was a veritable pack of the hyenalike dogs, ranging in color from near white to jet-black and in size from clumsy, long-legged pups to muscular, powerfully built adults.

Brill let out a piercing whistle, and several of the larger dogs abandoned their playful gamboling and came thundering toward us. Actually, they didn't seem especially interested in us; it was the small knot of sheep they zeroed in on. Exchanging enthusiastic greetings with Brill's brindled dog, the newcomers swiftly formed a kind of canine whirlwind, sweeping the hapless sheep on ahead of us. I was so fascinated by this spectacle that it took me a moment to notice that someone had stepped out of the shed behind the dogs; I didn't realize she was there until, with a single hand signal, she brought all of her frolicking dogs to instant attention at her heels.

The woman waved cheerily at us, and Brill waved back. We had caught up close enough to Brill then that I could hear the big Tachs say, "Well, I'm off to my place to pen these sheep; I guess you can't get lost from here."

Redding glanced back at the three of us as we came up beside him and Alexandria. "This is the woman who can help us," he explained needlessly, gesturing toward the approaching figure.

My first impression was that the woman with the dogs was the smallest Tachs I had ever seen; I don't think the top of her head would have even come up to my chin. But as she drew nearer to us, scattering the brilliantly hued poultry in her wake, I could see that she wasn't a Tachs at all. She had a lean, muscular body that was almost boyish-looking in the tightly fitted trousers and overshirt she wore. Her closely clipped dark hair did nothing to dispel that impression, but her face, smiling then in greeting, was almost delicate with its high cheekbones and wide mahogany eyes. The cavalcade of dogs followed her with absolute devotion.

"Alexandria!" she called out, her laughter giving the name a lilt I had never heard in it before. "By the Light, it's good to see you again!"

The smaller woman launched herself at Alexandria with such enthusiasm that her feet nearly left the ground. Murmuring something that was inaudible to me, Alexandria returned the dark-haired woman's embrace with genuine warmth. Then she had spun out of Alexandria's arms and into Redding's, repeating the exuberant hug and exclaiming, "You shameless pirate—they haven't caught up to you yet? I couldn't believe it when Harley told me you were with her!"

As she backed out of Redding's arms, still looking him up and down with obvious pleasure, I could see that this woman was considerably older than I had first assumed. Although she was in excellent physical condition and her normal face showed none of the telltale signs of plastic repair, she probably had a good ten or fifteen years on either Alexandria or Redding.

Still holding her hand, Redding began to introduce the three of us. Announcing our names to her, he nodded at the lithe little woman and told us, "This is Claire duFochs."

Lewis and I each shook hands with her, but Asplundh just stood motionless, a totally astonished look on her face. "*The* Claire duFochs?" she blurted out. "Of Neville's Planet? *The Theory and Practice of the Submolecular Basis of Cloning in Poultry?*"

A wide smile split Claire's tanned and fine-boned face. "The same," she confirmed, reaching out and finding Asplundh's still-dangling hand. "Though it's been a good many years since that thesis was very newsworthy. You must be the geneticist they told me about."

Torn between the mixed emotions of self-consciousness and pleasure, Asplundh vigorously pumped the older woman's hand. "It's still almost the bible in my discipline," she assured Claire, adding spontaneously, "But I didn't realize you were still on Earthheart."

"Oh, I've been retired from the rigors of academia for some time now," Claire replied with another crooked smile. As her band of dogs crowded around her slim legs, she made a broad gesture with one hand, encompassing the whole of the valley. "What better place to live out my waning years than here, where the living proof of my labors is everywhere around me?"

" 'Waning years,' my ass," Alexandria said, thumping Claire on the shoulder hard enough to almost cause the shorter woman to stagger. "You'll outlive the lot of us, you tough little runt!"

Claire's expression swiftly transformed itself from one of affable humor to one of nearly grim irony. "Sometimes I believe you're right about that, Alexandria," she said quietly, her gaze traveling over our faces in a rapid arc. At her feet, one of her dogs—a half-grown, clay-colored pup—whined impatiently for her attention. Without looking down, she reached automatically to fondle the soft ears, continuing, "My information network is still pretty much in place; I've been monitoring your progress since Springcamp." Her lean face was somber yet strangely sympathetic. "I know what happened out on the high plains; you've got trouble tied to your tail again, my friend."

Alexandria's expression had changed as well, from good-natured sarcasm to stony determination. "We've got no choice, Claire, not this time."

The brown-eyed woman met her gaze for a moment, her lips compressed. "That's what you said the last time, Alexandria," she remarked, "when you brought them here."

And as I watched the two women, those two old friends, as they confronted each other, I was painfully aware of the bittersweet flavor of their shared past. I also got the sense that the wiry little geneticist had already done Alexandria some disproportionate favor; it was surprising to find that there was anyone in the quadrant to whom Alexandria was beholden rather than the other way around.

But the silence lasted only a few moments. Then, abruptly and disarmingly, Claire suddenly smiled again, and I knew the matter had been deliberately set aside, unresolved, for a more appropriate and perhaps less public airing. "When's the last time you all had a chance to eat?" she asked us. "At Springcamp?"

"A Tachs-style breakfast," Redding said, his tone implying that he considered that description a contradiction in terms.

"Come on, then," Claire said, waving toward the buildings, "you're due some decent food." She flashed us a lopsided grin and actually winked at Lewis. "After all, what's the point of perfecting all these damned animals if you're never going to *eat* them, right?"

She made some small, subtle hand signal to her dogs, and the lot of them took off again, tussling and racing down the slope ahead of us. Alexandria and Redding walked beside Claire, bantering inconsequentially, but the three of us hung back a bit. Asplundh still had a somewhat awestruck look on her face, but Lewis wordlessly took my hand again.

He gently squeezed my fingers as if to reassure me, but through that strange, unspoken connection between us—that silent visceral sense of oneness—I could feel the tension that vibrated in him. We were perhaps nearer to our goal then than at any point since our reunion, and yet he was even more uneasy. Not that I was exactly unconcerned myself: I couldn't contact Handy and my ship; I was separated from Taylor and Raydor, two of my dearest friends; we were still in danger from both the A's and the renegades; and every direction we turned on that planet seemed to place our fate more and more securely in the hands of people I didn't know. But we were finally getting close to the rest of Lewis's people; I had thought he would be heartened by that. I knew what I was afraid of. I guess what disturbed me most about Lewis's apprehension was that I wasn't sure if I understood all of its sources yet.

Claire led us to the large structure that looked like a residence, the dogs playfully scattering the exotic fowl ahead of us. The building was predictably single-storied and partially set into the hillside it fronted. I was a little surprised when several of the panting dogs followed her right through the doorway with an easy familiarity that made it evident they were house pets as well as working animals. But the biggest surprise was the interior of the house. Although it was constructed of the same native rock and real wood as the buildings we'd seen in Coldwell, that was the only similarity. Inside, Claire's home was as well furnished as the luxury quarters on any of the more progressive planets I'd been on. It had both lushly upholstered and intricately carved real-wood furniture, deeply piled carpets scattered across the gleaming flooring, numerous paintings and other decorative objects, and, most surprisingly, the first Integrator access I'd seen since we'd left *Raptor*. Not only was the woman not Tachs, she didn't exactly live like them, either.

Asplundh spun in a semicircle, taking it all in. "You have such a beautiful house," she told Claire, an ingenuous sense of wonder in her voice.

Claire gave a short laugh, a sound of both amusement and pleasure. "You think so?" she replied. "The fruits of a long career here. Later, if you like, I'll show you my lab facilities."

Asplundh's face beamed even more brightly. "I'd love it," she responded immediately.

Claire gestured expansively at the grouping of couches and chairs in the commons area. "Just make yourselves comfortable," she told us, "and I'll see what I can come up with for us to eat."

She had just begun to move away, toward a doorway that led from the rear of the large room, when a huge Tachs Altered emerged from the same entrance. His broad face was set, its expression almost inanimate, but I noticed that his powerfully built body was clothed in a rather expensive-looking cream-colored jumpsuit, and he instantly halted when confronted with the much smaller woman.

"Jeck," she greeted him, "I'm glad to see you're here. Can you prepare us a meal?"

The crepey, flattened face was typically economical in its degree of expressiveness, but I was sure I detected there a subtle undercurrent of what I could only interpret as affectionate tolerance. Wordlessly, the big, blocky man directed a pointed look toward the trails of dusty footprints we had tracked from the entryway across the immaculate floor. From there, his gaze traveled to the group of dogs lolling indolently on the lush carpeting. Then, with gracious dignity, Jeck solemnly nodded. "Of course," he responded in a deep, raspy voice.

As the Tachs disappeared back through the doorway, Alexandria plopped down on one of the more capacious upholstered chairs and hooked a booted ankle over one knee. "So," she told Claire with a mocking little smirk, "I see you still don't have any trouble keeping good help."

Before Claire could reply, a second Tachs came into the room through the same doorway. This man was Normal but only slightly smaller than the first one. He had shoulder-length, rust-colored hair and huge, limpid dark eyes. He was dressed in herdsmen's clothes, leather breeches and a roughweave overshirt, but he was carrying a most domestic looking vacu-mop in his hands. Giving Claire an almost apologetic glance, he nodded toward the dusty bootprints and explained, "Jeck said the floor was dirty."

If it hadn't been for the relative urgency of our situation, I think I would have laughed aloud at the blatantly comic aspects of the little domestic melodrama. It was pretty obvious that those two Tachs were more to Claire than just the hired help; I had a vivid imagination about those things, and the incongruous trio they made should have been worth a broad smile at the very least.

Claire waved dismissively at the second man and said with a sort of fond annoyance, "You tell Jeck to confine his worrying to his kitchen and let me worry about the rest of this house." She actually gave the big redhead a gentle shove on the arm, adding, "You want to be of some use, Rudd, you help him get that meal together."

Hesitantly, glancing back over the rest of us, the Tachs reluctantly allowed himself to be ushered from the room.

"Sit, please," Claire reiterated, for only Alexandria had done so. For emphasis, Claire dropped down onto one of the plush couches, right across a low real-wood table from Alexandria's chair. Deferentially, almost shyly, Asplundh took a place beside her on the couch. Redding, as was his custom, rejected her suggestion and instead took a few paces away across the floor; he nonchalantly stepped over one of the sprawling dogs and stood before a tall wooden cabinet, casually studying its contents.

Before Lewis and I had even sat down, Alexandria bluntly resumed the more pragmatic aspects of our business there. "How are they?" she asked Claire.

Calmly converting to a similarly brisk tone, the elder woman replied, "They're well." She stretched her tightly clad legs out before her and crossed them at the ankles. "The news from Camelot was upsetting, of course." She paused, then made a small nonspecific gesture with her slim brown hands. "You know, she still blames herself for letting them be taken in the first place."

Alexandria's craggy face was tautly set, nearly unreadable to me; her rough voice carried very little inflection as she replied. "Yeah? Well, there's enough blame to go around and then some on that one."

Feeling conspicuous, I slipped down onto a padded chair at the end of the table. Lewis sat on the chair beside mine, his eyes lowered, his body broadcasting tension to me in strobing waves. I glanced sideways at him to see that his hands gripped the chair's armrests as if he were in an aircraft, expecting turbulence.

"They left here as soon as the word about the trouble came," Claire continued after a moment. She openly studied Alexandria's stolid face. "They would have tried to get off-planet if it had been feasible, even though I counseled against it." She shrugged delicately. "It's very difficult for them to feel safe here now."

"Where are they now?" Alexandria asked.

Much of the conversation, the contextual part of it at least, had been taking place over my head, and I had been left floundering for inference. This question, however, was straightforward enough, and Claire didn't hesitate or equivocate in her reply.

"The old embryotory at Flatstone. You could leave for there in the morning."

"The morning? We can leave yet today!" Alexandria countered imperiously, locking her thick fingers around her bent and raised knee.

"That would be too risky," Claire pointed out calmly. "The Commerce Commission's surveillance is at its most intense from dusk till dawn."

At that moment, the door at the far end of the room swung

open and the perspicacious Jeck reappeared, bearing a tray of
steaming ceramic mugs. "I will serve coffee," he announced
solemnly, but the brief little look he darted in Claire's direction
as he bent to pass her one of the mugs was anything but properly
obeisant. Moving with dignified grace, the huge Tachs skirted
one of the snoozing dogs and made the circuit of the low table,
dispensing the coffee and its accompaniments.

"What about our food?" Claire demanded in what I could
then see was a familiar and comfortable little ritual of teasing
insult.

Unblinking, Jeck merely replied, "Good food takes time to
prepare."

"Well, make it adequate food, then, and make it snappy!"
Claire retorted. "Let Rudd help you. These people are hungry."

Sketching the shadow of a courteous bow—an attitude as patently feigned as Claire's air of irritated impatience had been—
the huge Tachs proceeded to move unhurriedly from the room.
Then, as if the interruption in their dialogue had never occurred,
Alexandria went gruffly on.

"All of this is risky," she told Claire. "Waiting until morning is risky, too."

"What about the rest of your group?" Claire reminded her
quietly.

Alexandria never hesitated. "They can catch up later," she
said flatly.

Involuntarily but automatically, I felt my spine stiffen and my
jaw tighten. In the chair beside me I could sense rather than feel
Lewis's whole body just freeze, as if in anticipation. Although
I was familiar with this obsessive side of Alexandria's thinking,
it seldom failed to rankle me. She might have been willing to
leave Raydor and Taylor behind, but I wasn't; to me they weren't
expendable. And I sure as hell wasn't about to go trooping off
across the wilderness without Handy's relay. Just as words to
that effect were about to come from my mouth, I was saved from
saying something that would undoubtedly have been inflam-
matory; Redding stepped in for me.

He stood leaning almost nonchalantly against the cabinet, his
coffee mug slung loosely in one hand. There was a typically
indifferent drawl to his voice as he interjected, "We can go to
Flatstone any time you want, Alexandria, but we sure as hell
aren't getting off this planet without that ship."

Alexandria glowered at him, and not for the first time I found
myself wondering just how two such obdurate personalities as

she and Redding had ever become or managed to remain friends. Both of them were used to getting their own way, but I think Redding was able to achieve that goal only by a circuitous route where Alexandria was concerned.

I'm not sure what further acerbic arguments Alexandria would have unleashed, but I had no doubt the confrontation would indeed have gone on had not Claire's big jumpsuited Altered once again made a timely entrance. Effortlessly balancing two heavily laden trays, Jeck strode purposefully into the room, accompanied by a swirl of the most tantalizing aromas I had smelled since Taylor and I had been seduced by the street vendor's real meat on Porta Flora. Throwing Claire a smugly self-satisfied look, he presented the trays for our approval and then bent to slide them onto the low wooden table. Following closely behind him, the rusty-haired Tachs carried in plates and utensils. Rudd seemed a little awkward about his service, and I suspected this was not a part of his usual duties. As quickly as he could finish dispensing the flatware, he made an unceremonious exit, whereas Jeck busied himself for some time, arranging serving dishes on the table and announcing their contents for our benefit. Finally Claire literally shooed him away, waving her hands at him like he was one of her big slant-eyed dogs that had become overly familiar.

"That's good enough—just go," she scolded him with unconvincing irritation. I almost had to smile at her obvious enjoyment of his performance. "I'll call you when we're done."

For a time the passing and sampling of the food occupied all of us. Redding came back over to the table and dropped down onto the couch beside Claire. The sprawled-out dogs never moved, although I was sure it was more a matter of training than of genuine disinterest, because the food was irresistible. The various dishes were heavy on real meat, although some of them were succulent with only fresh vegetables in sauce, and all were remarkably delicious. It had been a long time since I'd had the chance to think of food as an experience of pure pleasure, justifiable on the basis of taste alone and not solely on the need for sustenance. I tackled the meal with a most uncultured enthusiasm. There was only one discordant thought to intrude as I heartily bit into a chunk of herbed and stewed beef: If only Taylor and Raydor could be here to taste this.

"I think this is the best real meat I've ever eaten," Asplundh said, raising a broiled chunk on her fork and waving it as if for emphasis.

"Yeah," Redding said, heaping his own plate, "and to think that at one time cattle nearly became extinct."

Apparently accustomed to this kind of dietary largess, Claire was conducting herself with a bit more aplomb than were the rest of us. "Actually," she remarked as she deftly sliced strips of carrots and potatoes with her knife, "the animals have probably benefited the Tachs as much as the Tachs have benefited the animals."

Swallowing a tender cube of beef, I looked curiously at her. "You mean because of the economics of real food?" I asked. As far as I could tell, if you discounted the existence of plain dumb luck, there were really only two reasons why the Tachs had survived and prospered on Earthheart. One was their natural group ethic of perseverance and hard work. But the other was that they had chosen, both by their history and by design, to raise the very things that had come to assume a disproportionate value in the rest of the galaxy—real things. Even the pettiness of the A's sanctions against them as a race and as a world had not been able to crush the power of that natural, renewable wealth.

Nodding, Claire continued. "That, too, of course. But in the beginning this planet wasn't well suited to agriculture. The Tachs converted it to productive use in a remarkably few generations simply because they didn't make the same mistake made on so many other worlds."

Asplundh had been chewing avidly; grasping Claire's point, she quickly swallowed the mouthful of food and interjected, "Microorganisms- -from the animals!"

"Exactly," Claire confirmed. "For Old Earth–origin plants to thrive, you need the type of soil microorganisms they depend on." She made a small gesture with her knife. "What better means of rapidly and economically spreading that kind of 'culture' all over the surface of the ground than through the constant excretions of herbivorous animals?"

Alexandria looked up from the half-demolished contents of her plate and pronounced sardonically, "Earthheart: the success story built on cow shit!"

But Claire just shook her head in tolerant admonishment. "Ridicule it all you want, Alexandria; the truth is, the Tachs have not only successfully propagated a lot of vital animal species on this planet, they've also managed as a sect to pull themselves back from the brink of extinction."

"Despite the A's best efforts to the contrary," Redding added.

The conversation was unwittingly leading in a direction that raised some troubling questions for me. I had never been entirely convinced of the innate sanctity of the Tachs way of life, not with what I had seen of its results. To me, Earthheart had shunned too many of her own, men like Raydor. "The A's aren't the only ones who discriminate," I remarked, spearing a chunk of sauce-coated potato. "It's the Tachs themselves who drive away thousands of their own Altereds every year, not the A's."

Claire's head turned sharply toward me, and I knew she would have responded to that indictment had not Alexandria beaten her to it. Setting down her fork, the big, burly woman slowly lifted her coffee mug. Regarding me for a moment over its rim, her dark eyes narrowed beneath the frizzled fringe of her unruly hair, Alexandria quietly said, "No one drives them away, Jo."

I gave an impatient toss of my head. "Well, unlands them, then, or whatever you want to call it. What the hell are they supposed to do?" I fixed her with a sharp stare. "You should know better than anyone. How many Altereds leave this planet every year?"

With a steady patience I would never have credited her with, Alexandria lowered her mug and replied, "It's a matter of survival of the sect, Jo. Do you realize how few female Tachs are born?" Without waiting for a response, she went on, essentially answering her own question. "The Tachs have suffered from a number of unusual sex-linked lethals. There's a high rate of embryonic death. The ratio of male to female live births is nearly twenty to one. Call it unlanding if you want, call it discrimination, but only the Tachs daughters are permitted to inherit land, and only the normal Tachs males are permitted to reproduce." Her craggy face was gravely set; surprisingly, there was no bitterness in either her expression or her tone. "The Tachs have always been condemned for their refusal to conform to the Code, but to do so would have been racial suicide for them. They have so few females that if they'd allowed Classification, they'd be extinct by now. The Altereds aren't driven out, Jo; not by their society, at least. The 'drive' comes from within, for the ones who want something more than this planet can offer them."

I met her steady gaze for a moment, then, dropping my eyes, I skewered another hunk of potato. No one spoke for a brief time, then the conversation gradually resumed around the low table.

I returned to my meal, but the edge had been taken off it for me. Luckily, I was not required to make any intelligent reponses to anything that was being said from that point on. After Asplundh studiously asked a few more questions about some of the dishes, the talk turned more general. Asplundh and Claire spent the last part of the meal on a detailed exchange of information about the various flora and fauna of the region, with Alexandria making occasional comments. Redding, like Lewis and me, remained silent.

Glancing sideways almost guiltily at Lewis, I noticed then that he had barely been touching his food. I don't think anyone else had been aware of his lack of appetite; the conversation had been too diverting, and Lewis had been fairly adept at concealing the fact, helping himself to most of the dishes and keeping his utensils in motion, moving the uneaten food about on his plate. When he lifted his coffee mug to his lips for the third time in less than three minutes, I slid my dusty boot across the carpeting beneath the table and gently nudged the side of his foot.

He shot me a quick apologetic look. Despite the fact that he tried to dampen it, his anxiety still strummed through the small space between us. I just raised one brow inquiringly at him: *Are you all right?* Then he lowered his eyes and determinedly redevoted himself to rearranging the food on his plate.

It was only when we all were sated and Claire was offering refills on coffee from a thick earthenware pot that the mealtime conversation gradually wound down. Leaning back against the plump upholstery of the back of the couch, Claire offered to Asplundh, "Would you like to see my lab facilities now? My meager facilities, I should add," she amended with a self-effacing smile, "I'm sure that compared to your lab on Heinlein, this will look pretty primitive to you."

"Yes, I'd love to see it," Asplundh said quickly, setting down her coffee mug. Despite the size of the meal she'd just consumed, the geneticist looked ready to leap eagerly to her feet.

Still holding her mug, Claire rose lithely from the couch. Her gaze made a circuit of the table. "Any other takers?" she inquired with some amusement.

Lewis stood up so rapidly that he startled me. "I'd like to come along," he told Claire.

Replacing my mug on the table, I also got up. "A little walk sounds like a good idea," I said casually. I was only mildly interested in the lab, but I was very interested in getting away from Alexandria for a while.

The four of us were halfway across the room, heading toward a rear doorway, when Jeck suddenly appeared in the entry to the kitchen. I was beginning to wonder if he could actually hear Claire think. That crepey, stoic face seemed set without expression, but I was developing the ability to read his mood right off his eyes. He gave Claire an intent, just slightly overlong stare and then announced, "I will clear the table."

"Yes, do that," she told him, thrusting her coffee mug into his hands. "And take the dogs out to the kennel."

I had never been much of a voyeur, but I had started to get to the point where I thought I would have paid good credit to see just what the hell went on in the private quarters of that house.

Claire led us through a large but cluttered room that looked like some kind of office or study. Its walls were liberally lined with shelves of vids and tapes, and there was a desk and some counters, all piled high with untidy stacks of both vid and printed material. Then we passed down a short corridor that served several smaller rooms; there was a smattering of equipment in some, but most of them looked empty and unused. Claire paused just long enough to wave inclusively at them, explaining, "I used to maintain a basic sort of infirmary here, years ago."

Lewis gave her a quizzical look. "But you're not a physician," he said.

She merely laughed. "No, but back when Coldwell was just a frontier town and this was the edge of nowhere, I was the best they had."

From the direction we'd taken when we had left the commons area, I knew we had been headed back toward the part of the building that was set into the hillside. As we went through the last doorway at the end of the corridor and entered a large, well-lit room, I realized we were probably completely underground.

I don't know what Claire would have considered an ample facility, but her use of the term "meager" to describe her laboratory seemed to me to be deliberately misdirecting. I was no scientist, so perhaps I was easily impressed, but the vast and orderly well-stocked chamber certainly looked modern enough to me. Asplundh's expression was as delighted as I had seen it when she had been out in the open fields, surrounded by growing things. As Claire guided us up and down the long rows of counters, equipment, and specimen cases, she kept up a wry and entertaining commentary on the collection of what she deprecatingly described as "the remnants of my reputation." Almost nothing that I saw looked familiar to me, and I understood the purpose of only about one-tenth of what we were shown, but Claire was still a fascinating lecturer, and I found myself thoroughly enjoying the tour. Even Lewis, walking easily along beside me, seemed to have relaxed once we'd gotten away from the table and out of the commons area. And away from Alexandria, I had to think.

At the far end of the lab my eyes were drawn to a huge floor-to-ceiling storage case that was built into the wall. The doors were broad panes of glass, and, peering at their opaque and hazy surface, I turned to Claire with a curious query. "What's this in here?" I asked her, pointing at the case.

Coming over, the dark-haired little woman glanced at the section of the case I had randomly indicated. "Ah, Gordon sheep, I think," she responded solemnly. "Or, next to them, the Athenas."

At my expression of startled befuddlement, Claire laughed good-naturedly and released the latch on the nearest glass door. As she slid the panel partially aside, I got my first good look at what was stored inside the case. Neatly stacked in row after horizontal row were tens of thousands of tiny, transparent bubblelike containers, each half-filled with an almost clear liquid. Scientist or not, no daughter of Heinlein would have failed to have recognized those vials.

I looked back into those deep brown eyes, my brows lifting in surprise. "They're embryos—in suspension," I said.

"Exactly," Claire confirmed, seemingly pleased, although whether by my recognition of them or by my surprise at them, I wasn't sure. She made a gesture. "This section is sheep; down there we have cattle; then poultry, and dogs, and—" She glanced up and down the case, then shrugged and continued. "I think we might still have some swine in here somewhere, too."

I was still perplexed, but I found myself automatically glancing quickly over to Asplundh before I asked Claire, "But why? Why suspend all these embryos when this whole planet is stocked with naturally reproducing animals?"

"Think of them as spares," Claire explained. She gestured again at the case. "This suspension case contains embryos of every pure strain of animal now raised on Earthheart." She flashed us that quick, quirky smile. "As well as certain . . . exotic strains, variations I developed myself, which were never selected for large-scale use."

"Like the birds outside," Lewis suddenly deduced, his expressive face alight.

Claire rewarded him with another generous smile. "My

hobby," she confessed, "an indulgence of my retirement years." She gave a small, dismissive shrug and concluded, "When you're struggling to build a planet's economic ecology, everything has to have a purpose or it's rejected. But in here I've kept a bit of everything I've developed, because in genetics, sometimes diversity can be a purpose in itself."

As I stood listening to Claire speak, my eyes were on Lewis and my thoughts were on another suspension case, in a medical complex half the quadrant away. He stood there calmly, his body tranquilly poised, with one hand on the frame of the case door, his fingertips lightly splayed on the cool glass. If Asplundh's expression during our tour of the lab had been one of wonder and delight, then Lewis's was one of nearly mystical contemplation. As he gazed, transfixed, at the countless rows of crystalline vials, each with its carefully suspended embryo, he was like a man who had just opened the door to his own fate. But I could not tell if that door led to the past or to the future.

As we stood in the aisle, I glanced sideways and saw that Asplundh was studying me. Our eyes met, but the look on her face was not that of a scientist considering some theorem. She regarded me as one woman might regard another when the two of them were friends and shared some common concern. Then her eyes cut away from me, and she said suddenly to Claire, "I'm fascinated by the strains of sheep you've developed here. Do you think the three of us could go out to the pens and get a closer look at some of them?"

Lewis looked up and turned from the storage case, his expression mildly puzzled at Asplundh's request.

Something in the incisive narrowing of Claire's dark brown eyes made me think the older woman doubted the irresistible allure of her sheep pens, but she merely gave Asplundh a faint smile and replied, "Of course; here, you can go out through the infirmary exit if you like."

Claire led us back across the laboratory, out the door, and down the short corridor. In one of the half-empty small rooms that branched off from it, a door in the outer wall led out into the rambling dwelling's side yard. As we stepped out onto the grass, I was surprised to find that it was almost dusk. The air was cooler, and the bruise-colored sky was streaked with purplish windrows of cirrus clouds. The air was so fresh, it was like inhaling a stimulant; there was the faint but pleasant scent of dung and dust and crushed grass.

Claire pointed toward the row of animal sheds, with their

attendant pens, about fifty meters from us, where small groups of sheep stood nearly motionless in the twilight. "Just don't wander off too far," she advised us with a dismissive wave. "The Ceecccc's surveillance remotes come through this area all night." Then she turned to go back into the house.

For a moment I wanted nothing more than just to follow her back inside. At that instant I would have given everything to avoid what I was about to do. But even as Asplundh took the lead across the side yard, I hung back only for a second, my hesitation scarcely noticeable. Because I was no good at running away from trouble, never had been and probably never would be. I was good at *thinking* about running away, good at *wanting* to, but I was no good at actually doing it. And so I fell into step beside Lewis and said nothing.

The three of us walked in silence down to the row of low buildings. Now that the temperature was falling, I was grateful for my Springcamp clothing. The short, bunchy grass was growing damp beneath my boots, and the sweeping limbs of the dusty looking willows hung limp and still. The only sounds were the sheep's soft, glottal mutterings and the faint sough of the wind. Beyond the small cluster of Claire's buildings, for 360 degrees around us, as far as I could see, there was no sign of any other human habitation. Even on the blizzard-whipped prairie I had not had quite the same keen sense of being so isolated. Reaching the junk-wood pole and woven-wire fence of the first sheep pen, I leaned forward, resting my elbows on the top rail. Unexpectedly and involuntarily, I felt myself shiver.

From behind me Lewis gently circled my waist with one arm. Even through our clothing, the heat of his body seemed to burn, inflaming me. I saw him glance quickly up and down the pen, his gaze rapidly skimming over the only slightly interested sheep. His eyes moved to Asplundh, who had stopped along the fence a few feet from us; then they finally came to rest on me.

"What is it, Jo?" he asked me softly.

Asplundh took a sudden step forward, abruptly enough that several of the big shaggy animals in the pen jerked their heads up in alarm. But she did not look directly at us, and the sheep did not move farther, and I could not evade Lewis's question.

Looking out across the pen, I wet my lips and said quietly, "You know those tests they were running on you and Alexandria and Redding when you got back to Heinlein? And the tests Asplundh was doing after the doctor saw you?"

When he didn't respond immediately, I had to turn my head;

I saw then that he was nodding. Elaborating, he asked, "The tests about the touch-healing, you mean?"

Because his expression was not just one of simple perplexity, because there was just an edge of wariness in his tone, Asplundh seemed to feel compelled to join me in my explanation. "Remember that I told you I'd found something interesting, Lewis?" she said.

He nodded again, his face still creased by a frown. "Something to do with the Talent? The microphysiology of how it might work?" he asked carefully, almost hopefully, I thought.

But Asplundh was shaking her head. She had placed both of her hands on the top rail of the fence; her pale fingers curled around the rough wood, gripping tightly. "No, the tests weren't just about your Talent," she told him, her voice low and reluctant. "Do you know what Riekert's Index is?" she asked him.

As if I were serving as a conduit between two electrical posts, I felt a current jolt through me, traveling from Lewis's hand and arm directly to my heart and then spreading thunderously in great bounding pulses to the very tips of my fingers and toes. I had thought I was becoming fairly acclimated to adrenaline, but this was nothing like that; this was a plain and primal lurch of pure dread that bypassed the usual neurosynapses; this was Lewis's fear, and against me, his body was frozen in silence.

Misinterpreting his lack of response, Asplundh started to go on slowly. "It's a method of classifying the—"

"No!" Lewis interrupted her, his voice sounding startlingly loud in the tranquillity of the dusky sheep yard. "No," he repeated, more quietly then, his eyes rapidly searching my face, his hand automatically rising to touch the curve of my cheek, the caress like fire. "I know what it is." His voice dropped even further, pitched softly, earnestly, those cerulean eyes fixing me with an intensity that was almost frightening. He spoke as though Asplundh weren't even there.

"Jo, on the truck—when I said there were things I wanted to tell you about, when—"

His anxious flow of words was abruptly cut off by a loud bellow from the direction of the house in a voice that was aggravatingly familiar to me. I could not understand what Alexandria had just shouted at us across the nearly darkened yard; all I knew was that the moment had been broken, shattered like glass. Lewis stepped back from me then as all three of us swung around, turning toward the looming silhouette of the bulky woman who was striding swiftly across the wet grass toward us.

"What the hell's the matter now?" I shouted at her, dismayed to find that I felt as much relief as anger at the interruption and perversely irritated at myself for the cowardice of that relief.

Alexandria did not have to be close enough for me to have seen her face to be able to read her mood accurately; as she approached us, the set of her blocky body and the furious tone in her voice clearly broadcast her belligerence. "I said, come on up to the house—*now*!" she repeated fiercely, her dark eyes like two sparks of jet in the dimness. "The renegades have just attacked the transmitter station at Coldwell!"

CHAPTER TWELVE

I guess that was one of the things I would never like about planets; places like Heinlein and even Earthheart had a way of lulling you into a false sense of security. Their textures, their rhythms, their diversity—the very kaleidoscope of their sights and sounds and scents and sensations—all seduced you, subverted your natural skepticism and caution. In space, you always knew that you were nothing more than a few centimeters away from death; there was seldom anything but the thickness of your ship's skin between you and the fatal oblivion of eternal vacuum. You didn't need to remind yourself or keep thinking about it; you just knew. But on those damned planets it was too easy to forget. You got out and moved around; you breathed real air; you planted your feet on the seemingly unshakable ground of some spinning ball of rock—and you began to overlook the universal fact that death could still be just a few centimeters away.

"Are they okay?" I demanded anxiously. But, her directive delivered, Alexandria had abruptly swung around and started back toward the house without even pausing to see if we were following her.

All three of us started after her, practically jogging to catch up. "What happened?" Asplundh panted, coming abreast of Alexandria, but the big woman's stride never slowed.

"Are they all right?" I repeated, nearly shouting again. I was close enough that I was about to reach out and grab the sleeve of Alexandria's tunic, willing to haul back on her really hard, and I think Lewis knew that. He caught my arms and held me back, his fingers squeezing tightly. I probably would have turned on him, too, none too gently and not very appreciatively, either. But at that moment Redding's lanky figure appeared in sharp

196

silhouette in the doorway, backlit by the house lights, and I rounded on him instead.

"What the hell is going on?" I demanded loudly, bypassing Alexandria as if she weren't even there.

Redding's lean face was grimly set, those gray eyes as cool and hard as gunmetal. "Someone attacked the transmitter station," he said tersely. "Three unmarked air cars. Looks like it was renegades." He directed his next piece of information to Alexandria. "Claire was able to contact Harley; he's already on his way out there."

"Is anyone hurt?" Lewis interjected quickly, still holding my arms.

Redding made a curt, frustrated shrugging movement. "We don't know yet. The message from the station was pretty garbled."

I swung sideways, pulling free of Lewis's grip. "Then why aren't we going out there?" I insisted angrily, starting forward as if to push past Redding.

Both Lewis and Redding caught me that time, although it was Alexandria who explained, in a voice harsh with the same helpless disappointment I felt. "Just how the hell do you think you're getting out there—ox cart?" Her heavily lined face was taut and stubbornly set. "Harley's got a hover car, and he's Tachs; he can travel out there even this time of the night without being questioned. We let him go," she concluded, although the smoldering look in her eyes told me that she wasn't any happier about it than I was. Alexandria hated being thwarted just as much as I did.

Claire appeared in the doorway, her finely boned face filled with compassion and concern. In that strange twilight zone between the brilliance of the house's lights and the darkness of the side yard, she suddenly appeared very much as what she had claimed to be: just an aging onetime teacher of the sciences, retired to the peaceful reward of her farm. We were the interlopers there, standing stiffly in the shadowy dimness on the wet grass, regarding her with such wary unease; we were the ones who had brought this plague of danger to her house.

"The station's channel has been shut down," she said quietly, her arms crossed over her thin chest. "But Harley hailed me on his car's transmitter. They'll be here in a few minutes."

No one moved to go back inside the house; there was no point in it. We moved around to the front of the building, stepping wordlessly across the dewy tufts of grass. There, light spilled from the entryway, and Claire's rusty-haired Tachs, Rudd, met us with a power lantern.

"Was anyone hurt?" Lewis asked doggedly. He had not tried to touch me again after I had twisted free of his hold a second time but he remained standing close by me, as if my nearness reassured him.

Claire shook her head almost apologetically. "Harley didn't say," she told us, "but he had to keep the transmission very brief."

Alexandria seemed more angry than apprehensive; her formidable face was set in an obstinate scowl. "It doesn't make sense," she complained to no one in particular. "How the hell would those bastards've known any of us had gone to that station? If they'd somehow managed to pick up our trail from Springcamp, they still shouldn't't've been able to tell we'd sent anyone to that chicken farm!" Her voice had risen from a coarse growl to a pitch that made the words "chicken farm" sound like an epithet. Her big hands were knotted into fists, pressed impotently into her ample hips as she threw out the bitter query to the group in general. "How the hell would the renegades've known they were there?"

It might have sounded like a rhetorical question, but with Alexandria, such queries usually weren't. It was Claire who spoke first, her voice calmly rational. "Maybe they inadvertently did something in their work with the relay at the station that was somehow detected by the renegades," she suggested.

"No," Alexandria insisted, shaking her frizzy head impatiently. "Raydor would never screw up like that." Her phrasing made it clear that she wasn't including Taylor in that blanket assumption of competence. In fact, the implication of her entire tirade had been just the opposite: that Taylor could and very well might have screwed up and that some blunder on his part could be the only reason the renegades had found them.

I felt the old rage rising in me then, pure and plain and somehow invigorating. Suddenly it seemed as if venting the pent-up accumulation of my grievances against Alexandria could, in some propitious way, not only lessen my own anxiety and make me feel better but also somehow miraculously remedy the precarious situation in which we once again found ourselves. It was a wonderful discovery; I almost smiled, however grimly, as I swiftly considered just where to launch into my attack against the big, obnoxious woman who stood across from me in the faint glow from Claire's house lights. But the moment I was set to enthusiastically begin, the oblique bluish beams of the running lights of Harley's hover car appeared over the crest of the long hill.

In both altitude and speed, hover cars fell just a notch above ground vehicles. Unlike air cars, they were limited to a point of suspension about a half meter off the ground; in terrain like that, it was usually adequate and they didn't need roads, but they kicked up one hell of a cloud of dust. As the sleek, oval-shaped vehicle glided down the slope toward us, it sent up a gritty roil of dirt and chaff ahead of it. The running lights pierced that cloud like beacons in a blizzard.

Without waiting for the hover car to shut down, Alexandria started forward, the rest of us right behind her. As the high-pitched whine of the car's engine trailed off, the chassis thumped down softly onto the sod and one of the front hatches popped open. The first person to emerge was Harley. Blinking against the lingering veil of suspended particles, the big Tachs turned to release the catches on the second hatch. Cam hauled himself out of the back of the car, pulling Taylor along after him. Almost immediately behind them, the two men scrabbling awkwardly with arms joined, came Traeger and Raydor.

Harley met Alexandria's advance, confronting her with a gruffly concise report, which he had to shout over the continuous low whine of the hover car's engine. "Renegades, all right!" he confirmed. "Place is a mess. Cam and I are going back over—see if we can put it all to rights before the A's come snooping around."

Cam had released Taylor once they had cleared the border of the car's downdraft. Then the stolid Altered plunged back through the fuming cloud of flying dust and ducked back into the vehicle even as Harley swung around and strode back to the driver's seat. Within moments the engine revved up again. The hover craft lifted to its cruising height, pivoted, and gracefully swept away again in a spray of whirling earth and fragments of dead grass.

I had been immensely relieved just to see that all four men had arrived on their feet, but my anxiety had not yet been completely assuaged. Alexandria and Redding were already crowding around Raydor and Traeger, and Lewis still stood with Asplundh, so I turned and hurried over to Taylor. Automatically, my hands went out, gripping the filthy sleeves of his blackened overshirt. He looked like hell, his clothing scorched and reeking of smoke, his face smeared with soot, but there were no visible signs of injury on him. For a few seconds I couldn't even force a word from my mouth; I was that damned happy to see him again. Then he flashed that crooked grin, his white teeth gleaming in his grimy face, and I just launched myself at him, hugging him hard and tight. If he had been injured, I could have punctured a lung, but his arms closed around me without hesitation.

As I clung to him, he murmured something several times. Finally I realized that what he was saying was, "I'm okay, Jo; I'm okay," repeated in a litany of reassurance. Pulling my head back, I quickly glanced over toward Raydor and Traeger. Following my gaze, Taylor assured me, "We're all okay, just kind of messy. Traeger's got a few nicks and bangs but nothing serious."

Straightening, I took a half step backward, still clinging to his dirty sleeves. "What happened?" I asked him a little shakily.

"Yeah, just what the joinin' hells *did* happen?"

In the sudden relative calm of the hover car's departure, Alexandria's icy demand hung in the hazy near darkness of the farmyard. In a half dozen or so imperious strides she had crossed the space between the others and the spot where Taylor and I stood. For one shocked instant I thought she was actually going to strike him; there was that much naked fury in her weathered face. I found myself taking a quick step in front of him, angrily and defensively.

But it was not a display of force or any loud rejoinder that defused the flammability of the moment. Rather, it was Claire, with her calm and quietly stern voice, who came between us both literally and figuratively. Cutting in front of Alexandria, she said brusquely, "This is hardly the time or place to hold an inquest, Alexandria." She turned slightly, gesturing to Redding and the others. "Let's get back in the house so we can get these men cleaned up a little and see to Traeger's wounds." She fixed Alexandria with one last incisive look. "Then I'm sure they all would be very happy to tell you whatever they can about what's happened to them."

Alexandria's expression was still belligerent, but, pointedly ignoring her, I guided Taylor past her and followed the others toward the pool of light flowing from the front door. In the stronger light, I could see that although Raydor looked as disheveled as Taylor, he appeared unharmed, and that Traeger, for all the tattered ruin of his clothing and his bloodied face, walked steadily and without hesitation. Whatever had happened at the transmitter station, they had been either well prepared or very lucky.

At the doorway, Lewis separated himself from those following Raydor and Traeger and turned back to Taylor and me. His helplessly expressive face was etched with anxiety and confusion, and he looked at Taylor's state of grimy disarray with obvious alarm. I reached out and briefly touched his shoulder, assuring him, "It's okay, he's not hurt. Can you help Traeger?"

Inside Claire's elegant commons area, the three sooty, bedraggled men made a rude contrast to the luxurious furnishings. Jeck appeared in the doorway to the kitchen, but despite the trail of dirt we'd tracked in and the scruffy condition of the additional guests, that broad Altered face held no trace of reproach.

Glancing up, Claire called to him, "Bring some washers and clean towels, Jeck." Wincing as she briefly studied Traeger's cut and bruised face in the good light, she added, "And bring my med kit."

But Claire wasn't going to need her medical palliatives. Even as she spoke, Lewis quietly approached Traeger and began automatically to reach for the ruddy-haired Tachs's smudged and battered face.

Startled by the action, Traeger reflexively took a step backward, his arms coming up to ward off what seemed to him to be Lewis's inexplicable advance. Moving forward, I quickly intervened between the two men.

"It's all right," I reassured Traeger, part of my mind seeing the ironic humor of my having to guarantee this hulking giant of a man that Lewis wouldn't hurt him. Hell, Traeger probably outweighed Lewis and me put together. I put my hand lightly on Traeger's torn sleeve, continuing, "He's a touch-healer; it's his Talent. Just let him—"

I broke off then because I saw that Traeger's wide dark eyes were not on me but on some point over my shoulder. He was looking anxiously to Alexandria, but the big, grizzled-haired woman merely nodded at him.

Lewis almost had to stand up on his toes to be able to reach Traeger's face; then, at the last moment, the big shaggy head bent, lowering itself for Lewis's strange benediction. It was over with so quickly that I thought at first Traeger doubted that anything had really even happened. It was only when he saw, with gape-mouthed astonishment, the fleeting shadows of his own injuries already fading like ghosts from Lewis's face that he realized his own face, while still streaked with dirt, was un-marked.

As the Tachs stared down at the smaller man with wide-eyed incredulity, Lewis just gave a small, slightly apologetic shrug and explained almost shyly, "To do the rest, I need to see what—to see where else you're hurt."

If there was one trait all Tachs seemed to share, it was a sense of personal modesty or public body-shyness, at least. Traeger was powerfully built, and I had no doubt that he had great cour-age as well, but he could no more have taken off his clothing in front of the lot of us than he could have flown. In fact, I think the power of flight would have come to him a hell of a lot easier.

Jeck reappeared in the kitchen doorway, his arms filled with towels and the prewetted disposable cleansing pads known col-loquially as washers; Claire's med kit was tucked under one elbow. Quickly interpreting the particular stricken look on Trae-ger's rugged, blackened face, Claire promptly instructed Jeck, "Here, give me those. Then take these two back to the kitchen with you and get Traeger some more washers and some clean clothes." As she reached for Jeck's load, she added, with a nod toward Raydor and Taylor, "And we'll need more clean clothes for these two fellows as well."

Jeck had barely started back across the room, Lewis and Trae-ger following at his heels, when Rudd came through the door-way at the rear of the room, carrying an armful of clothing. Claire masterfully concealed the glimmer of surprise that had just kindled in her eyes, but I swore I saw Rudd give her a hint of a self-satisfied smirk just the same.

Feigning impatience, Claire merely thrust the med kit at him and instructed, "Here, take this back; we won't be needing it now."

I guess Raydor had once had the Tachs sense of body-shyness, too, but maybe living off-planet had worn it off him. Or maybe I had corrupted him. At any rate, he seemed to have no qualms about stripping off his filthy clothes and standing in his suit liner in front of a roomful of people. And I knew very well that Taylor had never had any such inhibitions although out of deference to Asplundh and Claire, I don't think he would have shed his liner even if it had been dirty. Alexandria and Redding were helping Raydor peel out of his grimy garments, so I continued to assist Taylor. Asplundh seemed anxious to help but a little at loose ends until I suggested she try to sort out a set of fresh clothes that would fit Taylor.

I knew the temporary truce Claire had succeeded in calling out in the front yard would not last, and so when Alexandria, who was vigorously swabbing the back of Raydor's gritty neck with a washer, suddenly resumed her interrogation, I was not surprised.

"What the hell happened out there?" she grunted, her strenuous ministrations making Raydor squirm away from her like a small boy objecting to some odious bit of grooming.

"Three air cars," Raydor answered, turning to face her. He took a towel from Redding and began to dry his hands. "We picked them up on the station's security net."

"It's nothing but a damned booster station. What the hell were they doing there?" Alexandria asked, her beefy hands crumpling the soiled washer into a tangled wad.

"I don't know," Raydor said. He ran the towel over the hairless crown of his chamoislike head. "But we figured they couldn't be Authority vehicles, because they didn't respond to the station keeper's hail."

Claire had been silently gathering up the discarded soiled clothing that had been dropped on the floor. She glanced up then, observing, "Tark would have been suspicious of any air cars, I think; the Ceecees seldom make any patrols with manned vehicles in this region after dark."

"They attacked you?" Redding went on, passing Raydor a clean overshirt.

"Not exactly," Raydor said; it was a far more nebulous answer than he would have dared give had the question come from Alexandria. But as soon as he had pulled the coarsely woven shirt over his head, he further explained, "They posted themselves equidistant around the station, about a half kilometer out, and wouldn't respond to any transmitted queries."

"Then they *knew* you were there!" Alexandria interrupted. She tossed the crushed washer down to the floor with a furious swing of her arm, where the damp material landed with a satisfyingly loud splat. Then she spun to confront Taylor again, her black eyes glittering dangerously. "Damn it, this is the second time they've managed to find you," she hissed at him.

Taylor had been toweling off his damp hair while I had turned to Asplundh to take the clothing she was passing to me. I swung around so abruptly that Asplundh stepped backward in surprise.

"Just what the hell are you acusing him of?" I demanded furiously.

"Wait a minute," Redding cut in, grabbing the back of one

of Alexandria's tunic sleeves. "No one's accusing anyone of anything here." He looked to Raydor again and gave the big Tachs a quizzical look. "So, just how did this little stakeout turn into an attack?"

Alexandria promptly jerked free of Redding's restraining hold, but she didn't persist in assaulting Taylor. I noticed, however, that both Claire and Asplundh were keeping a wary eye on the two antagonists. I didn't relax my vigilance entirely, but I switched most of my attention to Raydor as he replied to Redding's question.

Raydor gave a slight, almost nonchalant shrug. "We figured it might be profiteers," he said with deliberate innocence. "The station has some short-range beam cannon—for defensive purposes, of course."

Redding grinned wolfishly, showing a glimpse of square white teeth. "You got two of them first, right?"

Blinking owlishly, Raydor nodded, his expression of feigned innocence turning more rueful. "It was the third one that almost fried us," he admitted. "Cam and Traeger took out the first two, but the third one had moved. We almost didn't get him." He shot Taylor a sympathetic glance and continued. "They had these incendiary grenades—set off fires everywhere." He made an economical gesture toward the pile Claire had made of their cast-off clothing. "That's mostly how we got so messed up, trying to put them all out before they set the prairie on fire. Except Traeger," he added, shaking his head. "When the last air car came down, it took out part of one wall of the station; Traeger had just gone back inside to get our stuff."

For a moment no one spoke. I was just letting out my breath, a breath taken deeply and held too long, when Alexandria put a further question to Raydor. Her voice was quiet and controlled, but there was a cold edge to it that still caused my body to tense.

"The third car—you and Taylor went after that one?"

Not pausing in the act of reaching for the clean pair of leather trousers that Redding was offering him, Raydor threw her a quick look and simply responded, "Yeah, but I had the cannon."

"By the Light!" Alexandria exploded, turning back to Taylor with such vehemence that her wild hair bounced in a crazy halo around her face. "It's *him*! Don't you see?" she said, gesturing emphatically at Taylor. "That third air car moved because you had *him* with you! Just like out at Dayne's, in that mother-joinin' blizzard, the air car that was tailing us stopped following when we dumped *him* off." Her voice dropped but somehow the decrease in volume only seemed to produce a simultaneous increase in menace as she harshly concluded. "Somehow those bastards are tracking *him*!"

There was a moment of silence when no one spoke, and it seemed that all I could hear was the roaring rhythm of my own pulse in my ears. Everyone's eyes automatically and will-lessly had been drawn to Taylor. He stood there absolutely motionless in just his suit liner, the damp towel still hanging from one hand. I tore my gaze away from him and fixed my eyes on Alexandria's rigid face, and suddenly a lifetime of unaddressed grievances boiled up through me like a fiery bolus of pure rage.

"You Classless *bitch*!" I snarled at her, stepping forward with my hands knotted into furious fists. "How *dare* you accuse—"

Then Taylor caught me from behind, his fingers biting through the coarse fabric of my woven shirt and then painfully into the flesh of my shoulder beneath. He pulled me back so sharply that I almost lost my balance and fell into him. He spoke in a voice I had never heard before. "No, Jo," he said, his mouth nearly at my ear. "She's right. I think they *are* following me."

I spun around so abruptly that I wrenched free of his hands. Studying his stricken face, I felt an icy numbness sluice through me. "What do you mean?" I asked him with total calmness while I stared helplessly into those soft, remorseful sienna-colored eyes and felt the dread of discovery wash over me like a drench of cold water.

Taylor licked his lips and glanced over my shoulder. I felt a gentle hand touch my back and turned my head to see that Lewis was directly behind me. He and Traeger must have been able to hear the shouting all the way out in the kitchen. I had not even been aware that he had reentered the room. But Lewis's physical contact with me steadied me, giving me a badly needed sense of emotional equilibrium in that turbulent situation. It literally gave me the ability to go on.

"What do you mean, Taylor?" I repeated softly.

The towel dropped silently from his hands, but Taylor did not move toward me or try to ameliorate what he was about to say by attempting to touch me. He met my eyes steadily, intently, as if we were the only two people in the room, and slowly began to explain. "On Porta Flora, after we left the Ombudsman's office and you went back to your ship, someone from CA Security tailed me and detained me." My brows must have climbed at that, but Taylor's gaze never wavered; he went on, his voice low but unfaltering. "They took me back to the Ombudsman's." He paused briefly but significantly. "But it was Leppers who'd sent for me."

I think I sensed rather than heard Alexandria stir then, but before she could interrupt with any question or comment, I darted a sharp, threatening look in her direction. Then I resumed eye contact with Taylor, wordlessly urging him to go on.

"Leppers told me what he had told you—about the renegades and about the threat to the Class Tens. He told me you were in terrible danger, Jo." For the first time Taylor's voice seemed to verge on failing him, but he hesitated only momentarily, his gaze holding steady, before he continued. "He asked me to go with you, to let him know where you went when you left Porta Flora."

My eyes must have betrayed my reaction even before I could have put words to it, for Taylor's eyes dilated, growing wide and helpless, and he suddenly reached out and gripped my shoulder, beseeching me. "Jo, I told him *no*—I wasn't going to do it! But then you—"

But then I had asked him to come along with me.

Taking a deep breath and rushing on as if he knew he probably would have a limited opportunity to speak before someone interrupted him with questions, Taylor resumed earnestly. "When you asked me to come along with you, I knew you really were in trouble—that Leppers hadn't been bluffing and you really did need help. And so I thought if I was going to be there to watch out for you anyway, then I could try to help Leppers, too."

I got out the first question, my voice unnaturally calm, sounding hollow even to my own ears. "Right before we pulled out from Porta Flora, you told Leppers we were going to Heinlein?"

Taylor nodded, closely watching my face. "When I made the call back to my lodgings. They had told me how to code my messages so it wouldn't look suspicious."

"And on Heinlein," I went on levelly but inexorably, "when you went up to Port to send the message to your boss?"

For the first time Taylor's eyes dropped away from mine for a second; his nod was scarcely more than a stiff little jerk of his head. "I coded it to Leppers, told him we were going to Earthheart." He swallowed with a visible effort. "Except by then—"

Except that by the time we'd pulled out from Heinlein, Leppers had long since been dead, and if I'd been honest with Taylor from the start, he would have known that, and the renegades—who had doubtless killed Leppers once he had served their purpose and had been summarily appropriating the coded messages from Taylor—would not have had our final destination handed to them on a silver platter. No wonder Taylor had been so stunned to find out that Leppers had been killed. What was it that Alexandria had said earlier to Claire about her culpability for the capture of the Tens? Well, there was more than enough blame to go around on this one, too.

I realized then that I'd been staring at Taylor, undoubtedly frowning. His expression was a pained mixture of guilt and earnest remorse, but at that moment there was not a bit of anger or recrimination toward him in me. I felt too strongly the weight of my own guilt, my own remorse, to be able to summon up any blame for him. Suns, all he had done was try to protect me, and by keeping the truth from him, twice now I'd nearly gotten him killed as well. About the only thing I could have faulted him for was not telling me about all this sooner, once he'd found out Leppers was dead and knew exactly what we were up against. But even then I didn't think it had been a matter of courage; I thought he just honestly hadn't seen that it could make any difference then.

Taylor's hand lifted from my shoulder and rose almost hesitantly to cup the side of my face. There was no guile in those golden-brown eyes; in all the time I'd known him, there never had been. "Jo," he said softly, "I just thought I was helping them protect you. I didn't realize—"

"I know," I responded, cutting him off. I also knew Taylor needed to tell me that and more. But I didn't want it then, not in front of the others. I repeated, more gently, "I know you didn't."

When Alexandria broke in, her manner was somewhat brusque but surprisingly evenhanded. "When you met with the A's on Porta Flora, did they want you to carry a transmitter?" she asked Taylor.

Taylor turned slightly so that he could face her squarely, his expression solid and unflinching. "No," he said, "I only talked to Leppers, and all he asked me to do was to go with Jo and report our destination back to him."

"Are you sure?" Alexandria persisted. "He didn't want you to carry some kind of tracer so they could follow you?"

"No," Taylor repeated, his jaw tightening slightly, a trace of indignation in his voice. "He didn't give me anything like that. And if he'd suggested it, I would have told him no."

One long, almost casual stride brought Redding right alongside Alexandria. As usual, his manner was offhand and quite matter-of-fact, and his lean face was noncommittal as he asked Taylor, "Remember anything funny happening to you while Leppers had you there?" At Taylor's blank look, he elaborated. "The security goon didn't hold a weapon on you, did he? Or prod you with anything?"

It was Alexandria's craggy face that provided the key to Redding's line of questioning; comprehension turned her creased frown into a look of grim irony. She glanced sideways at Redding. "You're thinking an implant?"

Redding shrugged almost amiably. "It's been done," he pointed out.

I looked from Redding to Alexandria and then back again. "You mean you think they could have stuck him with some kind of subdermal transmitter without him knowing it?"

"It's possible," Redding offered simply.

Torn between self-righteous denial and honest confusion, Taylor just threw me a helpless look. "Nothing like that happened," he told me unhappily. "No one touched me at all. I'm sure of it."

When Raydor suddenly spoke up, I was surprised. Not only did the Tachs seldom involve himself in those kinds of debates, I had expected him to side with Alexandria in his evaluation of Taylor's worth. Equally surprising, he spoke directly to Taylor and not to her or to the group as a whole. "From what's been happening, it seems real likely those renegades have got some way of tracking you," he said quietly. "No matter why it happened or how it happened, I think what really matters is putting a stop to it."

At least the simple pragmatism of his assessment was pure Raydor, and I don't think the logic of his conclusion was lost on anyone in the room.

Extending one slender arm to him, Claire said calmly, "Taylor, why don't you come with me for a bit?" She glanced over to Asplundh, who still stood holding the pair of leather trousers she'd selected for Taylor to wear, and added, "You, too, Asplundh, if you would."

Puzzled, Taylor took a hesitant step forward. I gave him an encouraging little nod to keep him moving toward Claire. I thought I knew what the geneticist had in mind, especially since she'd asked Asplundh to accompany them. She had a hell of a lot of equipment in that lab of hers; I was sure there was at least one med scanner equal to the task of ferreting out any unwanted additions to Taylor's person.

For a moment I thought Alexandria would try to follow them, too, and I knew it had nothing to do with any concern for Taylor's personal health, either. But despite her diminutive size, Claire was every bit the mistress of that house. One sharp, meaningful glance from her as she gently took Taylor by the hand and began guiding him from the room was enough to keep Alexandria from following. And when I took a closer look at the expression on that seamed and weathered face, it was not what I had expected. Alexandria did not look irritated or even suspicious as she watched Claire, Taylor, and Asplundh disappear through the rear doorway; instead, she looked strangely thoughtful.

Redding's mind had immediately progressed to practical matters. With typical bluntness, he asked Raydor, "Were you able to modify the relay?"

Raydor gave a little snort. "Just about," he replied, bending to retrieve his dirty shirt from the pile on the floor. From its pouches he extracted the compact rectangle of Handy's relay and a handful of assorted components, a few of which I even recognized. "We were interrupted," he said.

"But you were able to find what you needed?" I asked him hopefully.

"More or less," he said. "It shouldn't take too much more to rig this to amplify the broadcast range; the receiver might take a little more work." He looked over to Alexandria. "We're going to have to link this in with an Integrator; can you key me access to Claire's?"

Alexandria's bushy brows tented, and some of her old asperity returned to her tone. "I thought you could key yourself access into any Integrator ever created," she put to him.

"I can," Raydor replied simply and without conceit, "but I figure if anyone's going to crack her system, it should be you. After all, she's your friend."

I hadn't even noticed that Jeck was back in the room until he spoke. The meticulous Altered had been silently cleaning up behind us, scooping up the dirty clothes, used towels, and discarded washers from the once-pristine floor. Before either Alexandria or Raydor could make a start toward Claire's Integrator console on the far side of the room, the jumpsuited man said firmly, "I will key the access for you." Again, a nearly imperceptible hint of amused superiority touched his implacable face, then he glided toward the console, adding, "I have been instructed to give you whatever aid you require."

I felt that I should stay there with Raydor even though I had no real technical skills to offer, but I could not. I watched as my crewmate seated himself at the console bench and entered some preliminary data into the access Jeck had just keyed for him. Even in that exotic setting and dressed in the coarse homespun of his Tachs clothing, when he was bent over the Integrator's panel, his crepelike and hairless head bowed in concentration as his thick fingers flew over the board, Raydor suddenly seemed so familiar, so achingly right, that I felt overwhelmed by unexpected despair.

Redding was peering over one of Raydor's broad shoulders, Alexandria over the other. Studying the small collection of scavenged components, the brown-haired man pointed out one in particular and commented, "You think that's going to interface with your amplifier?"

Without looking up—indeed, without even pausing in his rapid process of entry—Raydor explained, "I wouldn't've thought so, either, but Taylor showed me how we could retool the primary facet and make it even more powerful than your standard booster."

Redding was asking another question, but only the sound of his voice and not the sense of it registered with me. I felt Lewis's hand move, slowly kneading my back; it had been resting there for so long, I had forgotten its constant and reassuring presence. His hand slipped to my upper arm, and he stepped alongside me. "Come on," he said softly, starting to guide me across the room.

No one seemed to notice as we left. Raydor, Redding, and Alexandria were engrossed in the relay. Jeck was still restoring order to the room, and Rudd and Traeger had never put in a reappearance. Lewis led me back to the kitchen doorway and across the spacious, deserted room. I got only a brief glimpse of Jeck's domain, but I noted that the kitchen was equipped as lavishly as that of a fair-sized public eatery. Then we passed through another doorway, and we were outside, out into the cool darkness of the side yard, beneath the star-packed night sky of Earthheart.

If Lewis had sensed and understood the turbulence in my emotional state and my urgent need to remove myself—

temporarily at least—from the scene inside the house, then I hoped he could also comprehend what it was that I was feeling at that moment. Powers knew, I wasn't sure I understood it myself. I had thought that I was going to cry. But once we got outside, I found, much to my confusion and frustration, that the tears wouldn't come. My throat closed, and my shoulders shook with a few dry, convulsive sobs, but that was all. Without a word, Lewis took me in his arms and just held me, the side of his head pressed against mine.

For a time his embrace was all that I was aware of: the firm hold of his sinewy arms, the way his chest and abdomen and hips molded to mine, the heat of his body, and the faint soap and smoke scent of his skin and hair. In a way it was almost more intimate than our joining had been, because sexual unity automatically offers a lowering of the barriers to true access, and this kind of unity was a premeditated lowering of those same barriers, deliberately sought. And I felt strangely vulnerable and yet ridiculously secure in his embrace. Even though he was the one person who had the greatest capacity to cause me pain— and I knew so clearly that he might before it all was finished— in that moment I felt totally and utterly safe with him, and that was everything.

Gradually, after some indeterminate period of time, I began to notice other things: the chill of the rising breeze, the glottal bleat of one of the penned sheep, even the rich organic smell of the dewy sod beneath our feet. When that happened, I knew that I wasn't going to be able to cry—not then, at least. But I also knew that I would be all right again. Lifting my head, I made an inarticulate little snuffling sound.

Lewis pulled back his face and studied mine intently in the dim light leaking from the doorway. His fingers tangled gently in the ends of my hair, where it brushed my shoulders. "What?" he asked softly.

I cleared my throat. "I was just thinking about something Alexandria once said to me," I explained with a self-deprecating little snort. "She said that she couldn't figure out why, with so many people looking out for me, I still couldn't seem to stay out of trouble. Well, I just realized that the people who've been trying to protect me can't even keep themselves out of trouble."

The observation did not require or even invite a response from him; Lewis merely continued to stroke my hair, those luminous blue eyes silently watching my face in the faint light. I gave a little shiver and dropped my gaze. "You know the worst thing about that?'' I went on, feeling the burn of bitter irony tightening my throat. ''Alexandria's been riding Taylor ever since we left Heinlein, damn her! Now it looks like she was—''

But Lewis's fingertips had slipped to my lips, preventing me from going on. ''No,'' he told me, his voice quiet but firm, ''she didn't know, Jo, no more than you did—no more than *he* did, for that matter.'' His leanly muscled shoulders hitched slightly in a fatalistic little shrug, then he concluded intently. ''Don't be too hard on Alexandria; this is so important to her. I know that she forgets not everyone can share her degree of commitment to it, but she still feels so much pain about what's happened.''

I lifted my eyes, and his fingers slid lightly from my mouth. Calmly and deliberately, I studied that perfect, ingenuous face. ''What happened when Hanlon's renegades captured you?'' I asked him levelly. ''Was Alexandria there?''

Almost instantly I regretted the insensitivity of the question; those were things we had never tried to discuss. Although his plain and level expression did not change, Lewis's eyes betrayed him, those sapphire irises constricting until his pupils nearly disappeared. ''No, she wasn't there,'' he replied, his voice amazingly steady considering the depth of the pain in his eyes. ''That's part of why she feels so guilty.''

His lean shoulders shifted again, a movement so sketchy that it could hardly even have been called a shrug. There was a strangely remote focus to those usually unshuttered eyes, as if he found it necessary to somehow distance himself from the brutal memories I had so bluntly evoked. When he spoke again, his voice was soft, almost vague. ''You know, I don't remember a time when there was a place I really could have called home. Sometimes it seems like I've spent my whole life trying to hide who and what I am. All of us, we've been running from the Authorities since the Insurrection and from renegades since—''

He broke off then, his gaze suddenly returning to me, as if he'd just remembered my original question about Alexandria. ''It was on Araphos where we were taken,'' he told me quietly. ''I didn't know then that she and Lillard had once been lovers. I didn't know what she'd gone through trying to get back to him before we were taken.'' His hand rested on my shoulder, his fingers still twined in my hair, while his eyes held mine. ''They intended to take all of us alive, of course,'' he continued, not without a touch of irony in his voice. ''But they didn't know we'd had some warning and that we'd be armed. So there were some losses on both sides, some friends of mine . . .''

His voice trailed off, those vivid blue eyes slowly focusing on some point beyond my face—perhaps, indeed, beyond that planet. And I knew that he would go on, but suddenly I didn't think I could bear to hear the rest. I began to shake my head, gently at first and then more vigorously. But Lewis could not stop; he still had words that he could not keep inside any longer.

His fingers tightened urgently on my shoulder; his other hand rose to touch my cheek. Then the words came out in a stream. ''There was someone there, Jo—someone I cared for very much—and I had to watch her die, because they held me back and wouldn't let me go to her, when maybe I could have saved her life if I would have been able to just touch her—''

At last his voice broke painfully, and he was forced to stop. Standing there, his fingers clutching me while those incredible eyes filled with tears, I realized Lewis was about to do for the friend he had lost the one thing I had just been unable to do for my own friend: He was ready to weep. *His friend and lover*, I knew then, belatedly and with a curiously detached stab of pain at the realization. But as the first helpless shudder ran through his slender body, even as I reached to pull him fiercely into a tighter embrace, the side door of Claire's house swung open the rest of the way, and the stinging light of a power lantern spilled across us.

A huge form filled the doorway. I had to blink for a few moments in the sudden glare to recognize who it was.

Nodding deferentially, Jeck told us, ''They're back from the lab. Claire says you'd better come inside again.''

CHAPTER
THIRTEEN

Inside the house, in Claire's luxurious commons area, the lighting seemed painfully bright to my night-dilated eyes, and it took me a few moments to orient myself. Raydor still sat at the bench in front of the Integrator access console. I saw no sign of Taylor or Asplundh, but Alexandria and Redding sat on one of the plushly upholstered couches, with Claire on a chair across from them. The three of them looked up when Lewis and I entered the room, but typically, only Alexandria appeared openly impatient. From her expression, I suspected Claire had told them nothing yet.

I needed a chance to compose myself, and so, ignoring them, I went directly to Raydor. "Anything yet?" I asked him quietly.

The big hairless head lifted, his wide-set eyes bracketed by a whole new net of lines and creases. He made a small gesture, his thick and callused fingers grazing the gleaming surface of the access. "We're transmitting a coded call," he told me simply. He didn't need to add the second half of the statement—that so far he'd received nothing. I knew that Handy'd had to pull out, otherwise we'd have heard from him long before. The only questions that remained were how far out the maneuver had taken him and just how much coast time he was still facing coming back in. And they were questions to which I knew Raydor had no answers.

Leaving the console, I rejoined Lewis, and we came around the grouping of furniture. I stood to one side of Claire, my hands gripping the back of the mate to her chair. "Did you find the transmitter?" I asked her.

The wiry little woman seemed to take my brusqueness in stride; Powers knew, considering her long association with Alexandria, my manner must have seemed downright genteel to her. Claire gestured for Lewis and me to sit, but when I ignored her suggestion, he also remained standing beside me. She clasped her fingers around one drawn-up knee and offered calmly, "Yes, in a manner of speaking . . . but it isn't an implant."

I took a step forward, moving to the side of the chair to speak, but Alexandria beat me to it. "If it's not an implant," the burly woman demanded, her big body automatically leaning assertively forward, "then just what the hell—'in a manner of speaking'—is it?"

Claire disengaged her linked fingers, spreading her hands before her in a vague and yet perfectly evocative gesture. "I guess the best definition would be to call it a biochemical marker," she said. "My scans show minute amounts of what appears to be some kind of tracer compound in the nucleic acid of all of his neural cells."

"Wait a minute," I interrupted, already anticipating with dread the explanation diverging off into some complicated medical mumbo jumbo. "What do you mean by a tracer compound?"

Patiently leaning forward, Claire continued. "I can't be certain yet that this is even the same thing, but in genetics research, a tracer compound is what we use to mark certain nuclear material before we introduce it into a tissue culture or an organism." She began to sketch an invisible diagram on the polished surface of the low table at her knees. "It's like a synthetic protein; certain cells will take it up and incorporate it into their structure, but it won't break down, so when we scan for it, we can use its presence to follow whatever genetic material we had marked with it."

Shaking her head impatiently, Alexandria leaned even farther forward, her dark eyes glancing from Claire's nonexistent drawing back up to the geneticist's composed face. "You're saying that somebody dosed him with some kind of chemical transmitter?"

Claire's slender hands turned palms up. "Essentially, yes," she confirmed.

At the Integrator console, Raydor had been bent in silent concentration over the access, but I knew he hadn't missed a word of what had been said despite his seeming preoccupation with the modified relay. At Claire's words of verification, his head lifted and his eyes briefly met mine.

Beside Alexandria, Redding shifted slightly on the couch. His shaggy head was cocked quizzically, his brows canted, those steel-colored eyes bright with speculation. "This stuff may work in the lab," he reminded Claire, "but could that kind of marker be detected in something as big as a human body and over the kind of distances we're dealing with here? Those renegades must've been at least twenty kilometers behind the caravan for us not to be able to detect them following us."

But Claire just nodded. "Theoretically, yes. Although the laboratory application of these compounds has required only a rather limited range of transmission, there's no reason why a compound couldn't be developed that would be detectable over a much greater distance." She shrugged and concluded almost reluctantly, "If a med scanner can detect the marker's presence from a few centimeters away, there's really no reason why a scanner couldn't be developed which could detect a particular compound over any range you desired."

Alexandria made a rude snorting sound. "What I'd 'desire,' " she noted acerbically, "is for those ball-less bastards to have never detected this little piece of chemical baggage in the first place!"

Still perplexed, I moved another step closer to Claire, facing her directly. "How did they get this stuff into him?" I asked her anxiously.

"I think maybe I drank it."

I had turned far enough so that my back was to the rear doorway of the room and had been so intent on the conversation that I hadn't even heard Asplundh and Taylor enter until he'd spoken. They both approached the rest of us; Asplundh hung back a bit, but Taylor came up directly. He was freshly dressed in clean clothes, and his manner was typically forthright, even if his expression was a bit sheepish as he offered his explanation.

"On Porta Flora, when I met with Leppers in the Ombudsman's office," he continued, "he offered me coffee." He hesitated a moment, as if suddenly struck by the inanity of the method, then he just shrugged ingenuously, flashing a self-effacing smile. "What can I say? It was real coffee—it was delicious, by the way."

"It also was probably laced with the biochemical marker," Claire concluded needlessly.

While Taylor had been speaking, although I had been paying attention to what he said, I had also been thinking about two other things. One thing was Lewis's touch, because nearly the whole time we had been standing there together, his hand had been resting lightly on top of my shoulder. There was something in that contact that piqued some memory; I was just not yet able to sort out in my mind exactly what that was. The second thing was Alexandria's expression, which had subtly but definitely changed since Taylor had come into the room. From her original scowl of acrid sarcasm, her demeanor had shifted, but not in the direction I would have expected. She was regarding Taylor with a strangely speculative look rather than her typical contempt.

"So, what are we going to do about this marker thing?" Redding said. "Neutralize it?" He had directed his question to Claire, but the older woman merely turned to Asplundh, giving her a slight nod.

Asplundh awkwardly cleared her throat. "I've done some work with nucleic acid markers—in my research on Heinlein," she quickly added. She shot a sideways glance at Taylor. "If that's what this substance is, it might not be possible to chemically neutralize it. These markers are specifically designed to get into certain target cells and to stay there; there really isn't any antidote for them."

"Then what you're saying is that he's stuck being a walking transmitter," Alexandria translated bluntly, but surprisingly without malice.

"No, not necessarily," Asplundh hastily went on. "What we can do is analyze and then try to synthesize this particular compound. Once we have an actual sample of it, we might be able to formulate a countermarker—a substance that would bind to this marker at all its cellular sites and mask it so that the original scanning equipment they're using to detect it would no longer recognize it in the altered form."

But it was Redding who quickly brought up the obvious flaw in Asplundh's methodical plan. "Just how long is that going to take?" he asked her. He had only voiced what all of us, Taylor included, had to have been thinking already: The renegades had found Taylor twice so far; how long would it be before they found him again, before he led them right there to us?

Asplundh bristled visibly at Redding's implication. No longer hesitant or self-conscious, she shot back, "I don't know how long it'll take, but standing around here arguing about it sure won't make it happen any faster!"

I felt my heart begin to thud rapidly, accelerated by the same sort of indignation. Redding's pragmatism seemed determined to reduce Taylor to a commodity—and a liability at that. I was on the verge of adding my own protest to Asplundh's, when I found that it was not necessary, because Raydor spoke for the first time then, addressing the other, perhaps less obvious limitation that we all faced.

Turning from the Integrator console, his gruff voice as impassive as his stolid face, the big Tachs reminded us, "We could leave him, and we could go to Flatstone. But we still aren't getting off this planet until we've got a ship."

Muttering some inarticulate, probably archaic curse, Alexandria lurched to her feet, throwing back her head so viciously that the frenzied mass of her grizzled hair swung wildly. She had no obvious, satisfying target for her impotent fury; I knew exactly how she felt. Once again it seemed our lives were being held hostage by circumstances beyond our control. But even as she stalked off, taking a few fierce but useless strides across the carpeting, Taylor spoke again.

"Maybe we're looking at this thing from the wrong angle," he said quietly, looking first from Claire to Redding and then to Alexandria's stiffly set back.

The big woman swung around, staring sharply at him. "What do you mean?" she demanded roughly, but for the first time her anger didn't seem to be directed specifically at Taylor.

Taylor spread his hands. "You said it yourself," he explained to Alexandria. "I'm a walking transmitter. I'm the one they're following." His voice was calm, completely normal in tone, as he finished. "Why not put that fact to some good use."

"No!"

I thought at first that the vehement denial had come from my own lips, because the word had just exploded in my brain, but it hadn't been me. It hadn't even been Asplundh, although her whole body had jerked around sharply when she had heard Taylor's almost casual proposal. No, incredibly enough, it had been Alexandria who had spoken, her voice harsh with admonition. Equally incredibly, Taylor just went on, much as though her astonishing outburst had not occurred.

"Face it, we couldn't have come up with a better diversion if we'd created this ourselves," he said. "If I set off tonight, before you leave for Flatstone, I could lead them on the biggest wild goose chase you ever—"

I stepped forward, pulling away from Lewis, but again Alexandria was already ahead of me. "No, *damn you*," she hissed. She reached Taylor in a few prodigious strides, her powerful hands seizing the front of his overshirt with such furious strength that for one shocking moment I was certain she was going to shake him like an old rag. But she didn't. She was a good half head taller than him and probably outweighed him by at least fifty kilos, but as she glared down at him, her face contorted with anger, I suddenly realized that he was not the actual cause of her considerable wrath. He was just the unfortunate target of it. She was so infuriated only because she was afraid. Glowering at him, she snarled roughly, "You go out there like this, we might just as well slit your joinin' throat where you stand!" Then she actually did give him a little shake, but the action was almost gentle, as if she were only trying to be sure that she had his complete attention. Her voice had fallen low and become a soft growl. "You want to be a joinin' *martyr*, you stupid ass-hole? I'll fry you right here—save you the trip!"

Although I stood beside them, I did not try to reach out and touch Taylor. And I certainly didn't try to pry Alexandria free—I was no joinin' martyr. I just eyed the incongruous pair cautiously as, for a moment, the whole room fell silent and the only sound was the thumping of my pulse in my ears.

Taylor was the first to move. Slowly, almost imperceptibly, he straightened in Alexandria's grasp, and as he took a half step back from her, her thick, clawlike fingers gradually released their iron grip on his shirtfront. His expression was calm and his voice surprisingly level as, looking up directly into that formidable face, he announced, "Good; I'm glad you feel that way." Automatically smoothing the wrinkled fabric across the front of his chest, he concluded, "I wasn't so crazy about the idea myself."

I think I could have cheerfully throttled Taylor myself at that point, but suddenly the tension in the room broke and came apart like rotted ice, and so I opted instead for quickly taking him in a hard, relieved embrace. It was only then, as those familiar strong arms came around me, that I realized my legs were actually shaking. And at that time, when I desperately didn't need them, the tears wanted at last to come. I thought of Lewis's grief for his murdered friend and how I still had that chance Lewis had been denied: the chance to tell someone I loved how much he mattered to me. I choked down hard on the sobs that threatened me. "You asshole," I whispered wetly in Taylor's ear, squeezing him fiercely.

But circumstances were not willing to wait for us. Claire was already propelling herself to her feet. "Let's get to it, then," she said energetically. She was halfway across the room before she even paused, turning only to gesture to Asplundh. "First, I want you to run another neural scan; I'll start fractionalizing the data we already have."

Claire was nearly through the rear doorway, with Asplundh hurrying after her, before Taylor released me and stepped back. He winked at me and, with a final squeeze, let go of me to follow the two geneticists.

"Another neural scan, huh?" I heard him ask Asplundh, his voice deliberately light and teasing. As the curly-haired woman paused for him to catch up, he rolled his eyes, complaining good-naturedly, "I want you to know that last one gave me one hell of a headache!"

I had not noticed that Lewis had stayed standing near Redding until then, when he suddenly moved. Stepping forward across the carpeting, he came to an abrupt halt at a point halfway between me and the departing pair. "Wait," he called out to them. Then he swung to me, his face alight with a strangely intense expression.

"Jo, do you remember on the incubator truck, when we— when you asked me if there were other things I could do?" he asked me earnestly.

Momentarily stymied, I hastily tried to put the two things into juxtaposition—what we had been doing on the truck and the question he had just posed—and come up with some connection that didn't involve sex. Instantly seeing my confusion, Lewis rescued me by elaborating further.

"You asked me if I could do other kinds of physical reorganization by touch-healing," he prompted. "Do you remember?"

And suddenly I did remember. Asplundh seemed to comprehend the intent of his question as well, because she turned back into the room, cautious encouragement blooming on her pale, oval-shaped face. "Of course," she said softly, glancing rapidly from Lewis to a somewhat puzzled Taylor. "I never even thought of that possibility."

Patience had never been one of Alexandria's strong points, and the frustrating constraints of our current situation tended to make her even less tolerant than usual of any obtuse or baffling behavior. Claire had reappeared in the rear doorway, a look of mild irritation on her tanned face as she confirmed that Asplundh and Taylor had not continued to follow her back to the lab. But before the older woman even had a chance to speak, Alexandria's sharp gaze swept swiftly across the room, from

Asplundh to Taylor, past Lewis, and finally to me. "What the hell are you talking about?"

Asplundh was the expert; even Claire would have been a more logical choice. But Alexandria was still glaring at *me*, and so I found myself doing the explaining.

"The research that Asplundh was doing on Heinlein with Lewis's touch-healing," I elaborated for Redding, Raydor, and Claire as well as Alexandria. "We know that the physical basis of his Talent is the ability to reorganize tissue at the submolecular level." I shot a quick look at Lewis, remembering our strained and truncated conversation in the incubator truck, and then went on. "With healing, it's taking damaged tissue and making normal tissue out of it again. But it might be possible for him to do other kinds of submolecular reorganization." Without volition, I glanced over to Taylor, who was listening with a calmly absorbed expression on his face. "It might be possible for Lewis to take cells with this marker in them and make them into cells without the marker."

For a moment no one spoke while the full implication of what I had just said sunk in. In the sudden silence, even the smallest of sounds assumed a unique clarity: the subtle hum of the house's heating system, some faint metallic rattle from Jeck's kitchen, the soft creaking of the wooden bench's joints as Raydor shifted before the Integrator console. I watched as slowly, almost will-lessly, Taylor's eyes moved to settle on Lewis's face. But it was Redding, ever the pragmatist, who first asked the obvious question.

The gray-eyed man got to his feet, leisurely and with elaborate nonchalance. He actually paused to stretch, extending his spine with a lanky grace. Then, turning to Lewis, he put it to him bluntly. "Well, can you do that?"

Lewis made a small gesture, his slender hands spreading. "I don't know," he admitted. "I've never tried to do anything like that before."

Alexandria gave a sharp snort. "Well, try it!" she said. "What've we got to lose?"

Stepping back through the doorway and into the commons, Claire moved to Asplundh's side and quietly intervened. "It may not be that simple," she pointed out reluctantly, her delicate face set in concern. "I'm no authority on touch-healing—" Catching herself, she shot us a quick, bemused smile and added parenthetically, "not that there *are* authorities on touch-healing, I guess, but technically we're not dealing with 'damaged' tissue here.'' She tipped her head toward Taylor. ''The marker has been incorporated into his neurons as a normal nucleic acid. As far as his body is concerned, those cells *are* normal.''

''You mean that trying to touch-heal him could actually damage his cells?'' I asked her, giving Taylor another and far more anxious glance.

''No, not necessarily,'' Claire said. ''In fact, that seems unlikely. What seems more likely is that Lewis wouldn't be able to 'recognize' the marked cells as being any different; I don't think that touch-healing would have any effect on them at all.''

''You think it's safe to try, though?'' Alexandria asked.

''That's not for me to decide,'' Claire replied, adding diplomatically, ''There's only one person here who can make that decision.''

Whether intentionally or not, all of us in the room seemed to find our eyes drawn to Taylor. With a toss of his head, he shook back his hair and said cheerfully, ''Well, what the hell? It's just neurons, right?''

Slowly and deliberately taking the last few steps that separated the two men, Lewis approached Taylor. His expression was intent, but those cerulean eyes were also filled with open compassion. ''Don't worry,'' he said gently, his voice almost a whisper. ''I won't hurt you.''

''Yeah, that's what they said before that damned neural scan,'' Taylor quipped. His voice was steady, and he didn't flinch, but I knew him well enough to sense the very real apprehension hidden behind the theatrical roll of his eyes as Lewis carefully lifted his hands and rested them on Taylor's temples.

My own experience with touch-healing had been brief and precipitate, seemingly eons ago. I didn't remember what it had felt like; actually, I guess what I did remember about it was that it hadn't felt like anything at all. As I watched the two men, momentarily linked by that light and tentative touch, my thoughts went more to what it was that Lewis might be feeling during the contact. His eyes were closed, his head slightly cocked, his mouth turned down in a frown. Then his lids lifted, and he dropped his hands from Taylor's head.

''Nothing,'' he said regretfully, shaking his dark head. He took a half step back, lifting his shoulders in an apologetic shrug. ''I'm sorry,'' he explained directly to Taylor. ''I know nothing is happening. It just doesn't feel . . .'' He trailed off, his glance bouncing over the rest of us waiting in the room. ''I'm sorry,'' he reiterated needlessly. "I don't even know how to explain this when it does work, but I know it's not working now."

"Hey, that's okay," Taylor said, reaching out and giving Lewis an encouraging clap on the shoulder. "You tried it; what more could you do?" He flashed that stellar smile and added wryly, "Besides, you got rid of my headache!" I couldn't tell if he was kidding Lewis or not.

"Come on," Claire said, motioning to Asplundh and Taylor, "back to plan A. The sooner we get started, the quicker we can solve this."

I wanted to go with them then. Not because I thought I'd be of any help—I had no illusions about that—but because I was no good at waiting, and I thought it might relieve some of my interminable anxiety if I could be where something, however unproductive, was happening. But in the end I just stood helplessly by and watched them disappear through the rear doorway and didn't try to follow.

Redding came up to Lewis, giving him a companionable pat on the back and murmuring something to him that I could not hear. Then the laconic freightman drifted off toward the far side of the room, where he seemed content to occupy himself with casually inspecting the contents of Claire's extensive cabinets and curio shelves. Alexandria prepared herself for the wait by planting herself in one of the lushly upholstered chairs, where she sat, unapproachable and silently brooding. For a time I hung around near the Integrator console, stolidly watching the blank screen over Raydor's broad shoulders. Lewis stayed nearby, but he did not try to intervene or touch me. I know that Raydor would have talked with me if I'd initiated any kind of conversation; perhaps he would even have welcomed it. But I found that I had no words to offer.

After a small eternity that couldn't have been more than a half hour, objective time, Taylor came back into the room. His face looked drawn and oddly tight, but when he saw me coming toward him, he gave me a quick smile and announced, "Well, I guess it's up to the great scientific minds now."

I put my hand out to touch his upper arm. Looking beyond me, to where Raydor sat at the console, Taylor asked, "You hear anything yet?"

Not deterred by his diversion, I gently squeezed his arm as I shook my head. "Not yet," I told him. "What about you; are you okay?"

"Sure," he responded, adding, "A little dragged out, I

guess.'' He glanced around the commons area, his eyes barely pausing on Redding and Alexandria, lingering a moment on Lewis, and then finally coming to rest on me. ''This'd be a great time for some of those golden oldies chips,'' he teased me. ''I don't suppose you brought any along.'' As I again shook my head, he continued. ''Much as Jeck and Rudd look like fun guys, I'd bet we couldn't scare up a chip of Stressed Metal's greatest hits around here, either.'' Then he yawned elaborately and announced, ''That being the case, I think I'll just find a corner somewhere and curl up for a while; my poor neurons aren't used to all this activity.''

After Taylor left the room, Lewis came up to me and lightly put his arm around my waist. Wordlessly, he urged me along over to one of the plush couches and got me to sit down there with him. The cushions felt seductively yielding beneath me. I didn't think there was anything exceptional in play, nothing like his Talent, but as he slowly and methodically massaged my tense neck and shoulders, I gradually began to relax against him. Then I felt my lids begin to droop. Murmuring a halfhearted protest, I nevertheless did not attempt to get up again or move away from him. His fingers continued to knead my knotted muscles, and I felt his warm lips lightly brush my forehead as I slumped bonelessly across his chest. Someone lowered the level of illumination in the room; either that or it was just my eyes shutting down. Lulled by the repetitive comfort of Lewis's touch, I slowly let myself go.

Once when I opened my eyes, my lids stupendously heavy, I realized that both Redding and Alexandria had gone from the room. But that seemed remote and very inconsequential to me. I knew that Raydor was still seated at the Integrator console, and I gave serious thought to offering to relieve him. For about five seconds. I had Lewis's body against me, Lewis's warmth and shape and scent; true sleep claimed me, dragging me deeply under.

When I awoke again, it was rapidly but without any sense of alarm or disorientation. My time sense told me I had been sleeping for several hours; it must have been the middle of the night. Lewis was leaning back, half reclining against the arm of the couch in what didn't look like a very comfortable position. His arms were still around me, his lips were slightly parted, and his breathing was slow and softly nasal. He looked so relaxed, so childlike, that for a moment I wanted to just forget where we were and why.

I also wanted very badly to stay where I was, but the volume of Claire's real coffee that I had drunk earlier had done its work, and I needed to find hygiene. It took some delicate maneuvering to work myself free of Lewis's embrace without waking him, but he was still deeply asleep and barely stirred when I slipped off the couch. I passed the Integrator console, where Raydor still sat on the bench, his torso slumped over the access, his big hairless head practically resting on the small maze of components he had rigged to Handy's relay. He was asleep but not off duty. There was no way he would have been able to sleep through an incoming signal in that position.

Negotiating my way through the dimly lit commons room wasn't difficult; finding Claire's facilities in the small labyrinth of rooms back in the private quarters of the house proved more tricky. I struck out on the very first place I tried, a room I had selected principally because its door was partially ajar. But the room was a sleeping quarters, and it was occupied. A haphazard trail of scattered and unidentifiable articles of clothing led across the floor from the doorway to the wide bed, where a completely identifiable activity was energetically taking place beneath the heaving bedcovers.

Pulling back into the corridor, I headed resolutely onward toward the next door. I felt a curious sense of emotional detachment about the scene I had just inadvertently witnessed, although I realized even then that perhaps later, with some thought, I would feel differently about it. For although the darkness and the bedcovers had hidden the details, there had been no mistaking the distinctive guttural voice of the woman I had heard moaning in that bed. It looked as though Alexandria had finally considered Redding worthy, after all.

It was Handy's voice that propelled me out of sleep the next time, some scant hours later. My awakening had not been quite simultaneous with his transmission, however, because I caught him in midsentence, and by the time I'd lurched to my feet and reached the console, he and Raydor were already in the midst of a typical conversational exchange.

"Any damage?" Raydor was asking Handy.

There was an infinitesimal pause; then Handy's deep voice reported, "Nothing major. I'm keeping Internals busy, though."

I leaned across the console and hit the switch that looked most like transmit on the cobbled-together conglomeration Raydor had made of the relay. "Handy, what the hell is going on?" I demanded, too deliriously relieved just to hear his voice again to be able to force any real conviction into what I had intended as a reprimand.

"Hi, Jo!" Handy responded. "Sorry I had to pull out on you. I tried to reach *Kestrel* before the renegades did, but they didn't even take time to hail her before they opened fire."

His deep bass voice dropped even lower then. In a human, the tone would have signaled anger, and because I understood just what it signaled in Handy—whether the emotion was theoretically possible or not—I didn't interrupt him to ask just where the hell he'd gotten the idea that protecting an unmanned ship was part of his programming. I interrupted him only to hasten the rest of the story.

"So you pulled out to avoid the renegades?" I asked him.

"Oh, no. Even though it was too late for *Kestrel*, I was able to take care of them without much problem," he corrected me matter-of-factly. "They only had three ships—no high-beams. No, I pulled out to avoid the A's."

Of course. In a convoluted sort of way, I guessed it made perfect sense. The renegades could be fried because they presented a direct threat to *Raptor*, a fact they had amply demonstrated on *Kestrel*. The A's arrival on the scene was just an inconvenience, and Handy's programming didn't bend far enough to allow him to fry them just for that. It had meant abandoning us, but then, he had known that we were in no immediate danger where we were. So he had run.

I really didn't want to have to think any more about that part, so I tried reverting to my command mode. "Ship's status?" I asked.

"Well . . . let's just say it's a good thing we're running without personnel right now," he came back smartly, "because the AG is still shot to shit, and I've got the damnedest collection of stuff floating around in here—"

Giving up any pretense of command, I interrupted him by simply asking, "Where are you now?"

"Six-point-seven-eight hours out," he said, all business then. "You have our coordinates here?"

"Of course, Jo," he replied. "We have contact, remember?"

For the first time since I had been catapulted into wakefulness, I became aware again of the other people in the room with me, and the universe necessarily expanded to include more than just me and that familiar voice coming over an unfamiliar speaker. Raydor sat hung over the console, his posture a typical one of absorbed concentration. Lewis had gotten up from the couch and followed me across the room to the Integrator; he stood right behind me. If the others had been asleep, the sound of our voices must have wakened them. I glanced quickly, almost guiltily, over to Alexandria and Redding. The burly woman looked even more disheveled than usual, her unfettered hair in frizzy disarray, but Redding managed to look barely rumpled. It was Taylor who still looked the most bedraggled, his homespun shirt still half-unfastened and his feet bare. He yawned hugely, blinking in the dim light, looking like nothing more than a little boy who had been dragged out of bed in the middle of the night.

Turning back to the boosted relay, I said quietly, "Handy, we've got a problem here."

"Yeah, I'll say. You won't have a ship for almost seven hours," Handy quipped. But then, before I could make any reproving remarks, his sonorous voice sobered and he continued. "I know all about it, Jo."

I guess that initially I hadn't been as awake as I had thought, because it took me until then to remember that from the moment he had been able to make contact with us by way of the augmented relay, Handy had in effect been connected with Claire's Integrator. In the time it had taken him to speak his first sentence—probably even his first word—to Raydor, his hypertrophied neurons had already scanned everything that was contained in the banks of his host unit, including the portion of the Integrator's function core that was devoted to Claire's laboratory use. In addition to the detailed status of the entire household, he knew everything about the situation with Taylor that Claire and Asplundh did, which was already a lot more than I knew.

Handy had paused for a few seconds, not to "think," because his artificially supplanted brain had already instantaneously moved on in its logical course, but merely out of courtesy, to wait and see if I had anything further to interject at that point. When it became evident that I didn't, he continued. "I have information that might be of some help; Claire and Asplundh are reviewing it now."

I didn't even want to know where the hell he'd gotten his "information," although the fleeting image of the renegades' three vessels exploding under *Raptor*'s high-beams did skitter briefly through my mind. I just lowered my gaze to the console and asked him, "Can you give us a visual from the lab?"

The resolution on the console's small screen wasn't of shipboard quality, but it was adequate to connect us with the lab. Claire was working at the Integrator access, her patrician face etched by a thoughtful frown as she studied the new data. In the background I could see Asplundh transferring a glass container from one cluttered counter to another. I didn't mind not being able to see exactly what might be in the container; it bore an alarming resemblance to a disembodied vertebrate brain and spinal cord. Both of the women turned toward the console speaker at the sound of my voice.

"Can you use what Handy's got?" I asked them without pre-amble

Claire's dark brows tented. "We can use *anything*," she said. "We were hitting nothing but dead ends here."

"It's turned out to be an entirely different class of compound than the genetic markers I've used in my research," Asplundh said, still holding the jar in which the spidery white tissue floated. "Same purpose, but completely different structure." High resolution or not, I could see the exhaustion pulling at her pale face. She made a gesture with the container toward the console, the ghostly tendrils undulating in their liquid support. "I don't know where your Integrator got this data, but I think it's the key to what's been blocking us."

With a deliberate effort of will I kept myself from glancing at Taylor. Instead, my eyes briefly sought out Alexandria's craggy face before I turned back to the screen and asked Claire, "How long will it take us to get to Flatstone?"

Behind me in the commons area, someone stirred slightly; a throat was cleared. The implication of my question was evident enough. In less than seven hours we would have a ship again; biochemical markers or not, the rest of our journey had to be planned.

On the Integrator screen, the image of Claire's face assumed a thoughtful expression. "I had Rudd and Traeger ready the ground carts; even during daylight they're the least conspicuous way for you to travel. The surveillance scouts are accustomed to us using them with the cattle." She paused, her expression astute and evaluating. "By ground cart, the trip takes about five and a half hours," she concluded.

I addressed Handy again. "You've got the coordinates for the embryotory?"

"Of course, Jo," was the prompt reply.

I had been sitting perched on the edge of the wooden bench before the Integrator; I shifted, leaning even farther forward over the console, with its bastard tangle of wires, as if my very posture could convey to Handy the urgent importance of what I was about to tell him. "You're still out, what—about six and a half hours? Whatever happens, I don't want you coming in all the way until you hear directly from me," I said flatly. "I want you to stay out completely beyond the A's scanner range—no matter what—until I call you in. Do you understand me?"

Handy sounded moderately aggrieved, as if I'd just treated him like either an idiot or a piece of machinery. "Of course I understand you," he responded, confirming my impression of his reaction by adding almost petulantly, "Who do you think you're speaking to, the food synthesizer?"

"No, Handy," I replied, my voice softly apologetic, "I'm speaking to an old friend and the one person I trust to save my ship—and my life."

I turned sideways on the bench, my eyes going momentarily to Lewis's face. I wanted to be able to linger there, to be engulfed by those blue eyes and just abandon the rest of it. But, of course, I couldn't. I wrenched my gaze away, settling it on Alexandria's solid, implacable face. "Once we're ready to leave for Flatstone and you get word to them, are they going to be ready to evacuate immediately?" I asked her.

I don't think a few hours' sleep alone could have visibly improved Alexandria's weathered face that much; maybe the vigorous joining with Redding had helped. Or maybe it was just the fact that events seemed to be increasing our possibility of reaching her goal. At any rate, she actually looked quite rested and reasonably composed as she responded to my question. "They're always ready," she said simply.

"We'll still be able to do it with only one ship?" I asked.

"We could do it with one air car and a skyhook if we had to," she said.

I let my eyes sweep from Alexandria to Redding. He stood beside her but not suspiciously close, his lean face typically unfathomable. I didn't have the luxury of time to try to interpret the change, if any, in the silent dynamics between them, but I mentally filed away his look for future analysis.

I looked then to Taylor, scanning his somewhat sleepy face, before I turned back to the Integrator screen. "How long till dawn?" I asked Claire.

The dark-haired woman replied without even looking up from her access. "About an hour yet."

"So that still gives us some time to—"

Coming over the speaker, Claire's whoop was stunningly amplified and slightly distorted as she interrupted me. "We've got it! By the Light—we were close all along," she added with a touch of wonderment. She gestured hastily to Asplundh, then both of them bent over the console, their fingers a blur as they furiously punched in data.

Without comment, Handy blocked off a strip at the bottom of the viewing screen and began running a stream of symbols and chemical configurations, all of which were completely incomprehensible to me. The looks on the two geneticists' faces told me more. They conferred in terse and rapid phrases, studying the readout even as they reran and confirmed it. But then, before I could so much as begin to formulate the questions I wanted to ask about their discovery, the expressions of jubilation and triumph began to crumble from their faces.

"Shit, this *can't* be right," Claire muttered, punching buttons on the console with what suddenly had become an almost belligerent intensity.

Asplundh's ivory-colored face was even more revealing. "I don't believe it—you don't put this kind of isomer into living tissue!" she sputtered. She looked up directly into the screen, repeating incredulously, "I can't *believe* they used this as a marker."

"*What?*" I blurted out.

Calmly and plainly, Handy explained for us. "The marker that was introduced into Taylor's body is a compound that can't be neutralized or altered to mask its presence without catalyzing a catabolic reaction."

Once again I had to fight the automatic reflex to turn and seek out Taylor's golden-brown eyes. Determinedly staring at the screen, I addressed myself to Handy. "You mean it would damage or destroy his cells?" I asked him, my voice concise and even.

"Yes. And you couldn't destroy the compound even by destroying the tissue that contained it," the Integrator elaborated calmly. "Even cellular decomposition wouldn't affect it."

It took a moment for Handy's final statement to penetrate, unwillingly, the barrier that I had erected in my mind, that innate line of defense I carried as protection against hopeless situations of any kind. Both the commons area and Claire's laboratory fell abruptly silent as the finality of the Integrator's blunt assessment was fully absorbed. For a minute or two the only sound was the cadenced rhythm of some small bit of laboratory equipment,

oddly filtered over the speaker as it toiled busily and uselessly
in the background.

I slowly turned from the console again, and this time I permitted my eyes to go to Taylor. One of his sorrel-colored eyebrows canted up crookedly, and the fleeting ghost of that
devastatingly droll smile pulled at his lips. "Then I guess we
can forget the part about slitting my throat where I stand," he
noted wryly. The rest of it was said with his eyes.

I was off the bench and reaching for him without the need for
any thought. I caught him hard by the upper arms and gave him
a furious little jerk. *"No!"* I snapped, shaking him again, grimly
then and with real purpose. "You're *not* going out there alone!"

Probably more to Taylor's surprise than my own, the second
pair of hands to grip him was Alexandria's. The big woman had
turned on him with nearly the same vehemence with which I
had, and she had the advantage of superior size and strength.
She seized two fistfuls of his opened shirtfront with a tenacity
that rudely dislodged my hold on one arm and then glared down
into his somewhat bemused-looking face with the steely command, "You're not going *anywhere*!"

To his credit, Taylor neither protested our assault nor tried to
free himself. Yet he didn't capitulate. As he stood there tractably
in our crude grasp, those sienna eyes just studied both our faces
with an indefeasible calm. Then, still unresisting, he quietly
pointed out, "It's not a matter of misguided idealism, believe
me—it's just a matter of pragmatism. Once they find me, I'm
dead anyway. Why should I be with you when that happens?"

"No."

The word was spoken scarcely louder than a whisper, yet to
my tautly stretched nerves, in that anxiously hushed room, it
could as well have been shouted for the effect it achieved. Still
clutching Taylor's arm, I snapped my head around and my gaze
found Lewis. And although I wasn't touching him, something
of the same sensation I had come to think of as Lewis's presence
within me—his *essence*, for lack of a better term—shot through
my body. Slowly my hand slipped from Taylor's arm, and I
pivoted to face Lewis.

"What?" I asked him, my voice as soft as his had been.

And I knew I had seen that look before; it just took me a few
seconds to remember when and where. A shudder ran through
me then, and my pulse began to bang, because the last time I'd
seen that intense but frighteningly abstracted light in Lewis's
eyes had been in the research complex on Camelot, when he

had reached so deeply within himself that he had plumbed a place where the Lewis I knew might not even have existed.

Lewis made a small, nonspecific gesture toward Taylor. Then, wordlessly, he was already turning toward the Integrator console. He reached out smoothly and purposefully, but I saw that his hand, when he extended it, was trembling slightly.

Raydor silently slid over on the bench, offering Lewis more space. As Lewis leaned over the console, the Tachs automatically reached for his questing hand and guided it toward the makeshift input like an instructor directing a pupil. Staring down at the access, Lewis quickly fitted his fingers to it.

"The compound," Lewis said to Handy, his voice curiously lacking in inflection. "Can you feed its configuration to me by Integration analysis?"

My pulse had been racing, but at that moment I was certain that it had suddenly halted. For a few crushing seconds I felt as though I had taken a staggering blow to the chest and that the breath had been forced from my lungs. Then everything started up again in a rush. I stared incredulously at Lewis, but something—that something inside me that was his, I knew—kept the explosive command, the vehement protest, from ever leaving my lips.

"If you want," Handy replied mildly.

I don't know whatever happened to "Integration analysis is not a legitimate function of my systems," and I didn't much care. Maybe after what had happened at Nethersedge, there was something inside Handy that was Lewis's, too.

Stirring, Lewis began glancing around the cluttered console. Raydor was the first to realize that what he was looking for was a set of cerebral leads. As the Tachs began to methodically search the console's compartments, the rear doorway swung open and Claire and Asplundh came into the room. When I saw the set of leads clasped in the older woman's hand, I realized that the two of them had been able to see and hear everything that had happened in the commons area since Handy had made his irrevocable announcement.

Lewis immediately turned toward Claire, but the wiry little woman dropped her hand, holding the leads down against her thigh while she regarded him with open skepticism. "What are you going to try to do?" she asked Lewis.

Catching himself then, as if just first remembering the presence of the rest of the people in the room, Lewis spread his hands in a spontaneous, evocative gesture. He spoke in response to Claire's question, but his clear and earnest blue eyes had gone directly to my face. "The problem before—when I tried the touch-healing—was that I couldn't feel what was wrong, what was out of place," he explained. His hands rose to his head, his sinewy fingers briefly bracketing his temples in a self-evident demonstration. "But if I had the formula, if I could *feel* what the compound is—" His eyes shifted suddenly, utterly, to Taylor. "Then I know I could do it."

But Claire still held back the leads, steadily scrutinizing Lewis's anxious face. "Are you sure that would be safe?" she queried pointedly. "If you triggered the catabolic reaction, the compound—"

"No, that wouldn't matter," Lewis interrupted her. Hastily, with another glance to Taylor, he tried to explain. "Even if the compound catalyzed that reaction, it wouldn't matter. If there were any damage, I could just heal it."

Claire's frown deepened. "Are you certain?" she repeated. "Even Integration analysis itself is—"

"Yes!" I cut in, the word hissing out of my mouth with a conflicting mixture of reluctance and urgency. "Yes, he's done it before!" I held out my hands for the leads, moved by a numbing sense of fatalism as I concluded, "It's the only way."

Still hesitant, I saw Claire's eyes sweep from Lewis to Alexandria and then to Redding. Neither of those impassive faces revealed any obvious emotion, but they were Claire's trusted friends, and she knew what she was looking for. I didn't know what that might be, what assurance she needed, but whatever it was, she must have found it there. Still frowning, she brought up her hand and slowly and unwillingly offered me the slender network of wires and pads.

I simply stood aside as Lewis turned to face Taylor. The quality of his intense gaze had subtly altered, becoming almost an entreaty, not a demand. Although the two men still stood several paces apart, Lewis's eyes had the force of a physical touch, and I saw Taylor, helplessly fixed, swallow soundlessly.

"You'll just have to trust me," Lewis told him quietly.

Taylor gave a small shrug, a jerky little hitch of his shoulders that betrayed him. "I guess it beats the hell out of the alternatives," he said with convincing aplomb.

But I knew Taylor, and he was scared shitless. It was not a matter of courage, for in his own way, enlightened self-interest or not, Taylor was one of the bravest people I knew. There was no doubt in my mind that he had fully intended to go out and play the wild goose for us, even though it meant certain death for him. Rather, it was more a matter of uncertainty; he was frightened then because he had no idea what might happen.

I had no idea, either, but I knew it wouldn't require an audience; that was something I could do for Taylor, even if there wasn't much else. Tearing my eyes away from the two men, I threw Claire a sharp, meaningful look. She understood almost immediately, and from the ease with which she communicated her agreement to the others, I think they had already considered the same thing.

Claire gave a small wave and addressed Alexandria. "I have some things to finish in the lab yet, and there are still some preparations to be made before you leave for Flatstone. Perhaps Rudd and Traeger could use some help," she suggested.

Before he slipped off the wooden bench, Raydor took the set of cerebral leads I held out to him and deftly inserted their contact in the console. Then he got to his feet and, giving my shoulder a gentle squeeze, silently followed the others from the room. At the rear doorway, only Asplundh hesitated, hanging back for a moment. Her reluctance to leave us might have been partially due to professional curiosity, but from the expression of unguarded concern on her pale face, I knew that most of her unwillingness to go had a far more personal origin than that.

Lewis did not even seem to have noticed that the room had cleared. He had turned away from Taylor again and was carefully untangling the wires from the leads. As he did so, he began to remind Handy, "I don't have much of a grounding in medical biophysics, so—"

Handy made an abrupt but strangely gentle snorting sound; I had heard that expression of dry humor before, and in that moment it was hard to remember that the Integrator was still an almost incomprehensible distance away from that room, slicing relentlessly through the cold vastness of space. "That's never been the basis of your Talent," he remarked casually.

Lewis gingerly pressed the adhesive pads of the temple leads to his forehead. "If you can phrase the compound's formula in such a way that I can—" Lewis broke off with a small, helpless gesture aimed reflexively at the blanked screen.

Handy did not repeat the snorting sound, but I was still somewhat suspicious that there was gentle amusement in the reassuring tone of his voice as he said, "Don't worry. I can translate it for you." Then, as I wordlessly assisted Lewis with the placement of the third lead at the back of his head, Handy placidly added, "Of course, whether or not you can find and alter it is another matter entirely."

To my surprise, Lewis flashed the relay a quick but genuine smile. "Don't worry," he echoed. "You just leave that part of it to me."

The big commons room whose very luxury had become comfortably familiar to me over the course of that long night was weirdly silent. Although he was linked with the Integrator by the leads, Lewis's expression endearingly remained entirely his own: He blinked, frowning slightly, like a man who suspected he was on the verge of an unpleasant headache. I reached out and, taking Taylor by the arm, gently propelled him those last few steps toward the console where Lewis stood.

In the subdued light, Taylor's sun-streaked chestnut hair looked like a tousled crown of red gold. As I released his arm, his fingers suddenly found mine and clung with a quick, unspoken desperation. "Aren't you going to wish me luck?" he asked me, his voice fiercely nonchalant.

Squeezing his fingers, I slipped my hand free and found myself holding back the stinging press of unexpected tears behind my lids. "You won't need luck," I assured him, but I turned my face and swiftly pressed my mouth to his anyway. Then I stepped back and let Lewis do what he could.

The other times I had witnessed the touch-healing, it had happened so quickly, so spontaneously, that it was positively eerie to see Lewis just stand there a moment longer, his dark head slightly cocked. It was almost as if he were actually listening to something audible through the leads rather than merely having information will-lessly force-fed to his cerebrum by the Integrator. Then, over a space of a minute or so, his expression came back into focus, and he took the additional quarter turn necessary to put himself squarely facing Taylor.

I didn't know exactly what I expected. I guess that was it: I didn't know what to expect. Maybe something along the lines of a brief, formalized laying on of hands—*Rise, my son, and be healed.* What actually happened then was, to my relief, almost more comic than cosmic by comparison. Lewis quickly looked Taylor up and down and then cleared his throat. He made a small, helpless gesture toward Taylor's opened shirt, beginning awkwardly, "I'm sorry, but I think you'll have to—"

The taut lines of Taylor's tensed body instantly relaxed at the unexpected diversion. "Oh," he said hastily, agreeably. "Okay, sure." Struggling swiftly out of the sleeves, he tossed the shirt aside. He wasn't wearing a suit liner beneath it, but he immediately started unfastening his leather trousers.

Incredibly, Lewis actually seemed uncomfortable having to ask Taylor to strip for him. "I'm sorry," he repeated, making another clumsy, essentially meaningless gesture. "It's just that I have to be able to—"

With what came as an equal surprise to me, I could see that Taylor was embarrassed as well. "No, it's okay," he assured Lewis again, his fingers fumbling with the unfamiliar closure of the pants fly. He tried for levity, remarking, "Of course, it's usually not this easy for a man to get me out of my pants on such short acquaintance." But the quip fell flat, and even a stranger could have read the anxiety so poorly masked behind Taylor's light tone. It was only then that I realized he was not embarrassed to have Lewis see him naked; he was embarrassed to have Lewis see how afraid he was.

Taylor kicked the trousers aside. It had been a long time since I had seen his long, lean body, but I was stunned at how familiar it still seemed to me. Taylor's was the first male body with which I had ever become intimately and utterly acquainted. I found it astounding how perfectly that residual memory had been preserved, for in my mind I still carried that almost intrinsic sense of everything he was. I could still remember with absolute clarity the particular coppery color of his flat little nipples, the exact velvety texture of his foreskin against my tongue, and the unique musky scent of shampoo in the hair on the nape of his neck. Yet as I saw him standing there before Lewis, my first thought was not even sexual; I just thought how golden he looked, as golden as Lewis was dark.

Lewis dropped down on one knee before Taylor. His hands moved so quickly, so fluidly, that it took me a moment to understand exactly what he was doing. Starting at Taylor's bare feet, his fingers traced a light and rapid trail over the honey-colored skin, from the tips of Taylor's toes to his knees, skimming so delicately that he barely stirred the fine red-blond hairs on Taylor's legs.

An involuntary shudder ran through Taylor's body. His arms hung limply at his sides, but his eyes—gone wide, unguarded, vulnerable—were cast downward, watching Lewis's every move with wary intensity. The room was warm enough; in fact, to me it had become almost uncomfortably so. But Taylor's skin was pimpled with gooseflesh, and only by an effort of will did he seem able to keep himself from actually shivering as Lewis touched him.

Lewis paused, his hands resting lightly on Taylor's kneecaps. There was a peculiar expression, intense and yet somehow tranquil, on his face as he cocked his head again, as if he were checking something through the feedback in the leads. Then, in one graceful motion, he stood. Moving even more quickly and surely now, his hands found Taylor's passively dangling fingers. Traveling up Taylor's arms, slipping over the pliant body with growing certainty, within seconds he had reached Taylor's bare shoulders.

Taylor blinked. I didn't think it was possible that he could actually feel anything happening, but perhaps that was enough, that he felt nothing. I was only beginning to have the dimmest understanding of just what his fears and apprehensions about the whole process might have been. But as Lewis went on, something had changed for Taylor. Subtly but perceptibly, I could see him begin to relax beneath Lewis's touch, even though Lewis's hands were systematically covering the more sensitive, more private areas of his body. The strong, slender fingers glided from the long planes of Taylor's back to the lean muscling of his ribs, skimming across his chest, his abdomen, his hips, and yes— then there, and there: slipping from the base of his spine to the rounded curve of his buttocks, the brassy curls of his pubic hair, the vulnerable weight of his genitals. It was a healer's touch, but for a moment, selfless and urgent, it was also like a lover's caress. And as I watched them together, I saw in the guileless depths of Taylor's eyes the dawning comprehension as he looked into that fathomless well of Lewis's capacity for compassion.

Life held so few moments of perfect clarity, but I knew that I had witnessed one of them. Lewis's hands rose even as Taylor's shaggy head bent. Like some confessor-priest of the Old Blood, his gentle fingers spread as if to absolve a penitent of his unwitting sin. Healer, mutant, lover, friend: for that instant the whole of the universe could be contained within the span of those two miraculous hands.

Then suddenly it was done. Lewis stepped back, dropping his hands from Taylor's head. He stripped off the leads' adhesive pads with one abrupt and clumsy tug; I saw that his pale forehead was beaded with perspiration.

I really didn't want to cry then, but I felt the tears leaking rebelliously across my cheeks as I moved forward, catching Lewis's waist with one arm and pulling his unresisting body against my side. And then, because I knew what the tears were for, I reached out with my other arm and encircled Taylor's bare waist as well.

It made for a peculiar embrace, especially since Lewis still seemed mildly dazed from what had happened and Taylor was endearingly chagrined to find that he'd been left with a partial erection. But I didn't give a shit, a fact that I think I repeated to them loudly and inanely several times. I know I said, "I love you," and probably several times as well. But I don't think either one of them was worried about to whom I was referring.

CHAPTER FOURTEEN

The one thing about living planetside that I guessed I could have learned to miss in space was the rich variety of ambient conditions. Shipboard, every day—however you chose to mark that period—and every part of that somewhat arbitrary division was pretty much the same. There was no dusk or night or dawn, and the temperature and humidity were whatever you set them to be. It was comfortable and reliable and utterly predictable. But the people who had chosen to live on planets—"muddy-booters," the freightmen called them, often with a tone of disdain—had adapted themselves to living in a bizarrely diverse array of climatic conditions, many of which were frankly unattractive or harsh. That morning, as I stepped out the side door of Claire's house and into the chill hush of Earthheart's dawn, I think I finally understood why.

The cool air, blushing with sunrise and still rife with shadowy wells of darkness, played over my face and gently lifted the tangled ends of my hair. As I headed across the side yard away from the house, my boots lightly skimmed the damp sod, where a star field of dewdrops hung spangled like diamonds in the short tufts of grass. From the willow-draped squares of the sheep pens, I heard the impatient bleats of the restless animals, and I could smell the rich, pungent scent of the earth they had trampled beneath their sharp hooves. Across the low valley, on the shallow face of one dark green and rolling hill, a dimly outlined grouping of the massive LaGrange cattle already busily grazed, their blunt heads slowly sweeping back and forth like mowing machines as they sheared off the grass.

For a time I had needed and wanted to be alone. I knew that Lewis and Taylor could answer all the questions put to them and that they would be all right without me, just as they had known that I needed to remove myself. Claire could run as many tests on them as she wanted; I knew they both were fine. Even though I wanted to see Redding again—and Asplundh and maybe even Alexandria eventually—I needed a small bit of space. Earthheart had thoughtfully provided me with the backdrop for my solitude, this muddy-booter's bucolic vision of paradise.

By the time I had reached the crest of the first long slow rise of land, the same hillside into which Claire's laboratory and part of her house had been built, the leading edge of the pinkish-gold sun was just visible over the rim of the farthest slope on the horizon. My tracks had made a trail of darker sweeps behind me through the glittering silver of the wet grass. Stepping around a flat of dried cow manure the diameter of a small throw rug, I crouched down, squatting on my heels to watch the gradual warming of the sky. Sacculated coils of cirrocumulus clouds looking like nothing more than cottony, rose-colored loops of bowel roiled across the mauve dome. All around me, like the gently undulant curves of a woman's body, the hills and valleys of that serene and fertile land spread in a seemingly endless sea of green.

As I watched the sky brighten and the light paint those peaceful slopes, I thought about what I had just seen happen and about what it meant. Asplundh's theory about the potential application of touch-healing was correct; Lewis had proved that the moment he had laid his hands on Taylor's body. A Talent could be trained to recognize and reverse genetic damage—the Alterations could be healed. A Class Ten like Lewis could become a resource of inestimable, unlimited value; he could become a hero, a pariah, a target. The incredible scope of it was almost beyond comprehension, but it was also the simplest thing in the galaxy. I felt as if I had just witnessed the successful detonation of the first nuclear bomb.

Gradually, both my mind and the sky cleared. And when I began to notice things again, it was small things, like the cramp-like tugging I was beginning to feel in the muscles of the backs of my thighs from the squatting position I had assumed and the fact that my boots were just about soaked through from having walked in the heavy dew. So much for paradise.

Although I hadn't heard footsteps, I was aware of someone coming up behind me a few moments before the big hand landed silently on my shoulder. I glanced around but made no move to rise. When I reached up as if to brush away the touch, the blunt fingers locked around mine; they were warm and callused and dry.

"We ready to go?" I grunted as Alexandria smoothly and easily pulled me to my feet.

To my surprise, she did not immediately release me but held my hand for a moment longer, those dark eyes moving over my face. Then her fingers slipped from mine. "We're ready—are you?" she responded.

I met her gaze squarely, studying that weathered face as if I had just met her for the first time. For suddenly I was able to see Alexandria for just what she was—and more. I saw her then for everything that she had been, because I realized the magnitude of what she had devoted her life to protecting.

Her thick, bushy brows quirked slightly, her expression mildly perplexed by whatever she was reading in my eyes. "Come on," she said, swinging away from me and starting back down the slope without looking back to see if I was even following. When we were partway down the hill, she added over her broad shoulder, "Look out for the cow shit."

Look out for *all* the shit, I thought, but I said nothing.

The side yard was a jumble of activity when we returned to the house. Four dust-streaked ground carts stood outside one of the smaller outbuildings, their pack-powered engines murmuring at idle. Redding and Raydor were going from cart to cart, checking gauges and making adjustments. Across the yard at the house, the side door from the area of the old infirmary swung open with a bang and Rudd emerged, struggling as he pushed along a large and loudly protesting sheep. The big Tachs had the woolly creature firmly clasped in a tight embrace, his powerful arms locked beneath its front legs, and was walking the bleating animal along on its hind legs in front of him like an unwilling partner in some weird dance. Behind him, Asplundh shouted encouragement over the sound of the sheep's bawling as the awkward pair progressed unevenly across the grass. The look on the geneticist's face was excited, even exuberant.

I would have asked Alexandria just what the hell was going on, but she had already outdistanced me, veering off toward the sheep pens. Claire and Traeger were both there, standing right inside one of the wide wooden rail gates. Just as Alexandria reached the fence, Rudd and his reluctant companion made it to the gate. Claire swung the gate open, and Rudd pushed the sheep inside. The instant he released the animal, it bounded off across the dusty ground to join the eight or ten other shaggy creatures that milled skittishly in the enclosure. Asplundh actually applauded as Claire closed the gate behind them.

Raydor was nearest to me, standing beside one of the carts. The moment I reached him, I immediately asked, "What's with the sheep?"

He snapped down the cart's engine hood and gave me a swiftly assessing look before he replied. "Wild goose," he said enigmatically.

I felt like giving him a good sound thump on that thick, hairless head; the last thing I needed then was some joining riddle. But Redding stopped my impulse by coming over from the next cart and elaborating for me.

"Claire and Asplundh synthesized that compound they found in Taylor," he explained. Then his lip lifted in that crooked, wolfish grin, and his chin jerked toward the sheep pen. "They gave it to that sheep!"

He didn't need to say any more. I almost laughed out loud. "So where is the sheep going?" I asked.

Redding shrugged, the grin still tugging at his mouth. "As far as those dogs will take it, I guess," he said.

Two of Claire's lithe, hyenalike dogs crouched in the long shadows of the fence rails. At some imperceptible sign from the dark-haired woman, they both sprang to their feet, instantly alert. Rudd pulled back the gate, and the dogs streaked into the pen, deftly working the spooky group of sheep into a tight knot. At another signal from Claire, they set them into motion, the shaggy creatures bounding out into the freedom of the yard. It took only about three seconds for the dogs, a pale dove-gray and a brindled dun, to swing the would-be stampeders sharply into line. Moving like blurs through the sudden cloud of dust, the dogs let the sheep run, but the animals ran just where the dogs wanted them to. Within moments they were streaming up the first slope, heading for the distant hills.

I couldn't help but appreciate the irony of it. The renegades had made a Judas goat out of Taylor, but it looked as though they'd have to settle for a plain old sheep instead.

I noticed that Redding was eyeing me thoughtfully. "You hungry?" he asked. "Jeck whipped up one hell of a breakfast—bacon and eggs, even. I'm sure there's still some left."

But I just shook my head, turning to Raydor instead. "You got Handy's relay?" I asked him.

Raydor dug into his tunic and withdrew a small object; the

relay, stripped of all its accoutrements, seemed strangely insignificant again.

"How far out?" I asked him, slipping the little rectangle into the pouch of my Tachs tunic.

"I just disconnected the whole hookup about ten minutes ago," Raydor replied. He bent to check something on the ground cart, continuing, "He was four-point-two-six hours out then."

Claire had said it would take us about five and a half hours to get to Flatstone—plenty of time for the ship to get in, especially since I'd told Handy to stay out beyond the range of the A's scanners until I called him in. That also meant, I reminded myself dourly, that there would be plenty of time for us to get ourselves in trouble, since the ship would not be able to reach us immediately, even once I'd signaled Handy. I suddenly found myself wishing that we still had the audio hookup so that I could at least hear the sound of that deep voice once more, no matter how far out he still might be.

Traeger and Rudd had disappeared back into one of the buildings, but Claire, Alexandria, and Asplundh were coming back down the slight slope from the sheep pen. A small flock of the geneticist's gaudy-colored birds scattered ahead of them, squawking indignantly at the disruption of their morning foraging. Asplundh's cameolike face was alight with a certain weary satisfaction; she looked tired but determined, and I remembered that she had worked straight through the night. I gave her a small, complicit smile as she approached us.

Claire gestured toward the far hills. Somehow, she had the kind of face that did not hide amusement well. "I hope your renegades like mutton," she said.

Alexandria had already begun to move on, striding down the line of ground carts, rapidly scanning the length of each. "Come on," she said to Redding, "let's get this dust run under way."

Asplundh traded quick looks with me, then she started to follow Alexandria again. I glanced around, looking for Lewis and Taylor, but I didn't see either man in the yard. If I knew Taylor, they were probably still at the breakfast table.

At the head of the line of vehicles, Alexandria had climbed aboard the first cart. Impatiently, she revved its engine, and more of the exotic poultry scurried across the grass in a flurry of bright feathers and startled hooting sounds. Throwing her a bland, unimpressed look, Redding walked up the line and mounted the cart parked behind hers.

"Come on," Raydor said, sliding onto the driver's mount of

the last cart, the one we still stood beside. He held out his arm, making a beckoning gesture.

Ground carts were intended to be one-man vehicles, but there was a benchlike pedestal behind the driver's mount for use as an equipment or cargo box. By straddling that pedestal and hanging on to the driver, a passenger could ride in relative security. There was no such thing as comfort on a ground cart, even for the driver; they had been created strictly as working craft, and no allowances had been made for physical ease. Asplundh had already climbed onto the rear of Alexandria's cart. Swinging my leg over the pedestal, I used Raydor's proffered arm as a lever to pull myself up onto the box.

I shifted slightly on the hard and unsympathetic seat, still scanning the yard. Just as I thought Alexandria might decide to leave without them, Lewis and Taylor came out the side door of the house, walking rapidly side by side. As they approached the line of waiting carts, their eyes quickly scanned the row of riders. The only empty cart was the one directly ahead of ours. Leaning past Raydor's broad back, I gave them a little wave as they came toward it.

"Hey, you missed breakfast," Taylor said over the murmur of the carts' engines.

"Yeah? Well, if you don't hurry up, you're going to miss the tour bus," I shot back, trying to conceal my embarrassing relief at seeing them both again.

Lewis gave me a little smile; then he and Taylor exchanged a brief, quizzical look over the empty cart. Lewis shrugged. "You want me to drive?" he asked.

Taylor scrutinized him skeptically. "You ever drive a ground cart before?" Without waiting for the evident answer, he climbed up onto the driver's mount, concluding, "I think I better drive."

Alexandria started her cart toward the first hill, and the engine noise settled into a soft hum. Redding moved out behind her, and behind him, Taylor and Lewis.

At the last minute, before Raydor put our cart into motion, I hastily turned to Claire. I had planned to offer some words of appreciation for all that she had done for us there, but when I turned, she was smiling gently at me, and there didn't seem to be any need for words of thanks, after all.

"What will you do?" I asked her, watching those level dark eyes.

I don't think that she misunderstood me, unless it was deliberate. There were deep lines etched into that deceptively young-looking face, and I was forced to think of all that we had put her through in the short time we had been there. I had to wonder once again just how the hell Alexandria ever managed to keep any friends. But Claire's expression was calm and unruffled as she thoughtfully considered my question.

"I've heard from Harley," she replied, "and they've managed to get the transmitter station put back together again without the A's being any the wiser." She glanced up at the cloud pocked blue bowl of the sky and shrugged philosophically. "I think I may just see if I can get some of the boys together today and see if we can get that new roof on my shearing shed," she decided.

Ahead of us, the other three carts were climbing the first slope; Alexandria was nearly to its crest. As Raydor slowly eased our vehicle into motion, I looked back one last time.

"Until I see you again, Jo," she concluded with a fey little wave.

She sounded cheerful, and yet I felt the words were not meant to be a mere pleasantry. I thought if anything they were a sort of benediction, a confident assertion that we would survive. So I put my arms around Raydor's broad waist and hung on, burying my face in the clean and sun-warmed back of his tunic as he accelerated to catch up with the other carts.

I was on the driver's mount when we first sighted the skimmers. Both the shape and the rigidity of the unyielding surface of the ground cart's cargo boxes had proved punishing; whatever shock-absorbing system there might have been seemed confined to the driver's seat. Alexandria had called a brief halt for relief when we had been traveling for about three or four hours. Before we started out again, when Raydor offered to change places with me, I gladly accepted the switch.

We had been riding with the four carts fanned out in a roughly wedge-shaped formation, staying as much as possible to the lower faces of the slopes. The landscape had remained monotonously consistent: long, rolling sweeps of green hills, barren of trees but knee-high in grass, glistening and undulating in the sunlight. It looked as if the Powers had simply taken the planet's surface and pushed it together until it had wrinkled up in an endless series of shallow ripples. The only animals we saw were occasional groups of the huge fawn and cream-colored La-Grange cattle, and they regarded our passage with only the vaguest of interest.

Because their operation was nearly silent, the skimmers came as a surprise. Skimmers were essentially one-man hover cars: cableless like the ground carts, but infinitely faster and more maneuverable. We were spread out along the gentle incline of a hill when the first of them darted into view from behind us and flitted down the narrow valley between two slopes like a projectile being fired down a slot. Even before the first had passed us, two more of the sleek little craft appeared from behind the cover of the hill's base. They never slowed or deviated from their direct course down the lowest lay of the land, and their riders never turned back to look at us. By the time we had braked the carts to a halt, all three skimmers were rounding the curve of the next slope, disappearing as silently as they had come.

"Shit!" Alexandria said, revving her parked cart's engine in a useless display of frustration. "Just what we needed!"

Asplundh tried to see past Alexandria's broad back. "Who were they?" she asked. But it was Redding who replied.

"Just a few independent merchants," he told the geneticist, his voice calm. Then, seeing Asplundh's blank expression of incomprehension, he explained, "Black marketeers—pirates."

"In the daytime?" Taylor asked, his brow furrowed. "But I thought they—"

"They take a hell of a lot of risks," Alexandria cut in, her craggy face still set with a scowl of disapproval. "With skimmers, if they stay down along the bottom of the hills, they can often avoid the Ceecee's scout ships." She paused, staring down the long, empty valley ahead of us. "This time, anyway—I hope," she muttered darkly.

Redding glanced up and down the course the skimmers had taken and gave a casual shrug. "Well, if they've got a scout on their tails, we'd probably know it by now," he pointed out. He looked down the depression before us for a moment, then added, "Let's just hope they aren't going where we're going."

"The embryotory?" I asked sharply, my hands tightening involuntarily on the cart's control stick. "Why would they be going there?"

"It's supposedly abandoned," Redding said, easing his cart into motion again, "and it's out in the middle of nowhere. Lots of these little half-assed pirates hole up wherever they can."

Conceding that he probably knew from experience, I began to move our cart out after him. Over my shoulder and practically in my ear, Raydor continued. "There are a lot of obsolete structures in the low hills, most of them left over from the early settlement days. Facilities like the embryotory were put out where they were needed, where the animals were, and then abandoned when they were no longer useful.'' I could feel his big shoulders shrug. ''The A's don't try to maintain surveillance on all of them; most are too remote.''

Great! I thought glumly, accelerating again to match the other carts' pace. It was bad enough we had to evade the renegades and the A's, but we had black marketeers to look out for, too. And even though the trio on the skimmers had displayed no interest in us, they might be a threat to the Tens at Flatstone. Pirates also had the unfortunate potential to attract, however unwittingly, the attention of both the Ceecees and the renegades.

''You think they're going to the embryotory?'' I finally had to ask Raydor after a few moments' consideration.

''I don't know,'' the Tachs replied. ''I guess we'll find out when we get there, though.''

Almost involuntarily my eyes were drawn to the next cart, where Lewis and Taylor rode together. Lewis was facing straight ahead, his black hair whipping out behind him. His body was poised in a curved arc, crouched to take advantage of the windbreak Taylor's back provided. He looked calm, but his tension was something that I felt more than observed.

''Thanks for trying to cheer me up,'' I murmured to Raydor, but my words lacked the necessary sting for effective sarcasm, and I doubted that I had even spoken loudly enough for him to have heard me.

It was something in the subtle shift of Alexandria's posture that made me look for the abandoned facility long before I would have noticed it on my own. As we came down across the rolling face of a slope—a hill virtually identical to the three or four million other such embankments we had surely traversed in the last five-plus hours—something in the cant of the burly woman's head altered and the set of her shoulders stiffened. Then she swung her cart at a ninety-degree angle to her previous course and slowed the vehicle, waiting while we caught up.

Even then, I doubted the significance of what I was looking at. About a hundred meters ahead of us, set into the rise of the opposing hill, there was a short enframement and a pair of blank-faced doors set into the sodded slope. The two doors were fronted in steel, but their framing was made of beams of real wood. There was no other exterior structure, no sign of vehicular or equipment access, not even a damned footpath leading up to the doors. It looked like the boarded-up entrance to a long-abandoned mining shaft or perhaps the gateway to the planet's largest root cellar.

As we all pulled our carts into idle, one glance around me assured me that I was not the only one who was obviously unimpressed. I voiced my doubts, accompanied by a deprecating gesture. "That's *it*?"

The question was patently rhetorical, more of an expression of disbelief than a call for confirmation. Alexandria just ignored me, studying something on her cart's control panel, and Redding had already begun to ease his cart forward again, farther down the side of the hill.

Both Taylor and Lewis looked mildly perplexed, but Asplundh's initial expression of disappointment and bewilderment had already turned to comprehension and might even have been well on its way to genuine appreciation. "Of course," she responded eagerly, "subterranean vaults would be perfect!" She waved toward the stout doors, nearly bumping Alexandria's wide back with her hand, and elaborated in an increasingly animated voice. "Don't you see? During the early settlement phrase, when this facility was in use, they didn't have the resources to supply power way out here. But they needed an environment where the embryos could be stored at a constant—"

From a dozen meters ahead of us, Redding interrupted her, his voice flat but imperative as, without even turning his head, he directed me, "Call him in."

I understood immediately what he meant, but still I hesitated, puzzled by the blunt demand. "Only when we're sure," I countered, my hand moving automatically to cover my tunic pouch where I had stowed Handy's relay. "First, we'd better—"

"Call him in," he repeated more loudly, the words a command.

I could have disputed his order further; I was of a mind to, and after all, I was the one with the damned relay. But something about the look on that lean profile—the way his gray eyes had narrowed and were fixed straight ahead, unblinking, on a point the rest of us still could not see past the edge of the slope—made the protest die on my lips. I started our cart forward again, easing it along until I could also see what it was that he was looking at. And when I could see that, I lost all desire to argue with him.

In the valley below the embryotory's doors, in the small depression that formed the lowest juncture of the two slopes, lay what was left of the three skimmers. More accurately, what lay there was three blackened trenches in the earth, three deep furrows where the scorched sod had been peeled back like burnt skin and where bits of matter, both organic and inorganic, were scattered across the valley like incinerated fragments of shrapnel.

My fingers clumsy with adrenaline, I groped to reach the relay. Just as I pressed the panic button, the emergency summons, a sound like the loud *thump!* of a wet sandbag hitting pavement from a great height shook the ground beneath our cart. Then that same cart, with no intervention on my part, went flying sideways through the air in a shower of grass and dirt.

I landed roughly but on a yielding surface of some kind, my ears still ringing fiercely. The total incomprehensibility of just what might have happened kept me helpless for a moment longer than I would have been from merely having had the wind knocked out of me. The first thing I was certain of, beyond the simple fact that I was still alive and relatively functional, was that what I had landed on was Raydor. Then he lurched to his feet, slinging me ignominiously over his shoulder like a sackful of laundry, and began to run. I coughed, my eyes stinging. My position and Raydor's thudding gait drove the breath from me again, but I finally realized that the reason I could neither see nor speak was that my eyes and mouth were full of dirt.

Redding's cart had been just ahead of ours, and the other two carts had been right behind, but a tremendous commotion had erupted, and most of it seemed to be concentrated in the area between where we had been and where we were going. I heard at least two more distinct explosions; then I felt the actual concussions rock us and felt the shattered sod pelting down in a fusillade of dirt and grass. Finally, I heard the distinctive thin whine of beam weapons firing, seemingly from all directions, the sound exacerbated by the still-painful ringing in my ears. The air was filled with the acrid stink of something burning.

Surprisingly, in all the chaos I heard only one shout. Someone had cried out, but I couldn't tell who or if the sound had been made in pain or in triumph. The next explosion hit right in front of us, and it wasn't just sod. I heard the brittle sound of wood shattering, a sharp crack that was almost like the rupture of glass. Fragments rained down over my back, stinging like whips even through the heavy fabric of my tunic. Then we were out of the sunlight and into a dimness that my blurry eyes could barely begin to penetrate.

Someone was calling my name, a voice steady but urgent, and I spit out another gummy clot of dirt. The rocking sway of Raydor's body halted, and I felt him tilt beneath me, bending forward to slide me gently to my feet. Feeling curiously detached from my alarmingly rubbery legs, I stood with my knees braced, still clutching the front of his tunic, and tried to focus on the indistinct forms I saw milling around me in the surreal haze.

"You're all right, Jo," a familiar voice murmured, Lewis's hand passing over my face from my dirt-smeared forehead to my chin. Abruptly, the tinny clamoring in my ears ceased.

Blinking with more efficacy now, I squinted up with smeary eyes at Lewis's dusty face. It registered only abstractly as he reached over my shoulder with an almost reflexive motion and plucked a wooden splinter the size of my thumb out of Raydor's arm, healing the wound with the same smooth, automatic pass of his hand. "What the hell happened?" I croaked indignantly.

The answer came in a voice I did not recognize, but there was no mistaking that tone. "Renegades! Those cod-sucking bastards!"

I swung toward the sound of that bitter female voice, moving far too quickly and regretting it as a wave of vertigo made the already chaotic surroundings swim around me like a poorly focused vid. I found that if I kept my head still and just moved my eyes, straining them to pierce some of the gloomy miasma of suspended dust and stinging smoke, I could dimly make out the rough dimensions of the structure into which we had fled. It was the forechamber or anteroom of the old embryotory, I thought. To one side of me was the partially shattered remains of the real-wood framing of the crumpled exterior doors, and to the other side was a solid wall marked with rows of hatchlike metal doors that resembled something you'd find in a cold-storage warehouse. I heard the muffled *whump!* of another blast from outside the facility and felt myself jump involuntarily.

Several figures loomed before me, wavering in and out of my bleary gaze, but Lewis's was the only face I recognized. He, too, had turned toward the woman who had spoken, but he had moved in recognition, his arms lifted and his hands spread palms up.

"I'm sorry, Chris," he said quickly, his voice sounding strangely hollow in that murky chamber. "We knew that we might be responsible for leading them here, but we—"

The woman stepped abruptly forward, suddenly coming into

focus for me. She was barely my height, but she seemed nearly as broad as Alexandria. She wore a jumpsuit of some kind of stretchy fabric that had once been gold; it clung to every ample curve of her buxom body. "Christ's blood, Lewis!" she said, effectively interrupting him in midsentence by simply encircling him with her beefy arms and pulling him into a crushing embrace that made the upper part of his body nearly disappear into hers. "Here I didn't think I'd ever see your smiling face again, and all you can do is give me some ass-kissing *apology*?" Setting him back again, she gave him an enthusiastic shake so vigorously that both her dust-colored blond hair and her bountiful breasts bounced along with him. Then she pulled him forward a second time and planted a wet and exuberant kiss directly on his dirt-smudged lips.

"Besides," someone said from behind her, "the renegades didn't follow you, Lewis." He was someone I didn't know and could barely see in the gloom of the chamber, a slightly built man with receding shoulder-length brown hair. Beyond him other figures were still moving, apparently mobilizing against the attack on the embryotory. There was more shouting and the sound of beam fire, its discharges sparkling beyond the irregularly shaped borders that marked what remained of the outer doors. Raydor squeezed my shoulder briefly and then moved away, following the man who had just spoken.

The buxom blond woman stepped back from Lewis and turned to me. Close up, I could see that her eyes had the pale, refractive quality of beach sand; she studied me openly for a few seconds, her scrutiny swift and astute. "You must be this freighter captain I've heard so much about," she said, sounding both pleased and amused.

"Jo, this is Christopher," Lewis hastily intervened.

I would have offered her my hand, grimy as it was, since hers looked even worse, but just then Alexandria appeared through the smoky murk, coming up behind Christopher and slapping her on the back so hard that the dust flew.

Viewed side by side, both women looked like they'd been wrestling in the dirt, but I was relieved to see that Alexandria was hale and unharmed. "You always did run a clean facility, Chris," she remarked sarcastically, brushing at her soiled tunic.

The lighter-haired woman was smiling broadly as she turned from us to give Alexandria a hearty embrace. "Yeah? Well, it's a hell of a lot easier to stay neat when you don't have uninvited

guests dropping in!'' Christopher said. ''Company is always
such a nuisance.''

Lewis had begun to try to introduce, or at least point out, the
other Tens to me, but it was difficult to put faces to the names
when everyone kept moving and the visibility in the anteroom
was so poor. At least I was able to catch glimpses of Taylor and
Asplundh, so I knew they were all right, although with Taylor
already bargaining with a woman for custody of a beam cannon,
I wasn't sure how long his good fortune would last.

A large, powerfully built man with dark skin and a mustache
loomed in silhouette against the dusty shafts of light from the
ruined doors; he called out something to Christopher. I couldn't
hear what his question had been, but her response was quick
and to the point. ''Keep back, Kell,'' she commanded. ''Can-
nons only to the fore!''

Redding suddenly appeared from out of the haze; his clothes
were filthy and riddled with wood splinters. He threw me a
swiftly assessing look even as he had already started to speak to
Alexandria and Christopher. ''Only two air cars,'' he reported
tersely, ''but they've got aft-mounted beam cannon and what's
starting to look like a lifetime supply of those fusion grenades.''

As if to emphasize his announcement, a new series of dull,
thudding concussions shook the poured-rock floor of the old
structure; beyond the breached doorway, clots of sod and dirt
rained down in a fresh shower. But Christopher's broad and
dusty face revealed no alarm. It was a strong face, naturally
ruddy and congenial despite the tartness of her tongue, and I
suspected that behind those pale, deep-set eyes was the steely
will of a woman who was not used to giving in. She was clearly
in charge, and there would be a reason for it. She would be at
her best with her back to the wall.

''Cod-suckers!'' she reiterated, making a hand gesture I'd
seldom seen used by anyone but dockworkers. ''I don't know
what's worse—those idiots on the skimmers, gutter-running in
broad daylight like a bunch of green punks, or those brain-blind
sheep-joiners out there playing soldier!''

''The idiots on the skimmers passed us about an hour or so
back,'' Alexandria said grimly. Her grizzled halo of frizzy hair
seemed to have achieved one uniform hue, a dirty grayish brown.
''Damn! I _knew_ they'd draw trouble!''

''Well, if it's any consolation, those assholes in the air cars
weren't tracking the skimmers,'' Christopher went on by way
of clarification. ''They must have been on an intersecting course;

they didn't fry the poor bastards until they got right outside our door."

I saw Alexandria and Redding exchange a quick, meaningful look. "You think they knew you were here?" Redding asked Christopher.

But the blond woman shook her head, sending dust motes dancing. "No, not then at least." She let her gaze slip sideways, taking in Lewis and me as well as she went on. "I think they were looking for you fellows," she concluded, to the background accompaniment of another round of grenade explosions.

For a moment no one spoke, and the only sounds echoing in the hazy twilight of that archaic chamber were those of the ongoing skirmish: the *whump* of fusion grenades, the thick pattering of falling dirt, the insistent whine of the beam cannon, and the confusing snatches of unintelligible shouts from the people fighting to repel the attack at the embryotory's doorway. Beside me, I felt Lewis shift slightly, his anxiety thudding in me like a second, dysynchronous heartbeat.

Luck: You could believe in it or not as you chose, but it seemed that either way, fate liked to play her little jokes. All the way out there to the embryotory we had managed to evade detection by either the renegades or the A's. The only ones to stumble across us had been those pirates on the skimmers, and they were the ones who had run out of luck. But because of them, the renegades had managed to trap both us and the Tens, and I was sure we had yet to feel the full brunt of their forces. Ironically, it was their own noisy assault on the hillside that was likely to bring in the Ceecee scouts. And no matter how well dug in we were or how many renegades we could hold off, once the A's arrived, we'd be up against an adversary with unlimited resources and all the time in the world. Surrender to the renegades or wait and surrender to the A's—those seemed to be our choices, I concluded glumly.

As if reading my morose thought, Christopher directed a question at me, her voice even but tight. "How close is your ship?"

I wanted automatically to reach into my tunic pouch for Handy's relay, the relay that was out there somewhere on that crater-pocked hillside, probably either melted into slag or buried under several tons of Earthheart's renowned fertile soil. The concussion had distorted my time sense somewhat, but I figured it had been at least ten minutes since I'd hit Handy's summons, possibly as long as fifteen. "Not nearly close enough," I replied grimly, my fingers tightening uselessly on the empty air.

Alexandria's dust-streaked face was set like a slab of weathered rock; she had just done the same quick mental calculations that I had. She jerked her broad chin toward the fray continuing outside. "You think we can take them?" she asked Christopher.

Equally forthright, the buxom woman shook her head, more dust rising from her hair. "Impossible," she said, raising her voice to be heard over the noise of another series of explosions. "We've got three beam cannon and a couple of pistols—that's all." Her voice dropped as the offensive noise did, sounding suddenly weary. "I don't even know how long we can hold them off, Lexie. If they get some reinforcements from the rest of their goons, they might just decide to cut to the chase and slag this whole hillside."

Alarmed by that prognostication, I quickly interjected, "But they would never take that kind of risk, would they? Some of you might be harmed."

Both Alexandria and Redding shifted slightly; even Lewis had glanced away from me. Of all of them, only Christopher seemed bemused by the apparent naiveté of my supposition: She was the only one who didn't realize how little I still knew.

"Honey, I don't think our welfare is a real high priority with these assholes," she began. Then she broke off as she studied the pained look of incomprehension etched upon my dirt-smudged face. Speaking slowly, as if to make certain she had not misunderstood my comment, Christopher said, "Did you think they wanted to try to take us alive?"

My feeling of uncomfortable uncertainty was rapidly giving way to a sense of chilling alarm. I darted a sideways glance to Lewis, whose eyes were still downcast, before I hesitantly replied, "But I thought that was why the renegades have been after you all along—because they wanted you, what you have."

Christopher coughed loudly, and I don't think it was solely because of the dust and smoke in the chamber's air. She shot both Alexandria and Redding a sharp look; then she addressed them in a calm and implacable tone of voice. "What about the other two?" she asked them. "I suppose you didn't tell them, either."

Alexandria gave an unrepentant shrug and said, "Ignorance is bliss, Chris."

Not deigning to dignify that with a response, the big blonde turned to Lewis. "Get me your blissful friends, would you?"

Then she reached out and took me by the elbow. "Come on," she said, her voice still steady and calm, "I'll show you just what it is the renegades want."

She led me across the anteroom's littered floor, its surface strewn with dirt and splintered shards of the shattered wooden beams. As we crossed the chamber, we passed the silhouette of the breached doorway, where I could barely make out Lewis scrambling to find Taylor and Asplundh in the midst of the other Tens. I caught a glimpse of Raydor, his big bulk stretched out on the floor with his elbows braced, methodically and deliberately firing one of the beam cannon. Then Christopher had guided me farther down the wall, away from the worst of the confusing sights and sounds.

Christopher opened one of the metal hatches on the anteroom's far wall; I stepped through it ahead of her. I found myself inside a huge, cool chamber, a literally cavernous room whose walls and ceiling were carved out of the flintlike rock of the hillside. The only lighting was provided by a few dim bars of pack-powered emergency illuminators suspended so far above us on the vast ceiling that they seemed to float eerily, like some kind of bizarre linear constellations in an unfamiliar night sky.

As I stood there a moment, my eyes adjusting, Asplundh and Taylor stepped through the hatchway. They both looked pretty much the way I imagined I must have: filthy, puzzled, apprehensive. Wordlessly, I moved farther into the immense chamber, blinking in the gloom.

The poured-rock floor of the room was neatly segmented by row after row of empty perforated metal racks. It took me a few seconds and a startling jolt of recognition to realize that they were the same kind of framework as the structures that had held the tens of thousands of vials of suspended embryos in Claire's laboratory storage case. Her plump arm over my shoulders, Christopher directed me several steps farther into the massive storage facility, along the nearest row of bare racks. There she paused, gesturing down at something on the floor.

My gritty eyes were still adapting to the weak lighting, and so I bent over, squinting to see what she had pointed to. Asplundh and Taylor came up behind me, trying to determine what I was looking at. It was a small rectangular case, about the same size and dimensions as a piece of overnight luggage. If not for the lock slot and the carrying handle protruding from the top, it would have looked like nothing but a simple metal-bound box.

Still not comprehending, I straightened up again, glancing past Taylor and Asplundh to give Christopher a quizzical shrug.

Christopher drew something from the snug hip pocket of her gold jumpsuit and held it out to me; it was a plastic card-key. Frowning, I dropped inelegantly down into a squat on the cool stone floor and fitted the key into the lock slot on the top of the case. The two halves of the box parted neatly beneath my hands, fanning out on their hinged struts like two stubby wings, displaying the contents of the case like a salesman proffering his wares.

For a moment I was too stupefied to look up at the others. I could only stare at the opened case, the distant, faint light of the emergency illuminators reflected off its symmetrical rows of tiny suspension vials like a series of glittering parentheses.

"This is what the renegades are after," Christopher said softly.

Automatically, protectively, my hands spread in the air over the rows of bubblelike vials. I looked up at her with an expression of awe and disbelief on my face, making an unnecessary but helpless gesture. "Then these are—"

"What's left of the Class Tens," Christopher confirmed, nodding gently toward the case.

Equally bewildered, Taylor waved his hand, indicating the outer chamber. "But you—and the others—"

A brief, self-deprecating smile played over Christopher's full lips. "No, we're just the leftovers, I'm afraid. There are only five of us left here—six, with Lewis." Sobering, her eyes dropped from our astonished faces to the metal case resting at our feet. Her mouth pulled into a firm line. "On Araphos they took the last of our best." Her quiet voice hardened resolutely. "Three were killed in the battle to take us; six were captured and taken to Camelot. Only Lewis survived that massacre."

My fingers touched the edges of the case's halves, the questions churning chaotically in my mind. But it was Asplundh, dropping to kneel beside me, who looked up to Christopher with the next partially formed query.

"Then—then these embryos contain the—"

"The same mutated DNA that we do, yes," Christopher told her. The hardness melted from her tone, her broad and rosy face softening with genuine warmth. "We're an aberration but a somewhat self-limiting one; most of us are sterile. Even in the Tens who have proven fertile, the traits are often recessive. The Talents don't seem to breed true." She glanced briefly toward the hatchway and the outer room beyond. "Lewis's abilities are unusual; his Talent is the most strongly expressed one that I have ever seen."

I realized I was staring at her. Still, I blurted out, "Are you a—"

Christopher gave a self-effacing shrug. "A rather mediocre telepath," she replied with a gently mocking smile. But when she waved at the case with its rows of gleaming vials, her obvious pride was almost maternal. "But these children represent the best choices we could make, the strongest genetic crosses." Although I had not consciously been aware of the thought, the look must have passed over my face, for she added softly, "And yes, some of them are his."

Suddenly I understood more than I wanted to. Alexandria's burning obsession, Lewis's pained ambivalence, the renegades' relentless tenacity—There were at least two hundred suspension vials in that spread metal case, defended by a mere handful of ragged survivors. It was not just a matter of genetic exploitation or even a matter of political control; it was a matter of potential genocide.

"Christopher!"

The shout from the hatchway jerked me from my thoughts and made Asplundh and Taylor turn around as well. A slender, gray-haired woman appeared in the opening; I remembered Lewis had called her Tess, and the last time I had seen her, she had been lugging chunks of broken wood out of the way in the anteroom. Her rumpled orange jumpsuit was streaked with soot and filth. "Christopher, you'd better come!" she repeated urgently.

With admirable calm, Christopher bent to close the metal case and retrieved her card-key. Then, taking both Asplundh and me by one arm, she straightened again, pulling us to our feet. I glanced over to the hatchway with a question on my lips, but Tess was already gone. I threw Taylor a quizzical look, then all of us started for the hatch.

I had just stepped through the hatchway behind Taylor when the first blast hit. Ironically, it was Christopher's inelegant phrase—"slag this whole hillside"—that was uppermost in my mind as we burst back into the hazy disorder of the outer chamber. But despite the frantic scrambling of the people who had been dug in nearest the outer doors, fighting back with their beam cannon and pistols, and despite the violent flare of orange light that burned beyond the ruptured wood and steel barrier, I immediately realized that the embryotory itself was not the target of that thunderous explosion.

A renewed pall of roiling dust and oily smoke poured into the dim chamber, making my eyes water furiously. Taylor grabbed my arm to steady me, but I tried to push forward. In the shifting confusion of milling bodies I saw Christopher reach out and take hold of the nearest Ten, the burly, dark-skinned man Lewis had introduced as Kell. He was covered with a fresh layer of dirt, and there were wood chips in his mustache, but he still clutched his beam cannon to his massive chest.

"What the hell is it?" she loudly demanded above the rumbling din from outside. "More renegades?"

"Not unless they're blowing their own vehicles!" I shouted back, finally breaking free of Taylor's grip and pushing past Christopher and Kell. "That last blast was—"

The combined sound and concussion of the second explosion nearly knocked me off my feet. I don't know if it was because I was that much closer to the outer doors or if the second air car was just nearer to the embryotory's entrance when it was blown; whatever the reason, the second fireball was so bright that in spite of the thick haze of suspended matter, I had to turn and, staggering, avert my face from the blaze. I stumbled and almost stepped on the outstretched legs of a man lying prone on the floor, his beam cannon still cradled across his forearm. But when he looked up at me, the whites of his eyes ringed with soot, he flashed me an impudent grin.

"You okay?" Redding asked with indomitable aplomb.

I dropped down onto my knees in the dirt beside him, craning my neck to try to peer out past the shattered wooden door frame. "What the hell is going on?" I asked him.

Following my gaze, he jerked his chin and replied matter-of-factly, "My guess would be that someone just blew those two air cars to hell."

Then he looked back to my face, and our eyes locked, for both of us were thinking the same thing: The A's had arrived.

I stayed on my knees beside Redding's prone body. A few of the others in the anteroom began to cautiously creep forward again, straining to see out of the entrance without making targets of themselves. I recognized Raydor's burly shape silhouetted against the wall on the opposite side of the entry, with Alexandria behind him. After the constant fusillade of the renegades' bombardment, the sudden cessation of the attack had left an eerie calm in the murky chamber. A familiar hand touched my bent shoulders, and I leaned back against Lewis's legs. Then the air began to vibrate slightly with the reverberant hum of a small vessel hovering in for a setdown.

From my position inside the ruined doorway I couldn't see much of the hillside or the shallow valley beyond, but I didn't really feel inclined to move any closer right then just for the benefit of a better view. The A's and I hadn't exactly parted company as the best of friends, and even though surrendering to them seemed almost inevitable, I was in no hurry to rush the process. The quavering hum grew progressively louder. Dust and what little grass still remained intact in the immediate area began to blow out like a flattened skirt from around the vessel's hovers as the Ceecee scout ship lightly set down at the foot of the slope.

Several people behind us began to stir, although no one said anything. I didn't move from my knees, however, even as the soft creak of the scout's settling landing gear faded away. I just waited. I waited because a Ceecee scout ship was a lightweight little vessel, with a two-man crew and a very basic armament of beam weaponry, and it sure as hell hadn't been that ship which had blown those two air cars into oblivion.

Even though it was much larger than the scout, the second ship was actually much quieter coming in. The familiar dull *whoosh* of landing retros firing was the first sound I could hear; then the high, thin whine of the hover stabilizers positioning the vessel as she gracefully lowered herself toward the small level area at the base of the hill. I crawled forward a few feet then to be able to see all of her as she set down. My surprise made the potentially risky maneuver worth it. For the second vessel wasn't the MA picket ship or Ceecee light troop carrier that I had expected: The sleek, wedge-shaped craft was a CA long-range courier, and she carried the distinctive logo of the Combined Authorities' Diplomatic Corps on her side.

Lewis had crawled up alongside me and knelt with his body lightly touching mine. "What do you think?" he asked me; his voice was composed, but I could feel the anxiety and confusion pouring off him like heat radiating from his skin.

Almost ruthlessly, I tried to damp down that flow of feeling between us. I desperately needed to be able to keep my mind clear. "Well," I said cautiously, scanning the still-smoking bits of wreckage that littered the torn-up hillside below us, "it sure doesn't look like more renegades."

Neither vessel had popped a hatch, but a sudden burst of static crackled from the belly-mounted speakers on the Ceecee scout. A short, unintelligible bit of garbled feedback followed; then the amplified voice of her pilot came on loud and clear.

"To all persons in the structure: Discard all weapons and exit immediately in an orderly fashion. You are trespassing on an Interdicted world and are now in the custody of the Commerce Commission of the Combined Authorities. I repeat: Discard all weapons and exit immediately in an orderly fashion."

I sat back on my haunches and turned toward the back of the chamber, where the Ceecee officer's pronouncement had produced the predictable effect. Christopher, Alexandria, and several of the Tens were carrying on a hastily convened and particularly animated discussion, punctuated by some displays of Alexandria's congenital pigheadedness, Christopher's colorful language, and lots of general dissent. Taylor was exercising his newly found and well-honed flair for antagonizing Alexandria; even Asplundh seemed inclined to argue. Redding, Lewis, and I just exchanged a meaningful look: Taking on the A's with a beam cannon would have been more peaceful. But anyone in the chamber could have predicted where the dispute was ultimately headed, because we really didn't have a lot of options, and the sooner we responded, the sooner we'd find out just what the range of our choices might be.

Finally, after the pilot of the scout ship had repeated his message twice more, Christopher pulled away from the others, shaking them off like a dog shaking off water. "I'm going out there—give me your weapons!" she announced. Alexandria started to speak, but the big blond just sheared her off, adding pointedly, "*Not* you! With your luck, you'd just get yourself shot!"

Another of the Tens, a slight dark-haired woman named Wynna, kept her beam pistol clutched tightly in her hands, lamenting, "Chris, no! We can't just give up like this!"

Redding pulled back, smoothly getting first to his knees and then to his feet. He stepped toward the others, slowly shaking his shaggy head. The front of his overshirt was crisscrossed with the telltale smudge lines from the beam cannon he was holding out to Christopher, and his hair was still clotted with dirt. "What do you think we're going to do, outwait them?" he asked Wynna dryly. He shrugged almost indifferently, as if the whole matter was really of small consequence but he was still curious. And he added, as Christopher took the weapon from his hands, "I want to see where we stand."

The speakers on the scout ship had just begun to blare their repetitive message for the fourth time when Christopher sidled through the broken door frame and stepped out into the warm yellow sunshine of the Earthheart afternoon. In her arms she carried the meager sum total of our weaponry. Casually, she stepped around the heaved-up clods of scorched sod and the still-sizzling fragments of melting plastics and slagged metal. Like some Madonna of the battlefield, she calmly made her way down the ruin of the gentle slope. When she reached a point about a dozen meters from where the two ships sat, she unceremoniously dumped the beam weapons to the ground. Then she held her empty hands out, palms up, and waited.

At the embryotory we all crowded forward into the doorway to watch. Only Wynna hung back, reluctant to leave the sanctuary of the dim chamber. I stood at the edge of the door frame, my hand resting against the rudely splintered wood. I was aware of the other Tens and of my friends around me, but most of all I was aware of Lewis. He stood behind me, one hand on my shoulder; the sharp sting of his apprehension was like the taste of acid in my mouth.

The twin hatches on the Ceecee scout cracked simultaneously. The pilot and his second, gaudy in the red and black of their Commerce Commission jumpsuits, both leaned sideways in their seats, beam rifles leveled in their hands. But neither man spoke or moved any farther; it was as though they were waiting for something.

Then, with a faint whine, the belly hatch on the trim CA courier slowly dropped open, the short boarding ramp peeling down like a bright tongue of silver. Briskly, one after another, a quartet of CA Security guards exited the ship and stood stiffly in pairs on either side of the ramp. Instead of the usual Security colors, they wore the yellow and sea-green jumpsuits of the Diplomatic Corps, and in their belt holsters they carried some rather undiplomatic-looking hardware.

For a moment nothing happened. I could see Christopher eyeing the armed men with a certain bemused expectation, but none of them made any move toward her. Then one more man came down the courier's ramp, an unimpressive-looking man, not even brandishing a weapon. But no man could have surprised me more, and I did not even realize that I had been clutching the shattered wooden beam of the door frame so tightly until the sharp splinters dug into my palm.

For the last man was Hidalgo, the Ombudsman.

CHAPTER FIFTEEN

His drab charcoal-gray robe swirling around his legs, the Ombudsman stepped off the courier's ramp and onto the scoured and furrowed sod. And for one weirdly framed moment, elongated by the sudden static silence on that remote hillside, I could have been back in his office in Porta Flora, my memories of that meeting were still so sharp. His face and his demeanor were exactly as I had remembered them—the hawklike angles and fierce bronzing, the swing of his coarse black braid, and the acute sweep of those live-coal eyes.

Lewis made a grab for me, but I was out the shattered doorway before his fingers could close on my shirt. "Hidalgo!" I shouted, crossing the torn-up slope with such heedless speed that I was nearly sliding along on a small avalanche of dirt and debris by the time I reached its bottom.

I was only peripherally aware of Christopher's look of surprised disapproval, of Lewis scrambling down the cratered hill behind me, or even of Raydor and Redding preventing Taylor from following as well. I was aware only of the man who turned immediately toward me, his strongly planed face tautly set. "Captain," the Ombudsman said quickly, "I am relieved to have found you." He let his gaze swing from me to Christopher, to Lewis, and then back up the littered slope to the dusty figures clustered in the blasted-out doorway of the embryotory. "You all are in grave danger here." He made a broad gesture. "These hills still swarm with renegade ships, and I cannot guarantee we have the firepower to repel them all."

"You seem to have been doing all right up to now," Christopher said dryly with a deliberate glance at the armed security men.

I swung toward the blond woman, surprised by her tone, and hastily began to explain. "Christopher, this is the—" But she

262

interrupted me, almost casually closing the small distance that still remained between us, her stride steady and sure.

"I know what he is," she responded, pointedly eyeing the distinctive robe of Hidalgo's office, "and he's Authority."

Lewis had reached us, but he approached warily, his glance darting from my face to each of the others. An annoying prod of unexpected irritation goaded me as I glared at Christopher's impassive face. What the hell had she expected, a host of the Mother's archangels? But I bit down on any sarcastic rejoinders and merely shook my head in frustration. She and her people had done their best, but we had been left with two choices: the renegades or the A's. Of the two, I figured our chances of coming out of this alive, which were a hell of a lot better with the A's, had just increased another notch with Hidalgo's presence. "I know him," I told her insistently. "He's Authority, but we can trust him. He helped me on Porta Flora, and he—"

This time it was the Ombudsman himself who interrupted me, making another impatient gesture toward the debris-strewn hillside. "Do you realize what you are up against here?" he said to Christopher, his voice firm but urgent. "These people would destroy you. You have no choice now."

The buxom woman met his impassioned gaze squarely, without flinching. "We have another ship coming in," she told him implacably.

"Another ship?" The Ombudsman turned to me, frustration clearly etched on that sternly wrought face, his very expression demanding an explanation from me.

"My ship," I offered promptly, still increasingly confused by Christopher's obstinacy. What was she trying to prove? *Raptor* was still too far out to be of any immediate help to us, and Hidalgo was right about the renegades; if they returned in force, we'd be in a nearly hopeless situation.

"Where is this ship of yours, then?" the Ombudsman was asking me, his patience with both of us slipping rapidly.

"She's close to coming in, maybe ten or fifteen minutes out."

Those were not the words I had intended to say, yet astoundingly, they were what came from my lips—will-lessly, automatically, as if they had been provided to me by another person inside my head. *Christopher*—damn her! A "mediocre telepath" indeed! I turned to glare sharply at her but found my gaze instead snared by Lewis; his eyes were wide with alarm. Quickly, I forced myself to look back to the Ombudsman as he spoke again.

"This is not an option," he informed us somewhat stiffly. "I think you are forgetting that you all are in direct violation of Authority law by even being on this planet." His head made a small, tight tip toward the two Ceecee officers, beam rifles still at ready, who were braced in the open hatches of their scout vessel. "I have received assurances that you will not be prosecuted under the Interdiction if you agree to leave under my auspices. But if you—"

"Authority law doesn't apply to me or my people," Christopher interrupted. "We're not Citizens, and we're here on Earthheart by invitation of its governing board."

The Ombudsman was speechless for a moment, his gleaming black eyes regarding Christopher's broad, bland face with barely concealed aggravation. It was an emotion that I felt I could have easily matched then, for the woman's obduracy was beginning to wear on me as well. I could understand why she was reluctant to surrender her fate to any representative of the Authorities— she had about as little reason to trust them as I did—but Hidalgo was offering us a way out. And any way out was more of a chance than the renegades would give us.

As if he had read my thoughts, the Ombudsman let out his breath in a soft, low hiss. "I understand your fear," he told Christopher quietly, forcing a patience he did not feel into his voice, "but you underestimate the extent of the forces against you." Again he made an all-inclusive gesture, waving at the hills around us. "Since the incident on Camelot, the effort to discover and abolish those who had plotted against your people has become a cross-quadrant priority to us." His gaze shifted, skimming over Lewis and then directing itself to me again. "With the investigation of John Leppers's death, we uncovered the crucial link the renegades had into the Authority network. By using that connection to track them, we have been able to follow them here, to you." That hawklike face tightened, his voice rising adamantly as he concluded, "This is of the greatest importance to us. We are the only ones now who can guarantee your safety!"

Amazingly, Christopher seemed unmoved. "Like you guaranteed it on Gaza 2?" she put to him. Then, before he could reply, she concluded simply, "I'll have to discuss this with the others." Turning away from him, she started briskly up the slope to the embryotory.

"*Dios!*" Hidalgo exclaimed, an archaic curse that I could satisfactorily interpret from context. His fists were clenched impotently, and he vigorously shook his head as if in disbelief. Since Christopher was already too far away to listen to him, he once again turned to me. "Captain, there is not much time. They *must* understand!"

Beside me, Lewis shifted restively, and I quickly glanced over at him. There was something in his expression that I didn't understand, and it vaguely troubled me. The apprehension and anxiety I understood just fine; in fact, I could feel them throbbing uncomfortably through my own body. But there was something else there, something just beyond my conscious reach that puzzled me. When Lewis studied the Ombudsman's sharply sculpted and bronze-colored face, it was as though he were seeing there something that I could not define or share.

"Come on," I told Hidalgo, turning abruptly to return up the slope.

Down in the scout ship, the two Ceecee officers both shifted, their beam rifles bobbing, as if they intended to follow us. But one negating gesture from the Ombudsman stopped them, keeping them seated within their ship. Instead, Hidalgo gave a brief nod toward the security guards stationed at the courier's ramp. Two of them split away from the ship, hurrying to catch up to us as the Ombudsman quickly climbed the hillside after me. Lewis followed only after a moment, and then from some distance, his eyes still going back to sweep over the gleaming hulls of the two craft and, uneasily, over the remaining armed men. I found myself, as I had so many times in the past, determinedly throttling down the insistent pang of his fear and doubt. It was the only way I could go on.

At the embryotory's unevenly gaping doors, Christopher was holding forth with both her people and mine, with predictably mixed results. The dissension did not have to be verbalized for its impact to be felt, and much of what had passed between them all as we approached was written more clearly on their faces than any words could have expressed. But even the naked hostility in some of those expressions did not deter the Ombudsman from repeating his earnest admonition.

"I have been sent as a neutral representative of the Combined Authorities to guarantee your safety—and your lives," he told that diverse and dusty group without preamble.

Wynna, the dark-haired woman who had been so opposed to laying down our weapons, waved deprecatingly at the two yellow- and green-suited armed security men who had followed us up the hill. "Neutral?" she snorted skeptically.

The Ombudsman's black eyes flashed, and for an instant I could see the bottomless fire of the Old Blood kindle in him. But he kept his voice tightly contained as he replied, "Would you expect us to face these renegades armed only with words? You have seen for yourselves what these people are capable of. Don't throw away your lives for old grievances."

To my surprise, it was Alexandria who spoke, her tone unexpectedly level. "Maybe they'd rather take their chances with the renegades," she said.

Hidalgo's deep-set eyes swept over the faces of the group, lingering perhaps on those of the Tens and definitely pausing on mine and Lewis's. "If you care so little for your own lives," he said quietly, his gaze shooting suddenly to Christopher, "at least think of the survival of your children."

I saw the volatile emotions wash across that broad, ruddy face then: surprise, alarm, denial, and finally anger. But before she could respond, the Ombudsman continued, that dark head slowly nodding.

"Yes, we know about them," he went on intently, his eyes softly gleaming. "We've known for a long time now. Why do you think we have done everything in our power to put these despicable renegades to rout?"

Christopher's face remained stoically set, her sand-colored eyes as hard as stone. "The A's have never done anything that hasn't served their own purposes," she countered stiffly.

"Perhaps," he responded. "But then you must believe me when I tell you that it serves our purposes to see your people—and your children—survive."

Christopher abruptly looked away, not at the other Tens, not at anything at all that I could discern, but just away, beyond the compelling hold of those coal-black eyes. For the first time I was able to understand at least something of the tremendous ambivalence that tore at her. Lewis had said something about the Tens having fled the A's for generations; he had not told me precisely why or how the Tens had remained hidden from the A's for all those years. But there seemed to be an almost insurmountable barrier there, a mutual distrust that had spanned the generations and still had the power to make Christopher consider risking death or enslavement by the renegades rather than agree to the Ombudsman's terms.

When Christopher looked back to the gray-robed man, her face was curiously blank, as if she had purged herself of all emotion to permit herself to deal with him. "If we came with you, where would you take us?'' she asked him, her voice flat, without inflection.

"Christopher, no!'' Wynna protested, but the man beside her—the thin man with receding hair, the man Lewis had called Mac—put a restraining arm around her waist even as Christopher held up her hand in a command for silence.

"Whore?'' she repeated to Hidalgo.

"The regional Authority complex at New Panama, at first,'' the Ombudsman responded immediately, "but only until we were certain that all of these renegades have been captured or eliminated. Then, for your eventual assimilation into whatever—''

But Christopher bluntly cut off his flow of words by sharply turning away from him. Gesturing toward a woman who stood near the shattered doors, she instructed quietly, "Get the case, Tess.''

The slim, gray-haired woman hesitated, obviously torn between her customary obedience to Christopher and her equally powerful reluctance to give up custody of the metal case. In Mac's arms, I saw Wynna writhe as if in pain. Christopher did not repeat the command—not aloud, at least. But the piercing look she gave Tess had nothing equivocal about it, and the reluctant woman finally turned and swiftly disappeared through the broken doors.

Mac, Wynna, and Kell were clustered together, just as the rest of my friends stood closely together. The tense apprehensiveness, the sense of siege, seemed every bit as high then as it had while the embryotory had been under direct attack by the renegades. And at last Alexandria, who had obviously kept her silence for as long as was humanly possible for a person of her voluble opinions, finally reached her breaking point.

"You don't have to do this, Chris,'' she said, stepping forward from where she had stood with Redding and Raydor to confront her old friend. "Hell, woman, you're not even *Citizens*!'' She dismissed the Ombudsman with one contemptuous wave. "Some Authority lackey in a dress can't make you do anything.''

The muted chorus of assenting murmurs that rose from behind Alexandria only confirmed my impression that hers was a popular consensus, and not only among the other Tens. But Christopher merely shook her head, a look of both regret and inestimable weariness on that broad and dusty face. "You're right, Lexie,'' she said softly, "he can't make us do anything. But circumstances can.'' She made a subdued but self-explanatory gesture, encompassing at the same time the ruined door frame, the devastated hillside, and her grimy band of survivors. "*This* can," she finished in quiet capitulation.

But Alexandria, as usual, was not particularly swayed by the constraints of logic, nor was her prickly demeanor ameliorated by Christopher's grim assessment of our circumstances. "We have a ship," she argued, still confronting the big blond woman. "We don't need these goons!"

The Ombudsman tried to intervene then, his tone far more placating than Alexandria's behavior would seem to merit. "You say you have a ship, but where is it now?" he put to her. "Where will it be when more renegades arrive here?" He waved toward the waiting courier at the foot of the slope. "My ship is here now, and I can guarantee you safe passage from this place—now."

"You want to guarantee our safety?" Alexandria demanded. "Then give us cover until our ship comes in. That's all we need from you!"

For a moment the Ombudsman did not speak; he just studied the bellicose woman before him, his dark eyes hooded. When he spoke again, his voice was still reasoning, almost conciliatory in tone, completely at odds with the barely banked fire that I saw then within him. "I cannot do that," he told Alexandria patiently. "The conditions of my auspices apply only if you accompany—"

"Bullshit!" Alexandria exploded, nearly spitting in his face. Despite the vehemence of her response, no one else moved to intervene. For in that moment the confrontation had clearly become something between the two of them: the soft-spoken, gray-robed Ombudsman and the indomitable woman with hair like a crown of thorns. Her voice lowered, dropping to a near growl. "Citizen or not, there're some of us here the A's would just as soon be shed of for good." She eyed him up and down with patent contempt, then shot a blunt look to the armed security men. "Or are you telling me your 'office' is guaranteeing my safety, too?"

I remembered thinking then that it was a good thing the Ombudsman wasn't armed, because it would have taken inhuman discipline for him not to have just fried Alexandria where she stood. As it was, those fierce and burning eyes fixed her with a scalding look. The standoff could easily have continued to some predictably dire end, fueled by that look alone. But before Hidalgo could stifle his fury long enough to frame another response, Tess reappeared in the embryotory's entrance.

The slim woman hesitated a moment, clutching the metal case protectively to her thin chest while her anxious glance darted from Hidalgo's forbidding face to Christopher's familiar one. Then she started toward her friend.

If I hadn't been standing so close to the Ombudsman, I don't think I would have been able to detect the slight signal that he gave to the two silent guards who had waited behind him. But as they began to come forward, Christopher reached out and quickly took the case from Tess, enfolding it in her strong, fleshy arms. She threw Hidalgo a warning look, her broad jaw stubbornly set. "Tell them no," she insisted.

Hidalgo swiftly raised his hand, the gesture almost appeasing. The two men immediately halted. "They are only going to take the case to the ship," he explained, his tone placating once more. "We must—"

"No," Christopher repeated, her voice low and harsh—like Alexandria's, a growl. "No, I will not be separated from this case for any reason."

I saw it the moment that something in Hidalgo ruptured, saw it with a curious sense of detachment, like a viewer scanning something on a vid. His meticulous tolerance, already tested by Christopher's original skepticism, had barely had time to recover before Alexandria's acid resistance had begun to eat at it. Christopher's direct denial seemed to push him beyond his carefully maintained control. "Take it!" he snapped at the security men, making a sharp, chopping motion toward the buxom woman with the case.

At the same time Christopher was stepping backward toward the other Tens, with the metal case tightly clasped to her ample bosom, Alexandria was lunging forward toward Hidalgo's throat. Only one thing intervened to stop both of them; it was a tactical maneuver that I might have taken the opportunity to admire had our situations been reversed. The Ombudsman dodged sideways, knocking into me so hard that I was shoved away from Lewis and nearly lost my footing. But although I staggered, surprised and angered by his rude evasive tactic, I did not fall. One of his arms, as sinewy and biting as an iron band beneath the soft gray of his robe's sleeve, locked around my shoulders, his fingers digging into my flesh. His other arm was crossed over my chest, and in it then was a beam pistol, its barrel buried in the soft skin at the angle of my jaw.

I was relieved and strangely grateful to find that my first reaction was not panic, not even fear; my first response, fed to me in a great, pounding surge, was rage. It was, I recognized just seconds later, Lewis's rage—a furious wave of anger washing over me like a hot shower. Like everyone else on that torn and littered hillside, he had suddenly frozen in place, but there was a part of him, the part that reached inside me, that roiled in silent, defiant fury.

The first action to take place on the slope after Hidalgo had seized me was the well-timed approach of the other two security guards from the courier and of the two Ceecee officers from the scout. The four men came trotting up the rubble-strewn hill, all with weapons at the ready. That seemed to jolt the two guards who had hesitated in front of Christopher back into motion, initiating a struggle with her for the possession of the metal case that she still clenched in her crossed arms. Like most Security, the men had not been chosen solely on the basis of their size and strength; they also had agility and a certain amount of ingenuity. The buxom woman grappled desperately to hold on, but the guards, guided by the Ombudsman's example, had both drawn their pistols and were using the weapons as pry bars. There seemed little doubt they would have used them as more had Christopher not released her hold on the case.

With a hoarse, helpless cry, Christopher was pushed backward as the two men wrested the case from her grip. Frustrated and outraged, she rounded on the Ombudsman, her flushed face contorted with anger and pain. "You cowardly bastard!" she spit at him. "You're one of them, aren't you? You ball-less little piece of—"

One of the security guards, a sandy-haired Normal with a blandly regular face, backhanded her then, cutting her off in midcurse. He stood just a little too far away from her for the blow to carry any real viciousness, but it had the desired effect. Christopher spun toward him, her eyes gone almost colorless with her fury, but she did not carry through and give him cause to shoot her. The Ombudsman jerked up on me with one arm, making me grunt involuntarily as his pistol meaningfully prodded my neck. And so Christopher held back, glaring furiously at both Hidalgo and the guard who had struck her.

Alexandria did not try to move, but she was unable to keep silent. With all the icy imperiousness only she could summon, she just coolly eyed Hidalgo up and down and then offered her withering assessment: "Yeah, you were a real waste of sperm."

It was perhaps the ultimate insult in our universe, and I felt the body that held me jerk reflexively with anger, but the Ombudsman did not give Alexandria the satisfaction of a retort. But I saw the glance, fleeting but momentous, that passed between Alexandria and Christopher, and suddenly I understood. It was a look of sisterhood, yes, but it was also a look of grim complicity, of bitterly knowing satisfaction. Somehow, all along, those two women had known, or at least suspected, what had eluded me so completely. Everything either one of them had said or done since those two ships had touched down had been carefully orchestrated with a single-minded intent—testing, probing, pushing. Even their bizarrely synchronized "advocate/adversary" routine, wearing down Hidalgo's facade of humanitarianism like a whetstone grinding away at steel, had been a ploy to make him show his true colors. And they had succeeded admirably.

The Ombudsman's grip around my shoulders had eased slightly then, although I was not fool enough to believe that he was relaxing his vigilance. I felt his head turn as his gaze moved slowly and deliberately from Alexandria and Christopher to the rest of the men and women standing together on the slope. "I would hope that you would all be sensible now," he said evenly to no one in particular. "There has been enough destruction here already."

I saw Redding shift, his typical, deceptively casual pose straightening fractionally. He was a man who was used to keeping himself under control; he was cool in a crisis. Because it was customary for him to reveal so little of what he was thinking, anyone who knew him less well than I did might conceivably have missed the strong undercurrent of contempt and loathing that stiffened his posture. Even his voice betrayed more disgust than indignation, and very little of either emotion, as he said to Hidalgo, "Those two air cars. You blew up your own men, then."

I wasn't able to see the precise expression on the Ombudsman's face, but his tone was one of matter-of-fact regret. "Yes, that was an unfortunate necessity," he responded levelly. I felt him give a little shrug. "But would you have believed me otherwise? I think not."

"We didn't believe you anyway, you asshole!" Alexandria snapped, unable to resist goading him.

I would have appreciated her witty repartee more if I hadn't had a gun at my throat. Again the arm holding me rose in a small shrug. "Perhaps," he allowed her, the beam pistol pressing—deliberately or not—more tightly against my jaw. "But ultimately I am still the one who now has what he wants."

Christopher's eyes moved from Hidalgo to the metal case, still firmly gripped in the hands of one of the armed guards, then back to the Ombudsman's face. "What could your people possibly hope to gain by destroying mine?" she asked him, her expression more frustrated than angry then.

Hidalgo shifted slightly, pulling me back against his chest with an abruptness that nearly made me stumble. His voice, almost in my ear, was surprisingly intense, almost impassioned. "Is that what you believe, that we wish to destroy the Class Tens?" he responded immediately. "My Lady, I have no intention of seeing these embryos endangered." His sudden use of the formal term of address from the Old Blood surprised me, but not as much as what he had yet to say. "Your children have a gift which I hope to see fostered—fostered and used to better my people so that those of the Old Blood will not fall into oblivion again."

As he spoke, a strangely focused expression had been forming on Christopher's face, a mixture of both wonder and despair. "Then you know . . ." she said softly.

The Ombudsman stood motionless; for a moment I did not even feel the man draw a breath. Then he let out a soft sigh. "Yes, at last we know," he told her, his tone almost gentle. "From the time the Authorities first sequestered their Class Ones on Gaza 2, they have kept your secret well. Only that small, exclusive cadre knew of the mysterious change that obliterated the Ones and created the Tens in their place. And even they did not understand the nature of the element that precipitated that change."

His attention momentarily moved to Alexandria, where she stood with Redding and Raydor. "Our friend Hanlon's research on Camelot led her to the discovery of the agent of that unique transformation when she isolated the living organism that has made the Tens what they are."

My pulse galloped, each heartbeat like an urgent slap. I knew there was at least one other person on that hushed hillside who shared my thoughts at that moment. I tried, without being able even to turn my head, to catch Asplundh's attention with my eyes. But she stood beside Taylor, partially obscured by his body, and in her very stance I could read her reaction of both shock and a kind of unwilling excitement.

Hanlon's illicit research had accomplished what the curly-haired geneticist's own fledgling attempts had only hinted at: Alexandria's old partner and nemesis had discovered the nature of the nonstandard substance in the Tens' DNA. And that substance—"the living organism," Hidalgo had called it—was present in the cells of every Ten on that hillside, just as it was present in the tiny bodies of every suspended embryo in the metal case held by that renegade guard—and yes, even in every cell of that nearly shapeless little bit of protoplasm I had left behind me, halfway across the quadrant, in a medical facility on Porta Flora. Their children, my child—our child; it was all the same.

For the first time then, during the whole ordeal of that seemingly endless, nearly hopeless mission, I found that I was forced to rely almost totally on Lewis to sustain me. The enormity of what the Ombudsman had revealed had stunned me: The mythical Class Ones, secreted by the A's on a remote world, somehow being transformed into the genetic mutants whom the A's then betrayed—

Hidalgo moved suddenly, sharply jerking me around as he gestured with a nod of his head for the security guards to start down the slope with the metal case. "Take it to the ship," he ordered briskly.

As the sandy-haired man and his partner stepped smartly to obey, Wynna burst forward from the group of Tens, a hoarse cry wrenched from her lips. *"No!"* she gasped.

Both the pair of Ceecee officers and the other two security guards immediately swung to cover her; Mac grappled for her and missed. But Christopher lunged sideways and caught the dark-haired and much smaller woman, wrestling her to a halt before any of the armed men fired. "Wynna! No, Wynna—don't!" Christopher commanded her, fiercely clinging to the still-struggling woman.

"Be sensible," the Ombudsman said. With the barrel of his beam pistol still buried in my throat, I didn't find his calm admonition reassuring; only Lewis's strength kept me from shuddering. "Accept it—there is no way for you to stop us now."

Over Wynna's dark head, Christopher's sharp and quartz-clear gaze met Hidalgo's hooded eyes with unflinching stoniness. "You don't realize what you're doing," she told him grimly.

"I understand more than you will ever know, My Lady!" he nearly shouted back at her, his arm tightening painfully across my shoulders. He jerked my whole body sideways to gesture at the two security guards who bore the case, already halfway down the slope to the ships, and concluded more softly, "I understand. The people who control the power of the Talents will ultimately control our universe.''

Then abruptly, without warning, he suddenly threw me aside, spinning me away from him as he stepped back. With the embryo case in his possession and four other armed men to back him up, apparently Hidalgo no longer felt the need for a hostage. I nearly fell but managed to keep my footing only because Lewis was instantly there, gathering me into his arms.

The Ombudsman's fiery gaze raked over our embrace, but instead of scorn, Lewis's fierce protectiveness seemed to elicit a more equanimous response from Hidalgo. "Yes, I am the one who now has what he wants," he murmured, his angular face strangely calm. Then he turned, addressing the two red- and black-suited men who constituted the crew of the Ceecee scout. "Be certain that your new cargo is securely stowed," he instructed them tersely. "Then you may lift immediately. Your only concern from now on is to see that case safely to the rendezvous point. Now go.''

As the Ceecee officers, their rifles still drawn, started back down the slope, I could see the first pair of security men waiting by the scout ship with the metal case. Beside Hidalgo, the final pair of yellow- and green-suited guards automatically moved to flank him, their beam pistols leveled. Oddly enough, I felt no real sense of fear then, even though death seemed imminent. Perhaps it was that I still felt so little of my own emotions and that the feelings that poured through me from my contact with Lewis were still of the incendiary sort—contempt, outrage, and a steely resolve to survive. No one else among us, Citizens or Tens, cringed away from Hidalgo's final piercing scrutiny.

The Ombudsman held his pistol almost casually, its barrel bobbing negligently in his hand. "I have to leave you all now," he announced solemnly. "I must put in an appearance at the Authorities' octospherical regulation base to make my report . . .'' His voice trailed off, then suddenly he smiled. It was a faint, tentative smile, but it was the first such expression I had ever seen on that warlike face; he wore it badly, like some borrowed item of clothing that was somehow too tight to fit properly. "I regret that I will have to inform them that my mission here failed, that I arrived too late to save your people from the renegades' attack. Yes," he added quickly, reading the surprise off our collective faces, "there are still several of my people's craft in this octant. We have been in contact even as my courier set down here." The ill-fitting smile widened, becoming almost ghastly, like a grinning death's-head. "Some of them were not particularly amused about the small matter of the sheep."

The Ombudsman turned, nodding to his guards, but he had not taken more than a few steps down the hillside before Asplundh suddenly exploded into motion. She had been standing beside Taylor, and he was the one who then reached out almost reflexively and prevented her from lunging after her quarry. *"Bastard!"* she spit, her face flushed as she struggled fiercely against Taylor's restraint. "Class bigot! You *used* a human being like a piece of equipment! Put an undegradable compound into his—"

The two security men had moved forward again, stepping in to shield the Ombudsman with their weapons menacingly leveled. But Hidalgo waved them back, his own pistol still plainly directed at our group. "Enough!" he said, his voice sharply admonishing. When she fell silent, he stared at her for a few moments as she hung pinioned in Taylor's arms. "Ah, you are the geneticist, the one who came from Heinlein," he remarked quietly. He lifted the barrel of his pistol slightly, using it to point in her direction. "And this is the young man whose misuse you protest. I was not the one who used your friend; your own dear Authorities did that. If it is any consolation, the man who authorized it is dead." He shrugged almost indifferently. "All we did was make use of the way they used him, just as we have been able to make use of everything they have known, all along."

Until that point I didn't think I had really fully understood the enormity of what the Ombudsman's betrayal had represented. I had been seeing everything that happened in a fragmented way, as a series of disjointed events without any necessary relationship to each other. But now I began to comprehend that all of it—from the moment that Rollo, the Authority liaison, had intersected me in that eatery on New Cuba—had been part of a frightening design that I had always been too close to for the pattern to have made any sense. The renegades had been behind everything that had happened to me since New Cuba; they had been on a collision course with the Class Tens from the beginning. And although I had skipped in and out of the picture, careening into events or being ricocheted off them— all with a probability I once would have thought was merely random, until I knew better—I realized then that ultimately I had always been destined to be caught between those two opposing forces.

The high-pitched whine of lifters firing filled the little valley, rolling up the surrounding slopes in quavering waves of sound. The Ceecee scout ship, with its stolen prize secured aboard, was lifting. Unwillingly but helplessly, the eyes of all of us were drawn to the sight of that sleek little vessel, the sunlight glittering off her hull, as she gracefully rose into the flawless blue of Earthheart's sky.

The Ombudsman, too, watched for a moment; then his dark eyes moved back to the ragtag little group that had been left behind. The expression on his face was strangely sober, and his voice was quiet and low. "And now I will leave you as well, my friends," he said softly, his lips twisting downward in a thoughtful frown. "No, I have no intention of killing you. I'm afraid there are others who will gladly see to that, and soon enough."

Abruptly, the gray-robed man turnēd on his heels, his black braid swinging as he started down the hillside again. He was flanked by the two security guards, who crab-walked sideways so that they could still face us with their weapons trained on us. Hidalgo himself no longer seemed concerned with us; he was intent only on reaching his waiting courier ship.

The scout ship was nothing more than a dot in the sky by then, rendered visible only by the sharp, crystalline sparkle of the sunlight off her gleaming hull. Still, my gaze was frozen to her, unable to give up that last connection with everything the Tens had been and could be. My own emotions were coming back, unwelcome and turbulent, leaking into the defenses of Lewis's feelings like dye spilling into water. I felt his arms tighten around me, but not in desperation. Incredibly, what Lewis felt was still outrage—outrage and an inhumanly calm resolve that we had not reached the end.

"Ombudsman!"

Christopher's sudden shout jerked my eyes back from the sky. Her broad and ruddy face as stolid and expressionless as the sod-covered hillside, she stood with one arm extended, holding something out to Hidalgo.

Some twenty meters down the slope the Ombudsman and his guards paused. He turned with a quizzical look on his darkly bronzed face.

"You may as well take this, too," the big blonde explained, tossing something after him.

I wasn't able to tell what the object was until he had deftly caught it and held it up; then I recognized it as the plastic card-key Christopher had used in the storage chamber to unlock the embryo case. Barely glancing at the shocked and indignant expressions on the faces of the other Tens, Hidalgo nodded slightly to Christopher and then quickly slipped the little device into his robe before he and his guards resumed their course back down the rubble strewn slope to the waiting courier ship.

Filled with frustration and despair, I looked back up to the sky, but the scout ship had slipped beyond visual range. I was still vainly searching for a glimpse of it against the backdrop of vivid blue when the distant fireball bloomed in an exploding starburst of orange and yellow. The reverberant concussion, the sheer volume of the detonation stunned me for an instant. How could anything that far away, so high up that I had not even been able to see the ship, have caused such a loud and immediate blast? Then an inchoate cry from behind me made me drop my gaze, and the reason for the discrepancy became shockingly clear.

The booming explosion I had just seen far overheard was not the explosion I had heard: Halfway down the furrowed slope, where only moments earlier Hidalgo and the two security men had been striding toward their ship, there was nothing more than a discolored circle of ground, a blackened ring of shapeless debris that was surrounded by widely strewn bits of scorched clothing and macerated flesh and still streamed a thick gout of putrid black smoke. And beyond that carnage lay the bodies of the last two guards, still whole but either stunned or killed by the force of the blast.

I did not need to turn around to know what was on the faces of the people behind me. It would have been like looking into a mirror at my own expression: astonishment, horror, incredulity. Yet, through Lewis, I felt something more, something that I could see reflected on Christopher's and Alexandria's broad faces as well, something that surprised and confused me. For the two women were glancing, much as I had, from the grisly scene of slaughter on the hillside up to the sun-washed sky, where long streamers of dark smoke still streaked down like incendiary markers from the flaming bits of wreckage of the destroyed scout ship, but neither one of them seemed shocked or horrified. If I'd had to put one word to that fierce gleam in their eyes, it would have been "vindication." And with a lurching sense of recognition, I realized then that it had been Alexandria whom I had heard cry out when the explosion had taken out Hidalgo and his guards and that the sound had not been a cry of alarm but a shout of triumph.

"Jesus—!" someone behind me breathed; it was Taylor, and he had made the single word resonate like a prayer.

My eyes went to Christopher's, digging in like grappling hooks. "The key—" I began breathlessly.

Her pale fingers were still clenched into fists, but the sand-colored eyes were bright and sharp like chips of agate as she met my gaze and nodded. "Spatially detonated microfusion explosives," she offered, her voice entirely matter-of-fact. "Primary charge in the case, secondary charge in the card-key."

Using a device very much like a set of detention cuffs, she had made the Ombudsman the unwitting second component in a two-part bomb. As soon as the charge that had been concealed within the embryo case aboard the scout ship had reached a sufficient distance from its counterpart in the plastic key she'd thrown to Hidalgo, the circuit had been tripped, and both explosive charges had been detonated. And so she had succeeded in stopping the renegades' unconscionable theft of the embryos, but in doing so she had also had to destroy the one thing she had devoted her life to preserving. To me it seemed an empty victory, bitter and without meaning.

A loud grumble rose up from the valley, and I spun abruptly to see exhaust jetting from the courier's lifters. Whatever crew she had left, at least one of them was a pilot, a pilot who saw no advantage to lingering in that place. The immediate question that occurred to me then, as the rising rumble of the diplomatic vessel's engines reverberated across the shattered hillsides, was very simple: Would the courier swing over to strafe us with some of that impressive Authority artillery that she carried under her belly or would she be content to leave our fate to the vengeance of those yet-incoming remnants of the renegades' forces on-planet?

Lewis seemed to have already made up his mind about the courier's likely course of action. He pulled me backward gently but firmly, saying, "I think we should find cover again."

But another familiar voice, one that I had long since learned to listen to, cut in. "Listen," Raydor said, stepping forward with his big head curiously cocked.

At first the only thing I could hear was the accelerating growl of the courier's lifters as the gleaming vessel began to rise steadily from the valley floor in a roiling wave of flying dust and debris. Then, even as that sound grew louder and more high-pitched, as the courier pulled up and away from the ravished slopes, I could make out another sound above it: the faint, hollow-sounding but distinct popping bursts of distant explosions.

Disregarding Lewis's caution, I slipped free of his hold. Hastily, I trotted obliquely across the face of the hillside for a few dozen meters, stumbling over the long trenches scored into the sod, my eyes fixed on the brilliant blue of that cloudless sky. I knew that I was being followed—by Lewis, by Raydor, and by others who were willing to ignore the wedge-shaped threat of the courier that was rapidly lifting above our heads. But the ship did not swing back around to fire on us; rather, she took a sharply angled trajectory on a course heading directly away from the slope where the embryotory stood and accelerated briskly.

Lewis caught up to me then, grabbing the sleeve of my filthy tunic and halting my scrambling flight. "Jo!" he cried out, his voice sharp with both exasperation and concern. He spun me around so abruptly that I felt my chin connect smartly with his shoulder. "Where the hell do you think you're—"

"Listen!" I commanded him, my head tilting back to scan the horizon.

The explosions were nearer now but less frequent. Lewis stood wordlessly for a few moments, listening, still breathing heavily, his fingers dug into the coarse weave of my tunic. I was peripherally aware of Raydor and Redding coming up behind us, and behind them, more of the others. Then, just as I sensed Lewis was about to speak again, the first of the incoming air cars became visible on the crest of a distant hill, winking with a jewellike brilliance in the slanting rays of the afternoon sun.

"God's breath, Jo! Those are more *renegades*!" Lewis exclaimed, jerking me backward again. I think he was about ready to just throw me over his shoulder and carry me off that damned hillside by force by then. It took a few seconds longer for the reason for my seemingly foolish bravado to become apparent to him and to everyone.

Another explosion, this one clearly audible, detonated just beyond that highest rise of land. A flashfire of golden light like a miniature sunset flared behind the hill. Then a sleek silver projectile rose predatorily into view, skimming over the crest like a soaring hawk riding a thermal current in a canyon. Narrow vanes swept back, her gleaming prow aimed like a missile, my own bird of prey closed in on the remaining renegades.

CHAPTER SIXTEEN

I guess it was a good thing you didn't have to believe in luck to have your ass saved by a fortunate set of circumstances, because *Raptor*'s arrival was nothing if not fortuitous. My mother had always believed that you made your own luck, and maybe that was the principle at work there. As the ship cleared the highest rise of land, twin spurts of almost painfully bright blue fire squirted from her belly. Seemingly simultaneously, the line of incoming air cars exploded in coruscating fireballs of orange flame, literally vaporized by the furious heat of *Raptor*'s high-intensity beams. Beside me I saw Lewis avert his face as if even at that distance the brilliance of their destruction could blind. I had to squint, but I could not keep my eyes from the sky.

The courier ship had leveled off then, forsaking altitude in favor of acceleration and offensive action in favor of flight. She was pushing hard to put some space between herself and *Raptor*. Her pilot was good and his judgment was sound, but his efforts were in vain. *Raptor* passed overhead, her long winged shadow undulating over the deeply gouged sod and scorched rubble and stinking smoke of the hillside. She climbed a few degrees, the adjustment smooth and nearly languorous, and for a moment it almost looked like she was breaking off the chase. Then her high beams fired again, the blue jets like spurts of liquid flame. There was a sound like the loud *whump!* of physical impact; then the courier ship erupted into a ball of incandescent gold.

High-intensity beam cannon were a remarkably clean weapon; very little solid debris was left to sprinkle down from the empty sky as *Raptor* peeled neatly around and swept back toward us. I gripped Lewis's hand and began to drag him after me as I plunged down the ragged hillside. High above us, the ship's retros cut in with a faint *whoosh*. Leaping chunks of scattered wreckage and stumbling through the long scours of upheaved sod, I lost Lewis's hand partway down the slope as I half ran, half slid to the bottom of the hill. Then, my breath coming in pants, my heart racing so crazily that I wasn't sure my heaving chest could hold it, I stood back from the largest level spot in that narrow valley and watched my ship come in. I didn't even care about the fresh, blackened scars on her gleaming hull or the jagged little wedge torn out of her tail vane; *Raptor* had never looked more beautiful to me.

Before the landing gear's cleated feet had even finished sinking into the plowed-up ground, I was ducking beneath the struts, racing for the access panel. I hit the ramp and hatch accesses simultaneously, hard enough to make my palm sting. The ramp began to drop in a graceful arch, the hatch quickly dilating. I pounded down the corridor to Control, heedless of the trail of dusty bootprints I was leaving behind on the deck plates. As Control's hatch whisked open, I threw myself into my chair, my hand coming down on Handy's curved access with an audible slap.

For a few seconds I was literally speechless, too stunned to think and too winded to be able to force the words out. When I was able to, I said, in a voice that was as steady as I could make it, "I just hope to hell those were all renegades and not Authority ships that you were taking out back there," although, in all honesty, at that point I really no longer gave a shit.

"Of course they were renegades," Handy rumbled, apparently unperturbed by either my doubt or my lack of a more conventional greeting. "Actually, all the legitimate Authority ships in this octant are already on their way back to the other side of the planet."

I heard Lewis and Raydor come into the compartment behind me, but they weren't the only ones, they were just the fastest. I didn't even throw them a glance. I just stared down at Handy's console, my brow furrowing, wondering if chronic exposure to the effects of adrenaline could cause premature senility. "What do you mean, the other side of the planet—and how the hell did you get down here so quick?" I demanded.

My second question probably seemed to have the greater priority to Handy, since by inference it called into question his obedience to my final orders about staying out of the A's scanning range until he was summoned by me. "I was able to take a little . . . shortcut to get here," he said. "I cut in across the

A's octospherical regulation base; it saved me almost fifteen minutes.''

Raydor had dropped down into the copilot's chair beside me. I darted a look at him then, but from the bemused expression on his seamed and dirt-smudged face, I could see that he was as confused as I was by the Integrator's explanation.

"Their *base*? What the hell about their *surveillance*?" I pressed him.

"That was no problem," Handy continued, "because on the way in, on my planetary approach, I took out a few of their relay satellites." He paused for a moment as if anticipating some protest on my part; when none was forthcoming, he made that odd little scritching sound that passed for his audio equivalent of a shrug and elaborated. "That courier ship had already taken out part of their surveillance net, and I figured it wouldn't make any different now, since we're leaving anyway. So I made a run over the base and knocked out their main comm station. Then I egressed into their emergency comm code and ordered all their survey and scout vessels to report to the southeastern octant at once to help quell a—"

"By the Holy Points of Light!" I exclaimed, uncertain whether I was about to start to foam at the mouth or dissolve into helpless laughter. At least that explained how he had known that all the ships he'd blown up had been renegades: His false priority call had already sent every genuine Authority vessel scurrying in the other direction. "You call *that* staying out of their range?" I just sputtered helplessly.

The deep bass voice sounded mildly indignant. "The relay went dead after you called me in," he reminded me pointedly. "I had to assume the worst. I wanted to save some time. Besides," he added, "that courier had already tapped into their comm system; Authority ships were being diverted left and right even before I got here."

Then I did laugh, not hysterically but appreciatively. From behind me, Lewis's arms came around my shoulders, squeezing me lightly. Glancing back at him, giddy with relief, I just told Handy, "Never mind—I don't think I want to hear the rest of this right now. Are all systems functional?"

"Of course," he responded. "Although there does seem to be a lot of stuff scattered around the cabins from when our AG was out."

"I don't care about that," I cut in. "Just get us the hell out of here!"

"Fine, Jo; you've got it," Handy agreed. He paused significantly, then reminded me, "Some coordinates would be helpful, though."

Before I could even consider that question much less answer it, an all-too-familiar voice intervened. Alexandria had wedged herself into the rear of the compartment, a space already crowded by Taylor, Asplundh, Redding, and, spilling out into the corridor, Christopher and the rest of the Tens. "Claire's," Alexandria said flatly. "We have to go back to Claire's, Jo."

I could appreciate Alexandria's desire to see her old friend once more and to assure Claire that in spite of the tragic loss of the embryos, the rest of us were safe. Claire had taken some tremendous risks to help us; once again Alexandria seemed to have come up on the debit side of the balance sheet with her. But above and beyond that I felt a sense of responsibility for the lives of the people on my ship and an almost overwhelming desire to lift from that planet as quickly as possible, before what was passing for our luck ran out.

I didn't turn to face Alexandria, because I didn't want to have to confront that implacable expression. I just began, reasoningly, "Look, our tail is clear right now, Alexandria; I don't think we should take any—"

Then another voice cut in, low and urgent. "Jo, it's important," Christopher said.

That time I did turn, catching Christopher's eyes where she stood at the hatchway. The look on her fleshy face was stolid and composed but strangely compelling.

Determinedly, I swung back to the console, but before I could speak, Handy said spontaneously, "We should have a little time left yet, Jo; it's going to take the A's a while to get things sorted out again over there at the base."

I considered that a moment, feeling the light, encouraging squeeze of Lewis's hands at my shoulders before I reached for the curve of Handy's input. "Okay," I said. "I suppose if we have to, we can always make another run for it."

"Yeah, but that probably won't be necessary," Handy noted ingenuously as he began to cycle up *Raptor*'s engines again. "When that courier ship first set down here, they already reported back to the base that the renegades had gotten here ahead of them—and that there were no survivors."

Someone—Redding, I thought—hooted loudly from the rear of the compartment. I had to choke down my own incredulous laughter before I managed to gasp out, "You mean the A's think—"

"Yeah," Handy confirmed, as the ship started to lift again from the little valley's narrow floor. "Officially, you're all dead!"

The trip to Claire's homestead, which had taken us hours by ground cart, was reduced by *Raptor* to a matter of minutes. I had Handy set us down as close to the house as he could without causing any major trauma to Claire's livestock. The LaGrange cattle, relatively removed from us on the rolling slopes, barely lifted their huge heads as we came in. But the small flocks of sheep that remained confined to the pens crowded to the far side of their enclosures, bleating piteously and packing themselves together like big wads of cotton batting. And Claire's exotic fowl seemed to be of two minds, either scattering in a frenzied flurry of feathers or squaring off, rigid necks extended, to confront the strange invader from the sky.

As the retros cut off and the hovers gently lowered the ship to the green and whipping grass, I left Raydor at the console and squeezed out past the people filling the compartment and the corridor. By the time I'd reached the outer hatchway, most of them were following me. I scrambled down the ramp before it had completely settled onto the ground. Ducking past a strut, I emerged from beneath *Raptor*'s belly and hastily scanned the yard. Then I just stopped, grinning and shaking my head in disbelief.

On the roof of one of the long, low buildings, a structure just beyond the sheep pens, a small group of Tachs had paused in their task long enough to straighten up and watch us come in. On the ground below, weaving her way between stacks of half-empty pallets bearing bales of sheet roofing, I saw Claire beginning to make her way toward us. Several of her herd dogs gamboled along ahead of her. I thought she had just been being facetious when she had told me that morning that she was going to get some of the Tachs together and reroof her shearing shed, but damned if she hadn't done just that. The irony of it seemed perfectly apt to me: We'd had to go out and face our destiny, but on Earthheart it had just been a good day to do another necessary chore.

I moved out to meet Claire, and as she drew closer, several more of her gangly dogs broke loose from whatever had been occupying them at the sheds. Frolicking across the sun-washed yard, they lazily scattered the last and bravest of the gaudy poultry and then ran up to stalk the ship, the coarse hair on their spines stiffening in a bristly display of unnecessary bravado.

I slowed and drew a deep breath, suddenly finding myself forced to stifle the rush of an emotion I could not even name. I glanced quickly across the entire sweep of the valley from the low green and gilt hills to the simple rectangles of the outbuildings and the unimposing facade of Claire's half-buried house. It seemed impossible to me that it had been only the day before when we had first walked into that place, following Brill as she drove her sheep home. I felt like I had spent half my lifetime there, or at least half of the part that really mattered.

Christopher had passed me and reached Claire first, capturing the lean little dark-haired woman in a fervent embrace. Then, one by one, the other Tens came forward to receive Claire's relieved and happy greetings. As I watched them all together, I thought again of the geneticist's words of farewell to me only that morning: "Until I see you again." Just a courtesy, I had assumed then; finally, I was beginning to understand.

"Well, come on, you'll have to eat," Claire urged us, starting to herd us toward the house as deftly as her own dogs directed sheep.

But Redding shook his dusty, shaggy head, explaining reluctantly, "We can't stay, Claire. There's no time."

"All right," Claire said quietly, "but at least come inside." And I noticed that she calmly continued shepherding us toward the door even as she spoke.

We followed Claire into the house, Lewis walking beside me, unselfconsciously holding my hand in his. As we entered the luxurious commons area, one of Claire's brindle-colored pups looked up from an upholstered couch at the sudden influx of people, then slipped guiltily back onto the carpeted floor. Jeck stood in the kitchen doorway, his massive forearms crossed, scowling unconvincingly at the slinking canine.

Claire glanced across the room. "Jeck," she called out, "get together some food, please—everything you have that's prepared and can easily be carried." She looked back to us then, shrugging and offering by way of explanation, "I've eaten synthesized food on ships before; you might as well take as much real food as you can." She gestured toward the large grouping of furniture. "Now sit," she went on, "and tell me what happened out there."

Despite Claire's suggestion, no one seemed willing to sit

down. But Alexandria began the narration, and I was happy to let her. By the time her account had reached the point where we had been blindsided by the renegades' air cars outside the embryotory, Christopher had joined in. Gradually, Alexandria's contribution concluded, and the buxom blond woman went on alone, relating the events of that afternoon with a simple and matter-of-fact dispassion that I doubted I would have been capable of given everything that had happened. The other Tens stood a slight distance apart, letting Christopher speak for all of them.

Only when she neared the end of her story did Christopher's tone and expression change. Her voice softened, gaining inflection as her ruddy face began to reveal the emotions she had kept stifled. But to my surprise, she seemed less outraged than just plain disgusted as she told Claire, "You were right—the embryos were what they really wanted all along." Her broad jaw tightened stubbornly as she added, "And without the explosives, they would have gotten away clean."

Claire gently patted the larger woman's arm in sympathetic support, her finely planed face filled with concern. "You did what had to be done, Chris," she told her quietly. "Using the Talents as political weapons—it would have torn the Classes apart."

Lewis's fingers were still gently twined with mine; he seemed calm, contained. But for several minutes I had been aware of Asplundh shifting anxiously behind us. I thought I knew what was troubling her, because it was a concern that I shared, exacerbated by the exchange between Christopher and Claire. And my suspicion was confirmed when the curly-haired geneticist cleared her throat and awkwardly interjected, "The Ombudsman—when he took the suspension case from you, he—" She broke off then, a faint flush washing across the pale oval of her face.

"It's all right," Christopher reassured her, her rose-colored lips lifting in a soft, quirky smile. "I think you've more than earned the right to questions."

But Asplundh only flushed more deeply and dropped her eyes for a moment, while beside her Taylor put a supportive arm over her shoulders. I thought that I understood Asplundh's reluctance; she felt that because she was a scientist, her burning curiosity was somehow out of place in that highly emotional situation.

"It's all right," Claire affirmed gently, encouraging her to go on.

"He—he said that Hanlon's researchers had discovered the 'element' that defined the Tens' DNA," Asplundh continued hastily and clumsily. "He called it a living organism, but—" She shook her head, dust still escaping from her curly hair, the gesture more one of confusion than one of disbelief. "I've done electrophorectosis on Lewis's DNA, and it couldn't—"

Claire quietly interrupted her, that delicate face thoughtful and composed. "Actually, Hanlon's researchers didn't 'discover' anything," she corrected Asplundh evenly. "They just uncovered something which select members of the Upper Council have known about for generations, ever since Gaza 2."

I studied that leanly sculpted face, my mind furiously wheeling. I remembered Lewis's pained explanation the night before, when we had stood in the side yard and he had described the fugitive nature of his life. "Gaza 2—the Insurrection . . ." I said slowly.

Nodding, Claire looked from my face to Lewis's, then to Taylor's, and finally back to Asplundh's. "Officially, of course, such a thing as Class Ones never existed," she went on. Her dark eyes continued to study ours as if for indications of our continuing comprehension. "But they were the last remaining pure racial strains in the galaxy, secreted on Gaza 2 by a Council commission, to be kept as a source of undiluted genes—breeding stock." She paused, her mouth crimping wryly. "You can imagine the uproar that would have resulted had the general public—even the rest of the Authorities—found out that there were members of the Council hoarding genes."

Yes, I could imagine; wars had been fought over far less. Much of the hard-won success of the A's right to govern had, from the very beginning, come from their ability to control and minimize the social devastation caused by the Alterations. The Genetics and Reproduction Code had never been widely popular, but it had been accepted and remained enforceable for the simple reason that it had been strictly and fairly applied to everyone, regardless of political or economic rank. If it had been revealed that any Citizens had been Classified as Ones and that their genes were being kept for exclusive reproductive use, the regulation of the Code would have collapsed and the Class system would have been torn apart.

"The ironic thing," Claire continued levelly, "is that the Ones nearly brought themselves to the brink of extinction by their own inbreeding. They developed certain lethal genes; there was a high rate of embryonic death and fetal malformation. There probably were less than fifty genetically sound adults left on Gaza 2 when the change came.''

The lean, dark-haired woman paused again, still studying our attentive faces. I realized then that Christopher and the others had gradually drifted farther away from us, moving to the other side of the commons, and that the four of us were really the only ones Claire was still speaking to. At the same time, it came to me just why: With the possible exception of Lewis, whose fingers were meshed with mine and who would not have left my side, we were the only ones who hadn't already known what the geneticist was revealing.

Asplundh's pale face was set and intense, her brow furrowed in concentration. "The change?" she echoed. "That was the—the organism the Ombudsman spoke of?"

Again Claire nodded. "Something happened on Gaza 2," she said quietly, "something that no one could explain. Over the span of a single generation, the Class Ones' genes were transformed—mutated into what we now recognize as the characteristic DNA of a Class Ten. It took the Authority researchers years to discover what caused that change." She gave Asplundh a quick, rueful smile. "Given the plethora of raw material they had to work with and our current methods, *we* probably could have defined it in a week." She sobered again, regarding the younger geneticist with thoughtful candor. "You would have discovered it yourself, Asplundh, given a little more opportunity," she told her. "You already knew that the DNA component was nonstandard, nonhuman. But it wasn't synthetic, either; it just wasn't terrestrial." Claire's voice was soft but perfectly clear as she concluded, "And it is an organism—a subviral aggregate."

Asplundh looked totally astounded; for a few moments she was literally speechless. I frantically indexed through my mental file, trying to drag up what little basic biophysiology I still remembered from my schooling. At least I remembered what a subvirus was, the smallest known living organism. For centuries that distinction had been accorded to viruses. But the discovery of subviruses not only had changed the order of rank and the medical taxonomy, it also had revolutionized human health by eliminating one of man's oldest scourges, the subvirus's greatest handiwork: neoplasia, or cancer. But I still couldn't juxtapose that textbook definition with Claire's explanation of the Tens'

DNA structure and come up with a logical match. Neither, apparently, could Asplundh.

"But—that's impossible!" she finally blurted out, staring at Claire in genuine bafflement. "Subviruses are entirely host-specific and completely host-dependent." She was looking at Claire then as if she almost hoped the older woman would correct her basic scientific assumptions, because otherwise the conclusion she was forced to come to was something she simply couldn't accept.

But Claire merely gave a gentle shrug. "Terrestrial subviruses are host-specific and host-dependent, but we're not talking about a terrestrial form of life," she reminded Asplundh.

Asplundh's tawny-colored eyes were wide with disbelief. "But how—how could the aggregate be nonterrestrial?"

I understood just enough of what they had said to be thoroughly confused. If the organism was alien, possibly something native to Gaza 2, then how could it have entered into a symbiotic relationship with a human being? Not only entered into such a relationship but actually altered that human's genetic structure—and, by effecting that change, radically enhance the host's psychic and somatic abilities? It was incredible, like something out of a science-fiction story. Lewis's fingers spasmed in mine, as I asked Claire bluntly, "Then the genetic alterations in the Tens—the Talents—are caused by an alien organism?"

Claire just nodded.

"So now all that's left of this organism is what's in the last of the Tens?" I concluded flatly, jerking my chin to indicate both Lewis and the five other Tens across the wide room from us. I just stared at Claire for a moment, hard and direct, almost wanting in my helpless frustration for her to reproach me in some way for the tactless candor of my blunt conclusion. But the steely little woman did not seem upset by my indictment; in fact, her tanned face wore a curiously calm expression, open and accepting.

"I think I can explain this better if you'll come with me," Claire said quietly. "There's something I want you all to see."

As she had spoken, she'd thrown one brief glance over our heads. I turned quickly to see that the glance had been directed at Christopher, who responded to Claire's wordless query with a single simple nod of acquiescence.

As the four of us followed Claire through the rear doorway of the commons, into the office area, Taylor spoke up for the first time. He still held Asplundh by the arm, and, typically, his voice was welcomely free of judgment. "If the subvirus was native to Gaza 2, could it still be there?" he asked.

Claire's mouth twisted down in a frown of regret. "I don't know if it was a native life-form, Taylor, and we'll never know now." She glanced over at him, her eyes narrowing. "Do you know what happened on Gaza 2?"

Taylor shrugged with boyish amiability. "Sure," he said. "The Insurrection."

But Claire just shook her head grimly. "That's what they called it. Someone in the Council commission with the knowledge of the discovery panicked. The so-called Insurrection was nothing more than a cover-up for a badly bungled attempt by outside forces to either abduct or destroy the Class Tens." Her voice hardened, her inflection flattening, as she tersely delivered her explanation. "Dirty weapons were used there—fission weapons. Gaza 2 was scoured by radiation." She glanced back at us as we passed the doors to the abandoned infirmary rooms. "Nearly three centuries later, and the A's don't even need to bother with Interdiction; a ship couldn't even get within orbital distance without receiving a lethal dose."

Asplundh's face looked as though someone had drained all the blood from her body. Beside her, walking with his arm linked with hers, Taylor's jaw was set, his golden-brown eyes as hard as cut glass. "Someone panicked?" he repeated, his voice harsh with incredulity.

But I had lost the capacity to feel surprise in those matters. When it came to whitewash, history wielded a pretty wide paintbrush. The Ones had never existed; neither, then, did the Tens. Gaza 2's Insurrection had been a civil dispute, an insurgency that had tragically turned into a nuclear holocaust. You were supposed to trust the Authorities—hell, you were supposed to trust *Ombudsmen*. But like an abscessed trail of rot, the festering track of the renegades had run through both the Military and Civilian Authorities, spilling out its pus into even their supposedly incorruptible adjuncts. Looking back, I could see how we had been used—all of us, at every available turn. If it had been possible to renounce my Citizenship, I think I would have done so then. Renouncing my membership in the entire human race was running a close second.

We had nearly reached the back of Claire's laboratory before I really noticed where we were. Once again we stood, as we had a mere day earlier, in front of the huge built-in, glass-fronted storage case, the same spot where Claire had displayed her "spares" and confessed to a weakness for genetic diversity. Stepping forward, the dark-haired woman released the latch and smoothly slid aside one of the big doors, its glass opaque with condensation. Then she stood back, those wide-set eyes flashing with an unexpected glint of challenge, almost triumph.

My mouth opening in soundless query, I leaned forward, peering warily into the case, at the seemingly endless rows of tiny vials, each reflecting the laboratory's lights in a series of curved images. Then Lewis's hand, nearly forgotten in my grasp, tightened almost painfully on mine, and as I turned, my gaze seeking his, I saw that his brilliant blue eyes were filling with tears.

"You were right, Jo," Claire said softly but without remorse. She gestured toward the interior of the opened case. "All that remains now of the subvirus is what's contained in the Class Tens, all 234 of them."

Something—a presence less distinct than Lewis's but compellingly direct—touched my mind then, and I wheeled around to find Christopher standing behind us in the laboratory aisle. She was smiling. I whipped back around, nearly knocking heads with Lewis, and stared again, this time in stunned incredulity, into the storage case. And I knew with utter certainty that Lewis's tears were from relief and joy, because mine were from the very same reasons.

"They were here all the time!" Asplundh exclaimed, breathless with disbelief. Her eyes darted rapidly back and forth from Claire to Christopher, but she was too dumbfounded to say more; Taylor just squeezed her happily, his jubilant face split by a helpless grin of relieved astonishment.

When I knew for certain that I could speak again without my voice quavering or breaking, I tried—uselessly and entirely transparently—to force a little irritation into the question that I asked of both those complicit women. "Then just what the hell got blown apart out there when that scout ship exploded?"

Claire just shrugged ingenuously and offered, with a definite touch of mischief in her voice, "Oh, about two hundred Mendellin swine embryos."

Taylor, too, tried ineffectually to feign aggrievement. "Great!" he snorted, giving Asplundh another enthusiastic hug and still grinning far too broadly for his aggravation to sound convincing. "You let us risk our lives out there defending two hundred *pigs*?"

Claire spread her hands in mock apology. "It's just a good

thing that all second-degree embryos look alike, anyway,'' she noted.

But the expression of regret on Christopher's face then was genuine enough. ''I'm sorry,'' she said quietly. ''I owe you four an explanation. But besides Claire and myself, only Redding and Alexandria knew.'' She looked to the storage case, her tone entirely serious. ''The more people who knew, the greater the danger was—to themselves and to the embryos.'' She turned to us again, quickly scanning our faces. ''But I wanted you to know now; it's part of the only way I can try to thank you all for what you've done.''

But I brushed aside her words of gratitude, uncomfortable with Christopher's expression of appreciation, because I had not done it for her. I had not even done it to save the Tens. I had done it only for one person, and even then it had not been an act of altruism. Lewis was so much a part of me that saving him had become merely an act of self-preservation.

And so instead, still clinging to the giddy triumph, the sense of satisfaction of the moment, I studied the neat rows of transparent little vials and asked, ''What will you do with them now?''

I had not specifically directed the question, but it was Claire who answered. ''Keep them here, I think, at least for the time being.'' I glanced over at her and saw her mouth lift wryly. ''At least until we can see what the Authorities will do with the Class Tens they're about to find out they still have.'' She studied me for a moment shrewdly and yet with a genuine fondness. ''And what about you?'' she asked. ''What will you do now?''

I grinned suddenly, tugging on Lewis's hand, catching him off balance and nearly pulling him into me. I answered Claire's question, but I was looking at Lewis as I did so. ''Back to Heinlein, I guess,'' I replied. ''For starters, anyway.'' I gave an elaborate shrug and added wickedly, ''Hell, if anyone's going to plan my funeral, I want to be there!''

CHAPTER
SEVENTEEN

I guess if I'd ever had to pick a planet to live on, Heinlein would have been at the top of the list. And it was moments like the one I was silently savoring that would have accounted for my decision.

I stood with Lewis in Heinlein's Central Services complex, at the broad window in the corridor outside Mahta's quarters, scanning the panoramic view that lay spread out below us. The neat tracery of walkways and throughways was already busy with pedestrian traffic despite the early hour, and the building fronts and glassed-in overheads glittered with the sun's bright, slanting rays. Every green space, deliberate oases captured within the city's geometry, glistened with a sliver sheen of dew. And beyond the settlement, the low foothills of the Koerber Range were still deep in shadow and shrouded in mist. It was a beautiful city on a beautiful planet, and for the first time I thought I understood just how much it meant to me.

Our coast time from Earthheart had been relatively brief, made to seem all the more so for me by physical exhaustion and an agreeable sort of emotion stasis. Nearly all of us had slept for most of the trip, bunched companionably together in the ship's few cabins, too fatigued to even try to clean up. We must have looked like a crew of colony planet refugees when we stepped off *Raptor*'s ramp onto the pavement of the hangar bay on Heinlein, but I don't think anyone really cared about neatness at that point. News of our deaths had preceded us, but fortunately, Mahta's comm network consisted of more than just what the A's fed into it, and she and the rest of Heinlein had been expecting us. I was glad, since I'd been in no shape to give long explanations when we'd come in.

It had been late night, Heinlein time, when we'd set down. I had been entirely willing to go back to bed, even if Lewis did insist on the removal of our filthy clothing and some basic hygiene first. I had also been entirely willing to go along with that particular gleam I saw light those bright cerulean eyes, but exhaustion made a poor aphrodisiac. He had fallen sound asleep on top of the bedcovers before I was even finished under the drier jets.

With my free hand I pointed to a distant structure amid the buildings that were arrayed below us; the surfaces of its curved and vaulted form reflected dazzlingly in the climbing sun. "The pool house," I said softly, squeezing the fingers that were twined with mine.

Lewis smiled, and I was almost embarrassed to find that the simple curve of his mouth still had the power to send a jolt of electric pleasure surging through me. Of course, the memory of what that mouth had been like in the predawn darkness—its texture, its heat, its taste, and its remarkable facility—helped conspire to perpetuate that feeling. But I smiled back at him with a deliberately suggestive directness that must have reminded him of a few things as well, because I saw that I could still succeed in raising a faint blush on that fair face.

"Sorry for the delay," Mahta said from behind us. She came through the doorway of her apartment, dressed in her customary ecru homespun, her pale hair unbound. As we both turned toward her, she continued with an amused little arch to her finely drawn brows. "More communiqués. If I thought the A's were being solicitous before—" She grinned ferally. "This renegade business has really gotten their balls in a knot!"

Lewis pretended to be shocked by Mahta's figure of speech, but I just flashed her an appreciative grin. I knew that she was delighted by the prospect of pulling that selfsame knot as tightly as she could before the whole matter was cleared up. We had just eaten an early breakfast with her and Jim and Mimosa, and both the discussion of the ongoing litigation and the matter of Heinlein having given sanctuary to the non-Citizen Class Tens and been viewed with relish and enthusiasm. Once the confusion with the Authorities' regulation base on Earthheart had begun to sort itself out, the need for immediate damage control had become obvious and urgent. The A's were extremely eager to keep the entire debacle under wraps; they were far more interested in conciliatory gestures than in prosecution. But Mahta loved a good fight, and she had the strength and tenacity of a glacier. The A's collective balls would never be the same.

As we strolled along the broad, carpeted corridor toward the lifts, I was aware of Mahta's appraising, almost wistful scrutiny. "I wish you two would reconsider," she said quietly, those wide, earth-colored eyes studying me with unblinking candor. "We really could use your help here, and I'll miss you."

But I just shook my head gently but doggedly, discounting the first part of her statement without doubting the second part.

Lewis reached out with his free hand and, with genuine affection, gave Mahta's slim shoulder a little squeeze. "We'll be back soon," he assured her.

Mahta covered his hand with one of her own and patted it fondly. "You'd better be," she responded wryly. "That Inquiry hearing is less than four weeks away!"

As we approached the lift station at the end of the corridor, the door on one of the lifts slid open and Redding stepped out. Clean and rested, dressed once more in the dusty green of a *Nimbus* flightsuit, he looked entirely like himself again and nothing like the dirty, disheveled onetime pirate and black marketeer in shabby Tachs clothing who had huddled over the console in *Raptor*'s Control compartment with me the previous night until long after the others had all shuffled off to sleep.

"On your way down to Port?" he asked, stepping into the corridor.

"Yeah, more or less," I replied. "I've got a few more people I want to see yet, but after that we're out of here."

Mahta had stepped up to Redding. She linked her arm through one of his and looked up at him with an appealing expression on her upturned face. "Can't you make her stay?" she entreated him playfully.

"Stay?" he echoed, his gunmetal-colored eyes going directly to my face even as he gave an amused little snort. "Hell, Mahta, I can't even talk her into going into business with me!"

"I told you I'd think about it," I told Redding, my voice suddenly quiet. Then, before the seriousness of the moment could stick, I swung away from Lewis, dropping his hand. "You want to go down already?" I asked him, but he recognized that it was more of a request than a question.

"Come on," Redding said heartily to Lewis, "you can come down with me. I guess if I want to see Raydor again before you go, I'll have to go out to the damned hangar."

I smiled, because he was right; Raydor had spent the night on *Raptor*, and it was likely that he and Handy had spent most of it fussing over repairing the remaining minor damage to the ship. But if *Raptor* was like a body to Handy, she was like a child to Raydor. Her burns and scars were like his own wounds, and he couldn't rest until he had made her right again.

As Lewis joined him and Mahta at the lift panel, Redding asked me, "Have you seen Chris and Kell and the others this morning?"

"Yeah, they and Asplundh came by earlier, when we were still eating," I replied, pushing the door release on the adjacent lift.

"They were on their way over to the pool house," Lewis added, his blue eyes bright with the memory of some secret bit of humor. "Mimosa went down with them."

As the door to my lift slid aside, Mahta looked up at Redding with an expression of mock petulance. "So I suppose now you'll be off, too?" she put to him.

But Redding shook his shaggy head. "Not right away," he replied, the corners of his mouth lifting in that quirky, crooked grin. "Not unless I steal another one of your ships, anyway!" He shrugged. "I'll be here until my ship comes in again—and what the hell, by then it'll probably be time for that damned hearing."

Mahta gave his arm a little shake. "I'll have you know 'that damned hearing' is going to be very important," she reminded him with poorly feigned severity.

As I stepped into the empty lift, Redding just gave me a casual little wave. "We'll see you down at the hangar bay," he said as the door swept closed.

Alone, I rode the lift to one of the complex's upper floors and stepped off into another wide, handsome corridor, this one with an even more spectacular view of the settlement. The sun had climbed higher then; below, the dew and mist were burning off the parks and squares and distant hills. It was a short walk to the apartment Mahta had indicated. I ran my fingers through my hair, brushing it back off my shoulders, and then pressed the summons buzzer outside the door.

Then I waited. When there was no response to the call within what seemed a reasonable amount of time, I considered my options: buzzing again or just walking away. I pushed the button again. Automatically, a little tendril of worry began to tickle its way up my spine. I knew that Taylor had been exhausted, but I also knew that normally he was a light sleeper.

Suddenly the door was pulled open. Just across the threshold stood Alexandria, her robust body elegantly wrapped like some

Egyptian queen in what only could have been a bed sheet, her wild, unfettered hair ringing her head like a frizzy crown. Her expression was more one of pleasure than one of surprise. "Oh, hi, Jo," she said. She stepped back, gesturing. "Come on in."

For a moment all I could do was just stand there, gaping stupidly at her. Then, hesitantly, I moved across the threshold, taking a few steps into the apartment's entryway. "I, uh—I was looking for Taylor," I said inanely.

Alexandria turned from closing the door and immediately bellowed out, "Taylor, come on out here!"

Still dumbfounded, I didn't make the obvious connection until Taylor actually appeared in the hallway leading from the bedrooms. He came around the corner yawning, his chestnut-colored hair boyishly tousled; he was clad in a pair of sleepers with only the bottom half fastened, so that the empty top part flopped along behind him like an amiably wagging tail. When he saw me, his entire face lit up.

"Hi, Jo!" he said brightly.

As I stood there, my stupefied stare moved back and forth between the two of them. It took me a few seconds to realize that the graphic image strobing through my mind right then was not my imagined fabrication of what had probably happened there in that apartment last night but was instead a memory of the night before, the night on Earthheart when, turning accidentally into a darkened bedroom at Claire's, I had seen what I had thought had been Alexandria and Redding, joining in furious urgency beneath the heaving bedcovers.

I knew that I was still gaping like an idiot, but not a single coherent word seemed to come to mind. Knowing Alexandria, I could see that despite the owlish look of innocence on that craggy face, she was thoroughly enjoying my stunned embarrassment and probably would have cheerfully entertained the idea of doing more to prolong it. But Taylor, also typically, was sensitive to my discomfort and equally eager to relieve it.

He came across the room and put out his bare arms, pulling me into a warm hug. "You're looking a lot better than the last time I saw you," he teased me. As he stepped back, his hands still at my waist, he looked me up and down. He tugged playfully at the silver piping on my fresh flightsuit. "So, are you all set to go already?"

"Yeah," I replied, finally finding my tongue, "we're just getting ready to lift." I glanced from him to Alexandria—who still looked like she was enjoying herself far too much to suit me—and then back into those familiar sienna-colored eyes. "I, uh—I just wanted to see if you needed a ride somewhere," I finished lamely.

But Taylor just flashed me his stellar smile, that smile whose abilities seemed to stop just short of being able to raise the dead, and responded, "Not this time, I guess." He made a small gesture toward Alexandria and explained. "I'm going to stay here, for a while, anyway. Mahta has talked Alexandria into serving as liaison between the A's and the consulate the Tens are establishing here, and—"

"*Temporary* liaison," Alexandria interrupted him, her amused smirk belying the abrasive tone of her deep voice.

"Temporary liaison," Taylor agreed with equanimity. "Anyway, I figured maybe I could help. Besides, my boss wants me to cover that hearing next month."

"What about Asplundh?" I asked, still confounded by the bizarre ramifications of his unexpected relationship with Alexandria.

Taylor's shaggy brows rose quizzically. "She wants to work with the Tens," he said, stating the obvious. "Although she's still talking about going back to Earthheart and trying to convince Claire to come out of retirement to help her with the genetics stuff."

That was not precisely what I had meant, and Alexandria knew it, even if Taylor didn't seem to. So I just looked from the big woman's sardonically self-satisfied expression to Taylor's bemused but contented one and mentally shrugged off whatever misconceptions I'd been struggling under. I gave them both a slightly rueful but genuinely pleased grin; then, leaning forward, I planted a deliberately wet and lingering kiss on Taylor's lips. "Good luck, Slick!" I told him.

Alexandria made a rude snorting sound, throwing Taylor a deprecating glance. "He doesn't need luck," she grunted.

That's what you think! I retorted mentally, but all I said, shaking my head as I gently cuffed his sun-tipped hair, was, "Well, I'd better get down there; I've still got to settle with Port."

"Wait, we'll come down and see you off," Taylor said. When he noticed the way I was staring at his and Alexandria's somewhat unconventional attire, he laughed and amended, "Well, we'll be down in a little while, before you lift, anyway."

"Fine," I said, turning back toward the door. "You know where to find me."

I had my hand on the door handle when Alexandria's voice stopped me, her tone purposely casual yet transparently concerned. "So, Jo," she said, stepping forward with the hem of her luxurious bed sheet trailing behind her on the carpeting. "Have you decided yet what you're going to do?"

I paused a moment, then looked back into that familiar weathered face, into the knowing depths of those dark and fathomless eyes. Alexandria was no Talent, no telepath; she had never needed to be. "Yeah," I told her with complete candor, "I've decided."

Out in the empty corridor, on the way back to the lift, I stopped again by one of the wide windows and looked out on that stunning vista one last time. The sun had risen high enough then to reach the flat pane of glass. I touched my hand to its transparent surface, warmed by the rays. Standing there, I had the strangest feeling, as if the sun could shine right through me as well, as if I were somehow translucent. I didn't think that I had ever felt such a sense of direction, of utter self-awareness. Because I realized then that for the first time in my life, I really did know what I was going to do.

And I was going to tell Lewis about the child.

ABOUT THE AUTHOR

KAREN RIPLEY, a Wisconsin native, was "born with the soul of a farmer in postagricultural America" and was an inveterate story-teller as a child. She learned to write at the age of four and, after discovering science fiction and fantasy in high school, had her first short story published in *Worlds of If* at the age of eighteen.

After graduating from the University of Minnesota in 1973 as a doctor of veterinary medicine, she went into private practice in her hometown. Her long-neglected interest in science fiction and fantasy was rekindled in 1983 when she discovered the world of organized fandom and SF conventions.

Besides reading and writing, her interests include "recreational bicycling, the Old West, and growing things." She still lives in Wisconsin, where she is the "sole support of several Arabian horses, a quartet of peacocks, and two large and otherwise useless dogs."

Her first novel, *Prisoner of Dreams*, was published by Del Rey Books in 1989. *The Tenth Class* is her second novel.